GRENELL 1893

A NOVEL

GRENELL 1893

BOOK 2 IN THE THOUSAND ISLANDS SERIES

Lynn E. McElfresh

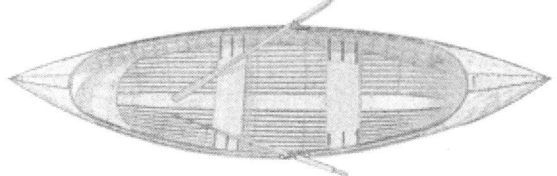

River Skiff Press
Grenell Island, NY

This is a work of fiction.
While real characters from history are represented,
their appearance, personalities, mannerisms,
and dialogue are imagined.

Copyright 2020 © by Lynn E. McElfresh

First paperback edition May 2020

Book design by Michelle Argento
Maps by Michelle Argento

ISBN 978-1-950245-02-4 (paperback)
ISBN 978-1-950245-03-1 (ebook)

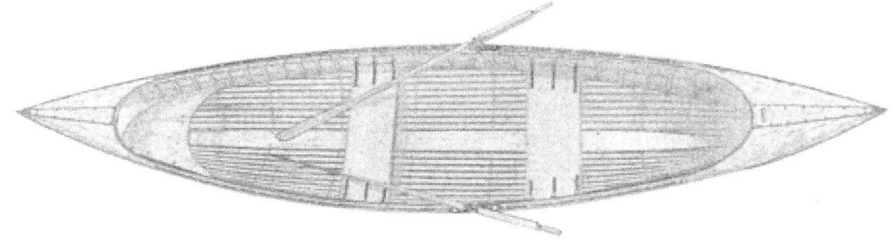

River Skiff Press
16439 Grenell Island
Clayton, NY 13624

To Alice Parker Pratt whose love and dedication is forever imprinted on Grenell Island.

Millionaire's Row 1893

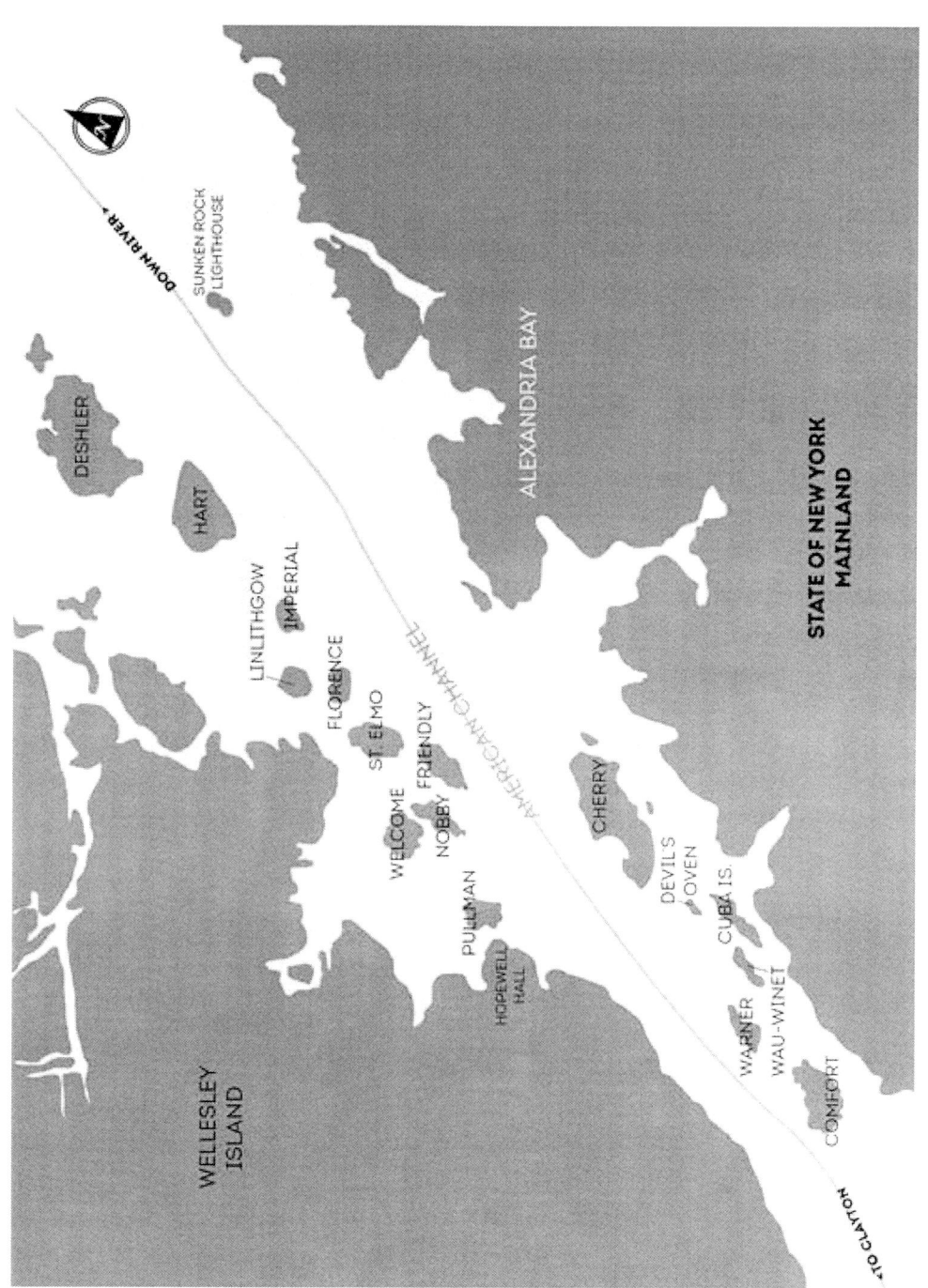

Thousand Islands Region 1893

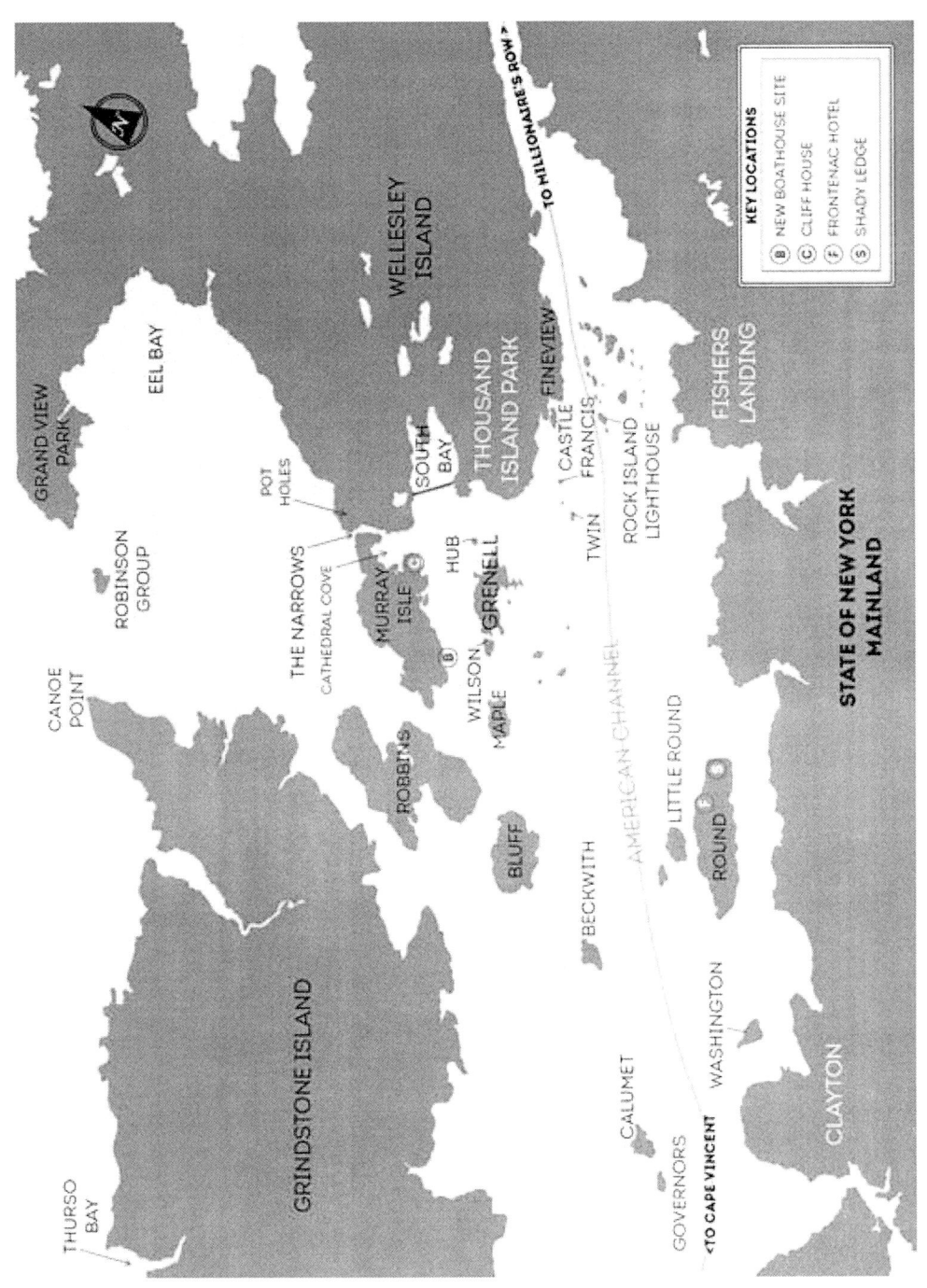

Grenell Island 1893

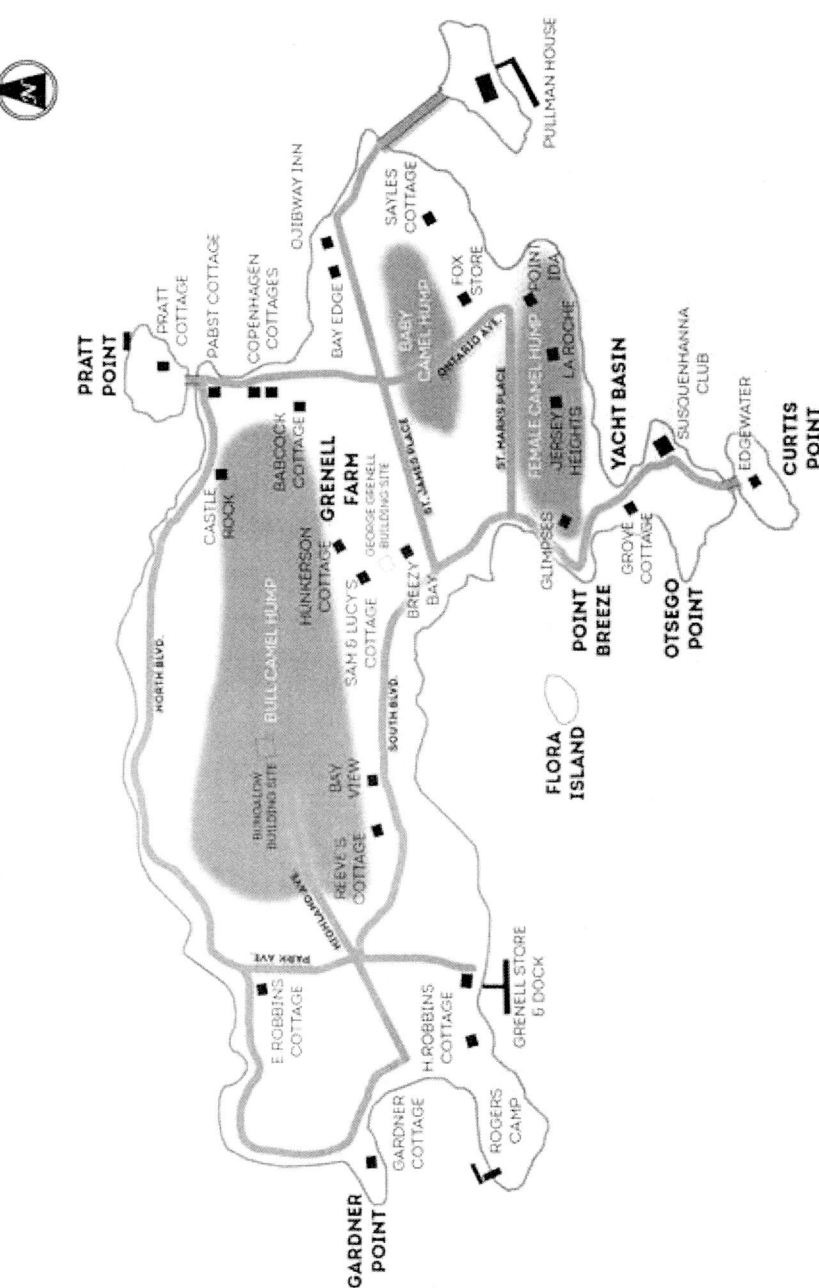

CHAPTER one

Wednesday, June 7, 1893
CASTLE ROCK, GRENELL ISLAND, THOUSAND ISLANDS, NEW YORK

"Marguerite!"

I stopped scraping and steadied myself on the ladder. Did someone call my name? I turned my head to the left and listened intently but only heard the lapping of the St. Lawrence against the rocks below. When I turned my head to the right, I heard the twitter of birds as they hopped about the pine boughs, sending puffs of yellow pine pollen into the soft morning breeze. I turned back to the blistered paint on the cottage eave above me and put the scraper against the wood.

"You've been on the island for only a day and you're already hearing *the Voice*," I scolded myself as I started scraping again. White paint chips cascaded around me.

I'd started hearing *the Voice* about ten years ago. But it was almost always at night when I was alone on the island. Those times were few and far between. Friend Anne and I usually arrived and departed together and each year we have a steady stream of guests. "When was the last time I was alone on the island?" I wondered aloud. I mulled that over as I continued scraping.

"Marguerite! Are you there? Miss Marguerite, you must come!

Hurry!"

The urgency in those words jolted me to a stop mid-scrape. A sprinkling of white paint chips blew into my face. I spluttered, spitting out the paint chips that had fallen into my mouth.

"Miss Marguerite?"

Was that Nat? I looked down the path that ringed the island, searching for the twelve-year-old boy who always kept me abreast of island happenings but did not see him. He sounded excited. I hoped nothing was amiss.

"There you are!" Nat cried out. "Hurry, or you'll miss it!"

I turned to see Nat descending from the little-used path that went up and over the towering ridge of rock that we referred to as the camel hump.

"Nat! What is it?"

"No time to explain. Hurry!"

I dropped the paint scraper. The metal part clanked on the granite below as I climbed down the stepladder, which wobbled wildly in my haste.

"Hurry," Nat urged as he ran up the steep narrow path that went over the top of the Camel hump.

I brazenly lifted my skirt to mid-calf and ran after him. I raised an arm to protect my face as I wove through a cluster of squat sumacs. The protruding branches grabbed at my skirt and clawed at my hair. I pulled off my mobcap and stuck it into the pocket of my painter's smock. As I swept past honeysuckle bushes in full bloom, my long skirt dislodged the yellow-and-white blossoms. Panic gripped my chest and a sick taste filled my mouth. What was happening? Was someone sick? Hurt? Uncle Sam? Aunt Lucy? Arnie? Nat's brother Arnie was on the island supervising the stone delivery to Mr. Sharples's cottage Bungalow. Had something happened to Arnie?

Unencumbered by a long walking skirt, Nat quickly outpaced me, crunched through a sea of mayapples, and reached the flat farm in the center of the island before I did. He paused there, turned back toward me, and, with frantic motions, he once again urged me to hurry before he continued on. Once free from the tangle of undergrowth, I thought I could keep stride with Nat, but he was twelve. At age twenty-eight, I was no match for his youthful legs. Again, he quickly outpaced me.

Besides, the flat section of Grenell's farm was fraught with peril. Recent rain had filled wagon ruts with murky water. I kept my gaze down as I maneuvered around puddles and cow pies.

"Look," Nat said, stopping short and pointing skyward. "There it is! Do you see it?"

In a few steps, I was on his heels. "Where? What?" I asked, trying to catch my breath.

"It just disappeared behind that oak."

"*What* just disappeared behind the oak?"

"A flying machine," Nat said, his eyes wide and a huge grin on his face. He grabbed my hand and tugged me toward the rocky ridge that we referred to as the female camel hump. It was smaller than the bull camel hump on the north shore that rises up behind my small cottage.

I stopped and pulled back against Nat's hand. "But that's private property. It belongs to Colonel Haskell."

"It's fine," Nat said. "He's rented out the place. The renters will understand. It's the best place to see the flying machine. Come! Before it's out of sight. You gotta see it! It's giant."

With that, I followed Nat up the path. As soon as I reached the top, I realized why Colonel Haskell calls the upriver tip of the female camel hump, Point Breeze. The fresh, cool air blowing from the prevailing southwesterly wind cooled my cheeks, which were warm from exertion. The small white cottage called Glimpses was tucked into the shade. It was a dainty cottage, swathed in gingerbread trim and wrapped with a deep porch on three sides. Colonel Haskell's sister-in-law, Mrs. Beardsley, who looks after the place in his absence, was on the porch with two maids. The trio of women did not notice Nat and me when we rushed by, as their gazes were fixed to the sky. Colonel Haskell's renters stood at the far end of Point Breeze looking and pointing at something in the sky over the channel.

"There it is!" Nat whispered to me, not wishing to draw attention to our arrival. "Do you see it?"

I looked up.

Immediately, my forward progress stopped. My feet seemed rooted to the spot. My mouth fell agape, and I was unable to respond. My eyes fixed in utter wonderment on the contraption in the sky. I've seen sketches of flying machines in newspapers and magazines. But seeing static black-and-white drawings was quite different than seeing the full-blown thing moving through the sky in front of me.

Mesmerized, I slowly moved forward until I was standing amongst the knot of people. I squinted into the bright morning light, hoping to bring the flying machine into sharper focus. The top was an airship made of grayish material. It was long, sausage-shaped, but pointed at both ends. It seemed to be as long as Twin Island, which it was slowly approaching.

Dangling beneath the airship, attached by ropes or wires—I couldn't tell which—were two wheelmen peddling safety bicycles. Apparently, the bicycles powered two huge paddlewheel-like things that churned and propelled them through the air. Behind the paddlewheels, at the stern of the craft was a huge rudder. My mind tried to make sense of what I was seeing, but my thoughts were coming so fast and furious that I couldn't sort them out.

The gentleman standing next to me passed a pair of field glasses into my hands without looking at me or saying a word. The field glasses were heavy. I raised them to my eyes and found first the silvery balloon, then moved the glasses around until I found the two wheelmen below and slowly brought them into focus. The wheelmen wore identical blue bicycle suit coats over matching bicycle trousers with golf cuffs. On their heads they wore leather skullcaps similar to what footballers wear and a pair of goggles. The two turned toward each other. They appeared to be talking.

I tipped the field glasses down to see if I could gauge how high they were in the air. Two hundred feet? Four hundred feet? Below I saw the steamer *St. Lawrence*, which had come to a stop in the water beneath the flying machine. Engineer Hammond and Captain Visger stepped outside the wheelhouse, and like their passengers who lined the hurricane deck, were staring up at the spectacle above them.

A collective gasp went up around me, and one of the women on Point Breeze stifled a shriek. Below on the hurricane deck of the steamer *St. Lawrence*, a woman had fainted. Passengers clustered around to support her fall to the deck. I handed the field glasses back to the gentleman, who immediately focused on the wheelmen.

"They've stopped pedaling!" he announced.

I looked up to see that the paddlewheels were slowing to a stop.

The rudder was at an odd angle, and the flying machine was inclined downward.

"Whatever are they doing?" asked one of the women from the small knot of people on Point Breeze. A flurry of other questions quickly followed.

"Do you think they are trying to land on Twin Island?"

"Whatever for?"

"Or are they crashing?"

"Oh! I can't look!" cried one young woman who hid her eyes. Another young woman put a comforting arm around her.

"Look! Look! They are peddling again," said the man with the field glasses. The paddlewheels began turning. The rudder angle changed. The flying machine had stopped its descent and was moving forward again.

I realized I'd been holding my breath and inhaled as deeply as my corset would allow.

The flying machine slowly turned to the south. Soon we could only see the back of the craft, the rudder, and the back of the two paddlewheels.

"They are headed for the mainland," one of the young men said.

I stared after the curious machine, my mind churning with disparate thoughts. I heard a dog bark, and my thoughts came out of the clouds and back to Grenell Island. The steamer *St. Lawrence* was landing at Pullman House. Guests had poured out of the hotel onto the dock. Perhaps a hundred people milled about, pointing to the sky.

The wake from the *St. Lawrence* had reached the boats moored in the deepwater basin between our perch at Glimpses and Pullman House. The Kerr's sailing yacht, *Tiger*, and Mr. Burditt's steam yacht, *Otsego*, bobbed at their their moorings.

The largest and most elegant of all the cottages on Grenell Island surrounded the deepwater yacht basin. To my left were three grand cottages. The porch at Jersey Heights was empty, but the Griswold sisters were on the porch at La Roche. Fanny Harnois and her daughter, Ida, were on the upper porch at Point Ida. All were staring after the disappearing airship.

Below on the Otsego peninsula, the southern most point of Grenell Island, the porch and dock of the Susquehanna Club was crowded with the families staying there. I only recognized the president of the Susquehanna Club, Mr. Burditt, who stood amongst the others on the dock.

Mr. Burditt cupped his hands around his mouth and called up, "Did you see that, T. B.?"

"Indeed I did," the man who lent me the field glasses called back.

"How far do you think they could go?" a young man next to him asked.

"Depends on how long the gas in the inflatable lasts," the man with the field glasses replied.

As the flying machine continued to shrink from sight, questions filled the air. Who were the wheelmen? Where did they come from? Why were they here? Where were they going? Did they mean to dive like that, or was it an accident? Was it all an experiment, or were they on a planned excursion?

"Have you ever seen such a sight?" a young woman asked me.

I shook my head. I wasn't able to converse right now. Everything was so jumbled in my head.

I had been invisible to the people on Breeze Point before, but now that the flying machine was a tiny dot moving quickly out of sight, I was suddenly noticed. Likewise, I began noticing the people around me. The middle-aged man who had lent me the field glasses was tall, clean-shaven, with hair combed straight back. He looked very business-like in his chocolate-brown sack coat. His simple fold-down collar was crisp and impeccably starched with a forest green silk necktie expertly knotted at the throat and tucked into his darker waistcoat beneath.

"What a wondrous age we live in! Wouldn't you agree, Miss . . .? I'm sorry, but I don't believe we've met," he said amicably, tilting his head to one side as he smiled at me.

"I'm sorry," I said, my cheeks coloring. "Please excuse my intrusion. Nat, the boy who works at the store, Nat Hunkerson . . . he . . . he alerted me. . ." I turned to point out Nat but only saw the top of his sandy brown hair as he disappeared down the path. "I'm Marguerite Hartranft. By the time we made it to the end of the Grenell farm, the flying machine was behind the trees. Nat insisted that I see it. Please forgive me for showing up uninvited."

"Not at all. You are more than welcome. How horrible if you had missed it! Point Breeze is the best venue for aero-machine observation. Nat is a bright boy."

"Miss Hartranft?" asked the younger of the two young women as she edged closer to me. "Oh! You have the cute little cottage on the north side of the island perched upon a rock. You were tenting in the same location the first time we arrived on Grenell."

"This is my daughter, Lois," the man said. "I'm T. B. Kerr, and this lively brood is my family. This is Mrs. Kerr. Next in line is my eldest, Mary Mason; my elder son, John; and my youngest child, just out of knickers . . ."

"Father! I've been out of knickers for a half-dozen years now!" The younger man protested.

". . . Clarence."

Ah, the Kerr family. I had heard of the well-to-do family from Englewood, New Jersey, who, for the past few years, had rented Glimpses or sometimes the Gardner cottage at the head of the island.

"Excuse me, ladies," Mr. Kerr said, nodding to his daughters and wife. "We have a date with some pickerel." Mr. Kerr motioned to John LaRue, their oarsman, who was patiently waiting for them by the skiff on the dock below. The three trotted down the staircase to the dock. Mrs. Kerr excused herself and returned to the cottage to supervise the staff, and I was left alone with the two Kerr sisters.

"Forget the pickerel! Bring back a fine catch of perch," Lois called after her father and brothers. "We only arrived last night, and I've been waiting all winter for some nice fresh perch from the river St. Lawrence." Lois's eyes brightened then as she seemed to be imagining her first forkful of the tender, sweet, fresh perch.

I smiled at that, for I'd hoped I'd have time this afternoon to put my line in the water and catch a couple of perch for my supper tonight.

"So this is your third season on Grenell?" I asked.

"No. Our fifth, actually," Lois said.

"We arrived in eighty-nine, the year before the Pullman House opened," Mary Mason said.

"I'm the reason we are here," Lois said proudly, her gray-blue eyes glittering. "We had stopped by to visit the Curtises. Mr. Curtis and

Father are law partners in the firm Curtis & Kerr. They represent Mr. Westinghouse in the many lawsuits brought against him by Mr. Edison. They argued before the Supreme Court—well Mr. Curtis did—but Father was there, too."

Her older sister, Mary Mason, nudged her. "Lois, you've gotten sidetracked again."

"Yes. Yes. Quite right . . . as I was saying, the Curtises were staying here on Grenell Island and we were only to stay one week and then move on to Atlantic City. But I was so enamored with the place. Who wants to go to crowded ol' Atlantic City when you could stay on this magical island in the middle of paradise? Well, I convinced the family to stay for the rest of the summer. And we've been back every summer since."

I smiled at the young woman's enthusiasm. "Reminds me of my first experience on Grenell," I told her.

"I've heard you share the cottage with another woman? A doctor?" Mary Mason asked.

"Yes. Dr. Ashbridge. But she prefers to be called Anne or Dr. Anne."

"I'm so happy to hear there is a doctor on the island in the event of a sudden illness," Mary Mason said.

Both Mary Mason and her sister had hair parted in the middle and pulled back gracefully in a low coiffure at the nape of their neck. Mary Mason's hair was a deep mahogany while her younger sister's hair was a light brown.

"Yes. Do feel free to call on Anne if you are ever in need of a doctor, but I'm afraid Anne's not here right now. She teaches at the Woman's Medical College of Pennsylvania. One of her students, Dr. Okami, just graduated. Dr. Okami is the first woman in Japan to obtain a degree in Western medicine. She will be returning to Japan at the end of the summer. Anne and Keiko—Dr. Okami, that is—have decided to go to the Chicago Exposition. They won't be arriving on the island until the first of July."

"I suppose we shall all have to remain healthy until then," Mary Mason said pleasantly.

"They're at the fair?" Lois asked. "Have you been yet? We are just back. We witnessed the opening ceremonies as guests of Mr. Westinghouse. We were in the front row when President Cleveland threw the switch and hundreds of thousands of Westinghouse Electric's incandescent lamps lit up the night. The buildings are all white, you know. That's why they call it the White City. And at night, when the lights come on, it's a veritable fairyland. Westinghouse Electric won the bid to furnish the Exposition's incandescent plant. Mr. Edison filed injunction after injunction, but Father's law firm batted each away like an easy tennis volley."

I smiled as Lois pantomimed a tennis player.

"The newspapers printed all this nonsense that the Westinghouse lamps would fail and ruin the Westinghouse company and the reputation of the fair—Mr. Edison pays for influence in the papers, you know—but it all went off swimmingly. It was spectacular." Lois threw her arms in the air to express how grand the event had been.

Mary Mason placed a calming hand on her exuberant sister's shoulder as she turned to me. "Will you be able to visit the fair later in the season?"

"I'm afraid not. I have commitments here on the island and will be returning for the start of the fall term at Penn at the end of September."

"You really must attend. It's not to be missed," Lois insisted.

"I wish I could. I will have to depend on those who have been fortunate to attend to fill me in on all the details. Could I persuade the two of you to come to tea and tell me more? Perhaps when Anne and Keiko arrive, and the four of you can compare notes about your visit."

"That sounds lovely," Mary Mason said, turning to see her brother John trot up from the stairs that led down to the dock below.

John rushed over and whispered something in Mary Mason's ear, then nodded toward me and said, "So happy to meet you." He raised a crooked finger to his head as if to tip a hat, although he wasn't wearing one.

"That's a splendid idea," Mary Mason called after him. "I'll do just that!"

As she turned back to me, Mary Mason's smile broadened, and a dimple in her left cheek sprang to life. "My dear, sweet brother just reminded me that you would be a perfect addition to our excursion tomorrow."

"Tomorrow? No, I'm sorry. I will be engaged in a painting project for the next few days. Regretfully, I will have to decline," I said.

"Painting? You're an artist? So that's why you're wearing a painter's smock?" Lois stepped forward to examine my smock.

"What?" I asked. I glanced down at my paint-stained smock and suddenly realized how I must look in my work clothes. Luckily, I had pulled the mobcap off my head and stuck it in my pocket during my run to Point Breeze. At that thought, my hand instantly went to my hair. As I suspected, my dark curls had come loose from the tight bun I had pinned them into this morning. They had sprung to life, sticking up every which way. When I smoothed a few errant strands back into place, a smattering of paint chips showered down on my bodice, so I quickly brushed them away.

"I so adore art and artists. Could I visit you at your studio? Or do you have your easel set up alfresco to capture your magnificent view of the river? Oh, how I wish I could paint or sketch!" Lois spun around with her arms outstretched, then hugged her arms to her as if to gather the surrounding beauty around her and capture it in her heart forever.

"I'm sorry to say that I'm not that sort of painter. I'm a house painter—or cottage painter, to be precise. I have guests visiting at the end of the week and hoped to have the cottage repainted before they arrive."

"Perhaps," Mary Mason said gently, reaching for my ungloved hand with her gloved hand, "you could take one afternoon off. My brother John will be a senior at Princeton next year, and as it turns out there is a bevy of Princeton students and alumni here in the islands this season. John has pressed me into service to organize *a fête champêtre*."

Lois giggled. "Don't let her fool you! There wasn't much *pressing* involved. Mary Mason loves to organize social events," Lois reported.

Mary Mason demurred but continued. "I booked the steamer *Nightingale* for a gala trip through the islands. We'll be picnicking at Grand View Park. I've covered all the details, except—and this is where you come in—I don't have enough attractive, intelligent young ladies."

My face must have expressed my surprise at being referred to as an attractive, intelligent *young* lady. At twenty-eight, as my mother and sister Rose often reminded me, I was teetering on spinsterhood.

"Please be assured that you won't be the only one. Lois and I will be there, of course, as well as a few young ladies I've already recruited from Thousand Island Park and a handful of girls who are staying at Pullman

House, as well."

I glanced over at the grand, four-story Pullman House, which occupied the area of the island where the more modest two-story Grenell House had stood when I first visited the island over a decade ago. The island on which the Pullman House stood was called Grenell Island, while the larger island it was connected to via a long narrow bridge was Grenell Island Park. Both islands were referred to simply as Grenell.

I could see John LaRue pulling hard on the oars of his St. Lawrence River skiff as he slipped under the bridge that joined the two islands. As if he knew we were looking his way, John Kerr turned and waved to us.

"Please say you'll come. John assures me we need to have a handful of the fairer sex to balance out the raucous collegians. I was hoping to invite the Hinds' girls. Do you know Jessie, Grace, and Addie? They summer on the south shore in the Bay View cottage," Mary Mason said, pointing to a white cottage with a double-tiered porch. "But they have yet to arrive on Grenell for the season. Perhaps they too are at the Chicago Exposition. You'd be doing me a great favor, and I would forever be in your debt."

"Well, I . . ." I started.

"It's settled then." Mary Mason beamed. She reached forward and took both of my bare hands in her gloved ones. I had the feeling that Mary Mason was used to getting her way. "Thank you so much. You can meet us at the new Grenell dock, the one in front of the Grenell Island Park store. Ten o'clock."

"Ten o'clock?" That would limit the amount of time I had for scraping and sanding. "What is the proper attire for this affair?" I asked.

"Oh, nothing special. A simple summer dress. Something like we're wearing today. I'm sure you've been on college outings before. You attend Penn, correct?"

"I . . . well . . ." I stammered.

I was too distracted to respond properly. What were Lois and Mary Mason wearing? My sisters, Rose and Lily, seemed to take in a woman's attire from hat to slipper in one glance. From that one glance, they could assess character, social standing, and other subtle nuances before they even uttered a greeting. I hadn't paid attention to what the Kerr sisters were wearing but now took a moment to appraise their apparel.

Lois's dress was decidedly nautical, Prussian blue with a bold white stripe at the base of her skirt. Another smaller white stripe lined the sailor collar, which laid flat on her back. A long white, tightly knotted tie dangled almost to her trim waist. Mary Mason wore a delicate white dress printed with rows and rows of tiny red roses. Finespun white lace edged both the high collar and the cuffs at the end of her long sleeves. Three rows of ruffles graced the bottom of her skirt. I wondered what my sisters would glean from their choice of clothing. More distressingly, I wondered what the Kerr sisters might have ascertained from my attire.

"The pleasure will be all mine," I said. "I have taken up too much of your time, especially for your first full day on the island for the season. Thank you so much for your hospitality. Please, thank your father for sharing his field glasses. Until tomorrow," I said with a little nod to the two sisters.

I turned on my heel, fought the urge to run, and instead walked calmly toward the path leading down from Point Breeze. Halfway down the path, I looked up to see Uncle Sam standing in front of his cottage. After he and Aunt Lucy sold Grenell House and the small island it sat on to Mr. Sayles, they'd built a splendid cottage with a double-tiered porch. On a clear day, they could see all the way up the channel to Clayton. Two years ago, another cottage was built one lot over by the Hudson family from Syracuse. They named their cottage Breezy Bay, an apt name today as a pleasant breeze was blowing off the river. Like Sam's cottage, it had a double-tiered porch. Mrs. Hudson had insisted that as many of the trees remain, including a young maple tree very close to their front steps. "Just think how this maple will shade and cool our cottage someday." Mr. Hudson had grumbled but complied.

The Grenell cottage and Breezy Bay were only two of a handful of cottages on the south side of Grenell. A boardwalk stretched from the Grenell cottage to the store. Between the Grenell cottage and the store, I could see the Hinds cottage, Bay View, and the Reeve's cottage beyond that. Our little island was turning into a lovely summer community.

"Welcome back to Grenell for the 1893 season," Uncle Sam called out once I was within earshot.

"Thank you. How was your winter?" I asked as I joined him on the porch.

"It was a cold one! The ice was solid and thick. Good thing. I had four tons of wood timbers to transport the six miles from Clayton on the ice."

"I heard you built a splendid dock. I've yet to see it. Captain Taylor picked me up in Clayton in the *Minnehaha* and brought me straight to my dock."

"Ah! Well, we have two other captains on the island now. Both of them are Robbins—Captain Hy and Captain El," Uncle Sam informed me.

"Are they related?" I asked. Hyland and his young bride moved permanently to the island last year.

"Well, his uncle Eldridge bought a lot in February and dragged a house from Robbins Island—s'pose people are calling it Emery Island now. Between you and me, it'll always be Robbins."

"They brought the house over on the ice?"

"Used sleds and a team of dray horses. Hauled the house right over top a little sapling oak tree. Most say it won't survive, but take a look at it when you walk by. It's startin' to straighten up. Lookin' mighty fine, it is," Uncle Sam said, stroking his white goatee thoughtfully. "But go see my dock first! She's a beauty!"

"I can't wait to see it," I said.

"It's a marvel! Recovered the timbers from the old timber station dock in Clayton. That lumber'd been underwater for fifty years and none the worse for it. She's a fine steamship dock. Told you I'd build one someday. First the store, then the post office and now a steamship dock." Sam hooked his fingers behind his lapels and rocked back on his heels.

"I'm sure it is a fine dock," I said.

Sam stroked his white goatee, leaned forward, and added in a conspiratorial whisper, "There's been complaints the past few years about Mr. Sayles at Pullman House chargin' cottagers eye-waterin' rates to land at the Pullman House dock and have their belongings transferred to their cottages. Vowed to remedy that particular predicament and I did! Gotta keep my island family happy," he said with a wink.

In January of 1891, Sam had a team of dray horses drag Britton's old store on a sled from Fishers Landing across the frozen river to Grenell Island and renamed it the Grenell Island Store. That spring, Mr. Sayles recruited E. A. Fox of LaFargeville to build a provision store in the little harbor on Grenell Island Park just opposite Pullman House. When

Uncle Sam found out, he was furious. He stamped his feet and could barely speak. I thought perhaps he would twist himself into a knot and tear himself in half like Rumpelstiltskin. It was not lost on me that the more people Uncle Sam brought to his dock, the more chances he had of making sales at the store.

"Did you see that flying machine this morning?" Uncle Sam asked.

"Yes. Nat ran to collect me to make sure I didn't miss it."

"Not much gets by Nat. Kinda like his pa that way."

I smiled. Nat was perhaps more like Hunk than any of Hunk's other offspring.

"Maybe I should've built me an aero-ship dock instead of a steamship dock. I hear some day in the future, folks'll be traveling by aero-ship. Makes me think I should've hung on to those nine lots at the crest of Grenell instead of selling them to the Quaker colony."

We both looked up through the trees to the crest of the island. Uncle Sam pursed his lips in concentration. "I'd thought we'd be knee-deep in Quakers by now. When they bought them lots, they were supposed to build nine cottages and a shared boathouse on the north-side shore.

"I think the Panic scared everyone off that idea."

"Not your Mr. Sharples."

"No, Mr. Sharples seems to be doing quite well, especially after he won that gold medal at the Paris Exposition for his cream separator. He was more than happy to buy the lots from his friends."

"Hear tell he's calling that castle-sized cottage he's erecting 'Bungalow.'"

"That's true," I said. When Mr. Sharples first showed the plans for the grand summer home and told me he was calling it Bungalow, I'd laughed and said if his cottage were a bungalow then our cottage was a castle. Mr. Sharples presented Anne and me with a sign for our new cottage the very next week: Castle Rock. The name stuck. After a dozen years of referring to our place as Camp Anne, we now referred to it as Castle Rock.

"Arnie's doing a fine job for Mr. Sharples. Worked all winter building a road to transport the quarry stone to the buildin' site. Got a delivery later this morning. You should watch Arnie in action."

"I'll have to do that. Where is Aunt Lucy?"

"Tendin' to her chickens, I believe. Spends more time with them birds than she does with me. Not quite how I envisioned my retirement."

"Retirement! I'm sure she can say the same of you—starting a store, building a steamship dock. What's next?" I asked.

"Got a hotel on the way!" he said, rocking back on his heels and tucking his thumbs behind the lapels of his frock coat again.

"Do tell! You are full of surprises, Uncle Sam. Please give Aunt Lucy my best wishes. I'll be by later to see her myself."

"Don't dilly dally! She'll wanna latch eyes on you as soon as possible."

"Certainly. I can't wait to see her either. Farewell for now," I said as I descended from the porch.

Seems hotels were popping up everywhere. I thought when Captain Taylor had transported me to Castle Rock that he'd pointed out the huge construction project near Oak Point on Murray Isle as we passed between the two islands. Two years ago Captain Jack Taylor had rafted and towed timber to the island to build the one-hundred-and-fifty-foot dock for a grand hotel planned for Murray Isle. The construction of the boathouse for the future hotel was in full swing.

My list of things I must do had multiplied in the short time I had been away from our little cottage. Somehow, I needed to visit Arnie at the Bungalow building site, visit Aunt Lucy, finish scraping and sanding the cottage, catch fish for supper, and most importantly, find suitable attire for a Princeton *fête champêtre* aboard the steamer *Nightingale* . . . all by ten tomorrow morning.

CHAPTER
two

    Perspiration dotted my forehead. I raised my wrist to mop my brow with my sleeve and thought better of it. White paint chips coated my sleeve. I reached instead for a tea towel and dabbed my face. Who was I fooling? I'm sure my face was splattered with paint chips. I probably looked like a speckled hen. My arm ached as I raised my scraper to attack the last section that needed to be scraped.

    The sun was nearly at its zenith and, despite my unexpected visit to Point Breeze, I was nearly finished. I'd returned from the aero-machine sighting full of frenetic energy. As I attacked the blistered paint of our two-year-old cottage, thoughts, and images of the aero-machine filled my head as paint chips filled the air. I pondered over the details. How exactly had the safety bicycles been attached? What kept the wheelmen from falling off those dangling safety bicycles to the abyss below? Had they been strapped to the safety bicycles in any way? How useful would the footballer skullcap have been if they had fallen? When they landed, did the aero-machine roll along the ground? My mind leapt ahead to the future. I wondered if someday I'd fly on an aero-machine from Philadelphia directly to an aero-port on Grenell Island. Oh, what a wondrous, marvelous age we live in!

    As I pried blisters of paint from the clapboard siding, my mind flitted to snippets of my conversation with Mary Mason: "*a fête champêtre,*" "attractive, intelligent young ladies," and "a simple summer dress like mine." As usual, my mind focused on the words and their etymology. *Fête champêtre* was a French term that literally meant rural party. Nowadays it generally referred to a garden party. The outing was on a boat, so I guessed it was a social interaction out-of-doors. I had fought the urge to correct Mary Mason's pronunciation. While her pronunciation of *fête* was good, the ending on *champêtre* should have been more closed. But who am I to correct her? My French is far from perfect. My expertise lies with Greek and Latin.

I laughed at myself as I paused to swat away a swarm of gnats. Here I was dithering over language when the more pressing issue was what to wear. My wardrobe consisted of dark-colored walking skirts and mostly white shirtwaists, although I did own several black and brown shirtwaists that were certainly not suitable for a summer outing. I sighed heavily. I had the wardrobe of a schoolteacher.

Knowing that Mary Mason had invited "summer girls" from Pullman House and Thousand Island Park did not help matters. These girls arrived at the hotel with four or five Saratoga trunks and stacks of hat boxes. I would be a drab thistle in a bouquet of dainty primroses.

"For heavens sakes!" I chastised myself, attacking the weathered paint with renewed furor. "You are not a simpering summer girl who worries about hats and dresses to attract a summer dalliance or even better, a husband," I mumbled to myself as I gave the wall a final scrape. I climbed down from the stepladder, put the scraper down, and brushed the paint chips from my hands. "I have a home, a summer home, and a teaching position at the University of Pennsylvania. I don't need a husband," I reminded myself.

That last sentence came out louder than I intended and the words stung as sharply as the sweat that dripped into my eye. I looked around to see if there was anyone on the path or out in a skiff who might have overheard my outburst before I wiped the sweat from my eye. I was not opposed to marriage, but I hadn't met anyone who seemed suitable.

I swatted those pesky thoughts away along with another swarm of gnats. I needed to focus on the task at hand. I stepped back to survey my work. The scraping was finished, and I needed to sand next. I had sandpaper. Nat suggested I ask Arnie for a block of wood to wrap the sandpaper around to use as a handle. I took off the painter's smock and mob cab, brushed paint chips from my clothes, wiped the perspiration from my face, and headed toward the Bungalow worksite. I chose the north shore path along the backside of the island to avoid the posh south side as I wasn't wearing civilized attire. Uncle Sam had named the north shore path North Boulevard. I laughed to myself at the thought. This boulevard was still no better than a cow path from field to manger.

 A cacophony of sounds swirled in the air above me as I turned onto a path that led from North Boulevard to the Bungalow worksite. I heard grunts of men as they pushed and shoved, shouted and whistled to the horse team. Sledgehammers rang out as they struck metal wedges. The sounds grew louder as I climbed the steep, narrow path to the crest of Grenell. Uncle Sam was right. This would be the perfect spot for an aero-port. When I finally reached the top, I was surprised that there were only fifteen or twenty men toiling away. It sounded like a hundred. The scene was dirty and hot. Dust stirred up by the horse team swirled in the air. Thankfully, a cool breeze wafted through just as I saw Arnie. I hadn't laid eyes on Arnie since last September. He seemed taller, his shoulders broader. His face was stern as he shouted orders to the men, but it softened when he caught sight of me.

 "Miss Marguerite! Nat said you'd arrived. I hoped to see you today," he said as he waved me over.

 "Oh my! Look at this," I said. "You've made great progress. Uncle Sam said you'd accepted a delivery of stone today."

 "Yes." Arnie turned, let out a sharp whistle, and then shouted, "Delaney! Move those draft horses! Find a post in the shade for them and get them a drink. They're done for the day."

 He turned back toward me and continued. "This is our third delivery. We finally have a smooth system for unloading the stones. As you can see, we have the foundation laid and we're moving up. It'll be a grand building."

 Over the winter, I hadn't received many letters from Arnie. He had been knee-deep in a huge project for Mr. Caswell, who was the contractor for the Bungalow project. Knowing he would start contruction in the spring, Mr. Caswell directed Arnie to turn the path called Highland Avenue into a road. I was proud to learn from a letter that Arnie sent in

April, that Mr. Caswell had been so delighted with the completed road, that he asked Arnie to supervise stone deliveries.

"I'm keen on seeing the road you built over the winter," I told Arnie.

"Yes. Come see."

We walked around the foundation of the house.

"Do you think you'll finish this season?" I asked.

"God willing. The Sharples family is hoping to move in by next season. I only need to keep this work crew on task. Did you see the flying machine this morning?"

"Yes. Thanks to your brother, Nat."

"Work came to a complete standstill for nearly twenty minutes. I thought it would put us behind schedule but somehow seeing that apparatus spurred the men on. The sight of men flying through the sky made it seem like anything was possible."

"Is Friend Helen here?"

"No. Mrs. Sharples likes to be onsite to help supervise but she is in West Chester this week. Arriving sometime around the middle of the month."

I sighed and my shoulders drooped a bit. I'd hoped Helen would be able to lend me something appropriate to wear to the Princeton *fête champêtre*.

"Is there anything I can help you with?" Arnie asked as a look of concern crossed his face.

"No, no," I said, straightening again. "How is the little one? Alma, is it?"

"Alma Mae! What a little darling she is! Between you and me, I wasn't sure if I'd like being a pa. Babies cry and fuss and require so much attention. But at the end of every day, I can't wait to rush home and hold that sweet little bundle in my arms."

"And Mavis?"

"Doing well, especially now that Alma Mae is sleeping through the night. Mavis'll be happy to see you. Hope you can stop by soon."

"I'll make a point of it."

"Well, there it is," he said, pointing to a steep road that descended through the trees.

"That's amazing! How long did that take?"

"Started last fall and worked all winter on the project, weather permitting of course."

"Heard it was a cold one."

"Brutal. I would have liked a gentler slope—say a six percent grade perhaps—but that would have required switchbacks, and I didn't have enough land for that. I decided that a smooth roadbed would make it easier for the draft horses to pull a load of granite blocks up to the crest."

As we walked down the road, he told me how he had cleared the trees and then the brush. Barges brought crushed rock and then dirt, which he applied a wagonload at a time. Each load was tamped down and smoothed out before another load was applied. I smiled at him. Arnie was no longer that sullen twelve-year-old boy I had met my first year on the island. He had metamorphosed into a tall, strapping, confident young man.

"Oh, I almost forgot. I was hoping you had a block of wood I could use as an anchor for my sandpaper. I've chipped all the blistered paint and I'm ready to sand."

"Of course. I'll have one of the workmen deliver it to your cottage."

"Oh, I don't want to add to your workload."

"Believe me, whoever I pick to run it over to Castle Rock will think of it as a welcome break. I'll walk you to North Boulevard," he said.

We walked down the road as Arnie described the routine for unloading a scow of granite blocks and moving them to the top of the road. We stopped at the bottom where the new road met up with Park Avenue, the path that connected Uncle Sam's store on the front side of the island with North Boulevard on the backside of the island. Uncle Sam had promised that someday these footpaths would be paved. Arnie said he would walk me to North Boulevard and was telling me that Alma Mae had just starting to crawl when I stopped dead in my tracks.

"What's this?" I asked, pointing at a farmhouse that stood at the corner of the Park Avenue and North Boulevard paths. Workmen were building a new porch around what was obviously not a new cottage. It was as if it had dropped out of the sky and landed on the shore of Grenell.

"Thick, thick ice this winter. Captain El brought this over the ice in February."

When Sam said that Captain El had drug a house here I was thinking of a small shed, not a huge two-story farmhouse.

"Moved it from Robbins Island. Not too far away. Emery bought Robbins Island. He's quarrying rock on the north side for his new summer house on Calumet Island. Captain El was in charge of moving Emery's old summer house from Calumet Island to the head of Robbins and decided to move the old Robbin's homestead here. Think he did it to give himself a little breathin' room. Captain El has a house in Fishers Landing. Owns a boardinghouse nearby, mostly filled with relations. It burned down around Christmastime and they all came to live with him. Think that was motivation to buy the lot here and move the house to Grenell. Bought the lot in January; moved the house in February."

"I thought I saw construction on Calumet Island."

"Yes. Sharples's Bungalow will be a little smaller than the castle Emery is building on Calumet. Since we started about the same time, I'm spurrin' my crew into a little competition. Which castle will be finished first? Bungalow or Calumet Castle? Meanwhile, you should see what Emery is doing to Robbins. Cleared much of the interior to make orchards. Took a delivery of two thousand fruit trees this month. A Mr. Shoemaker is in charge of the project. Which reminds me. Mr. Shoemaker has asked about bees. He's hoping Miss Anne can advise him. When is Miss Anne returning?"

"Friend Anne is in Chicago. She won't be here for a few weeks."

"Visiting the fair?"

"Yes, with Ruth and our housemate Keiko Okami. Dr. Okami wanted to visit the fair and then the Thousand Islands before returning to Japan. I've taken enough of your time. Give my best to Mavis. And I can't wait to meet the newest member of the Hunkerson family. Oh, and don't forget, I need a block of wood. I need to start sanding."

"Sure you don't want me to find someone to sand and paint it for you? I can find a boy or two."

"I don't need any Tom Sawyers to whitewash my fence. I'm perfectly capable of doing it myself."

"Looks like you've already started . . . you're covered in paint," he said as he turned to leave.

"Paint chips! I've yet to start painting." I called back over my shoulder to him.

With a wave, Arnie was trotting back to the worksite. "I'll send the block of wood. Be there within the hour."

I paused and looked out at Murray Isle, where I could hear the ring of hammers as a troop of men worked on the large boathouse for the future hotel. Before I left West Philadelphia, the newspapers spread the gloom of our country's economic woe: railroads bankrupted, banks failed, and businesses closing their doors. Panic had sent a paralyzing shock through the country earlier this year. Yet here in the islands, there was construction everywhere. Not all were in financial ruin.

"Now what am I going to do?" I muttered to myself as I walked back along the North Boulevard path. There was no point going back to Castle Rock, so I followed North Boulevard beyond Sentry Rock and through the dark lot into what used to be the ice house-laundry lot for Hub House.

Hub House burned down in December of '83. Hard to believe that it will have been gone for ten years as of this December. What a quiet season it was the next year. No banter between the workers as they hung laundry and retrieved ice from the icehouse. Hub House's owner, Mr. Best, vowed to rebuild, but the icehouse-laundry lot next-door remained empty. Later in 1884, George Pabst, a friend of Mr. Pratt's, came to visit and ended up renting the property. He tent-camped that year, purchased the lot the next year, and built a small two-story cottage with a double-decker porch.

Mr. Pratt and Prof. Pabst both belonged to the Masonic lodge in Syracuse. Both had built their cottages to face due east, which apparently was important to the Masons, though for what reason I'm not sure. Prof. Pabst was the official organist for the Masons, and he taught music to a wide array of youngsters in the Syracuse area.

George Pabst's parents, four brothers, and two sisters were frequent visitors. The Pabst family loved two things: fishing in the morning and making music in the evening. How lucky am I to have a concert next-door nearly every night?

I saw a skiff tied to the dock at Prof. Pabst's cottage. I looked around but didn't see him. The Pratts had hired the Pabst brothers to dig a channel between their properties to increase the water flow in the little bay and to keep Sam's cows off Pratt Point. It had taken the brothers two years to dig the channel. Arnie had built a bridge that was high enough and long enough so that high water wouldn't wash it away and winter ice flows wouldn't rip it away during the spring thaw. I looked and saw a woman standing in the middle of the bridge. Is that Alice? I wondered, then realized with a start that it was Olivia. She was fourteen this year and her once chubby toddler face was now long and narrow.

"Good morning, Olivia," I called out, so I wouldn't startle her.

"Miss Marguerite. How nice to see you," she said, but her eyes were sad and no smile sprang to her lips. She was wearing a mauve dress of half mourning. Her hemline was much lower than last year. Her face seemed devoid of joy.

"I heard about your father. I'm so sorry for your loss. It was quite a shock. How are you getting on?" I asked.

"As well as can be expected, I suppose," Olivia said, looking at the cover of the book she'd been reading. Her words seemed empty, as if she were repeating a well-practiced line.

"How is your mother doing?" I asked.

Olivia inhaled deeply but still did not raise her eyes. "She's well," Olivia murmured, studying her hands.

"Is your mother accepting visitors?"

"I'm sure she would be happy to see you. She's up at the cottage."

"What are you reading?"

"*The Iliad.*"

"In Greek?"

Olivia nodded.

"I didn't know you were studying Greek."

"I am."

"Let me know if you need any help."

Olivia shrugged again, as if she didn't know how to respond.

"Miss Marguerite!"

I turned to see Olivia's younger sister, Edith, bounding toward me. I thought she might throw her arms around me and give me a hug, but she stopped short and put her hands behind her back as if trying to bridle her excitement.

"My! How you have grown," I said, noting that although she was taller, her hemline was still short, about mid-calf. Unlike Olivia who was now wearing her hair up in a style more befitting a young woman, Edith's hair was plaited in two long braids that hung down her back, each tied with a black ribbon.

"Mother will be so happy to see you. How was your winter?" Edith asked as she took my hand and pulled me toward the cottage.

I turned to say goodbye to Olivia but she had resumed reading, seemingly oblivious to my departure.

"Mother! Mother! We have a visitor," Edith called out as we rounded the little cottage and approached the front porch. Alice, who was busy mending a stocking, put her mending aside, and rose as we approached.

"Marguerite," she said, reaching for my hands.

Alice was dressed in widow's weeds. Her dress was of black crepe. It was customary for widows to wear black for a year and one day, though some women mourned for years beyond that. My mother, a widow for five years now, still wore black crepe and often a black veil over her face when she ventured from the house.

I hadn't been sure if Alice would be here this season. Widows were not supposed to go into society for at least a year. But then, Grenell wasn't exactly society. My first few summers here, I considered our little corner of Grenell as an escape from society. But society had intruded on our island world in the form of the Pullman House.

I didn't object to how much easier it was now to keep in touch with the world beyond our little island. It was nice to have a telegraph office at the hotel and a post office at the store. The hotel brought society to the island in the form of hops and balls and though I had never participated, I could hear the music and the laughter wafting through the night air.

I took both of Alice's hands in mine and gazed into her pale blue eyes and asked, "How are you getting along?"

I had been startled to receive a black-edged envelope with black sealing wax from Alice last February, for it could only mean one thing—a death announcement. Alice informed me that Otis had for several years suffered from heart trouble and indigestion. He had retired at about ten o'clock on Monday the first of March, feeling poorly. She'd awakened shortly after midnight and found him awake as well. She'd asked him how he was feeling and he replied that he was feeling about the same. When she awoke again around seven o'clock the next morning, he was lying lifeless by her side. He was fifty-five years of age.

"When you marry someone seventeen years your senior, you assume you are going to outlive him." Alice paused and inhaled deeply as if to bolster herself. "Still, I thought we would have a few more years together."

"I wasn't sure I would see you this summer."

"I wouldn't dream of missing a season on the river. It's what Otis lived for. Besides, I have two girls to raise. I sold his business. I'm prepared to sell the house and move to more modest quarters before I would give up this place." Alice motioned for me to sit. "I hope you have time for a cup of tea."

"That would be lovely."

"Edith, would you prepare a pot?"

Edith nodded and retreated inside the cottage.

"This was our special spot. We spent our honeymoon here in seventy-five and every summer since. I know he would want to keep the place for our girls and perhaps for our grandchildren someday. I'm thinking of building a rental cottage to pay the taxes and expenses."

After tea had been served, I ventured onto the topic of tomorrow's *fête champêtre*.

"A what?"

"An outing on the steamer *Nightingale* with a group of Princeton students and alumni as well. The Kerrs have invited me, and I'm afraid I have nothing suitable to wear," I said, my cheeks reddening. Looking at her widow's clothes, I suddenly realized how inappropriate my question about clothing might be.

"I'm afraid I can't help you. Fashion isn't exactly my forte."

"Fashion! Wait! I can help," Edith said, dashing onto the porch from the interior of the cottage. "Wait! Wait!" She held up a finger to emphasize that she would return momentarily and dashed back into the cottage.

Alice sighed. "Olivia is so serious about her studies. Edith, on the other hand, reads endlessly on fashion and coiffure."

Edith returned momentarily with a stack of *Harper's Bazar* magazines. "Isabelle, my half sister, shares them with me when she's finished reading them. These can help," Edith assured me.

"Edith, Miss Marguerite and I are visiting just now. Why don't you play something for us?"

The smile drained from Edith's face. She took the magazines back inside the cottage and moments later I heard a practice scale from a piano.

My eyes widened. "You have a piano?" The Pratt cottage, like our cottage, had started as a tent platform. During the past decade, they had added rooms, but the interior central room was still very small. How had they managed to squeeze a piano into that small space?

"A square grand. Prof. Pabst—George Pabst, that is—helped Otis find it. He purchased it at a great price. George and Otis brought it over the ice at the beginning of February. Otis caught a cold and well . . . The doctors said it was his heart, but I'm sure that nasty cough didn't help. Weakened him perhaps."

Inside I heard the shuffling of sheet music, and then Edith started playing a slow, moving melody.

"That's a song that Prof. Pabst composed called, 'Rustling Leaves.' A shame that Otis never got to hear Edith play the square grand. He talked endlessly about how lovely it would be to come home from a day of fishing and have Edith play for him." Alice's eyes filled with tears.

I said nothing but put my hand on hers.

Alice smiled at my gesture and gave my hand a little pat before dabbing away the tears that threatened to overflow onto her cheek. "Yes, well then—I have no time to wallow in self-pity. I have stockings to mend."

"And I have a cottage to paint. I will let you get back to your mending. Thank you for the tea," I said, rising to my feet. I wanted to call in to thank Edith but did not want to disturb her while at the piano.

"Yes. It was lovely talking to you. Do stop by any time. The girls and I always enjoy visiting with you," Alice said as she picked up her mending.

The bridge was empty when I returned. I paused for a moment and looked around hoping to say goodbye to Olivia. I saw her sitting on the west rock looking out toward the river and decided not to disturb her.

"Miss Hartranft?"

I turned to see Prof. Pabst on his dock.

"How was your winter, professor?" I asked as I walked to join him on his dock.

"Good. And yours?"

"I had a good winter," I said. "Quite sad about Otis."

Prof. Pabst nodded solemnly then turned toward the Pratt cottage. "Edith is progressing nicely in her lessons. Ahh . . . that's the piece she played at the recital earlier this year, 'Erika' by Gustav Lange. Edith tends to rush through songs like it's a race. She's finally playing 'Erika' the way Lange intended: slowly, strongly, with meaning. She's finally perfected it."

"Seems she has a good teacher."

He bowed to me.

"Professor," I said with a nod, turning to take my leave.

"Wait . . ." he called to me just as I stepped off the dock. I turned and saw him pull from the fish box a large stringer of fish. "Caught too many fish. Can't possibly eat them all today. I'm giving some to Alice and the girls, but I have enough if you'd like a perch or two."

"Perfect! I was craving a perch meal."

"Professor," he said, bowing to me in return, and I walked back with the beautiful sounds of piano music floating on the June breeze.

After an afternoon of sanding, I cleaned up and fried the perch for supper. My arms ached as I washed up my supper dishes. As I dried the last fork and put it away, I heard footsteps on the spiral path.

"I hope I'm not intruding," Edith said. She held up a basket filled with magazines and other things. "I brought a few things to help you plan your wardrobe for tomorrow."

I invited Edith inside the cottage, and we spent the next ten minutes pulling walking skirts and shirtwaists from my trunk.

"Miss Kerr said a simple summer dress would be appropriate, and, as you see, I don't have a simple summer dress."

"Don't worry. It's all about the accessories. Look what I have here! Ribbons, sashes, gloves, an enamel pin, and a parasol. *Harper's Bazar* says that a parasol is the accessory of the season. Perfect for framing your face. See!" Edith popped the parasol open and tilted her head this way and that.

Edith paged through the magazines pointing out possibilities.

"You seem to have a flair for fashion, Edith. Thank you for your suggestions."

Her eyes brightened. "I love fashion. Would you like to see some of my sketches?" She pulled a sketchbook from the basket and showed me sketches of dresses and hats.

"Mother wants me to pay more attention to my music. It never really mattered to her before, but Papa loved music, and he wanted both of us girls to play the piano. Olivia was all thumbs at the piano. Papa used to take my hand and look at my long fingers. I may have piano fingers, but my heart isn't into the music. It's not that I don't like music; it's just that I want to be an artist. I want to study in Paris and maybe design fashion or hats."

"Who knows! Maybe someday."

Edith's smile wilted. "Mama says that isn't possible now. She assures us we will be educated, for that is important, but studying in Paris is out of the question."

I smiled. I wanted to tell Edith that anything could happen. Just look at me.

I put my hand on hers and thanked her for her help.

"I really must run. Mother is expecting me. Have fun tomorrow!"

After Edith left, I pulled the great yellow book from the shelf above my bed. This yellow book had brought me to the Thousand Islands and set my life on a different course. I ran my fingers across the embossed letters on the front: Walt Whitman. The Good Gray Poet had died in March of 1892. I paged open the book and looked at the inscription. There, in Mr. Whitman's immense, heavy-stroked handwriting was written, "Resist much, obey little."

I suppose that could apply to fashion as well.

I felt calm for the first time all day.

CHAPTER
three

I hung the small oval mirror on the wall opposite the window so light would reflect into the room. This morning, the light bounced off the water and flashed shimmering reflections around the room. I'd never realized before how small the mirror was until this morning. Smaller than a dinner plate, the mirror barely showed my entire face in it. I took it off the wall and looked at my face from all angles, stopping now and then to take a moistened flannel to wipe away a speck of paint dust.

"There," I said to my reflection. "I'm reasonably well-scrubbed." An hour ago I wasn't sure if that would be possible. I'd shot out of bed at first light and carefully covered my hair with my mobcap. Next, I'd donned my painters smock and work gloves. The walls and eaves of the cottage were festooned with cobwebs. An army of spiders must have toiled all night. Before I could start sanding, I had to wipe away all the cobwebs and the debris amassed in the webs. There were enough pine needles to start a new tree. After two hours of sanding, fine white powder caked every inch of my body. I'd gasped when I first saw my ghostly pallor. After two pitchers of water and lots of Ivory soap and rubbing, I joined the ranks of the living.

I changed out of my work clothes and into a plain white shirtwaist and hunter green walking skirt. "It's all in the accessories," I said to my reflection, parroting the phrase young Edith had repeated as she showed me sketches in *Harper's Bazar*.

Instead of a schoolmarm bun, I spent a little extra time taming my dark curls into a roll at the nape of my neck. I placed a Sennett straw boater with a low crown and wide double brim on my head and checked my reflection to make sure it was on straight. Edith had helped me attach a black velvet ribbon at the base with a pink ribbon and bow above. I secured the boater to the top of my head with a long hatpin. I wrapped the mint green and white sash around my waist as Edith's words echoed in my ears: "Mint green and white is a particularly popular color combination this year." I decided the crocheted gloves would be a nice accessory but left the parasol on my bed and rushed from the room. I choose North Boulevard thinking it would be quicker as I would likely meet someone along the more civilized south side boardwalk and might be delayed by conversation.

I glanced at the watch pinned to my bodice and realized I needed to hurry. But the panic over being late did not supersede my growing anxiety of meeting the throng of young men from Princeton. "Remember to be yourself," my younger sister, Lily, had advised me before any outing arranged by our mother's friends who fancied themselves as matchmakers. There had been many such outings in the past few years. Finding a suitable match for me seemed to be the sole interest of Mother and her many friends.

Of course, my older sister, Rose, usually gave me the exact opposite advice. "For heaven's sake, don't blather on about Greek and Latin. And by all means, don't quote any poetry," she would remind me. Rose had a point. When I'm nervous, I often blurt out foreign phrases or quote poetry, for I find ancient languages and poetry comforting. "Better yet, say nothing at all! Smile and nod. Smile and nod. Pretend to be totally enthralled by what the gentleman is saying. Men love to be the center of attention."

I hurried along the path, carefully raising my skirts where the path was not cut back as there was still a little dew clinging to the top of the grass. When I walked around the store and crossed the bridge that attached the new store dock to the shore, I found Uncle Sam standing in front of me with arms spread wide. "There you are!" he said as if I had arrived at his invitation. "Here to see the new dock at last! Come! Come," he said, taking me by the elbow and leading me to the center of the dock. "You may recall that on that very first season you visited Grenell, I told you that I would have a steamship dock."

"Surely you did!"

"It's jim-dandy, wouldn't you say? Mighty proud of it. 'Course I had a steamship dock for Grenell House before I sold out to Sayles. But that dock was carried away in a storm in eighty-five. High winds and high water, you know. It'll take more than a storm to move this baby. It's a hundred feet long, thirty feet wide. Built on ten cribs. Each crib is ten feet square and filled with hard head stone from bottom to top. Some fifteen feet of stone anchoring her."

"It's marvelous," I said and inhaled deeply. The top layer of cedar planks still smelled as aromatic as the day they were cut.

"The underpinning—the twelve-by-twelve timbers—were recovered from the old mooring place in the upper bay of Clayton back when timber rafts were floated down to Montreal and beyond. Although the timbers have been underwater for the past fifty years, they were well-preserved and as sound as ever." He knocked his walking stick on the board to prove his point. "Good thing the ice was so thick this past winter. The horses were pullin' loads of three to four tons, showin' the remarkable strength of the ice."

"There's our girl," Mary Mason gushed when she saw me. The dimple in her left cheek reappeared as she smiled at my approach.

Mary Mason was wearing another white summer dress, this one with lilies of the valley printed on it. A lacy rounded collar framed her kind face, and at her throat was a pin with an enameled painting of lilies of the valley. Around her waist was a spring green sash. Her gloves were the same lovely shade of green. Pinned on her head was a straw boater with two fresh daisies stuck in the headband.

"I knew that I could count on you! You are a lifesaver," she said as she reached out and grabbed my gloved hand in hers, and gave it a little squeeze. As she leaned close, the fresh, springlike, calming scent of lily of the valley wafted over me. She even smelled green.

"I'm honored to be included," I said, trying to think what my sister Lily would say.

"I want to introduce you to the young ladies from Pullman House, but

I have a few details to check on first. Lois!" Mary Mason waved a hand over her head and attracted the attention of her younger sister, who rushed over at her sister's behest. "Lois, could you check with Mr. Grenell—the younger Mr. Grenell, not Uncle Sam—about the ice and lemonade? And cups! We'll need cups!" she called after Lois, who rushed off to do her sister's bidding.

"The younger Mr. Grenell?" I asked, turning to Uncle Sam. "Your son Myron is here on the island?"

"No. My nephew, George—my brother Jason's son," he said nodding toward the man who had come out onto the store porch to talk to young Lois. "I brought him to the island last month to help his cousin, Herb. Expanding the operations. Here! Let me introduce you. George!" Uncle Sam shouted, snapping his fingers to get George's attention, then motioning him over with a wave of his hand.

George raised a hand in recognition, nodded to Lois, then strode our way. He was a tall man with sandy brown hair, broad shoulders, and an easy smile."

"George, this is one of our cottagers, Miss Hartranft. She has the white cottage high on the rock off the path on the north shore."

"Good day to you, miss," George said, beaming broadly. He touched his fingers to his forehead then bought them out in an energetic salute.

"George!" Herb called from the porch. "Where in the blazes are the ice tongs?"

"Be there in a minute," George called back over his shoulder.

George was as different from his cousin Herb as day is from night. Herb Kilborn was a small, wiry man with dark hair. Herb was the son of Uncle Sam's sister, Mary Anne Kilborn from Lafargeville, seven miles southeast of Clayton. Herb and his wife, Theresa, had moved to the island in 1891 and have had charge of the store since then.

George clasped his hands in front of him and nodded toward me intently, "Look forward to serving your needs, Miss Hartranft. We have everything you need here at the Grenell Island Store. Speaking of which. . ." he said slowly, turning toward his uncle. "Miss Kerr says they are stopping at Grand View Park for a catered picnic. If we had picnic tables on our empty lot, we could be catering picnics here."

"George! The ice tongs!" Herb called from the porch, his arms raised in desperation. Never had I heard the mild-mannered Herb raise his voice before.

George turned back toward his cousin. "In a minute!"

Herb stomped back inside the store.

"I think we're missing an opportunity here," George continued. "We could be—we should be—catering to fishing groups and other excursionists. We have the dock to take large steamers now. You and Aunt Lucy have the reputation for fine food already . . . at least you had a reputation. It's been four years since Grenell House closed."

"Quite right. We have the lot but not a kitchen large enough to prepare food. Once we get the hotel built, we'll have the kitchen. All in due time, my boy. All in due time. Now, better get back to the store and find the ice tongs for Herb before he has a conniption fit."

"Pleasure to meet you, Miss Hartranft," George said with a genial nod in my direction before he trotted back down the bridge that joined the long steamship dock with the boardwalk leading to the store.

"Please apologize to Aunt Lucy. I've been preparing the cottage for painting. And now this— I motioned toward the *Nightingale*. I promise to stop by for a visit soon."

Uncle Sam nodded and waved. "I'll tell her."

I turned and hurried over to Mary Mason who was eager to introduce me to the summer girls waiting for the *Nightingale* to arrive.

Obviously, this group of girls subscribed to *Harper's Bazar* and had read the same articles as young Edith. All of them had leg-of-mutton sleeves puffed up and starched. Every single one had a parasol open to frame her bright shiny face. Even from a half dozen paces away, I could tell I was probably a decade older than most.

The first two young women we approached were dressed exactly the same. Each wore a two-piece gown of cream-colored silk with coral pink stripes. Flounces of beige lace trimmed the hems of their skirts. Their parasols were made of the same fabric and tipped with a tortoiseshell finial.

"Excuse me, ladies," Mary Mason said.

I blinked back my surprise as the girls turned and two identical faces with bright blue eyes peered at me over aquiline noses. Their rosebud lips were nearly the same shade as the coral pink velvet ribbon that trimmed the neck and waistline of their summer dresses.

"I'd like to introduce Miss Hartranft, who has a cottage here on Grenell Island Park."

The girls nodded demurely, inclined their heads together, and said in sugary-sweet unison, "A pleasure to make your acquaintance."

"Miss Hartranft, may I present to you Etta and Gladys Upton?"

"The pleasure is mine, I'm sure," I said, nodding back to the two girls whose rosebud lips bloomed into chaste smiles.

Mary Mason took me by the elbow and led me to the next group of four girls. They were engaged in lively banter as they checked the condition of their attire.

"How does the hem of my dress look?"

"Is my hat on straight?"

"Why couldn't the steamer have stopped at the Pullman House dock?" a pert blonde asked. "I think I might have muddied my hem on that long walk to the Grenell Island Store dock."

"Ladies, I would like to introduce Miss Hartranft, who has a cottage on the north shore of Grenell Island."

"You live here? On this island? The whole year?" asked a girl with chestnut hair coiled into an elegant, high coiffure.

"I summer here," I replied.

They continued primping, barely looking in my direction.

Their constant primping made me self-conscious of my own attire. Immediately, Lily's voice came to mind. Lily would comfort me by saying, "When in doubt, wear a wonderful smile. Your whole face changes when you smile. Your eyes brighten, and your whole face glows. Your smile is quite disarming, you know." My dear sweet, sister Lily always knew what to say to make me feel safe, secure, and loved. The thought alone made me smile.

Rose, on the other hand, gave alternative advice. "Try not to think too hard. Better yet, don't think at all. When you're pondering a question or trying to remember one of those lengthy quotes you're fond of inflicting on others, your face turns prune-ish, like you are sucking on a lemon. You get two deep furrows between your eyebrows. If you're not careful, those furrows will permanently age you overnight."

I ran a gloved finger between my eyebrows now, hoping to smooth any prune-ish look away, and smiled at the girls.

Miss Kerr rattled off their names, and I tried to assign the name to the girl but came away only thinking of them as the blond with the pug nose, the brunette with elegant eyebrows, the chestnut-haired girl with the elaborate coiffure, and the mousy-haired girl with the large vacant eyes.

The girls nodded and murmured, "pleased to make your acquaintance" but it was clear they were not interested in me, but only the men we were about to meet.

Mother would have been horrified at their lack of attention during an introduction. "They should at least feign interest," she would have said. While being introduced, Mother had instructed me to stand straight with shoulders back and chin held high, "to show off that lovely swan-like neck of yours."

I took a big breath, pulled my shoulders back and held my head high, though I was certain not one of them noticed anything about me.

"What do college men talk about?" the mousy girl asked.

"Sports. I heard the Princeton group is particularly fond of their football and crewing teams," Miss Brunette said knowingly.

"Football! I know nothing about football!" Miss Blond moaned. Her voice bordered on panic.

"I think they can all speak about rowing or fishing, always popular topics for excursionists in the islands. Don't fret, girls! Just relax and be yourselves," Mary Mason suggested.

"Oh, Miss Kerr, when are they arriving? I'm afraid I might melt in this torrid sunlight," Miss Chestnut asked, readjusting her parasol for optimum shade.

"Soon," Mary Mason assured them. "They're due any moment now."

"I do hope so! I'm afraid I might freckle if I get much more sunlight," Miss Blond said.

"Come, Miss Hartranft. I have one more introduction to make," Mary Mason said, nodding to a woman standing near the far corner of the dock. I had noticed the woman there but had assumed that because she stood so far away that she wasn't part of our group. She was wearing a muted yellow dress with soft moss-colored trim. A matching moss-colored reticule dangled from her wrist. No lace. No gold braid trim. Her sleeves did not have a stylish puff; they were more straight and narrow like mine. I smiled at the simplicity of her dress.

"Miss Caldwell," Mary Mason called out as we approached. The lone woman turned, and her sharp eyes locked with mine. "Miss Caldwell, this is Miss Hartranft. She summers on Grenell Island Park in a cottage on the north side of the island."

"Miss Kerr! Miss Kerr!" Miss Blond called out in obvious distress.

"Excuse me, ladies," Mary Mason said and hurried off to the knot of young girls to soothe some newly found angst.

"A cottager?" Miss Cadwell asked, raising an arched eyebrow at me. "That accounts for your sensible dress. Appears you are the only one of us dressed for a picnic. That's what *a fête champêtre* is, isn't it? Just a fancy French word for picnic?"

"I suppose," I said, wondering if her "sensible" comment was meant as a slight. Perhaps she was just being observant. I glanced back at the Pullman House girls who were in a dither about something. I turned back toward Miss Caldwell who was eyeing me warily. She seemed more mature than the other Pullman House girls, perhaps nearly as old as me. Was this why she was standing so far apart from them?

"I'm certainly not dressed for such an event, especially with these silk slippers. The walk over nearly ruined them. I had no idea there was a farm between the hotel and the store. But then I never intended to leave the Pullman House veranda for my entire stay. However, Miss Kerr, the older one, that is—Mary Mason, is it?"

I nodded.

"She can be quite persuasive. So here I am being spirited away on some ill-conceived outing instead of relaxing with tea on the veranda or playing whist in the parlor."

Miss Caldwell turned away from me then and stared out at the river as if looking for some escape. My head was flooded with questions. Who was this Miss Caldwell? Where was she from? Was she traveling alone? Did she have money of her own? Was she employed—therefore having money to fund summer excursions? Or was she traveling with family, perhaps with a maiden aunt as an escort? Though I had the notion that, like me, she was approaching the age at which she might soon be the maiden aunt designated to escort younger nieces on trips.

Mother had worked a lifetime to squelch my penchant for asking too many questions. I wondered if those deep furrows Rose referred to had reappeared between my eyebrows and reached up to rub them away with my index finger. Thinking of Lily, I smiled broadly then. But the smile felt unnatural, more like I was an escapee from a lunatic asylum, smiling inanely at nothing in particular. I was thankful Miss Caldwell was still staring intently at the river far beyond the Grenell Island Store dock. I leaned forward slightly to see if I could ascertain exactly what she was staring at but saw nothing but the dazzling blue water of the St. Lawrence.

We stood there in a bubble of silence as the Pullman House girls continued to fret and prattle. Perhaps Miss Caldwell thought I had left. I considered slipping away and leaving her to her ruminations. I took a small step back, but before I could turn and go, she asked, "Have you had previous encounters with college men?" She had not turned to face me. She asked the question as she stared out at the river.

The inquiry perplexed me. What an odd way to word that question. Encounters? The Latin roots literally fixed the meaning at "meet as an adversary." That definition has softened through time, and today's meaning was not quite as adversarial. But how to answer? I had spent the bulk of the last dozen years at the University of Pennsylvania, a rare woman in a sea of college men. I had *met* many college men, but had I had any *encounters*? "A few," I replied tentatively. "And you?"

She turned and focused her hawklike eyes on me then smirked. "A few," she said, parroting my response.

A titter arose from the knot of Pullman House girls, as the steamer *Nightingale* appeared from around Front Island. "Here it comes. That's it! The *Nightingale*!" Miss Brunette said.

"Look there! My, what handsome young men. And so many of them," Miss Chestnut purred.

Crowded aboard the open deck at the bow of the steamer was a group of fresh-faced, clean-shaven young men. The ones wearing boaters tipped their hats. The others waved their arms.

The Pullman House girls twirled their parasols and tilted their heads coquettishly this way and that. Miss Brunette withdrew a lacy hankie from her reticule and began waving it daintily at the approaching steamer. Seconds later, the entire group had handkerchiefs fluttering in the morning breeze like surrender flags on a battlefield.

"This is it, girls," Miss Blonde declared. "Our future husbands may be aboard that steamer."

Miss Caldwell made a disapproving click of her tongue. "Such a spectacle," she grumbled and then as if to distance herself from any association with the Pullman House girls, she moved even closer to the end of the dock.

"Miss Hartranft! Miss Caldwell! This way," Mary Mason called out as she waved to us to join the rest of the girls.

"After you," I said, gesturing toward the waiting gangway.

"Oh, no . . ." Miss Caldwell said with a shake of her finger. Then, with a grand gesture indicating that I should proceed, ". . . after you."

CHAPTER
four

As soon as the steamer was tied to the dock and the gangway rolled up to the aft deck, Captain H. S. Johnston disembarked and greeted our parasoled group. His handlebar mustache stretched clear across his face and made his perpetual smile seem like it went from ear to ear. "My! My! More ladies at this landing than at the last. I want to welcome you aboard the steamer *Nightingale*. She has three salons. The one in the aft is the gentleman's salon, the center salon is a gathering place for all, and the front salon is for the ladies. All are welcome on either the bow or the aft open decks, but I will warn you ladies that the back deck is for smoking."

Miss Brunette scowled and whispered back that there were already girls aboard.

"No fair!" Miss Blond whispered to her friend. "They had a chance to meet them first."

Her friend put a gloved finger to her lips and nodded toward the captain.

"I am the master of the vessel, Captain H. S. Johnston. Mr. Knight is the engineer in the wheelhouse, George Bennett is the purser, and Arthur LaRue is the deckhand. Please feel free to alert any one of us if you need assistance. Welcome aboard, ladies."

Mr. Bennet and Mr. LaRue stood on either side of the gangway and handed us aboard.

The steamer *Nightingale* launched in September 1890 and was owned by the veteran shipbuilder Captain S. G. Johnston of Clayton. She was run by his son, Captain H. S. Johnston. The *Nightingale* had a distinctive happy chugging sound to her steam engine and a sweet, high-pitched whistle. She was a smaller steamer, with no upper deck, but due to her fine equipment and the courteous treatment accorded to her patrons by the crew, she was a favorite charter steamer for large parties. Though I've seen her many times up and down the river in the last two years, I'd never been aboard. I was curious to see her interior.

The long, narrow interior of the *Nightingale* was divided into three salons that were paneled, trimmed with elaborate molding and painted white. The ladies boarded first onto the open aft deck and were hastily ushered through the men's salon that served as a smoking room. Though no one was presently smoking, a miasma of cigar smoke hung in the air. The main salon was the biggest compartment. There were plenty of wicker chairs and settees around the perimeter of the salon, and three round tables with chairs occupied the center of the long room. The ladies' salon was in front, where those feeling faint or weary could recover. An open deck on both the front and back of the long narrow boat offered the best venues for viewing the islands. By now, the young men had filed back into the main salon where we were all herded together.

Somehow I ended up on the same side of the center tables as the three sisters from Thousand Island Park. The Pullman House girls, including Miss Caldwell, were on the other side of the tables. I stood straight and tall with my chin raised as I greeted the clean-shaven, fresh-faced Princeton students.

John Kerr asked for our attention. John and Mary Mason introduced themselves first. Then, John introduced the young men, identifying them by what year they were in school or by the year they had graduated. Mary Mason introduced the young ladies by the island where they were summering.

The Pullman House girls had closed their parasols and now I could see their heavily flowered hats. Only then did I notice that Miss Caldwell was considerably taller than the other girls for she peered at me from over a garden of hat flowers.

Miss Blond was wide-eyed and deep in concentration while Mary

Mason introduced the young ladies. I could see her lips move as she counted while the young men were introduced.

Mary Mason had barely finished her introductions when Miss Blond turned to Miss Brunette and announced in a loud whisper. "Great odds! Young men outnumber the young ladies almost three to one."

Miss Chestnut gave her a warning nudge to remind her to lower her voice. The "odds" were slightly better than that, but I didn't correct her. Miss Caldwell looked at me then, crossing her eyes slightly before rolling them in exasperation.

I pressed my lips together and raised my gloved hand to my mouth to suppress a laugh.

"Excuse me," one of the Thousand Island Park girls to my left addressed me as the *Nightingale* pulled away from the Grenell Island Store dock and headed to Round Island. "I'm sorry I missed your name. Miss Heart, was it?"

"Hartranft," I said. "And you all have the same surname—Sawyer—was it? Are you sisters?"

"Yes. Our parents have a cottage on Coast Avenue at Thousand Island Park," the one next to me said.

"We've practically grown up there," the one next to her said.

"Now who is who?" I asked. The three girls looked remarkably alike. They all had light brown hair, bright blue eyes, dazzling smiles and were dressed in white summer dresses with different laces and frills. Like many island girls, they were hatless. "I'm Carrie, and these are my two younger sisters, Bertha and Yvette."

"Oh! I think I've seen you out rowing. I have a cottage on the north side of Grenell."

"The one upon the rock?" Carrie asked

"Yes!"

"You must have a lovely view of the Narrows," Bertha mused.

"I do," I said.

"Well, I'm afraid you'll only see two of us out rowing this season," Bertha confided.

"Yes," Carrie agreed.

Yvette rolled her eyes.

"Why is that?" I asked.

"Yvette is passionate about wheeling these days. I doubt we'll be able to get her in a skiff at all," Carrie reported.

"I'm amazed we got her off her safety bicycle long enough to go on this excursion," Bertha teased.

"I'm surprised she didn't insist we bring the bicycle with us!" Carrie said. Carrie and Bertha laughed and Yvette smiled broadly.

"Now that I think of it, that would have been a splendid idea! I'd love to go wheeling on other islands. How about Grenell? Is it suitable for wheeling?" Yvette asked.

"I think Grenell would disappoint you. We only have one short road and a series of paths. The paths are crisscrossed with roots and chock-full of rocks. Too hazardous for wheeling. I think you might enjoy Grindstone, though. Grindstone has proper roads."

"See! Miss Hartranft agrees with me," Yvette chided her sisters.

"The three of you are welcome to visit me on Grenell anytime. If you see me on the porch or dock, please feel free to stop by."

"Oh look! Miss Blond called out. "They are all lined up on the dock. The more the merrier!" I looked out and saw a dozen or more young men standing on the Round Island dock. "Too many to count. All I know is our odds just improved."

The boat landed. The young men streamed aboard. John and Mary Mason made introductions again and as the *Nightingale* trilled her whistle and lumbered away from the dock, the noise in the central salon grew louder and louder.

Perhaps it was my years at Penn, but I could easily pick out the students from the alumni. The younger set embraced the trend toward clean-shaven faces and while a few of the students were mustachioed, they couldn't hide their fresh-faced boyish looks. Men out of college almost always had mustaches, and many were bearded with small goatees or trim Van Dyke beards. Only one or two had full beards.

The center salon was filled with laughter and conversation. It was too loud and held too many people for me, so I pushed my way into the next salon.

The ladies' salon was empty, and I paused, drinking in the quiet. Staying here might lead others to think I was feeling unwell. So I pushed my way out the door onto the front deck and breathed in the fresh river scent of the St. Lawrence. I've always found river air to be most salubrious and calming. I shut my eyes and inhaled again and came up coughing. Acrid cigarette smoke burned my nostrils and chafed my lungs. I raised my hand to my mouth to suppress another ragged cough. There were a half dozen gentlemen crammed into the bow. Four were smoking.

"Gentleman! There's a lady present. Captain Johnston made it very clear that smoking was to be confined to the men's salon and the back deck." The broad-shouldered young man threw his hands up and shooed the smokers toward the back of the ship as if they were a flock of hens.

"Sorry, miss. Freshmen never know how to behave," he said to me over the heads of the smokers.

Three of the offending freshman hung their heads and turned to leave. That left three young men on the bow: the broad-shouldered fellow, a scrappy-looking cigarette smoker, and a lanky chap leaning on the railing and looking out over the port side of the bow.

"Sorry, miss," said the first freshman as he passed. He took another puff from his cigarette but refused to exhale as he passed me. Two more cigarette smokers squeezed by. The scrappy-looking fellow inhaled deeply and then blew the smoke into the broad-shouldered man's face and said, "We're not freshman anymore. We're sophomores now, so stop pickin' on us."

"I don't care if you're a senior. Rules are rules. Go on! Get out of here and take that foul cigarette with you."

The scrappy sophomore with the cigarette balled up his right fist and reared back. "I oughta knock you into next week." He punched his fist forward, a good half-foot shy of the broad-shouldered fellow's face. Nearly a foot taller than the scrappy lad, the broad-shouldered fellow didn't flinch. Instead, he put his balled fists on his hips and stared at the little guy who had struck a pugilistic pose.

The broad-shouldered fellow rolled his eyes, clucked his tongue, and waved a warning finger at the smaller man. "If you're not careful, I'll leave you looking like James, Poe, and Wheeler."

"Ha! Try it. I'll even give you a free shot. Go ahead. Give me your best shot," the cheeky sophomore challenged as he flicked his lit cigarette into the river and jutted his chin forward.

I stepped back, not sure if the two were about to engage in violent fisticuffs right here on the open deck. I suddenly remembered Mary Mason's comment about needing a "handful of the fairer sex to balance out the raucous collegians." I had not taken that comment literally. I looked to the other fellow leaning on the port rail. He hadn't moved. He didn't look back. He continued staring out at the river as if he werethe only person onboard.

The broad-shouldered fellow raised his fists and advanced.

"You don't scare me!" the little guy said as he backed away.

The two swatted at each other with open hands.

I inhaled sharply, put my hand to my bodice, and turned, wondering if I should summon Mr. Kerr.

"Preston, what are you doing? You're scarin' the poor girl. She's gonna go home thinking Princeton men are all ruffians and thugs. Apologize!" the broad-shouldered fellow demanded, motioning toward me.

"Why should I apologize?" the scrappy fellow asked, dropping his arms to his side. As soon as he dropped his arms, the broad-shouldered fellow struck like a snake and wrapped the scrappy fellow in a headlock.

"Ow! OW!" the scrappy fellow yelled out.

"Because I'm an upperclassman and you're a lower classman. Now apologize."

"Sorry, miss," he squeaked. The broad-shouldered fellow released the scrappy-looking fellow, who scurried off. Once past me, he turned and shouted, "James, Poe, and Wheeler were upperclassman and we made them look like they lost a prizefight."

The broad-shouldered fellow didn't bother to reply. Instead, he swatted the comment away like a swarm of flies and then focused his attention on me, beckoning me forward. "My apologies, miss. Sometimes we spend so much time roughhousing together that we forget how to behave in civilized company. I'm Thomas Quigley, junior in metallurgy and mining. At your service," he said with a slight bow. While his mannerisms were like that of a middle-aged man, his face still had a large boyish grin. He had thick, dark-brown hair he had tried to subdue with pomade but a cowlick at the crown stuck up mischievously.

I looked at him quizzically. Had he called me a poor girl? This manchild seemed to think of me as a young girl in need of his protection. I was probably a good eight years older than he was. Perhaps ten.

"Does the student body often resort to fisticuffs?"

"Just horseplay."

"Didn't sound like horseplay for James, Poe and Wheeler."

He tossed back his head and let out a loud, hearty laugh that ended in a girlish titter.

"No. No. Those lads looked like they had lost a round with a prizefighter. Whew!" Mr. Quigley grimaced at the thought of their mangled faces. "But it was snowballs that caused the damage, not fists. It was the annual freshman-sophomore snowball fight, one of the many long-standing traditions at Princeton. Got a little out of hand this year."

The lanky gentleman leaning over the railing shot a glance over his shoulder, let out a huff of displeasure and then turned away again.

"Where are you from?" Mr. Quigley asked.

"West Philadelphia."

"West Philadelphia? I know it well. Was there last November for the Princeton-Penn football match."

A small smile sprang to my lips. I've never been to a football game at Penn but know that Princeton is a huge rival.

"Are you a footballer?" I asked.

"On the junior varsity team last season. On the varsity team next year. Our varsity team did pretty well last year, finished with a twelve-two record, with twelve shutouts and a combined total of 473 points to eighteen."

"Except against Penn."

He dropped his chin to his chest. "Except against Penn," he muttered to his chest. He raised his head again, his eyes bright. A huge smile lit up his face. "But believe me! Things will be different next season when Penn comes to New Jersey! I'll make sure of that."

I had the feeling that Mr. Quigley would personally make sure of that.

"Are you familiar with the islands?" he asked, turning to look out at the river.

"Somewhat," I said.

"Can you point out Grindstone Island?" he asked.

We had steamed between Round Island and Little Round and were in the channel now. I pointed at the distant shoreline to our starboard side which was Grindstone Island.

"That is an island? I assumed it was the Canadian shore."

"No. Grindstone is one of the large islands. Why do you want to know?"

"We're going there next. Taking a tour of the Forsyth Granite quarry."

"Really? I had no idea. Miss Kerr hadn't mentioned that stop."

"It's the only reason I came. I'm studying metallurgy and mining, but geology is my passion. I especially enjoy learning about the origin, formation and mineral composition of rocks."

"Oh, lithology."

Mr. Quigley stepped back, and his brown eyes widened. "How did you know? Do you study geology?"

"Not geology. Greek. *Lithos* is the Greek word for rock."

The lanky fellow on the port bow rail turned to face us. It was the first time I saw his face. It was long, with small eyes and a small, tight-lipped mouth. He cocked his head quizzically, but when he saw me looking at him, he turned back to looking out at the river again.

"What's that island over there?" Mr. Quigley asked.

"That is Bluff Island, and that one over there is Beckwith Island," I told him. "We're approaching Clayton. See the silver steeple of St. Mary's Church?"

I didn't tell Mr. Quigley that when I first arrived on the river, St. Mary's was a small wooden building on James street with a truncated tower and no steeple. The beautiful granite church replaced the wooden church in 1889. On a clear day, islanders at the head of Grenell could see St. Mary's silver steeple gleaming in the sun.

We steamed close to Calumet Island, and I told Mr. Quigley that this island was owned by Charles Emery, the tobacco tycoon and largest stockholder in the Frontenac Hotel.

"He's just now building a summer home, is he?"

"No, he had a lovely wooden summer home that he had moved to Robbins Island."

"Is he getting his stone from the Forsyth quarry?"

"No. He has his own quarry on the north side of Robbins Island, though, I suppose he's calling it Emery Island now since he recently purchased the island."

I told him about Governors Island and about Thomas Alvord, former lieutenant governor of New York, who had a cottage at the head of the island. "Mr. Alvord had a 6-pounder pointed upriver at the top of the steep precipice that he liked to set off several times a day to salute passing ships. Mr. Emery also purchased Governors Island. He had no interest in the cottage and allowed Alvord to remove that and his other buildings. I think they moved them to somewhere on Grindstone," I told him.

"It's like moving a cottage from one mountaintop to another."

I blinked, looking at him with surprise, unsure of his meaning.

"That's what these islands are, you know. What we are looking at here are the tops of an ancient mountain range—some of the oldest rocks on the North American continent."

Instantly, I wanted to tell him how Flossie, my roommate from Penn, and I liked to lie facedown on Castle Rock and try to feel the heartbeat of Mother Earth. I had imagined Mother Earth as being a young mother, but now perhaps I might envision her as a lovely, doting grandmother. Not just old rock, but the tops of old mountains. What a fantastic image that was! "How wonderful to know that I live on a mountaintop."

"You do?"

"Yes! I have a cottage on the north shore of Grenell Island."

"Tell me. I've heard there are potholes in the islands. Have you any knowledge of them?"

"I know precisely where they are. I love to take visitors there."

Mr. Quigley moved closer to me and lowered his voice. "How about a metallurgy and mining student?"

"Well, perhaps." His tone made me feel a little giddy. I backed away and pointed to the passing scenery. "We're now going through the cut between Wolfe and Grindstone," I told him. I pointed out the Canadian islands of Wolfe, Goose, and Hickory on the left and the American Islands of Grindstone, Club, Papoose, and Whiskey on the right.

"I do hope you can come ashore and visit the quarry with me," Mr. Quigley said.

"Miss Hartranft. There you are." I turned to see Mary Mason approaching. "I forgot to tell you that we are stopping at Thurso this morning. Some of the Princeton men are visiting the quarry, but we've organized a tour of Thurso for those who are interested."

"How lovely. I've yet to see the new church they built there."

"You'll go ashore then? Some prefer to stay aboard."

"No. I'd love a tour of Thurso."

"I know your preferences," Mary Mason said to Mr. Quigley, then turned to the fellow on the port side of the bow. "Mr. Bartman, what's your pleasure?"

I'd been so involved with pointing out the sights and islands to Mr. Quigley that I'd quite forgotten that the lanky fellow was still there leaning on the railing looking out across the water.

He turned and stretched to his full height, and I could see that he was quite tall, perhaps a hair taller than Mr. Quigley. Mr. Bartman bent toward Mary Mason and spoke in soft whispery tones.

By now we had turned downriver again, threading our way through the tiny islands that lie off the north shore of Grindstone. Mr. Quigley asked which islands were on the American side and which belonged to the Dominion of Canada. There were so many islands on this section of the river that I had to confess that I did not know their names, nor which side of the international boundary they were on. Soon we were tied to the dock at Thurso preparing to disembark.

CHAPTER
five

𝒥ohn Kerr stood at the end of the gangway. "Tour of Thurso to the left. Those going to the quarry please stay to the right."

Most of the young ladies stayed aboard to have tea with Mary Mason in the ladies salon. The Sawyer sisters from Thousand Island Park, Miss Caldwell, a trio of Princetonians, Mr. Bartman and I gathered on the left side of the dock, awaiting our tour.

"What! No!" Mr. Quigley called out when he noticed that I was on the other side of the divide. Just as his group was leaving, he dashed to my side, took my hand, and pleaded with me to come on the quarry tour with him.

My cheeks flushed. He was making such a spectacle. "Stop. You're embarrassing me," I whispered.

He went down on one knee. "Whatever I need to do to convince you."

Clearly, he planned on using embarrassment as a tool to compel me. This tactic only fortified my resolve. "Stand up and move along. I'll see you back aboard the *Nightingale*," I whispered to him.

"Good morning," a man with a strong Scottish brogue shouted above the small talk. He then asked for our attention. "I am David Black, postmaster of Thurso and your tour guide. Welcome to our bonny settlement."

Although not physically imposing, but of medium height and build, Postmaster Black exuded authority. Perhaps it was because he was urbanely dressed in a checked country suit or perhaps it was the well-trimmed, prodigious black beard that jutted from his raised jaw. But more likely, it was the combination of both along with his deep baritone voice tinged with a Scotsman's brogue, which commanded attention. "Behind you is Thurso Bay and to your right the Forsyth quarry."

I glanced to the right and saw a high granite dome dotted with derricks, small shacks, machinery, and workmen. I could see the mass of Princetonians shuffling along the dirt path in that direction.

"Quigley! Come on," a fellow at the end of the quarry group called back.

I nodded toward Mr. Quigley, then motioned for him to follow his group.

He placed a hand over his heart and gave me a pout that made me smirk.

Mr. Quigley turned, ran at breakneck speed toward the fellow who had called for him, jumped on his back, then down again, then slowed to a matched pace as he threw an arm around his friend's shoulders and continued on his way. Mr. Quigley looked back only once to give me another sad pout.

Mr. Quigley's actions caught the attention of everyone in our small group. Postmaster Black put his clay pipe in his mouth, took a puff, smiled, removed the pipe from his mouth, and indicated Mr. Quigley using his pipe as a pointer. "Yon's a right chancer." Then noting the puzzled look on our faces, he elaborated. "A person who takes risks and is a wee bit cheeky. Glad he decided to go on the quarry tour."

The group laughed, all except Mr. Bartman, who scowled, and scuffed the toe of his shoe in the dirt path.

"Come along, then. This way," Postmaster Black said, pointing the way with his pipe.

We followed a well-established path that crossed an empty lot and led us between two houses. Postmaster Black was in the lead, followed by the Sawyer sisters and three Princeton fellows walking closely behind the sisters. Miss Caldwell and I were next, walking side by side. The sullen Mr. Bartman trailed behind all of us, hunched over, hands in pockets, and with a hangdog air about him.

Postmaster Black stopped in the middle of the road that fronted the houses and motioned for us to gather around him. "The Forsyth quarry is named for Robert Forsyth, an immigrant from Scotland, which, if you haven't noticed from my brogue, is where I hail from, as does half the population of our fair town. Mr. Forsyth is my uncle. Like him, I was born, raised, and educated in Thurso, Scotland, the northernmost town on the Scottish mainland. You might recognize the name," he said with a wink and tip of his straw hat which revealed a shiny bald head.

The group slowly continued south on the dirt road. When the road widened, the three boys joined the Sawyer sisters. It was immediately evident they were more interested in the charming trio of sisters than they were the tour of Thurso.

Postmaster Black continued to talk as we shuffled along the dusty road. "The quarry was established in 1880. There are three quarries on the island, but this one is the most prodigious."

"How many people live here?" Carrie asked.

"Four hundred souls reside here in Thurso. Most, of course, are consumed with work in the quarry, but we have a few entrepreneurs as well: several boardinghouses, two shopkeepers, a barber, and a blacksmith. The men outnumber the women three to one."

"Our Pullman House girls would be thrilled to hear that," Miss Caldwell whispered to me.

"Most of the single gentlemen live in boardinghouses. As you can see, the heart of the community is clustered around Thurso Bay."

I had noticed the buildings and the many docks as we entered the bay.

"What parts of town you can't access by boat you can access via one of our two roads. We're currently on Cross Island Road. The public area of the town is centered around the intersection of Cross Island Road and North Shore Road."

Cross Island Road was lined with small homes, some painted nicely with well-kept yards and picket fences, others unpainted and unadorned. There were several tall boardinghouses and I noticed a saloon or two along the street, shuttered against the morning sun. I imagined with nearly three hundred men in town—many unmarried—the saloons would be filled with roistering young quarrymen most evenings. I doubted if the Pullman

House girls would be interested in quarrymen, but I did not share this thought with Miss Caldwell.

"There's been substantial and solid growth on Thurso as of late. Quite a few houses built in the last three years. We have a school now," Postmaster Black said, pointing to a small one-room schoolhouse. "One of three on the island. Miss Lottie McDonald, started her tenure as teacher here just last year. School's currently out for the summer, of course."

Next Postmaster Black pointed out a neighboring building. "This is the Thurso readin' room, which is used for all sorts of activities. Most importantly, it is used as a night school for quarry workers who want to improve their readin' and writin' skills. We have a debatin' club in the winter. We also have a dramatic club. Last April they presented *The Limerick Boy*, a comic drama in five acts, in the I. O. G. T. Hall at Thousand Island Park."

"The I. O. G. T.?" I asked.

"The Independent Order of Good Templars, a fraternal organization against the evils of alcohol. Frankly, we were surprised those do-gooders would invite boozers from Grindstone to the sanctimonious confines of Thousand Island Park. Perhaps they were trying to convert us to the temperance cause," Postmaster Black shared with a touch of sarcasm in his voice.

Miss Caldwell stifled a snicker.

"Whatever the reason, the steamer *Junita* ferried a boatload of Thursonians to the event. There was a large crowd from Thousand Island Park as well. Mighty proud of all the Thurso talent we have."

At the intersection of Cross Island Road and North Shore Road, I could see a little white clapboard church. The steeple on the right side loomed much higher than the tower on the left. It rose to the sky in stages. A rectangular tower provided the base. Above that was a square belfry that housed the church bell. Atop the belfry were two more stages that narrow into a point. A white cross graced the top of the spire.

Postmaster Black told us that the church originally had been on La Rue Island, a Canadian island near Wellesley island and the International Rift. Rev. Shorts arrived from Canada in 1883 to establish a Methodist ministry. He had the church dismantled and rebuilt here in Thurso. The Rev. Alexander Short stood in front of the church to greet us and take us on a tour of the church. Postmaster Black introduced Rev. Shorts as "a strong and convincing speaker and an able exponent of the Scriptures."

We walked into a small vestibule. It took a while for my eyes to adjust to the dim interior after the bright sunlight outside. The vestibule led to a small Sunday school room. After Rev. Shorts told us about the Sunday school program, he led us into the main part of the church. Sunlight flooded in through narrow gothic windows, striping the interior with bright light. On either side of the center aisle were straight-backed pews stained dark mahogany. I ran my hand across the top of one, thinking they were the most uncomfortable looking pews I'd ever laid eyes on.

"Hammered them together myself," Rev. Shorts told me proudly. "Stained them, too. If you'll follow me, miss."

I followed the reverend onto the low platform at the front of the church.

"This, of course, is the pulpit," he said. It was made with similar lines as the pews and I could only assume that he had made and stained the pulpit himself. "On the other side, we have a fine oaken reed organ. Last Christmas, Will Carleton, the celebrated poet, gave the church a fine organ as a Christmas present."

Carrie Sawyer tugged at my sleeve, slipped her gloved hand into my gloved hand, and whispered in my ear, "Have you heard of Will Carleton? He's quite famous, most notably for his ballads. He has a place on Coast Avenue."

"Yes," I whispered back.

"I'm hoping he will give another talk this year at the Tabernacle. You'll have to come as our guest if he does."

"That would be lovely," I whispered into her ear and gave her hand a little squeeze before releasing it.

I looked up to see Mr. Bartman staring intently at me. Had he been listening? Was his glare a rebuke for whispering during Rev. Shorts's tour? Or did he have an interest in Will Carleton, too? Mr. Bartman turned away before I could ascertain the meaning of his look.

Rev. Shorts continued his talk. I couldn't wait to tell the Sawyer girls that I'd already heard Carleton speak at the Tabernacle. I even owned an autographed copy of his anthology *Farm Ballads*. I was quite jealous when I learned he had penned his first poem, "The Dying Indian Chief," when he was only thirteen. I spent the early part of my first summer on Grenell striving to become a poetess. After a youth spent reading poetry with my father, I thought it would be easy. It was not.

Rev. Shorts told us that the Thurso Ladies Aid Society was a staunch supporter of the church. During the summer months, the ladies hosted weekly ice cream socials on the lawn at the side of the church. He then passed the hat and collected donations from our small group for the church's building fund.

"In the past, Grindstone has garnered a reputation for being lawless and full of liars, backbiters, and scoundrels. And while there may be a little smuggling carried on between here and Canada, I have found that due to the vigilance of our efficient customs officer, John Black—no relation to our illustrious postmaster, David Black—we are a quite upstanding community."

We thanked Rev. Shorts for his tour and exited the church.

As soon as the door closed, Postmaster Black took out his clay pipe and lit it again. "Well well, I suppose Rev. Shorts is right. It is too true that there is a class of people in every community who continually meddle with other peoples' affairs, and this place has more than its share of them," he said as he puffed on his pipe. "We have a few scoundrels, but mostly we have quite a few God-fearing, community-minded people. A few years back, a new society was formed here in Thurso called the Gentleman's Aid Society. Now, some of the womenfolk got their feathers ruffled thinkin' the gents were trying to overshadow their long-standin' Ladies Aid Society of Thurso, but the gents reassured the ladies that the purpose of the two societies were the same. The men hold a ball once a year and the ladies hold bazaars to raise money for the church, the readin' room, and such."

As we walked down the church's front steps and turned onto North Shore Road, Postmaster Black directed our attention to the new barbershop across the street. "Mr. Spink opened this barbershop a few years back to keep us looking trim and well-shaved throughout the year. A most welcome addition to our fair community."

As we passed the corner of the church, I glanced at the carriage house set back from the road and was stunned to see a horse-drawn glass hearse. I stopped, shaded my eyes from the sun, and squinted into the carriage house to examine the elegant hearse. Purple curtains with large tassels hung on the inside of the glass enclosure. Inside, the casket would sit on a purple velvet dais. Large carriage lamps hung on each corner of the hearse. Things have certainly changed since my first funeral on Grindstone Island, I thought. The memory of my friend Dempsey's funeral came to mind. It had been held in the lower schoolhouse as there wasn't a church on the island then. His coffin had been loaded onto the back of a buckboard and taken to his parents' homestead. I sighed at the memory.

"Miss?" Mr. Bartman asked. "Are you well? Are you ill?"

"No. I'm fine," I assured him.

"We had better catch up," he said.

The others had already climbed the stairs to the larger of Thurso's two stores. The sign above the store read Est. 1888. There was no name, but we were told that Greg Burgess ran the store. On either side of the door were two large windows crammed with an incongruent array of products: perfume bottles, Ingersoll dollar watches, men's work shoes, pots, pans, and fishing gear.

Inside was more of the same, except darker and dustier. A wood stove stood in the center of the room and a long wooden bench sat in front of it. To the right was the post office, "where I spend a fair amount of time," Postmaster Black confided.

Beyond the post office window ran a long counter. At the end was a red coffee grinder with two big wheels for turning it. The rich smell of coffee was mingled with the pungent smell of tobacco. Behind the counter were floor-to-ceiling shelves with rows and rows of shoeboxes and bolts of fabric, some plain and some flowered.

The back of the store was lined with shovels, pitchforks, bucksaws and other tools unfamiliar to me. Crowded into the far corner were rain gear, work clothes, and more fishing gear. On the right side of the store were canned goods and dry cereals. Buckets, barrels, and glass jars were filled with cookies, crackers, and candy. In front of the stove was a large crate that I recognized from the Grenell Island Store. It was from the Clayton bakery and was jammed with loaves of bread wrapped in blue waxed paper. Near the door was a cabinet filled with medicinal needs: cod liver oil, castor oil, tincture of larkspur, cough syrups and of course Carter's Little Liver Pills.

I blinked as we came out into the sunlight again and took a deep breath of fresh river air after the dank, dusty interior of the store. There was a storage building on the east side of the store. The first floor, Postmaster Black told us, was for selling oil and kerosene. "The second floor is known as the Hall. Don't use it much in the summer, but it's our community hall in the winter. The entertainment season runs from November to April here at the Hall."

He told us about the Thanksgiving Day party they'd had last November. The Gananoque orchestra furnished the music for that occasion. "On Christmas, old Santa makes his usual Christmas evening appearance to the great delight of the young people. All through the winter, the residents of Thurso gather for homespun vocal and instrumental music in the Hall. Of course, there is always the New Year's Dance with an oyster supper. Last January, a Boston gentleman gave an exhibition in the Hall about one of the greatest inventions of the age, Edison's phonograph. In February, Bill McClusky, the distinguished traveler and eloquent orator, gave a lecture on Oriental customs illustrated with magic lantern slides. This is also where we hold our town meetings. In April, the farmers decided to build a cheese factory in the center of the island."

Beyond the hall was a field that Postmaster Black referred to as the Sandy Soil Fair Grounds. "Last Saturday, an interesting game of ball was played on the fairgrounds between the Thurso Professionals and the celebrated Farmer Club. The latter achieved seventeen scores while the former made only three. Great pitching by Will Johnson, only to be topped by Harwoods' catching. The umpire was ruled out on account of his unjust decision. Saturday afternoon another game will be played between the teams."

Postmaster Black pulled a gold watch from his waistcoat watch pocket, popped the lid and checked the time. "It's time to head back."

We headed west on the North Shore Road. "Thurso is just a small part of the great island of Grindstone, which is mostly rural." Postmaster Black indicated with his pipe the road ahead of us.

Yvette Sawyer grabbed my arm and squeezed it affectionately. "You are right, Miss Hartranft! I think Grindstone would be a wonderful place to go wheeling!"

She pointed at the road ahead of us. "What a wondrous countryside! I can't wait to explore." Past the church was a deep swale, and then the road slowly rose, and I could see a well-kept homestead with a green house. If I squinted, I could see another farm in the very distance, another homestead, this one with a yellow house. Yvette ran ahead to join her sisters and the three young men who hovered around them.

I heard hammering as we approached the church and noted a familiar figure bent over on the front steps, his toolbox by his side.

"Hunk?" I asked, and he stood and gave me that lopsided smile.

"Miss Marguerite! Well, you're a sight for sore eyes! The boys said you were back on the river. Heard tell you were fixin' to slap a new coat of paint on that cottage of yours. Fancy meetin' you here in Thurso of all places."

"I finished sanding the cottage this morning. And I'd planned on painting it this afternoon, but I was invited on this outing. What are you up to? I thought you'd be out fishing. You're only the most popular guide on the river."

"Oh," he said, shoving his hat back on his head with one hand and stroking his long face with the other hand. "I prittin' near put my foot through this here step last Sunday. Must be all the winter weight I'm carryin'," he said, patting his midsection.

I smiled. Hunk is beanpole thin.

"Anyways, thought I better get over here before some God lovin' churchgoer breaks their neck. Besides, the winds in the north. . ."

"Do not go forth," I said in unison with Hunk, and his face broke out in a huge smile. Hunk was the consummate riverman. If anyone knew a good fishing day from a bad one, he did.

"You best catch up with your group there, missy. They're darn near outta sight. I'll catch up with you later."

I waved goodbye to Hunk, then hurried to catch up with our group. I was startled to notice that Mr. Bartman was almost walking shoulder to shoulder with me. Where did he come from? Had he been waiting for me? I glanced over at him and gave him a little smile. It seemed he had something he wanted to say, he opened his mouth, but nothing came out. He clamped his lips tightly together, shoved his hands in his pockets, put his head down and picked up his pace. I was now the last of the group. I looked around for Miss Caldwell. Where was she? Perhaps she had gone on ahead of us. Now that I thought of it, I didn't recall seeing her after I entered the church.

"Where is everyone? I've barely seen a soul," Carrie Sawyer asked when I caught up with the group.

Postmaster Black puffed on his pipe and removed it from his mouth before he replied. "Most are busy at the quarry. And the rest?" He shrugged. "Once spring comes, attention returns to the river. More fishin'. More boatin'. Farmers are busy with plantin'. But we still make time at Decoration Day to plant flags on the graves of the boys from Grindstone who fell during the War Between the States. We're now making arrangements for the Glorious Fourth. I'm sure we can attract a big crowd. Grindstone Island has a host of orators, anyone of whom could make an eloquent address."

As we walked on the path between the houses that led to the dock, I could hear Mr. Quigley's loud booming voice regaling his classmates with stories. As his voice faded, and a crescendo of laughter ensued. Mr. Quigley's boisterous guffaw boomed over the others.

"It sounds like the quarry tour made it back before we did," Bertha Sawyer said.

When we arrived at the dock, I could see a few of the quarry tour group by the gangway. The rest had already boarded the *Nightingale*.

The three Sawyer girls clustered together, their white day dresses forming a shimmering, diaphanous cloud. I looked again for Miss Caldwell. Perhaps she was already aboard, but I worried that we had left her behind somewhere inadvertently. I was about to say something to Mr. Black when I spied her standing on the aft deck of the *Nightingale* surrounded by smoking men. When she raised her moss-colored glove to her mouth, it almost looked as if it held a cigarette. Surely, I must be mistaken. The end glowed reddish-orange the instant she brought the cigarette to her mouth. She inhaled, then tilted her head back and exhaled a long, sinuous stream of smoke into the air.

"What's that?" Yvette Sawyer asked Mr. Black, pointing to a brass contraption bolted to the edge of the dock.

"That is the newest addition to Thurso Harbor. A hand-pumped foghorn for those foggy days we have in late spring and early fall." He swiveled the horn so that it pointed out over the bay, raised the plunger and slowly pushed down. A long, mournful bellow echoed out over the water.

"The Forsyth Granite Company did a big business the last year and the shipments were simply immense. The stones go principally to Detroit and other western cities where it is used in the construction of the finest buildings. The quarry is rapidly making a market for itself down around Albany and New York. It is confidently claimed to be the best building stone from the state of New York—perhaps in the entire country. It is free from the common weakness of granite, that of chipping through the action of frost and rain. It's both strong and beautiful, ideal building material and destined to be more extensively used than any other. It has been demonstrated by actual tests that this entire track is underlaid with granite to the depth of two hundred feet and there is every reason to believe that further drilling would show a still greater thickness of the formation, perhaps to a thousand feet. Ladies and gentlemen, thank you for your kind attention. Pleasant journeys."

We thanked Postmaster Black for his in-depth tour and turned back toward the *Nightingale*.

"Miss Hartranft! There you are," Mr. Quigley called out as I neared him. "The quarry was amazing. The equipment—gigantic! Cogs and derricks—amazing! Did you know that the workmen there swing their sledgehammers about twenty times a minute? That's once every three seconds. And two of them will go at it at once, hitting the same wedge. The timing is inconceivable! Like clockwork. Something like you'd see on a glockenspiel. And then there were the stonecutters, who showed us how they use feathers and pins to precisely cut a piece of granite to the exact measurements provided. They also showed us where tugboats push schooners into the dock, load them up, and then tow them out to the Wide Waters to sail off to western ports."

I smiled at his enthusiasm. In the distance, I could hear the ringing blows of the sledgehammers and the clinking and clanking of big metal cogs that seemed to punctuate his description. He was covered in dust and I was grateful I hadn't let him talk me into the tour.

"But the best was the glow of red granite. The granite we saw on our way here was lichen- covered and looked gray and old, but the inside is a brilliant red—like the beating heart of the Earth itself."

I thought of afternoons with Flossie as we lay with our ears pressed against granite rock and wondered briefly if the frenzied Mr. Quigley could ever slow down long enough to try to hear the heartbeat of the Earth.

"Mr. Forsyth, the quarry owner, told us that in the evening the setting sun shines directly on the amphitheater-shaped pit they've carved into this dome of the rock, and the rock glows red. Everyone standing there is bathed in red light. Perhaps after you take me to visit the potholes, we can come back at sunset and experience that ourselves."

I felt something thrum inside me at the thought but before I could reply, Captain Johnston called out and motioned for us to return to the *Nightingale*.

By the time I made it to the gangway, Miss Caldwell was gone from the aft deck. I held my breath as I walked through a cloud of cigar and cigarette smoke, but it clung to me and followed me through the gentleman's salon and into the central parlor.

The central salon was crowded with young people, each talking about their experiences here in Thurso. I caught sight of the back of Miss Caldwell's hat. Instantly, as if she knew I was looking at her, she whipped around and stared directly into my eyes, a knowing smirk on her face. Had she seen me observing her on the aft deck with a cigarette in hand?

CHAPTER
six

"I see you latched onto a Princeton man," Miss Caldwell said as I retired to the ladies' salon to rest my feet for a while.

"Heavens, no!" I said. "He's much too . . . I mean . . ." I flushed as I did not want to divulge that the brawny Mr. Quigley might be nearly a decade younger than I.

"You seemed to be in rapt conversation during our entire transit to Thurso," she said.

"He's a geology enthusiast and was asking about different geological sights in the islands. That was all," I replied. I felt my cheeks grow warm.

"Oh, I think he's interested in more than geological sites," Miss Caldwell said, her lips spreading to a sly, tight-lipped smile.

"How did you find Thurso?" I asked in hopes of redirecting the conversation.

Miss Caldwell hid a yawn behind a gloved hand. "Goodness, could you imagine living in a godforsaken place the entire year? The winters must be horrific!"

Now I wore a sly smile. I felt a little tingle from deep inside my heart because there had been a time when I had considered living on Grindstone Island all year. Back in 1881, I had been offered a teaching position at the lower Grindstone school. "I don't know. The weather may be cold, but the people seem warm."

Miss Caldwell raised a hooked eyebrow and shot me a surprised look. "Really! Do tell!"

I lifted a shoulder. "Not much to tell," I said and left it at that. I didn't know how to explain to Miss Caldwell how Grindstone Island filled with good honest people always drew me into its orbit. It was a Grindstone young man, not quite as old as Mr. Quigley is now, who was the first to ask for my hand in marriage. The teaching position offer had been a lure to get me to stay, so that he could court me properly. I'd almost taken that teaching position. In the end, I'd decided that I wasn't ready to teach because I still desired to be a student. More than once I had pondered how different—perhaps better—my life would have been if I had taken that teaching position.

My mind fluttered back to that August night in 1881 when we were tossed into the water when our skiff overturned. I could hear Dempsey's friend calling for him over the sloshing of the water and shrieking of the wind. The memory sent a quiver down my spine.

Miss Caldwell's keen eye appraised me. "My goodness. You have such a faraway look in your eye. Dreaming of your future with the geology man?"

I gave myself a shake and looked down at my hands. "No, nothing like that." No point thinking of that now: Dempsey was gone—dead and buried under a tree within sight of the kitchen window of his childhood home so his mother could keep watch on him as she washes the supper dishes.

Miss Caldwell stood and smoothed the front of her dress. "Nothing? I don't believe that for a minute. But then again, I suppose we all have our little secrets." She gave me a pointed look, then opened the door and joined the throng in the central salon.

Moments later, Mary Mason stuck her head in the door. "Marguerite? Are you unwell?"

"No. I'm fine, just resting my feet after our long walk."

"I was hoping to introduce you to someone, but it can wait."

"No, I'm well rested," I said rising to my feet. I smoothed the back of my hair, straightened my hat, and followed her out the door.

Mary Mason was a consummate hostess. She introduced me to a Prof. Corson, class of '87, who is currently the head of the English Department at Cornell University. Once we were engaged in pleasant conversation, she excused herself and circulated throughout the room making sure each young woman of our group was happily conversing with a member of the Princeton group.

I watched Mary Mason thread her way through the crowded salon, then turned my attention back to Prof. Corson. He was a little man with a hooked nose and serious countenance. "I'm intrigued with the innate curiosity of excursionists," he said. "It is evident every day at the Thousand Island Park dock. Upon the arrival of each boat, from one hundred to a thousand eyes peer eagerly onto the decks of the incoming steamer. The average person is not content to sit down and draw upon his own resources for enjoyment. On the contrary, they must continually be on the move to see something and behold new 'phenomena'."

As Prof. Corson continued to describe what he called "The Age of Phenomena," I looked across the salon and caught the eye of Miss Caldwell. She was talking to an older, barrel-chested man with a Van Dyke beard. Or rather, I should say, she was listening to him. Her part of the conversation seemed to be confined to a nod and smile. The moment he looked down or away, she would indicate with a slight nod of her head that she wished me to join her.

I made my excuses to Prof. Corson and threaded my way to the other side of the salon.

"Oh look!" Miss Caldwell said to the barrel-chested man mid-sentence, "It's my dear friend Miss Hartranft."

The man, who was speaking with a heavy German accent, stopped and looked at me. "Hartranft is it?" he asked with interest. "Any relation to the former governor of Pennsylvania?"

I smiled, for now I knew for certain that this gentleman was far older than most on the steamer if he remembered my father's distant cousin, the former general of the Grand Old Army, John F. Hartranft, who had served as the seventeenth governor of Pennsylvania from 1873 to 1879. "Not a close relation," I said.

"Miss Hartranft, may I introduce to you Herr Brittlinger," Miss Caldwell said. And with that she excused herself, whispering a sing-songy, "good luck!" in my ear as she brushed past me.

Herr Brittlinger nodded his head toward Miss Caldwell, clicked his heels together with military precision as if punctuating the exchange and turned a discerning eye to me. "So! You are no relation to the former Governor."

"No. Only a distant cousin." I told him.

"But you are German then, with a name like Hartranft."

Oddly enough, I never thought of myself as German, though I knew that my father's family came from Germany generations ago.

"I am an American with German ancestors—on my father's side at least," I said.

Herr Brittlinger's eyes crinkled. The corners of his mouth followed the ends of his mustache that had been twisted and waxed into sharp tips. He didn't seem disappointed. In fact, he seemed very pleased.

"You know the origin of your name then?" he asked.

My breath caught at the question. I placed my splayed hand on my bodice and inclined my head toward him. "I do not, but I'm intrigued."

Herr Brittlinger leaned toward me then and said in a low voice, his warm breath heavy with the scent of cigar smoke, "It is an old name from the Middle Ages. A word—how do you Americans say—oh, yes! A nickname for a pauper, an urchin on the street who begs scraps of food. *Harte* for 'hard' and *ranft* for 'rind' or 'crust'."

He eyed me cautiously, watching for my reaction.

Pauper? Beggar! My mother would be horrified. That was my first thought, but instantly my mind turned to work through the languages I knew. Latin, Greek, and French were so different from German. I was astounded. Me! The one who finds comfort in looking at the etymology of words had never thought to look into the etymology of my own name. "How fascinating!" I said.

He raised his head slightly, tilting it to one side, and eyed me warily. "I am not a student, as you can see," he said, patting his barrel chest.

"A graduate of Princeton then?" I asked.

"No. I attended university in Berlin. I'm a professor of astronomy."

"Ah," I said.

"You know what astronomy is, no?" he asked.

I smiled. "The word *astronomy* comes from the Greek words for 'star' and 'law'," I said.

Herr Brittlinger patted the tips of his fingers together in rapid succession and moistened his lips. "That is very good," he said. "You have studied astronomy then?"

"No. I have studied the Greek language. And the Greeks were avid astronomers. The word planet is derived from the Greek phrase *planētēs astérē*, which means 'wandering star'. Eventually, the second-word, *astérē* or 'star,' was dropped. I find it fascinating that the word *planet* literally means 'wandering.'"

Herr Brittlinger raised his chin and looked at me from beneath bushy eyebrows. He tapped the tips of his fat fingers together three times and pressed his lips together as if in deep thought.

He looked leery. I thought of Rose's advice and bit my lip. Had I said too much?

"Do you also have knowledge of the constellations?" he asked, tilting his head to the side and narrowing his eyes.

"A few," I said. I loved lying out on the great granite rock on a clear night and looking up at the stars. I could pick out a few constellations: the Big Dipper, the Little Dipper, Cassiopeia, and Orion. My favorite constellation was Pleiades—the Seven Sisters—but that was a constellation best seen in the autumn, although I first learned of the Pleiades here at the river. I had since studied the mythology associated with the constellation. I left all this unsaid.

Herr Brittlinger leaned forward slightly as if he could discern there was more going on in my head than I was sharing. I smiled sweetly at him and resisted the urge to rub at the furrows that might be entrenched between my brows. Rose's advice rang in my ears: *Try not to think too much! Don't blather on about Greek and Latin!*

"You know of the comet?"

"Comet?"

"A new comet was recently discovered at the Dudley Observatory in Albany, New York. It is receding from the Earth at a very rapid rate. It will be dimly visible for a week yet. The Columbian Hotel has allowed me to set up my telescope on the tower. At night, I can see it—although it is forty million miles from Earth. It is extraordinary. You must come to see it."

"I've never seen a comet," I said.

Herr Brittlinger looked at me intently and leaned forward with an outstretched hand as if he intended to escort me to the hotel now. "I would love to show it to you. You must come."

His hand grazed my arm, and his pinkie came in contact with the small patch of skin on my wrist that showed between my glove and my sleeve. It lingered there for an uncomfortable second. I smiled nervously, slowly pulled my hand back, and clasped my hands together in front of me demurely.

I felt someone's eyes on me and looked up expecting to see an amused Miss Caldwell but instead caught the sulky Mr. Bartman glaring at me. He inhaled deeply, brought himself to his full height, furrowed his brow and twisted his small mouth into a disapproving scowl.

"Attention! Attention!" Mary Mason announced. "May I have your attention please!"

Herr Brittlinger looked at me intently, stroked his Van Dyke into a fine point, then turned with military precision to face Mary Mason.

"We are approaching Grand View Park. They have set up tables for us on the lawn; a picnic luncheon will be served. Please feel free to sit wherever you like."

"Hear! Hear!" a group of students called out and the banter in the center salon swelled. Excitement grew as Grand View Park came into sight. Many of the students and young ladies looked out the windows on the port side to watch our approach. Soon the steamer was safely tethered to the dock and we were allowed to disembark. As the crowd surged to the door, Herr Brittlinger and I held back, patiently waiting our turn.

Once the salon was half emptied, Herr Brittlinger donned his Trilby hat, turned to me and offered me his arm. "May I escort you ashore, *Fraulein* Hartranft?"

I'd never been called *Fraulein* before, and it sounded so natural to my ear.

"How kind of you," I said.

"It would be my pleasure." He bowed deeply from the waist as he clicked his heels together, then gently tucked my left hand into his right elbow. We were shoulder to shoulder as we proceeded across the central salon. Herr Brittlinger turned sideways and gracefully eased us through the narrow door and onto the gangway.

Miss Caldwell caught site of us just as we stepped off the gangway. Her eyebrows shot up in surprise and she raised a gloved hand to her mouth to hide a mirthful smile. She shook her head, turned, and walked toward the tables.

I had rowed past Grand View Park many times but had never visited. Although not quite as big and definitely not as new as the Grenell Island Store dock, the Grand View Park dock was inviting with a dock house for the reception of baggage and to shelter guests as they waited for steamers to arrive. I was surprised to see their toboggan slide was nearly twice as tall as the Pullman House slide and situated on a sandy shoreline. Grand View Park was famous for its fine bathing grounds. To the left was an ample boat livery.

The proprietor, Mr. Childs, met us on the dock and pointed out the picnic grounds situated on the north side of Grand View Park in a well-shaded area. The grass had been cut and the low branches of the trees trimmed away to afford patrons of the hotel a good view of the river while providing shade for the picnickers.

There was one long table and three or four smaller tables.

"Will you join me for lunch?" Herr Brittlinger asked.

"I'd be honored," I said.

"If you don't mind, we shall sit at a small table."

"I suppose that would be alright," I said.

Herr Brittlinger led me to a table far from the main table. We had a great view of the river and the rest of the tables.

"As a professor here, I must remove myself from the students so as not to—er, how do you say in English? Impact their freedom of fun-making."

I smiled and nodded. "I understand," I said. I wanted to add that I too was a professor and had students but wasn't ready to disclose my situation quite yet.

He pulled out a chair for me and I sat down. The view from the table was astounding. Grand View Park is situated at the northwestern foot of Wellesley Island. From this vantage point, I could see both the main shorelines at oblique lines—miles in the distance of course. It was indeed a *grand view*.

A waiter visited the tables and offered us bottles of ale, ginger-beer, and soda-water. He was followed by another waiter with a pitcher of lemonade. We watched the younger people fill their cups and converse with each other. Mr. Childs moved among the tables setting out large baskets of biscuits and rolls. The rolls were still warm and melted in my mouth.

After the biscuits and rolls came sandwiches on freshly baked, thinly sliced bread filled with various cheeses, meats, and fruit. I particularly enjoyed the Welsh rarebit. Herr Brittlinger enjoyed the tongue sandwich. For dessert, waiters offered us a platter stacked with servings of pound cake and gingerbread.

A bit removed from the group, I had the opportunity to observe the others. The Upton twins were the only young ladies at the far end of the table; they were the center of attention. Miss Caldwell was speaking with Prof. Corson, though she shot me sly, quizzical glances during lunch. Miss Blond had attached herself to Mr. Quigley. It seems everything he said made her dissolve into giggles. Mary Mason was deep in conversation with a young man whom Herr Brittlinger identified as Seward Prosser. I overheard John Kerr and Yvette Sawyer discuss safety bicycles. Mr. Bartman sat talking to no one, and it seemed every time I looked his way, he was glowering at me from underneath knitted eyebrows.

I noticed Herr Brittlinger had impeccable manners, dabbing at his mustache after nearly every bite to make sure it was clean. Unlike most of the students, who were wearing sack suits, Herr Brittlinger was wearing a frock coat over a double-breasted waistcoat. On his head, he wore a felt Trilby hat with a curved brim. The silk band on his Trilby was the same burgundy as his cravat, which was precisely knotted beneath a freshly starched wing collar and held in place with a pearl stickpin. Two bits of gold occasionally caught the sunlight: a watch chain with an elaborate fob and a gold signet ring on his right hand. Herr Brittlinger and I had a pleasant conversation about constellations. And sometime between the tongue sandwich and the pound cake, I finally confessed my favorite constellation.

"The Pleiades? Really. And why is that?"

I resisted the urge to tell him about the symposium of 1881 during my first year on Grenell at which I met seven women passionate about education and learning. Instead, I told him only that the Pleiades were fraught with personal meaning. "As someone who is passionate about the classics, I love the stories the Greeks told about the Seven Sisters. Even one of my favorite poets wrote about it." Then I proceeded to quote from

Whitman's poem "On the Beach at Night."

> *The ravening clouds shall not long be victorious,*
> *They shall not long possess the sky, they devour the stars only in apparition,*
> *Jupiter shall emerge, be patient, watch again another night, the Pleiades shall emerge,*
> *They are immortal, all those stars both silvery and golden shall shine out again.*

As I recited the stanza, Herr Brittlinger steepled his fingers again. As I finished, he tapped the tips of his fingers together rapidly almost as if he were applauding.

"Perhaps you would love to come to see your beloved Pleiades through my telescope. Tonight promises to be a clear night," he said and moistened his lips with the tip of his pink tongue.

I tilted my head quizzically. "But the Seven Sisters—the Pleiades—are best seen in the autumn, especially in November."

He stopped tapping his fingers and leaned forward, "You forget. I have a telescope. I assure you I can bring all seven stars into sharp focus for your viewing pleasure."

"Thank you for your kind invitation, but tonight is out of the question as I have a pressing engagement early tomorrow morning," I said.

"Another time perhaps," Herr Brittlinger said, leaning toward me, and laying his wide hand over mine. The tips of his fingers brushed across the top of my wrist.

I resisted the urge to jerk my hand back. The gesture was very gentle but felt somehow invasive.

Now at the great table, the Princetonians rose and sang out, "Tune every harp and every voice." Someone had rolled the piano out onto the veranda of the hotel. Soon all were on their feet, arm in arm, singing Princeton's alma mater, "Old Nassau." The song went on for seven verses.

Herr Brittlinger sighed heavily and leaned back in his chair, wove his fingers together and rested them on his massive chest. "European universities have none of this silliness," he said.

When the last note ended, a classmate dubbed Slide Rule jumped on a chair. After declaring himself poet laureate for the class of '93, he regaled us with a poem.

The Nightingale that all day long,
Cheered the village with his song;
The Nightingale, the Nightingale,
That sung so sweetly in the vale.

Did you ever ride on the Nightingale?
She will take you safe through wind and hail,
And land you safely over her rail,
Wherever you want to go.
We all went aboard at Round Island Park
To go to Thurso for a little lark.
There was Moll, and Bell and Doll, and Kate
And Dorrety Draggle Tail.
And John, and Dick and Joe, and Jack
And Humphrey with his flail.
So John kissed Molly, kissed Dick kissed Betty,
Kissed Joe, kissed Dolly kissed Jack, kissed
Kitty, kissed Dorrety Draggle Tail.
O, we had such a lovely time on the Nightingale!

The kissing part drew roars of laughter and flushed-cheeked giggles from the girls. I have no idea to whom or what Dorrety Draggle Tail referred, but when Slide Rule jumped down from the chair, the group gave three cheers for Dorrety Draggle Tail, Slide Rule, then Captain Johnston and crew of the *Nightingale*, and Mr. Childs for his hospitality. Everyone seemed quite out of breath from all the hale and hearty cheers. John Kerr stood and said we had an hour or so to explore the grounds before we needed to board the *Nightingale*.

Mr. Childs's stopped by our table, and I complimented him on the breadstuffs.

"We have a bakery just there on the other side of the hotel. It's open to the public. You can purchase baked goods to take home with you," Mr. Childs said.

I thanked Herr Brittlinger for his company and excused myself to do just that.

Having purchased a loaf of rye bread, I was not two steps outside of the bakery shop door when Miss Caldwell took hold of my elbow and eased me around the side of the bakery, out of sight of the others.

"Whatever are you doing?" she asked.

"I just bought a loaf of rye bread to take home with me," I said.

"No. With Baron Von Butterfingers," she asked, her eyes wide.

"He asked if I would join him for lunch, and I thought why not?"

"Why not! You do realize he is a bounder, don't you?"

"A bounder?" I asked, unsure what she meant by that term. I could not see the hefty Mr. Brittlinger jumping or leaping.

"A masher," she said.

I shook my head, unsure what she was telling me.

"Where did you grow up—in a convent?"

Her question startled me. I was dumbfounded.

Miss Caldwell took a step back as her hands covered her mouth. Her eyes were wide under arched eyebrows. "Goodness gracious, I was joking. But it's true, isn't it! You grew up in a convent!"

"Of course not," I sputtered, uncertain what this conversation was all about. "It wasn't a convent . . . I attended Mater Misericordia Academy, a Catholic girls' boarding school."

"Which was in a convent with nuns as teachers," she said and threw back her head and laughed.

I pressed my lips together and let out an exasperated huff. "I don't know what this has to do with Herr Brittlinger."

Miss Caldwell inhaled deeply. "And here I thought you were sharp-witted, definitely not like those parasol-twirling simpletons. Well . . . you may be intelligent, but you certainly aren't worldly. Since I introduced you to Baron Von Butterfingers, I feel I need to warn you. He is not what he seems. Be careful!"

"How do you know?"

Miss Caldwell took a step forward, leaned toward me, gave me a long, pointed look, then said in a low voice, "How do you know the sun rises in the east?"

She turned and ambled away, her skirts swaying back and forth as she walked.

I blinked hard, trying to take in what she had said.

"Marguerite!" I heard a voice call out. It was Lois, running toward me.

"I need you!" She took my hand and pulled me toward a group of young Princetonians. "Tell them," she said, excitedly pushing me forward. "Tell them about the flying machine."

"What?" I asked at the sudden shift in conversation.

The college men broke into laughter and slapped each other on the back.

"She saw it, too! Didn't you, Marguerite!"

"Does this one have a very active imagination like her friend?" one lad with slicked-back hair asked with a wink.

Lois advanced on him. "Just because you didn't see it, doesn't mean that I made it up," Lois insisted, her face crimson with indignation as she jabbed a finger into his chest to press home her point.

"Flying machines. Ha!" another chortled.

I leaned toward Lois and whispered in her ear. "Clearly they are teasing you. It was in the papers. It's been the talk of the islands. Don't let them get your goat."

I straightened my spine, raised my chin, and in a calm but authoritative voice said, "Apparently these poor lads were too far down river and missed the event of the season. The flying machine was spectacular. It flew straight over the channel in plain sight of Grenell Island, turned south near Fishers Landing, and headed inland. Pity you missed it."

"You were right! This one's got an imagination, too" one snickered to another. The group guffawed. Lois tensed and balled her hands into fists. I put a calming hand on her forearm.

"By the by, were you there when Princeton came to Penn last November? Did you see it? Well, if you didn't, let me tell you that your Tigers lost. That too was in all the papers. I didn't see it, but I know that it is true."

The knot of Princetonians did not have a snappy response for this. Several stood slack-jawed, not believing that a member of the fairer sex knew about the Princeton-Penn football game.

"I want to take my bakery purchase to the *Nightingale*. Care to join me?" I linked arms with Lois and we headed toward the dock.

We were halfway to the dock when I heard someone call my name and turned to see Mr. Quigley rushing our way with Miss Blond close on his heels. "Miss Hartranft, might I have a word with you?" he asked.

"Certainly."

"I'll take your bakery goods to the ladies salon," Lois said, taking the bakery bag from my hands and hurrying off toward the *Nightingale*. After a few steps, she stopped and turned toward me again. "Oh, and thank you for that. You really put them in their place."

By now, Mr. Quigley had caught up with me. "We are at the foot of Wellesley Island, are we not?"

"Yes," I said.

"I'm certain you told me that the potholes are at the foot of Wellesley. Could you take me to them?" he asked.

By now Miss Blond had caught up with Mr. Quigley and looked very displeased.

"The potholes are on the opposite side of Eel Bay. Wellesley is a very large island—the largest on the American side. I'm sorry, but it's much too far," I said.

"Mr. Quigley," Miss Blond said, crossing her arms in front of her, and sticking her bottom lip out in a pout. "You promised to push me on the swing."

Mr. Quigley turned to Miss Blond. "Right, of course. Momentarily," he said and turned back toward me. "I would really like to see the potholes. Perhaps another time?"

"Perhaps."

"Mr. Quigley, we must hurry before someone else takes a turn," Miss Blond said, narrowing her eyes and scowling at me.

Miss Blond hooked her arm through Mr. Quigley's arm and turned toward the hotel. I watched them walk away from me. On the south side of the hotel, a swing was strung between two stately basswood trees that stood about eight feet apart. Miss Blond pretended to struggle to lift herself onto the swing until Mr. Quigley put his hands around her small waist and lifted her onto the wide plank. She giggled and laughed as if tickled by his touch. She let out a squeal at the first push. As Mr. Quigley pushed the swing higher and higher, her squeals grew louder.

I turned to look out on the river and felt drawn to the shore. I could see so far from here. I wandered along the shoreline and stopped near a willow that leaned out over the water. I shut my eyes and savored the sound of the river lapping against the rocks. A soft breeze tugged at the ends of my curls. I took off my glove and smoothed my hair back and up under my boater. I closed my eyes and inhaled deeply, drinking in the cool freshness of the river. The rich scent of the river filled my nostrils.

Someone cleared his throat, and I jumped.

There on the ground leaning against the opposite side of the willow trunk was Mr. Bartman.

"Oh! Excuse me! I didn't see you there. My apologies for intruding on your solitude," I said, turning to leave.

"No, please don't go. I mean, I did come here to be alone. I saw you there and figured you were here for the same reason. I didn't want to startle you."

"How very kind, but I will leave you to your thoughts."

"Wait! This mossy bank is more comfortable than a velvet-covered settee. Won't you join me?"

I looked at him quizzically as he patted the thick moss next to him. He had been scowling at me most of the day leaving me with the feeling that, for some reason, he didn't like me. Now his face seemed kind. He looked at me with pleading eyes and pressed his lips together.

"But wouldn't you rather be alone?" I asked.

He shrugged and looked perplexed. "I didn't want to come at all. I'm staying with the Clarks on Comfort Island. I'm working on a book. My hostess, Mrs. Clark, thought it would be good for me to get out and be around 'people my own age'." He clucked his tongue and rolled his eyes. "Truth is, I've never felt all that comfortable around people my own age. I never know what to say. I prefer to be with my books and studies."

"I know what you mean," I said and sat down on the mossy bank. "I too have always felt more comfortable with my books and studies."

"You speak Greek."

I looked at him, surprised. "How do you know that? Have you been eavesdropping on me?"

"Well, not eavesdropping, but I've overheard you now and then. I am an art historian, class of '91. The first class of art history graduates. I specialize in Greek and Roman art."

"Ah!" I said and repeated one of my many favorite Greek quotes. I love the feel of Greek words on my tongue.

"Which means?"

"A quote from Hippocrates. It means: 'Life is short, the art long.' I'm sure he was speaking of the art of healing, but it applies to the visual arts as well, don't you think?"

He stared at me, gulped hard, and nodded. "I'm so jealous. I'm not that good at languages. I've studied the classics—obviously—but I'm not that good at the Greek language. My Latin is only just so-so. Where did you obtain such a solid grasp of the Greek language?"

"At Penn," I said.

He raised an eyebrow. "Yes. I heard they were admitting women. Do you consider yourself a Platonist or an Aristotelean?"

"Socrates isn't in the running at all?"

"So it's Socrates, is it? You're the questioning sort?"

"Well, initially it was Socrates. I think I nearly drove my mother mad with all my questions. But then I read Plato's Dialogues. Spent most of my sixteenth summer translating it. Reading Plato's Dialogues was a seminal point in my scholarly pursuits."

"So you are a Platonist?"

"I was. I'm leaning more toward Aristotle these days."

"There is a lovely painting that illustrates the differences between Plato and Aristotle. *The School of Athens* by Raphael. Have you seen it?"

"Oy! There you are, Miss Hartranft," John Kerr called out as he approached us. "Mary Mason has asked me to fetch you. There is someone she wants to introduce to you."

John helped me to my feet, tucked my hand into the bend of his elbow and ushered me away. "Sorry, Bart!" John called back over his shoulder.

I looked back at Mr. Bartman. His face looked sullen and dark again.

Once out of earshot, John apologized. "Sorry. I came as soon as I'd seen that Black Bart had trapped you into a boring conversation."

"Trapped? By Black Bart? The stagecoach thief?" I whipped my head around but couldn't see Mr. Bartman's form behind the willow tree trunk from this angle.

John laughed. "I never realized the irony of Black Bart's nickname before. Black Bart, the stagecoach thief, was a charmer. Left poetic messages for the ladies he robbed, right? No. No. *Our* Black Bart is no charmer. No, he got that nickname at Princeton because he is so dull and serious. He's a bit of bookworm and once he starts yammering on about Greek art and pottery . . . well, there's no stopping him. I thought I'd better rescue you before he bored you to tears."

We both turned back to look at Mr. Bartman, who had risen to his feet, hands in pockets, head down, as he slowly paced back and forth on the shoreline.

"Look at him. He has all his classmates to talk to and he prefers to be alone, staring out at the water."

It was obviously lost on John that Mr. Bartman wasn't alone until he dragged me away.

CHAPTER
seven

"*Marguerite.*"

A whispering woke me. I heard the sloshing of the water below. The trees outside stirred, sending the refreshing scent of pine and cedar wafting through my window and into my dreams.

"*Marguerite.*"

It was just one word. My name. Not beckoning. Not threatening. It was somehow reassuring—calming—like someone I loved letting me know that they were here next to me always and forever. That I never had to feel alone.

The wind had shifted to the north and cool air surged through my window: cool, moist, fresh, exhilarating air. I got up, put on my bed jacket, and tiptoed out to the porch quietly shutting the door behind me, even though there was no one else in the cottage to wake. I could see the dark shape of Murray Isle across from me, silhouetted black against a midnight blue sky. The moon was hanging in the western sky—just a sliver of a moon—like the sky was winking at me. Its reflection floated like a silver boat sailing in the windswept waters below. Somewhere in the distance, I heard the call of a loon, a haunting moan that echoed through the inky darkness.

I had been asleep, hadn't I? I had laid awake for hours after sunset, the events of the Princeton outing sloshing around in my mind. Just then,

I heard a passing steamer chug past. I had heard the music of the harp orchestra first, followed by the laughter and chatter of the excursionists. The music and laughter grew fainter. Just as the thrumming of the engine faded into the night, the remnants of their wake met the rocks below, reminding me that I was alone again. It was just me, the moonlight, and the river.

As much as I had fretted over the *fête champêtre* and feared I would fall hopelessly behind schedule and not get the cottage painted before Rose and Mother arrived, I was glad I'd accepted the Kerrs' invitation. Mary Mason was right: the food was superb, and having the outing on a steamer was less stuffy than the gatherings at Penn. But then, those were for faculty, and there was a strong need for decorum. The exuberance of the Princeton students and alumni was contagious. The Princetonians brimmed with self-assurance and swagger. I thought of Mr. Quigley, how his face brightened when he spoke of rocks and mines. He was so young, the same age as the students attending my lectures at Penn. To have any other sort of relationship with Mr. Quigley felt unseemly. Mr. Bartman, on the other hand, was an alum, out of school for two or three years. That would put him around age twenty-three? Twenty-four? Closer to my age, at least, but perhaps still too young for me. Mother had always insisted on the importance of finding an older, established man, one who could support me in the "manner I have become accustomed." I hadn't thought of that phrase for a long time and I was suddenly aware that I had been supporting myself for some time now. And "the manner to which I have become accustomed" had changed drastically from that of my youth.

Then there was Herr Brittlinger. He was certainly "established." I was puzzled over Miss Caldwell's warning, however.

In the distance, I heard the loon again, not the long, sad mournful call but its loud, raucous jabberwocky call. It almost sounded as if it were laughing at me. The corner of my lips turned up. The loon was right if it were laughing at me. What was I thinking? I would probably never see any of these men again.

Still, they were more engaging than the men from Our Mother of Sorrows' congregation that Mother and her friends dredged up for me month after month in an attempt to get me married off. Most were widowers and much, much older than I.

Grenell 1893

I stretched, raising my arms to the sky, opening myself to the moonlight, drinking it in. I wanted to hug the rich beauty of the night. The gesture reminded me of Lois Kerr. Her love of the islands was infectious.

I trundled off to bed again. I needed my rest as tomorrow I would start painting.

After a morning of painting, I paused for lunch. I sliced the rye bread from the Grand View Park bakery, slathered it with butter, and topped that with three pieces of sharp cheddar cheese. The comingling of flavors and textures was divine. I savored every morsel. I couldn't believe I'd been here for nearly three days and hadn't written Anne, Ruth, and Keiko. I dashed off a quick note about my progress on painting the cottage. I would leave the description of the Princeton outing for another time. Nora, my classmate from my boarding school days, however, cared not a whit about my painting chores but would enjoy every tidbit about yesterday's excursion. I wrote to Nora once a week. I was sure she grew weary of hearing about classes, paper grading, and lectures. Finally, I had something that I knew would catch her interest.

I hurriedly folded the letters, stuffed them into envelopes, and scribbled on the addresses. I'd have to hurry if I were going to get these letters posted before the arrival of the three o'clock mailboat. Herb was on duty in the Grenell Island post office. I caught him just in time. Herb quickly processed my mail and included it in the outgoing mailbag, then ambled out on the dock to wait for the mailboat. No sooner had Herb left than his cousin George appeared from the back room. "Good day, Miss Hartranft. How was the Princeton outing?"

"Exceptional," I said.

George was full of questions then about Grand View Park: How many tables? What did they serve? What did I like best? When I mentioned the bakery, and that they not only baked breadstuffs for the picnic they served but sold bakery goods to the cottagers on the island, his eyes brightened.

By now the mailboat had exchanged mailbags and Herb had wandered back into the store to sort the mail into each individual mailbox. George danced around him excitedly. "Miss Hartranft has just given me a great idea."

"Great. More ideas," Herb sighed. He didn't even feign interest.

George ignored his cousin's grumbling and poured out his plan in an excited torrent of words. "A bakery. We need to build a bakery. Just think of it. We don't need a big hotel kitchen to prepare lunches. We could make bread and sandwiches. We could provide fire pits for guides to prepare the fish, and we could supply them with the shore dinner fixings: sandwiches, tarts, and cookies for the excursionists. Shore dinners and picnics will be our specialty. We can get started on that this week. We don't have to wait to raise the funds for a hotel. Tables, chairs and a small bakery is all we need. It's a great idea, isn't it!"

I thought how wonderful it would be to have a bakery on the island with fresh baked goods but said nothing.

"Look! Uncle Sam brought you on—out of the goodness of his heart—to help me run the store for our cottagers and to cater to smaller islands around us. Focus on that idea."

"But with the new dock, why not bring hundreds of people here each day instead of me going out to a few cottages here and there in a skiff?" George asked.

"Can we talk about this later? I have the mail to sort. Here you go, Miss Hartranft, you have a mitt-full today."

The two continued to banter as I exited. I had quite a handful of mail. I didn't look at it though. I wanted to savor my correspondence over a cup of tea later. I placed all the postcards and letters inside this week's edition of the *Friends' Intelligencer* and started back toward Castle Rock. I decided to take South Boulevard and stop and visit Aunt Lucy.

"Good afternoon, Miss Hartranft," Mr. Reeves called out from his porch as I passed. "Has the afternoon mailboat come yet?"

"Yes, Herb is busy sorting the afternoon mail now."

"Excellent. I'll take my daily walk and retrieve my afternoon paper."

"Please give my regards to Mrs. Reeves."

"I will," he said.

"And how are young Harry, Jessie, and Edna doing these days?"

"Healthy and well. Healthy and well."

I looked up and saw that the Hinds's cottage, Bay View, was still shuttered for the winter. The Hinds family had purchased the lot next to their dear friend Mr. Reeves and built a beautiful cottage with a two-tier porch. If anyone would know the status of the Hinds family, it would be Mr. Reeves. I inquired about the Hindses and I learned that—as Mary Mason had guessed—they were at the fair in Chicago and weren't expected for another week.

Uncle Sam was sitting on the porch when I reached the end of South Boulevard and he called out to me, motioning me over. "Miss Marguerite, I hope you have time to stop in and visit with the missus. She could use some cheering up."

"Oh no! What happened?" I asked, pausing at the bottom of the porch steps.

Uncle Sam put a finger to his lips, then whispered to me, "A fox got into the hen house last night, and the missus lost a passel of hens—including her two best layers. She was mighty attached to them birds."

"Oh, I'm sorry to hear that."

Uncle Sam again put a finger to his lips, indicating that perhaps I should not say anything about the calamity. He creaked open the screen door and hollered into the house, "Lucy! Get on out here! You got a visitor! The fair Miss Marguerite has come to brighten your day!"

Within moments, Aunt Lucy appeared at the door, drying her hands on her apron. "My lands! Look at you! You're a sight for sore eyes. Come here now and give me a hug!"

Aunt Lucy hadn't changed her hairstyle in the dozen years I'd known her. She wore her hair pulled back sharply from her face and gathered in a tight knot on the very top of her head. In the past few years, she'd started wearing wireless spectacles which only emphasized the wrinkles around her eyes.

"I hear you are on your own for the month. Sit! Sit! Tell me all about it."

"Yes. Friend Anne is at the fair. She'll be here before the Fourth. I'm so sorry I haven't been to see you here before."

"Fiddlesticks! Hear you are painting that cottage of yours. Can't believe it is time to paint it already. Seems like you just built it yesterday."

"Yes, time flies."

"Our Myron is at the fair, too."

"He is? How wonderful. Did he take Susan?"

"No, he's there on official business. He was appointed to the

Columbian Guard. The organizers of the fair asked for the best of the best from all the police departments around the country and from the military as well. Myron, of course, has been with the Lifesaving Service in Luddington, Michigan, for years now. He said that all the men were chosen not just on their exemplary service record but had to look the part—tall, strong, and muscular. That's our Myron! He sent us a photograph of himself in his Columbian Guard uniform. Wait! Wait, I'll go get it."

Aunt Lucy stood and rushed to get the photograph. Uncle Sam rocked back in his chair and gave me a little wink. "Mighty proud of our son, she is."

"Just look at that uniform!" Aunt Lucy said, offering the photograph to me when she returned.

I put my bundle of letters down on the little table between us and picked up the photograph.

"Myron says his uniform is navy blue. The fancy epaulets are black as is the braid and the cording. The buttons and the six-point star on his chest are brass. Says he buffs 'em every day to keep 'em shiny. The hat is blue too and has a red cord just above the brim. He's not especially fond of the black pompon on top. Says it makes him feel like a bit of a dandy. It takes my breath away to see him!"

"He's quite handsome." I shot a look at Uncle Sam, who was grinning like a Cheshire cat.

"Oh, my!" Aunt Lucy said, noticing the black-rimmed letter in my stack of mail. "Is that a death announcement? My dear! Please don't let me keep you from pressing news."

The return address was from my sister's home on Mulberry Street in West Philadelphia and the handwriting was my mother's.

"Don't worry. . . it's just a letter from my mother."

"She still usin' mourning stationery?"

"And still wears her widow's weeds."

"Really . . . How long has it been since your father died?"

"Five years now. I'm hoping a visit with Mrs. Pratt will help Mother realize that it is time to move on."

"Yes, Alice seems to be managing quite well under the circumstances. But then again, she has two girls to raise, no time to wallow in the self-pity.

Oh, I almost forgot! I have a pot of jam on the stove. I need to give it a stir."

"I should be on my way. I have so much to do to prepare for my sister's visit. Mother and Rose arrive next week."

"Wait here for just a minute. I'll be right back."

I gathered my mail and waited on the porch steps.

"I knew you would cheer her up. Thanks for stopping by," Uncle Sam said to me, rocking back in his chair. Sam was almost always rocking away on the porch, pondering over business schemes. Aunt Lucy rarely sat; she was always cleaning, cooking, baking, milking, or tending to her chickens.

When Aunt Lucy came back, she offered me a small plate covered with a clean tea towel.

"What's this?" I asked.

"Just a little something to welcome you back to the island."

I lifted the towel and inhaled the rich molasses aroma of Aunt Lucy's spice drop cookies.

"You know the way to my heart," I said, giving her wrinkled cheek a little kiss. "I'll be sure to get this plate back to you."

CHAPTER
eight

Midmorning of the third day of painting, I heard what sounded like a cowbell. Had Uncle Sam's cow wandered all the way to the north side of the island? I looked down at the path below and saw nothing. I heard the clatter of tin again. No, not a singular cowbell: it sounded like several cowbells, and they were rattling together at a rapid rate. If a herd of cattle were thundering past, I would surely hear their hoof beats or mooing.

I looked down again and saw a shimmering halo of frizzy, blond hair.

"Flossie! I called out," I put the wet paintbrush on top of the paint can, descended the ladder, and met her at the top of the path with open arms.

"Don't you dare hug me!" she exclaimed. "Who is that beneath all that paint spatter? Did you get any paint on the cottage?"

Flossie had written before I left West Philadelphia and asked if she could stay with me for a few days before the start of the American Canoe Association's annual meet and regatta on Grindstone Island. While I'm sure Flossie owns a calendar, I don't know if she really knows how to use it. I never quite know when Flossie will show up, nor when she plans to leave. Regardless, she always seems to show up when I need a lift in spirits.

"Me? What about you? What a racket! I thought you were an escaped cow. A herd of escaped cows. What are those receptacles? Are those candle boxes?" I asked.

Three elongated metal boxes, each with its own strap, dangled from each shoulder—six tins in all. They clunked together as she continued to the top of the rock outside our cottage door.

"They do look like candle boxes with straps, don't they? But they're not. Guess again," Flossie said, lifting the strap of the three boxes off her right shoulder and dropping them to the granite rock below in a clatter of clinks and clanks. She repeated the process for the boxes on her left side.

I lifted one of the boxes and examined it. It was a flattened cylinder made of tin. There was a hinged door on the top, which I slowly opened. Flossie is quite fond of snakes and spiders, and I was a bit terrified at what might pop out at me. Thankfully, the interior was empty.

"I give up. I have no idea what these are for."

A river breeze rippled the water below and set Flossie's shimmering hair bouncing around her smiling face. "That, my dear, is a vasculum."

"Hmm. Diminutive of the Latin *vas* for 'vessel.' But a vessel for what?" I was hoping she would not say for serpents.

"Perhaps the French name would be a better hint. In France, it is *une boite à herboriser*."

"A botanical box?"

"Where would you like your things, miss?" I turned to see Nat at the top of the spiral path with a valise in each hand.

"Good morning, Nat," I said and smiled. "How are you today?"

Nat smiled. "Fine, miss."

Flossie rushed over to Nat. "Oh, thank you, Nat. I'll take them."

"And the two crates?" Nat asked.

"Two crates? Are you moving in for the season?" I asked.

"On the porch, please," Flossie called after Nat, who was already sprinting down the path to retrieve said crates.

"Don't be silly," Flossie said, swatting at my arm. "One crate has all the botanical papers, for pressing and drying, and the other crate contains the flower press."

"Flower press? Botanical papers? Are you changing studies again? This time from anthropologist to botanist?"

"No, I'm still an anthropologist specializing in the Six Nations of the Iroquois Confederacy. As I go into the field, many interviews revolve around the natural world. Therefore, I decided to collect plant life from the area and create an herbarium, a collection of dried plants and flowers, so we can discuss plants and trees."

"I see."

"I'm counting on your help. I hope to get started bright and early tomorrow morning," Flossie said.

"I'm afraid that is out of the question."

"What! Oh, no, please! I have so much to accomplish before the American Canoe Association meet and regatta," she said as she opened the crate that Nat had just set on the porch before he ran back to the dock to retrieve the next crate.

"Rose and Mother are coming."

Flossie dropped the lid back onto the crate and splayed her hand across her chest as if her heart might leap from her body. "Your sister, Rose. Here? Tomorrow? Oh, dear. I won't unpack then."

"No, not tomorrow, but in four days. Four days! I still have this entire side of the cottage to paint and the inside of the cottage to clean. It must be spotless. No dust. No pine pollen. No cobwebs," I said, trying not to sound frantic.

Flossie patted my hand. "Don't worry, I'll stay and help you get ready. But I'll go to the Grand View Hotel before Rose arrives."

"Flossie, there's no need for you to leave. Rose and Mother aren't staying here," I reminded her.

Flossie gave me a pointed look. "Oh, but I do have to leave. I don't need another run-in with Rose. That won't help anyone," Flossie said.

I opened my mouth to protest but Flossie waved a dismissive hand. "No time for quibbling. Let's get started!" Flossie picked up her two valises. "Door, please," she said with an impish grin.

I opened the door, she marched inside and emerged ten minutes later dressed to paint.

"I trust you have another paintbrush," she said.

"I do."

The rest of the day flew by. We didn't stop for lunch or tea but instead talked, laughed, and painted. By late afternoon, the cottage had a fresh coat of paint. I was certain it would take me three days to finish, but somehow we had magically done it all in one day. I looked over at Flossie. Sometimes I wondered if she were half sprite. Other times I thought perhaps she was all sprite.

While I cleaned the brushes, Flossie disappeared inside and emerged moments later in her swim costume.

"I'll finish up here while you change."

"Flossie, it is early June, I'm sure the water is a tad too chilly."

"Good! It will feel refreshing. Go! Go!" she said, shooing me toward the door."

"But . . ."

"Go!"

By the time I had changed, the brushes were clean, the ladders put away, and Flossie was standing on the dock urging me to hurry.

"I don't know, Flossie. I think if I just dangle my feet in the water that would be refreshing enough."

"You'll thank me for this later," Flossie said, and with one push I was in the water. It was so cold it took my breath away. I came to the surface gasping for air.

Flossie jumped in next to me. "Ah! It feels heavenly!"

"To a polar bear perhaps."

"Oh, stop whining and relax," Flossie said. She put her face in the water and swam away from me in strong, confident strokes.

Instantly, Friend Anne's words came back to me. "The river is thy friend. Relax into the arms of the river. Go with the flow of the current and trust that an island will catch thee."

Flossie had taught me to swim a dozen years ago, but it was Friend Anne who had taught me to float and to relax in the river. Those words had saved my life.

I laid back on the surface of the river and felt all the tension melt out of me. I looked up at the bright blue sky and felt the warmth of the sun on my face and the silky arms of the St. Lawrence wrap around me.

By the time Flossie had swum to Pratt Point and back, we were both ready to get out of the river. We pulled ourselves up onto the dock, then dashed up the spiral path, dripping and laughing. Even though I was wearing a mobcap, my hair was soaked. It would take hours before it was dry again. I pulled off my mobcap, unplaited my hair, and let it fall down my back almost to my waist.

Even though the heat of the day had passed, the rock still radiated heat. We lay facedown on the rock. I could feel the heat of the rock warm my stomach. The lichen that covered the rock scratched against my cheek. The warmth of the rock felt good. We lay there in silence for a long while till I almost dozed off. Somewhere in that magic moment between wakefulness and sleep, I thought I heard—felt—the heartbeat of Mother Earth below us.

An ant crawled across my hand and roused me to wakefulness.

"Flossie?" I murmured.

"Yes?"

I told her about Mr. Quigley, how we were on the top of ancient mountains and that at sunset the Forsyth quarry glows red.

The story energized Flossie, who sat up straight. "We have to row over and experience that some evening."

"And row home in the dark? I don't know."

Flossie tilted her head and gave me a disappointed look. She was about to launch into a lecture when we heard voices on the path below.

"Yoo-hoo! Miss Marguerite? Are you here?" a woman's voice called out.

We rose and walked to the top of the spiral path and saw on the path below the two Kerr sisters.

"Mary Mason! Lois! Please, come up!"

"May I get you a glass of water?" I asked, motioning for them to sit on the wicker chairs on the porch. "No, thank you," Mary Mason said. "Please forgive our intrusion so late in the day, but we have a pressing matter."

Meanwhile, Flossie had retrieved two chairs for us from inside the cottage.

"Mary Mason and Lois, may I introduce my college roommate, Flossie Bixby."

"Flossie, these are the Kerr sisters I spoke of, Mary Mason and Lois."

Everyone murmured their pleasure at meeting each other.

"We have a telegram for you. Actually, it was sent to John as Mr. Bartman was unsure of how to reach you," Mary Mason said, tightly holding the opened telegram envelope in her hands.

"Mr. Bartman?" I asked.

"Yes, he was one of the alums on the Princeton outing. Do you remember him?" Mary Mason asked.

"He remembers you," Lois murmured.

Mary Mason gave Lois a warning look, then turned back toward me.

"This is perhaps a bit awkward," Mary Mason said, pressing her lips together.

"Did something happen to Mr. Bartman?" I asked.

"No. Nothing like that. It's just that the telegram was sent two days ago, but John didn't retrieve it from Pullman House until this afternoon."

While Mary Mason looked disquieted, Lois was bursting with enthusiasm. "Mr. Bartman would like you to accompany him to Frank Taylor's campfire this evening," Lois blurted out.

"Frank Taylor? The illustrator for *Harper's Weekly*?" Flossie asked.

"Yes! He has a cottage at the foot of Round Island. His weekly campfires are famous. He always has captivating entertainment and engaging guests," Lois said.

"The telegram says that there was no need to reply. The Clarks are traveling from Comfort Island to Round Island in their steam yacht the *Mamie C.* and will stop at the Grenell Island Store dock around seven-thirty. If you wish to attend, he will pick you up there," Mary Mason said handing over the telegram.

"It's a most sought-after invitation," Lois said as I read the telegram.

"If you don't wish to attend because you don't have time to get ready, or because you have a guest," Mary Mason said, motioning to Flossie, "I will be happy to meet Mr. Bartman and convey your regrets."

"I would like to attend, but . . ."

I looked at Flossie.

"Seven-thirty, you said?" Flossie asked.

Mary Mason nodded.

"Of course she will attend," Flossie said, rising to her feet. "It was very nice meeting both of you. If you will excuse us, ladies, we have a lot to do to prepare."

CHAPTER
nine

"Hold still! I have a few more hairpins to stick in," Flossie said.

"Thank heavens you are here, Flossie. I'm all thumbs when it comes to trying to tame my wild curls into a civilized coiffure. Well, anything beyond winding it into a simple schoolmarm bun."

"There," Flossie said, securing the last hairpin and stepping back to admire her handiwork.

"Do you think I need a little pomade to keep it in place?" I asked.

"Absolutely not! Besides, it's still a little wet in the back!"

"No thanks to you!"

"I did not get your hair that wet!"

I rolled my eyes at her and took the small oval mirror from the wall and held it as far away as I could, but I could only see my face. "Here. Hold this, I want to see how I look."

Flossie took the mirror from my hands and backed out of my tiny bedroom and halfway across the main room before I said stop.

The image was small but I could see myself from head to toe. "I look like a schoolteacher," I moaned, smoothing out the navy blue walking skirt and straightening the high lace collar of my white shirtwaist.

Flossie dropped the mirror to her side. "And what's wrong with that? You forget that I was a schoolteacher before I got my degree in anthropology."

93

"I guess the part I had left off was the *old maid* part as in *old maid* schoolteacher. I didn't mean to insult you or the former profession. I suppose I'm nervous about rubbing elbows with the set from Millionaires' Row."

"Who is this Mr. Bartman anyway, and how do you know him?"

"I really don't know him very well. I met him on the Princeton outing. He's staying with the Clarks of Comfort Island."

"Which island is that?"

"It's downriver near the town of Alexandria Bay. It's the one with the huge, soaring tower with a walkway around the top."

"Sorry, that doesn't narrow it down for me. So many huge castles with towers on the islands around Alexandria Bay," Flossie said as she re-hung my mirror above my washstand.

"There are a few castles being constructed on this end of the river as well," I said, smoothing my hair back again. "There is Castle Francis on One Tree Island, that was built a few years back. And this year, Mr. Emery is constructing a stone castle on Calumet Island across from Clayton." I held a black belt to my waist. "Doesn't really add any color or flair, does it?"

"My goodness! I can't believe it! You've turned into a simpering summer girl trying to snare a beau for the summer season. Do you have designs on this Mr. Bartman? Is he moneyed?"

"Actually, I don't know. I don't think so. He's an academic."

"Hmmm. What field?"

"Art history. Specializing in Greek and Roman art."

"Ah! I see."

"You see what?"

A curious look crossed Flossie's face, and then she said, "Well, maybe I have something to help you."

She went into the main room, pawed through her valise, and returned with a dark blue shawl. She draped it over my shoulders. I didn't need her to hold the mirror. I didn't need to know how it looked. It felt perfect. Just the weight of it made me feel royal and regal.

"This is an Akwesasne ceremonial shawl. I was saving it for a campfire evening at the American Canoe Association, but since you're going to a campfire, you can give it a try first. And I have a pendant for you as well."

She pinned it in the center of my high collar. It was a silver pin with a raised Indian motif. I peered at it in the little mirror and ran my finger over the motif.

"Is it an eagle?" I asked.

"No, a thunderbird."

I had no idea what a thunderbird was, but I liked the sound of it.

"Oh, Flossie, thank you! It's perfect." I reached out to give her a hug, but she checked her watch pinned to her bodice and let out a little *eeek*!

"No time for hugs. Look at the time! We must hurry!" she grabbed me by the hand and pulled me out the door. As we descended the spiral path and hurried along North Boulevard, she told me about the shawl.

She stopped outside the back of the store. "I'll say goodbye here, my dear. Have a lovely evening," she said.

"I'm sorry for leaving you alone your first night on the island," I said.

"I'll be busy setting up my flower press," she said as she kissed my cheek. "Now hurry along!"

I was glad to see Mary Mason and John waiting for me on the dock.

"What a beautiful shawl," Mary Mason said.

"Miss Bixby loaned it to me. Are you going to the campfire as well?" I asked.

"Well, no. We weren't invited. We felt it was our duty to see you off. John and I feel responsible. After all, we are the ones who introduced you to Mr. Bartman in the first place. We wanted to make sure that you were properly escorted. Besides, I was looking forward to meeting the Clarks," Mary Mason said. "John will be waiting on the dock tonight with the skiff to row you back to your cottage. It's a new moon tonight and it will be exceedingly dark. We didn't want you walking home without a lantern, and Mr. Bartman doesn't know his way around Grenell."

"Besides, Black Bart . . ." John started. Mary Mason gave him a gentle nudge. "I mean, Charles doesn't know the river at all."

A steam whistle tooted, and we turned to see a small steamer round Curtis Point, the southernmost tip of Grenell Island.

The steamer docked, Mr. Bartman disembarked, and without fanfare introduced the Kerrs and me to Mr. and Mrs. Clark and their three teener sons—Mancel, Alson, and Edwin. Then, with an awkward gesture, he invited me aboard.

"Why don't you join me in the salon?" Mrs. Clark offered as we settled in the small, but elegant enclosed salon. The menfolk stayed on the bow as their boatman pulled from the dock. It looked terribly windy out there and I was grateful to be out of the wind so I didn't have to worry about my hair disassembling before I even got there. Mrs. Clark was a pleasant-looking woman. I was pleased to see that even though she was the wife of a millionaire she was dressed very sensibly in a nautical dress, very similar to the one Lois wore the first day I met her—straight sleeves, simple lines, a broad sailor collar on the back and a long tie in the front. I'm not sure what I expected—perhaps that she would be decked out in silks, draped in diamonds, and wearing a tiara.

"Charles—I mean, Mr. Bartman—tells me you attend Penn," Mrs. Clark said when we were settled.

"Yes. I am at Penn," I prevaricated. It was an accurate statement but the words left a tinny taste in my mouth.

"You study the classics?"

I nodded, reminding myself that while I taught the classics, I still studied new things every day.

"Mr. Bartman tells me you are quite proficient in Greek."

I fought the urge to rattle off a Greek phrase but instead merely nodded again with a forced smile on my lips.

She leaned over, touched my knee, and smiled broadly. "When Charles came home from the Princeton outing, he talked of nothing but you. I was thrilled. I had been feeling guilty for forcing him to attend. I've come to think of him as one of my sons in the past few weeks. His parents live down the street from us, though we don't know them that well. We met Charles at the Art Institute. Anyway . . . I hope you don't think it too forward to be invited on such short notice, but when I heard you summered on Grenell and Grenell was en route to Round Island, I thought it the perfect opportunity for you two to get together again."

"Not at all," I said.

"Charles just needs a little nudge. He is—well—shy and a bit bookish. I can see my Alson being the same way seven years from now."

"Alson is your middle son, correct? How old are the boys?" I asked.

"Mancel is nineteen, Alson is seventeen and Edwin is fifteen. Like Charles, Alson thinks of only one thing—art. For Mr. Bartman it is art history. Alson showed talent in art even before he entered grammar school. He drew on every blank piece of paper he could find, including the frontispiece to the hymnals at church." Mrs. Clark smiled broadly at the memory.

"Oh my," I said.

"We had to check his pockets for pencils before we left for church on Sunday mornings. Sometimes we still do," she said with a wink. "In 1889, we took the family on the grand tour of Europe. It was educational for all of them, but the primary purpose was to expose Alson to European art. He was enthralled. But we all missed the river so. We first came here in 1882. The boys grew up here. When they weren't gamboling about the island playing pirate or explorer, they were out on the river rowing, fishing, and swimming. When Alson finishes secondary school, he'll attend the Art Institute in Chicago, where Mr. Bartman works."

I inclined my head, trying to remember our brief conversation on the shore at Grand View Park. Had he mentioned working at the Art Institute? "In what capacity?" I asked.

"Mr. Bartman is in charge of the classics wing . . . well, the future classics wing. The Art Institute will be moving into one of the buildings of the fair after the fair ends. Charles has this theory that there will be a renewed interest in the classics because of some French fellow who is pushing for the re-establishment of the Olympics."

"A renewed interest in the classics?" I asked. This news was thrilling to me as well. "But what did this have to do with France?"

Mrs. Clark waved a dismissive hand. "I really wouldn't want to speak out of turn. You can ask Charles all about it. Sometimes it's hard to engage him in conversation, but he will speak endlessly on classical art and his new project."

I nodded as I recalled our conversation under the willow about Socrates, Plato, and Aristotle. It was the first time I witnessed him engage in conversation all day.

"It's grand to be back on the river," Mrs. Clark said, looking out at the water. "It was tempting to stay in Chicago with all the excitement of the fair, but we couldn't endure missing another season on the river. When Charles heard we were leaving Chicago for the Thousand Islands, he asked if he might join us. He hoped to escape the frenzy of the fair and find a quiet spot to work on his book. He's been a delight. Alson has learned so much from him."

Mrs. Clark paused and looked out the window. "It appears we're almost there."

I looked out the row of highly polished brass portholes of the *Mamie C.* and could see the Frontenac dock, where several other private steam yachts were moored.

"Have you been to the Frontenac before?" Mrs. Clark asked as deckhands secured our lines.

"Yes, years ago, back when it was called Round Island House." My cheeks reddened. Mr. Emery had purchased the property only two years later—ten years ago—and he had renamed the property Frontenac. Would my slip alert Mrs. Clark that I was older than I perhaps seemed?

I studied her face as Mr. Clark helped her disembark. She showed no signs of alarm.

I stepped off the *Mamie C.* and stared in wonder at the Frontenac. Of course, I'd seen it from afar, but I was overwhelmed by the grandeur of the half-moon flower beds that scalloped either side of the walkway to the entrance of the grand hotel. The meticulously maintained beds were brimming with orange, white, and yellow blossoms. I thought Round House was grand, but the new Frontenac was huge! Mr. Emery had enlarged the Frontenac to be two or three times larger than the original Round Island House.

"Come along, boys," Mrs. Clark said. She shooed the boys in front of her, and they walked along the narrow path leading from the Frontenac dock toward the foot of the island. Mr. Clark linked arms with Mrs. Clark and they followed the boys, leaving me alone on the dock with Mr. Bartman.

He looked at me and shifted from foot to foot, clearly unsure of what to do or say next.

"How was the trip over?" he stammered finally. "Were you comfortable in the salon?"

"Quite. Mrs. Clark is a charming hostess."

"Yes, well. I suppose we should follow," he said, indicating the path to our left.

I walked ahead of him.

I wanted to ask about this book he was working on. I turned to speak to him, stepped on a stone, and stumbled a bit.

"Careful! Careful! It's rocky here. Watch your step!" He rushed forward then and took my elbow, walking beside me on the river side of the path so I wouldn't tumble into the river on my next misstep.

"Are you alright?" he asked after we had walked a few steps in silence.

"I'm feeling rather foolish right now. I summer on Grenell and our paths on the north shore are more rugged than this path. I of all people should know to watch my step."

"The one word I would never ascribe to you, Miss Hartranft, is foolish," he said, tightening his light grip on my left arm.

"Oh, here they are," Mrs. Clark exclaimed when we approached. "Mr. Taylor . . . Mrs. Taylor," Mrs. Clark said, nodding to each of them in turn, "may I introduce Mr. Charles Bartman from Chicago and Miss Hartranft from West Philadelphia."

"A pleasure to make your acquaintance, I'm sure," I said.

"Miss Hartranft attends Penn," Mr. Bartman offered. He seemed proud that I was a college woman.

I bit my lip and did not correct him.

"Oh, the Taylors also hail from Philadelphia," Mr. Clark said.

"Actually," Mr. Taylor interjected. "I'm not from Philadelphia. I was born and raised in Rochester, New York, but I currently reside in Philadelphia. Well, my home and family are there, but I spend most of my time on the road. I've been traveling almost nonstop since '78, producing tourist guidebooks. The only time I stay put seems to be when I come to our lovely summer place here on Round Island. We call it Shady Ledge."

"Thank you for your kind invitation," Mr. Bartman said.

"I hear you're attached to the Art Institute of Chicago, Mr. Bartman," Mr. Taylor said, stepping closer to Charles.

"Yes, curator for the Classical Arts wing," Mr. Bartman replied. He still had my hand tucked firmly into his elbow, and as he talked I could feel the tension increase in his arm to the point that I thought my hand would go numb.

"I was about to show young Alson my studio. Would you care to join us?"

"Indeed," Mr. Bartman replied, and, with relief, he released my hand and motioned me ahead of him. I gently shook out my hand as we followed Mr. Taylor to his studio on the second floor of the boathouse. The studio was lined with windows on three sides, which afforded Mr. Taylor wondrous views of the river. An easel stood in the corner that faced the channel. A large worktable strewn with sketches dominated the middle of the room. The wall to our back was lined with shelves crammed with paints, brushes, and blocks of wood.

"What mediums do you work in?" Alson asked.

"Watercolor, pen and ink, and woodcut engravings, mostly," Mr. Taylor said as I spun around the room taking in the different works displayed nonchalantly on shelves and table tops. "Watercolor is probably my favorite medium, but pen and ink, as well as woodcut engravings, are my bread and butter."

"What's this?" Mr. Bartman asked, indicting the many sketches strewed about the work table.

"I'm currently working on *Estes' Standard Guide to the Thousand Islands*, due out next year."

"I really like this one," Alson said, indicating a sketch of a steamer shooting the Lachine Rapids. "How do you get the feeling of movement?"

"Practice. I was lucky. I started my career as a 'special artist' doing illustrations for newspapers. It taught me to work fast and to zero in on meaningful details."

"Frank," we heard a female voice call from below. "The crowd is getting restless."

"Coming, Maggie," Mr. Taylor called down to his wife. "Come, gentlemen, Miss Hartranft, we must hurry or we'll miss this evening's entertainment."

Mr. Taylor led us to the staircase. Alson and Mr. Bartman preceded me down the stairs, and Mr. Taylor followed.

"Tell me, Miss Hartranft," Mr. Taylor said before we reached the first landing. "Are you any relation to General Hartranft?"

"Distant cousins," I said over my shoulder.

"I served in the War Between the States. Joined the Rochester Grays Battery Light Artillery in '63. I had the great honor of meeting General Hartranft at the Battle of Bullrun. He won the congressional medal of honor at that battle. The Hartranft name holds a lot of weight with me. I was disappointed when Rutherford Hayes beat him out for the Republican presidential nomination in '76. General Hartranft would have made a valiant president of these United States."

We approached an amphitheater that had been carved into the hillside. Three rows of seating—planks on log rounds—looked down on the small stage area. A cozy fire had been lit to the side of a stage. The first two rows were already filled with about thirty people waiting for the entertainment to begin. "Speaking of cousins," Mr. Taylor said as I settled into a seat in the third row, "I have a cousin on Grenell. Perhaps you know him. Mr. L. L. Carlisle from New Jersey?"

"Indeed I do," I said, turning to Mr. Taylor. The Carlisles were the first to build a large cottage on a bluff on the south side of the island overlooking the American channel. Now there were four large rambling summer cottages perched on the female camel hump, high above the water. Starting at the end closest to Pullman House was Point Ida, built in 1890. Next came La Roche, with a short tower and crowned with a cupola, built for the Griswold sisters in 1882. The Carlisles built a large rambling home they called Jersey Heights in 1889. Glimpses is to the west of Jersey Heights, tucked onto the back end of Point Breeze under the shade of some towering trees.

"I hear Mr. Carlisle is feeling poorly, which is why he hasn't arrived yet," I said.

"Yes. He's hoping to convince his doctor to allow him to make the trip. I believe the island air would do wonders for his vitality. If you'll excuse me, I need to introduce our first performer."

The first performer was R. T. Sperry, a sleight-of-hand artist trained by none-other-than Hermann the Great. He fascinated the crowd with dazzling coin and card tricks. He made a coin disappear right before my eyes and then pulled it from behind my ear. Sperry was followed by an actor in blackface who called himself William the Darkie, who gave an impersonation of porter-life in a sleeping car that had us laughing so hard I had to dab away tears of mirth with my handkerchief. The last tidbit of entertainment was the renowned travel writer Earnest V. Ingersoll reading from his newly published book, *Crest of the Continent*. Ironically, he read a chapter, that described an Indian campfire in riveting detail.

"I see we have an authentic Indian shawl at this campfire," he said when he finished and invited me down to the stage so everyone could get a good look at it. I was grateful that while walking me to the dock, Flossie had informed me about the shawl.

"It's an Akwesasne shawl," I said hoping I had pronounced the tribal name correctly. "The Akwesasne are a Mohawk tribe that straddles the St. Lawrence. The motif on the shawl represents the Hiawatha belt. The five sections represent the five original members of the Iroquois Confederacy."

When he asked about the choice of colors—the dark blue of the shawl and the felted pieces of cream and orange that comprised the Hiawatha Belt—I told him that I didn't know.

He presented me again, and I gave a bow and the small crowd applauded.

Once settled back on the bench next to Mr. Bartman, he leaned over and whispered in my ear, "It's a beautiful shawl." His warm breath on my neck and the smell of his sandalwood and vanilla shaving oil made gooseflesh erupt on my arms. I shivered despite my close proximity to the campfire.

"We have refreshments for all." Mr. Taylor announced. "Lemon pound cake."

As the guests rose and shuffled toward the refreshment table, Mr. Ingersoll climbed to where we still sat and asked if he could join us. "You spoke most eloquently about the shawl. Have you studied Indian lore long?"

"No, my roommate from Penn is an anthropologist specializing in the Six Nations. The shawl belongs to her."

"Really? How very interesting."

"She is staying with me. But only for a few days. She will be attending the American Canoe Association meet which starts in a few weeks. Tomorrow, Chief Two Buttons is delivering an authentic Mohawk canoe for her to use at the A. C. A."

"Are you staying here on Round Island?"

"No. I have a cottage on the north side of Grenell."

"Perhaps I can meet this Miss . . ."

"Miss Bixby," I filled in.

"I would love to see this canoe."

Grenell 1893

"I believe Chief Two Buttons will be there in the fore-noon."

"My interests lie in art. But art history and anthropology do intersect. This shawl, for instance, is a work of art. I can see how it mimics some of the symbolism we have in Greek and Roman art," Mr. Bartman said as we walked toward the refreshment table.

The Taylors' staff served us cake and lemonade, and we sat back down in the amphitheater. Remembering my mother's instruction to take dainty bites, I cut the bite I had intended to take in half. I felt giddy, excited, and a tad light-headed. I wouldn't have been surprised to learn that the lemon pound cake had been laced with rum.

CHAPTER
ten

    I was sitting on the porch watching peach light streak across the morning sky when I heard the tea kettle hiss. I jumped up, went inside, wrapped a tea towel around my hand, and removed the kettle from the stove before it shrieked and woke Flossie.

    Flossie was fast asleep when I arrived back at Castle Rock last night. She had left a lantern on low in the main room, which I carried with me as I tiptoed to my room. I quietly disrobed, pulled my sleeping gown on over my head and readied myself for bed. I extinguished the lamp but didn't even attempt to sleep. Images of Mr. Taylor's campfire entertainment buzzed in my head. Instead, I slipped out onto the porch, into the night air, and eased the screen door shut. I couldn't remember such an auspicious gathering: a conjuror, a minstrel, and an author. Such a diverse entertainment selection. Somehow, each had made me feel special.

    Wrapped in fragrant darkness, I relived the evening. Eventually, my thoughts drifted to Mr. Bartman: how I caught him looking at me through the evening, how he proffered his arm to help me along the path, and our moment on the dock when he said good night.

    I sat on the porch surrounded by darkness for an hour, then plodded back to bed barefoot but didn't sleep much. I decided I might as well rise, dress, and watch the sunrise.

    "He said I could call him Charles, and I had said he could call me

Marguerite," I whispered to myself as I poured the steaming water into the teapot. I plopped in the tea ball.

Mother would be aghast if she knew we were already calling each other by our Christian names. I could hear her now, "Marguerite, one must not allow such familiarity." Perhaps it had come from my years of living with Quakers. They are decidedly less formal and eschew titles, opting for no title at all or, after a long while—and only if earned—using the desired title of Neighbor or Friend.

I hurried the brewing process along by dunking the tea ball up and down.

Mother would again chide me for being impatient and tell me that there are things in this world that cannot be rushed. Certain things require time to unfold and develop, steeping tea being one of those things.

I poured the tea into my cup and put in my customary clove and two cinnamon imperials. In the light of pre-dawn morning, I stirred the tea, watching the candy swirl and tint the tea red.

"I see you're up and dressed already," Flossie said from the bedroom door.

Sitting out on the porch in my sleeping gown felt decadent at midnight, but it was positively indecent to do so in daylight. "Thanks for leaving the lantern lit for me in the main room," I said.

"That path must have been treacherous last night. With no moon, it was very dark," Flossie said, sliding into a chair. "Could you pour a teacup for me?"

"Of course. John and Charles rowed me home in a skiff," I said

"John and Charles?"

"Yes. Charles wanted to make sure I was properly escorted home, so he spent the night on Grenell at Glimpses with the Kerrs. He may be dropping by this morning," I tried to keep my voice neutral, as if Charles was in the habit of dropping by, and I wasn't excited about the opportunity of seeing him again.

"Oh, I see," Flossie said knowingly.

I looked up from my cup and saw her smirking at me.

"What?" I asked.

"Charles? We're on a first-name basis? Already?"

"Yes, well . . . it's the Quaker influence, I suppose," I said, trying out my theory on Flossie.

"How about your red cheeks? Do you attribute that to the Quaker influence as well?"

"Stop! This is all so new to me."

"What? Courting?" Flossie asked coyly.

"I don't know what it is yet. We've only just met. Oh, and by the way, a Mr. Ingersoll is coming by sometime this morning to see you," I said, hoping to re-direct the conversation.

"Who is coming to visit me? And, whatever for?"

"Your shawl was a hit. Mr. Ingersoll was there reading from his book about an Indian campfire. He wants to talk to you about your shawl."

"What book?"

"Uh—I think it was titled—oh, what was it? Something about the continent."

"The *Crest of the Continent*?" Flossie asked

"That's it!"

Flossie dropped her cup to the saucer with a clink, put her hands on the table and leaned across at me with eyes wide and mouth agape. "You mean Ernest V. Ingersoll is coming here?"

I nodded.

Flossie pushed herself from the table, her chair scraping loudly across the wooden floor. "When?"

"Shortly before noon, I think."

"Ernest V. Ingersoll! I can't believe it," she said, pacing around the room, and shaking her hands excitedly. "I can't wait to talk to him about Mesa Verde. He and William Henry Jackson were the first to investigate and describe the cliff dwellings there. Really, truly—you're not teasing me? Ernest V. Ingersoll is coming here? This morning?"

"Hmmm. Now who sounds like a simpering summer girl?"

"Oh, this is not the same at all," Flossie said. "This is purely academic."

"Is it?" I teased.

"I don't even know what he looks like."

"You read his book. I'm sure there was a sketch of the author in the frontispiece. "

"I don't recall."

"I can see you now staring at the frontispiece, hoping to meet the dashing Ernest Ingersoll someday," I said before taking another sip from my teacup.

Flossie stopped pacing, and whirled around, and rolled her eyes. She slid back into her chair and took another sip of tea. "Don't be silly. I'm not like you. I don't need a husband," she said.

"Who said I need a husband?" I said, carefully replacing my teacup in its saucer.

"Your mother and your sisters," Flossie said, raising the cup to her lips.

She had a point there.

Flossie took a long sip, then set the cup down again. "Thank goodness that I'm an only child whose mother died when I was young and was reared by a father who has never been concerned with marrying me off. I wasn't raised to think that marriage was my only option. You, my poor dear, were. Not just raised but bombarded constantly by the notion that you need a husband to make you whole. And speaking of bombarding, when is your sister Rose arriving?"

"At the end of the week."

"Will this Mr. Bartman meet her expectations?"

I hadn't considered that someday I would have to introduce Mr. Bartman to Rose and Mother. The idea unnerved and haunted me as we ate breakfast.

After breakfast, we started on our morning chores.

"I'll get water," I told Flossie after I'd stoked the fire, "if you'll take care of the chamber pots. Tomorrow you can get the water, and I'll deal with the chamber pots. Whoever finishes first can clean the lamp chimneys and trim the wicks."

Every morning I retrieved two buckets of water from the river: one for washing and cleaning and the other for drinking water. Several years back, Anne had insisted we boil our drinking water. No sooner had I descended the spiral path and reached the end of the dock then I saw Nat rowing this way.

"Mornin', Miss Marguerite," Nat called out. "Got a visitor for you."

I quickly filled the buckets, carried them to the end of the dock, then returned to help tie up the skiff. "Greetings, Mr. Ingersoll. Welcome to

Castle Rock," I said as I helped him from the skiff.

"I hope I'm not too early. I took the first steamer available from Round Island to Grenell. I didn't realize you were so close. This lad was gracious enough to offer to row me to your place."

"I was makin' an ice delivery anyway," Nat said, pointing to the ice blocks in the front of the skiff, safely tucked away from the morning sun under several gunnysacks.

"I was just getting our daily supply of water," I said, picking up the two buckets.

"May I help you with that? I can carry one or both for you," Mr. Ingersoll offered.

"Thank you, but no. Two balance me out, and, besides, I'm used to it. Follow me. Miss Bixby is anxious to meet you. Flossie!" I called out when I reached the top of the path. She was just returning from her trip to the privy up on the hill behind the cottage. "Mr. Ingersoll is here."

"I'll be right there. I need to wash up. Please, settle him on the porch if you will," Flossie said. She returned momentarily, all smiles, with her shawl in hand.

The two settled on the porch and soon became absorbed in deep conversation. I helped Nat chip away the rough edges of my ten-pound block of ice and squeezed it into our small icebox. Ice chips skittered across the wooden floor, and I scrambled about to retrieve them. I thanked Nat and sent him on his way. Then I set about boiling drinking water for the day and scrubbing out the chamber pots. The strong carbolic soap stung my nose with its turpentine smell and made my eyes water. I noticed a little water on the floor. I figured it was from melting ice chips, then realized I'd forgotten to empty the icebox drip tray last night. As the ice diminished, meltwater collected in the drip tray beneath the wooden icebox. Ordinarily, I emptied it twice a day, but last night I had been . . . distracted. Now it was overflowing. As I slid the tray from underneath the icebox, more water sloshed out onto the floor and caused a huge mess.

By the time I had finished cleaning the kitchen floor, Mr. Ingersoll and Flossie had switched from talking about the mysterious Mesa Verde and were comparing Hopi and Aztec cultures. They didn't even notice me when I walked out the back door, past the porch, and down the spiral path on my way to drop off this week's laundry to Maggie Robbins. Laundry was such a time-consuming endeavor. I was thrilled when Maggie moved to Grenell last year after marrying Hy Robbins and started taking in laundry.

As I left the Robbins' cottage, I looked out between Murray Isle and Grenell and saw in the distance a canoeist towing another canoe and determined that he must be Chief Two Buttons.

"I think Chief Two Buttons is approaching," I called out as I ascended the spiral path.

Flossie seemed surprised at my arrival as she had not noted my departure.

Mr. Ingersoll and Flossie descended the spiral path as Chief Two Buttons paddled toward our dock. Flossie explained to Mr. Ingersoll that in the past few years, Indians canoed about the islands selling their hand-woven baskets to summer residents. This is how we had met Chief Two Buttons. Last year, Flossie had visited their encampment on Grindstone Island. That is when she had made the arrangements to borrow the canoe for this year's American Canoe Association annual meet and regatta.

I opened the folding camp table that I use as my writing desk and penned a letter to Keiko and Anne as I listened to the three talk below. Chief Two Buttons explained how the Mohawk made canoes from birchbark. Mr. Ingersoll took a notebook and pencil from his vest pocket and furiously took notes and drew diagrams. After I finished with my quick note to Anne and Keiko, I took out another sheet of stationery to write a note to Nora, noting with amusement that while both letters said essentially the same thing, the tone of the letters differed greatly. To the doctors, my tone was very matter-of-fact. My letter to Nora was filled with emotion, vivid details, and snatches of dialogue.

Below on the dock, I heard Flossie ask if Chief Two Buttons would be willing to teach her the Indian paddle stroke. This interested me as well. I closed my letter to Nora, put my paperweight on the pile of papers so that they wouldn't blow away in my absence, and hurried down to the dock. Chief Two Buttons demonstrated the stroke, moving through the water silently with no sloshing or splashing sounds. "It is a silent stroke used for sneaking up on prey or enemies," he said. "The blade of the paddle stays in the water at all times. You rotate the handle with your wrist drawing a large oval in the water."

"May I try?" Flossie asked.

Chief Two Buttons nodded solemnly toward the empty canoe. She knelt in the canoe, took the paddle, and quickly and silently paddled out to the middle of our little bay.

Mr. Ingersoll wanted to try as well. Chief Two Buttons climbed out on the dock and offered Mr. Ingersoll his canoe. Mr. Ingersoll took off his suit coat, then handed his suit coat, notebook, and pencil to me.

While of similar size to Chief Two Buttons, Mr. Ingersoll somehow seemed far too big for the little birchbark canoe. Then, I noticed that instead of kneeling in the canoe as the Flossie did, he sat with his knees up. He seemed all knees and arms as he struggled to negotiate the waters of our small bay.

I noticed that the little demonstration had attracted a crowd. Across the bay at Pratt Point, the Pratt women were watching. I waved to Alice, Olivia, and Edith who waved back.

I had always thought that Indians, both male and female, wore their hair in long braids. However, Chief Two Buttons' hair was cut short and didn't show under his soft, felt hat. Suspenders held up pants that seemed to be a size too big. Tucked into his pants was a red calico shirt. Only his large, hook nose and complexion betrayed him as an Indian. As he stood next to me and shouted directions to Flossie and Mr. Ingersoll, I noticed his regal bearing.

Chief Two Buttons called to Mr. Ingersoll and waved for him to come back to the dock to change positions. Mr. Ingersoll must have misunderstood and tried to shift from sitting to kneeling in the middle of the bay. The little canoe rocked violently left, then right, and then there was a huge splash. Flossie immediately paddled over to help. The water is not deep there and Mr. Ingersoll stood, righted the canoe, and attempted to climb back in. Each time he tried, the canoe tipped again, spilling him out. Eventually, he gave up, swam to Pratt Point, and got out on the rock there.

Flossie towed the canoe back to our dock and then paddled out to retrieve Mr. Ingersoll's hat, which was slowly floating away.

The Pratts walked Mr. Ingersoll back to Castle Rock. Alice handed me a stack of folded clothes. "I think Otis's work clothes will fit Mr.

Ingersoll. Something for him to wear until his clothes dry out."

I thanked Alice for her thoughtfulness. Flossie thanked Chief Two Buttons for the use of his canoe and the lessons, then helped Mr. Ingersoll up the spiral path to our little cottage so he could change into dry clothes.

I was about to follow them when I heard someone talking to the Pratts in the shady lot between Castle Rock and the Pabst cottage. But the large Sentry Rock prevented me from seeing who it was.

"Good morning, Marguerite," Lois called out as she appeared from behind Sentry Rock. Mary Mason and Charles were right behind her.

"What's this?" Lois asked, indicating the birchbark canoe."

I explained the morning's events to the trio of newcomers.

"I'm so sorry we missed that . . . well, not the falling out of the canoe part, but the Indian stroke demonstration. Mr. Bartman wanted to speak with you, and I tagged along hoping to see the Indian shawl you wore last night and hear a little of the story around that," Lois said.

"Certainly," I said indicating the spiral path. Mary Mason, Lois, and I went first, and Charles followed closely behind.

"You slept well, I hope," he said to me as we reached the top.

"Yes," I lied. "And you?"

"Fairly well," he said.

By now Flossie was on the porch and was explaining the shawl to the Kerr sisters.

"I was hoping you could join me on another outing," Charles said, biting his lip and shifting from foot to foot. "It's called a watermelon party, hosted by the Sawyer sisters at Thousand Island Park. Seems they've taken a liking to you. They sent word over last night and asked that you come along as well."

"A watermelon party? Goodness me, I've never heard of such a thing."

"Nor I, but, well . . . I would love to spend more time with you. We weren't able to finish our conversation about Plato and Aristotle."

Lois looked up from the shawl and asked, "Did you ask Marguerite about the watermelon party yet?"

"He did. When is it?" I asked.

"Friday afternoon. It sounds like great fun. Mr. Sawyer is having the watermelon sent by freight all the way from Georgia. Too early for local melons."

"Oh, I'm sorry. I'm afraid I won't be able to attend. My sister, Mother, and four nephews arrive Friday," I said, looking at Charles.

"It's a great family event. You can bring them along. The Sawyer sisters said, 'the more the merrier.'"

I thought of Rose and Mother meeting Charles and swallowed hard.

"I'm sorry. I'm sure they will be exhausted from their trip."

"Perhaps we can get together another time next week. I would love to show you that Raphael painting. I have a photograph of it in one of my books."

"I . . .er . . . I rarely see my family and time on the island together is precious for us. Perhaps after they leave," I said.

"Certainly, I understand," Charles said, looking like a deflated balloon. "How long will they be staying?"

"Two weeks," I said.

Charles said nothing, but the thought of not seeing me for two weeks seemed to distress him greatly.

"I'm eager to see the photograph and resume our discussion on Plato and Aristotle," I assured him, peering up into his small dark eyes. "I'm in the process of cleaning, trying to get things in tip-top shape before my mother and sister arrive, otherwise I would give you a tour of our cottage. Though small as it is, it wouldn't take long. Perhaps after my family leaves," I said to the entire group.

Mary Mason stepped forward then, taking charge of the small group. "Thank you for showing us the shawl, Miss Bixby. We will leave you to your chores, Marguerite. Come along, Lois and Charles. Good day!" Mary Mason called as they descended the spiral path.

It took nearly five hours for Mr. Ingersoll's wet clothes to dry, but the time flew by for Flossie and Mr. Ingersoll, who spent the time on the porch in rapt conversation. Meanwhile, I was inside cleaning baseboards and polishing furniture, and wondering what one would wear to a watermelon party.

CHAPTER
eleven

I pulled on my borrowed crocheted gloves, buttoned the pearl button through the opening at the wrist, checked my bodice watch, then turned to appraise the cottage's interior one more time. My eyes were immediately drawn to the vase of lilacs and ferns in the middle of the table, and I smiled. The cottage looked neat as a pin, cozy and welcoming. Once outside, I surveyed the exterior. The new paint looked dazzling in the morning light. I'd spent an hour with a broom clearing away last night's cobwebs.

The cottage was so quiet since Flossie left last night. I had begged her to stay but she insisted on securing a room at the Grand View Hotel. "I can't trust myself to be civil in front of your sister Rose," she said. "If you need me, I won't be too far away. Have fun with your nephews and good luck."

I was ready. I straightened my hat, smoothed the front of my shirtwaist, descended the spiral path, and started off toward Pullman House. It had been nearly a month since I'd seen my nephews. I was looking forward to reading stories, playing games, and teaching the boys to fish and swim.

I nodded to Prof. Pabst who was reading on his porch. When I went up over the rocky outcrop beyond the Pabst cottage, I called out a "good day" to the knot of people at the next two cottages. This section of Grenell could be called Copenhagen Cove. The first is called the Copenhagen cottage as it is always filled with avid fishermen, from Copenhagen, New York, a small town fifty miles south of Clayton on the Rome, Watertown & Ogdensburg Railroad line. The next cottage beyond was built in 1884 by Charles Chickering, who was then a hardware merchant in Copenhagen. He became a New York State assemblyman soon after he built the cottage and is now a U.S. Congressman. Currently too busy to spend much time on the island, Charles had his cousin take over the cottage, sharing it with two doctors from Copenhagen. The doctors are rarely here at the same time. One always stays in Copenhagen to attend to the health needs of the community.

I heard laughter in the distance and looked toward Pullman House to see where it was coming from. I saw a group of young women on the bridge between Grenell Island Park and Grenell Island. Their hair was not worn loose around their shoulders like girls, but pulled up in neat coiffured hairstyles like young ladies. Their giggles told me otherwise.

I turned onto what had once been a marshy area filled with tall trees and cluttered with underbrush. The underbrush had been cleared away, and some of the trees removed. Now two cottages stood at the foot of the bridge that led to Pullman House. The cottage closest to the bridge was built more than a decade ago for Reuben Fuller and has changed hands twice already. It currently belonged to a jeweler from Utica, New York, Mr. Schiller and his wife, Lena. I'm not sure which of the three owners had decided to call the cottage Ojibway Inn. The name thrills Flossie, who tells me that the Ojibway are an Algonquian-speaking group sometimes referred to as Chippewa, who live predominately north and west of here.

In the fall of 1890, Mr. Worden, a grocery salesman from Syracuse, hired E. G. Robbins to build the second cottage on this side of the bridge. Mr. Worden named his two-story cottage Bay Edge and moved in the next June with his wife, Eva, and daughter, Mable. Olivia was delighted to have a girl her age right across the bay, and the two became fast friends.

When I reached the bridge, the three young women were leaning over the railing and dropping something into the water below. The tallest of the three, who was wearing a small-brimmed straw hat with artificial currants clustered on the front, turned to me and said, "Miss Hartranft!"

Startled that she knew my name, I stared into the young woman's face.

"Mable?" I asked.

"Yes! How was your winter?"

"It was lovely," I said, wondering how long the winter had been for Mable Worden to change from a girl in pigtails into a charming young woman in long skirts. It seemed like only yesterday Mable and Olivia had been crafting paper dolls and had come to Camp Anne begging for stray bits of lace or ribbon.

"These are my friends Miss Bessie Hale and Miss Jennie Luce."

"I'm pleased to make your acquaintance," I said, nodding to Bessie and Jennie.

"Miss Hartranft is a teacher at the University in Pennsylvania. She has a cottage on the north shore," Mable said.

Bessie and Jennie curtsied.

"How are your parents, Mable? I didn't see them when I passed your cottage," I said.

"They are well. My aunt from Illinois will be visiting next month. Mother is in a dither sprucing up the place," Mable said. "We're on our way to see the monkey at the Pullman House dock. Come along, girls."

"Wait," the dark-haired Bessie called out. "We have to throw our daisy discs into the river or our predictions won't come true."

The three giggled. I looked over the railing. Daisy petals floated on the surface of the water below.

"He loves me," Bessie whispered, and her cheeks turned scarlet as she threw the denuded daisy center into the water below.

"He loves me," Mable said as she kissed her daisy center and tossed it over the railing.

Jennie rolled her eyes and without looking down, tossed what remained of her daisy in the river, then turned toward Pullman House. "He loves me not. Now let's go see the monkey."

"You did say monkey. I thought perhaps I had misheard. There's a monkey at Pullman House?" I asked.

"They decided to get rid of that offensive cannon and have replaced it with a monkey," Mable informed me.

"It's adorable!" Bessie squealed.

Last year, the manager Mr. Lewis and the owner Mr. Sayles had installed a yacht cannon on the dock and fired a ceremonial round at the passing of each steamer to call attention to the newly improved Pullman House. The canon was not popular with the cottagers, as it shook napping gentleman from hammocks, roused babies from their slumber, and aggravated nearby fisherman, who insisted the constant cannon fire was frightening away the fish.

Mable's father drew up a petition, collected signatures, and presented it to Mr. Lewis. Apparently, the petition worked. The canon had been replaced with a monkey.

"It was just a baby when they acquired it from a sailor. The first day on the dock, it attached itself to the dock boy's dog. Petey . . ."

"The dog's name is Petey?" I asked.

The girls giggled and blushed.

"No. The dog's name is Prince," Jennie informed me.

"Prince belongs to a dock boy named Petey," Bessie added.

Mable bit her bottom lip.

Jennie batted her eyes.

"Oh, and the dog is such a prince! The little monkey clings to Prince's back as he runs up and down the dock. When Prince stops and sits down the monkey slides off his rump and nestles next to his side," Mable told me.

"Always with one of its arms up over Prince's back . . . like it's hugging Prince," Bessie added.

"Prince doesn't chase the monkey away. It is so adorable," Jennie said, clasping her hands in front of her.

"Since the little monkey is so attached to Prince . . ." Mable explained

"Literally!" Bessie said, her brown eyes wide.

"And Prince belongs to Petey . . ." Mable continued. A wave of giggles erupted from the girls again as they hid their faces behind gloved hands.

"Petey has been placed in charge of the monkey. He sells dog biscuits to feed to the pair. A biscuit for a penny," Mable finally finished.

"A penny?" I asked, not certain if I had heard Mable correctly. A penny could buy a good supply of licorice sticks or hard candy, but it could also buy a couple of fresh eggs or a loaf of day-old bread.

"I know. I know. It's expensive. Being a grocery man and knowing the fair price of things, Father strictly forbids me to pay such an exorbitant price. Luckily, Jennie's father gave her some spending money," Mable explained.

"And Petey . . ." Bessie began.

His name evoked another titter of laughter from the girls.

" . . . Petey lets each of us have a biscuit for a penny. We each feed half to Prince and the other half to Jambo," Jennie finished for her.

"Jambo?" I asked.

"The monkey," the girls said in unison.

"I think it's African for hello," Bessie said.

I smiled at this comment and thought of telling the girls that there are nearly two thousand different languages spoken in Africa, but there is no language called *African*.

"Come on, girls! We need to get there before the next steamer so we will have Jambo, Prince, and *Petey* all to ourselves." The three linked arms, headed toward Pullman House, and started singing a parody of the popular song "Daisy Bell."

Petey, Petey
Here is my answer true.
I'm not crazy
All for the love of you.
If you can't afford a carriage
There won't be any marriage.
'Cause I'll be loather"
If I'm betrothed
On a bicycle built for two!

Seeing the three girls so happy and carefree reminded me of my two sisters and how we used to sing together in the garden. We loved singing. Rose is two years older than I am; Lily is two years younger. There was a time when we were eight, six and four that we were the best of friends. Rose still played with dolls then and we would have mock tea parties and play ring-around-the-rosy in the garden. I smiled at the memory. When had things changed? I'd gone off to Mater Misericordia Academy, Rose had married, and poor little Lily had been left all alone. She still complains to me about that—being left alone without a playmate in our big house on Cherry Street. Rose and Lily were both married now. We were no longer three little girls playing in the garden.

By the time I arrived on the dock, Mable, Bessie, and Jennie had already purchased their biscuits from Petey. He was a strapping youth with straw-colored hair. He tipped his cap to the girls and they giggled.

Prince was a large, older dog with a light golden coat. Jambo seemed to think Prince was its mother and clung to the dog for dear life. Prince tolerated the little monkey as it jumped on and off his back. Jambo landed facing backward, its feet pushing against Prince's floppy ears. Prince sat down, and the little monkey slid face-first off Prince's rump. As Prince stretched and laid down on the dock, Jambo nestled next to the patient dog and threw an arm over Prince's side.

Bessie kept her distance, leaned over, and held out of a half-biscuit for Jambo.

Jambo reached longingly for it, and tentatively inched from Prince's side.

"Come on, Jambo. It's alright," Bessie coaxed.

The little monkey bounced three steps toward Bessie, grabbed the proffered biscuit from her hand, dashed back to Prince's side and gobbled down the biscuit.

Once the monkey had his three treats, the girls went to Prince and let him eat from their gloved hands as they petted his head.

I wish I'd known about the monkey; I would have brought a penny for each of my nephews. I reminded myself that the boys would be here for two weeks, and we would be able to feed the monkey and Prince many times during their stay.

I heard rhythmic sloshing of the paddles as the sidewheeler *St. Lawrence* approached the dock. Prince lumbered to his feet, and Jambo jumped on his back. Prince trotted back and forth the length of the dock and barked as the steamer approached. Jambo clung to Prince's back like a jockey on a thoroughbred.

Bessie, Jennie, and Mable clapped their gloved hands, their girlish enthusiasm belying their more adult attire. I shaded my eyes and scanned the hurricane deck looking for Mother, Rose, and my four nephews: Dickie, Miles, Thad, and Martin. I was certain that Rose would be traveling with the governess for the older boys and the nurse for the younger ones. A group of four grown women and four young boys should be easy to spot. But even after the steamer was at the dock and the dock boys scurried about securing the lines, I still hadn't laid eyes on the Tidwell party.

"Auntie Marguerite!" I heard a tiny voice call out and looked to see Miles peering over the rail. I waved my handkerchief at him.

"Ahoy!" I called out.

Miles waved back. The tall child standing stoically next to Miles must be Dickie. Where were the others?

I stepped to the other side of the gangway to avoid the crowd of onlookers that clustered around Petey, Prince, and Jambo. At last, after about two dozen passengers disembarked, I caught sight of Rose. My heart jumped a beat.

"Rose," I called out, waving my handkerchief above the heads of the people swarming about the dock. Startled, Rose looked up and caught my eye. Her mouth twisted into a tight rosebud of disapproval. The dock boys handed her down from the steamer onto the gangway.

"Rose!" I said, rushing forward and embracing her. I stepped back to appraise her outfit. She was wearing a traveling dress of moss green with bright heliotrope trim. Perched atop her mound of light brown hair was a moss green toque, a brimless hat crafted from coils of velvet ribbon. On the back of the hat, two moss green velvet bows with fish-tailed ends stuck up like two small wings. A cluster of pinkish-purple silk heliotrope flowers brightened the center. A veil of moss netting with small star patterns covered Rose's face. Behind the veil, I could see Rose's eyebrows scrunched together in vexation.

"Miss Hartranft," she said to me in a low, stern voice. "Please address me as Mrs. Tidwell in such a public place. Mother would have been horrified to hear you shouting out like a peddler on the street."

"Where is Mother?" I asked, peering over Rose's shoulder, and expecting to see her on the gangway. Instead, I saw the dour governess, Mrs. Gruder, herding two young boys in front of her.

"Obviously not here. She chose to remain in West Philadelphia with Thaddeus and Martin," Rose informed me.

A wave of disappointment washed over me. This would have been the first time that Mother had come to visit me on Grenell Island since Father's death, and I had been eager to show her our new cottage. Then

I saw the bright shining faces of my two older nephews, and my dashed hopes were whisked away.

"Miles! Dickie!" I said, welcoming my nephews, who both wore dark blue velvet Fauntleroy suits. Large lacy collars surrounded their cherub faces. Flouncy cuffs stuck out from their short, cut-away jackets. They wore white stockings beneath their velvet knee breeches. Long matching velvet ribbons dangled from the backs of their broad-brimmed Fauntleroy straw hats. Both boys looked exceedingly hot--like they would wilt into little puddles of velvet at any moment.

Little Lord Fauntleroy suits became popular after the publication of Frances Hodgson Burnett's book of the same name. Thank goodness Rose's obsession with the style did not extend to the long ringlet "love locks" that some of the young Fauntleroy look-alikes wore.

Miles brightened and pointed toward Jambo. "Look! A monkey!"

Rose quickly slapped down the offending finger. "Miles! How many times must I tell you? Pointing is vulgar!"

"But Maman, that boy there is selling biscuits to feed the monkey. Can we feed the monkey?" Miles asked.

I smiled at Miles's botched French pronunciation. *Maman* was the French word for mother. Rose had decided while the boys were still in swaddling clothes that they would call her Maman even though Hartranfts were of German descent and the Tidwells were of English descent. I suppose to Rose, French seemed far more proper and respectable.

"May we. . ." Rose corrected Miles. She took Miles by the hand and led him away from the crowd of people clustered around Jambo and Prince. ". . . and no. No! You may not. You are forbidden to approach that filthy, flea-bitten beast. Do you understand?"

Miles nodded and hung his head.

Rose jerked at his hand. "Miles! I asked you a question, and I expect a response."

"Yes, Maman. I understand," Miles replied as his head sunk further onto his chest until all I could see of Miles was the crown of his Lord Fauntleroy hat.

Rose sniffed the air as if she smelled something foul, then leaned toward me, and whispered in my ear, "That filthy thing better not break loose and find its way inside the hotel." She shuddered at the thought, then stopped short, wheeled around and pushed Miles toward Mrs. Gruder.

"Mrs. Gruder," Rose said sharply.

"Yes, Mrs. Tidwell?" Mrs. Gruder asked, rushing forward and taking Miles's hand.

"See to it that our trunks are taken to our rooms. I've reserved two rooms: one for you and the boys, and a room for me. I'll be just across the hall."

"Yes, Mrs. Tidwell," Mrs. Gruder said, taking Miles by the hand and patting it gently as he was still upset about not being able to feed Jambo. Mrs. Gruder reached for Dickie's hand.

"As soon as you get to the rooms," Rose continued, "I want the boys bathed. Then have them take a nap so you can unpack their things."

"Maman!" Dickie said. He pulled away from Mrs. Gruder's grip, stomped to his mother, placed his hands on his hips, and tossed his head back so he could see from beneath the broad brim of his Little Lord Fauntleroy hat. "I'm ten now, far too old to be taking a nap." Dickie punctuated his pronouncement with a stamp of his right foot.

"Then have Mrs. Gruder give you a lesson if you prefer," Rose replied, unswayed by Dickie's impudence.

Dickie stamped his foot again, crossed his arms in front of him, and scowled. "A lesson? Maman! We are on an excursion. Must I really take a lesson the instant we arrive?"

"Alright then, read one of those adventure stories you so love. Just go," Rose said and waved Dickie away with a flutter of her heliotrope gloves.

With the boys safely shepherded away, I linked my arm through Rose's.

"Would you like to walk to Castle Rock, have a cup of tea, and catch up?"

"All that way for a cup of tea when we could have tea right here on the Pullman House veranda? Besides, the last time I walked to your rock I was besieged by swarms of bugs." The very memory of bugs made Rose swat the air around her. "After such a long journey, I just want to sit down."

"Certainly," I said, motioning Rose toward the Pullman House veranda. "I forgot how weary you must be after your train journey."

"Train travel is so dirty and wearisome. I think I may have train-brain," Rose said raising a gloved hand to her forehead for emphasis.

I smiled at this. For over a decade now, the papers have been full of theories that the fairer sex may succumb to train-brain, an addled condition caused by the jostling of women's more fragile brains while on trains. Friend Anne has repeatedly told me that women's brains are as strong as men's brains and neither are addled by train movement.

"Truly, dear sister," Rose said, placing her gloved hand on mine, "I would like to remove the netting from my hat and wash my face of the grit and grime of the train. Would you order tea for us on the veranda? I'll join you in just a minute."

I found two wicker chairs and a tea table at the far end of the veranda, settled myself, ordered tea and waited. From the Pullman House, I had a great view of the American channel. In the distance, I could see the tower of the Rock Island Lighthouse rising from the rock ledge behind the lighthouse keeper's house. The lighthouse had once been atop the keeper's house, but a new lighthouse keeper's house had been built in 1882, and the tower had been moved to the rise of rock in the center of the island behind the keeper's house. Several ships have gone down in the channel near the light since the move, and there has been talk of relocating the lighthouse from behind the keeper's house closer to nearer the shore.

The island that lay between Pullman House and the lighthouse was once called One Tree Island and now called Castle Francis. One Tree Island, or Lone Tree Island, as it was sometimes called, stood empty for decades, save for its one towering tree. Then in 1884, H. S. Wright of Depauville built a pavilion that housed an ice creamery and confectionery. The One Tree Island pavilion did a brisk business due to its proximity to Thousand Island Park and Grenell Island House. It was a pleasant row from Grenell Island. Friend Anne and I would row guests there for a sweet treat. Quite a fervor arose several years ago when Rev. Chase purchased One Tree Island and cut down the sentinel pine that had served as a guidepost for sailors for over a century. The white pine was mammoth. I dare say that the tower of Rev. Chase's castle, Castle Francis, is just as tall and more substantial and should serve as a channel guidepost for eons. The Chases sold the property a few years back, and I've yet to meet the new owners.

The teapot arrived along with a tray of savories and sweets, but I did not partake. Instead, I covered the tray with a napkin and waited for Rose. A half dozen steamers crisscrossed the waters in front of me before Rose returned.

"Feeling a bit more refreshed, I trust? May I pour you a cup of tea?" I asked, hoping it was still warm enough.

"That would be lovely," Rose said.

"Lemon?" I asked.

"Only a little sugar."

Sitting here with Rose, Mother's endless tutorials on tea etiquette came flooding back. *Lemon and sugar are placed in the cup first. Then the tea. Milk goes in after the tea and never never at the same time as the lemon.*

"Milk?" I asked.

"Yes, please."

Mother's words returned to me, and I said them aloud, "'To put milk in your tea before sugar is to cross the path of love, perhaps never to marry.' Such a silly superstition. I never take milk in my tea, so I don't have to worry about that."

I poured, then passed the cup and saucer with a spoon properly placed behind the cup, and not in front. Rose silently stirred her tea without clinking the spoon once against the edge, then tucked it behind the cup again.

"So we can't blame the milk for the reason for being unmarried at age twenty-eight," Rose said before she took her first sip of tea.

"No, it's not the milk," I said, trying to sound light and cheery. I had hoped that we would be able to pass our two weeks together without discussing my marital status, but I had foolishly opened that door by reciting that silly superstition.

"Marguerite," she said, looking into her teacup, and not looking over it. She took a sip, then placed the teacup and saucer on the table. "How do you expect to attract a suitor dressed as you are?"

I looked down at my perfectly ironed and starched shirtwaist. "What's wrong with what I'm wearing?"

"Well, you look like a New Woman. Next, you'll be wearing bloomers, a suffrage ribbon and marching down the street with a placard proclaiming that you want to be a man."

I took in a sharp breath, then sighed. Another subject I'd hoped to avoid.

"Tell me you have not become a suffragist!" Apparently, Rose took my silence as an affirmation.

"No, not at all."

I pressed my lips together to quell my desire to correct Rose. Instinctively, I wanted to point out that a New Woman was not necessarily a suffragist. A woman could be one without being the other. But I did not wish to get into a battle of semantics on our very first hour together. "Perhaps you could take me shopping. I would love your sartorial advice. Maybe later this week?"

"What? Here? At this far-flung outpost?"

"Alexandria Bay is swarming with the moneyed set. They call that section of the river 'Millionaires' Row.' I heard Tiffany's has opened a jewelry store in Alexandria Bay now. We're not as far-flung as you may think," I told Rose.

"Could you afford shopping at Tiffany's? On a schoolteacher's salary?"

"I'm not a schoolteacher, Rose. I'm a teaching fellow at the University of Pennsylvania Women's School of Graduate Studies."

Rose said nothing but gave me the same look Mother had given me as a child that let me know that I was being impudent. It totally unnerved me.

I put my right hand on top of my left in my lap in an attempt to tamp down my rising agitation and took another deep breath. I said nothing but straightened my back, raised my chin and smiled pleasantly back at Rose.

Rose took another sip of her tea. "Really? A teaching *fellow*? That sounds worse than a schoolteacher. And pray tell, does your position at the University of Pennsylvania afford you a salary commensurate with the moneyed set that would be shopping at Tiffany's?"

"Of course not," I said, keeping my tone light-hearted.

"My point entirely. Call it what you will, my dear Marguerite, you are nothing but a schoolteacher," Rose said, picking up her teacup and saucer again and giving me a smug smile before taking another sip.

"So how is Mother?" I asked, changing the subject. "Why didn't she come? I received a letter from her on Tuesday. She wrote that she was looking forward to her trip to Grenell. What changed her mind? She is not unwell, I hope."

"No, no. Mother is fit as a fiddle. It's just that she feels her mourning period is not yet over, and it is too soon to take such a journey."

"Too soon? But Father has been gone for nearly five years now."

"Really, Marguerite. You have never had a husband so what would you know about losing one. Besides, Mother felt she needed to stay in West Philadelphia to watch over the house and the staff," Rose said then she rolled her eyes. "Servants will run amuck if left alone too long. A household does not run itself. One must be constantly vigilant, but you wouldn't know anything about that, either."

The comment was sharp, and I wanted to protest—again—as I not only taught at the university but also, in lieu of paying rent, managed the Ashbridge household on Woodland Avenue. Again, I took a deep breath and pushed down my protestations.

Rose screwed up her lips into a tight disapproving pucker. "I'm too exhausted from our travels to try to explain to you how tedious it is to organize and run a household. You are so out of touch with how proper people live."

There was no way to respond amicably to that comment, so I said nothing. Instead, I feigned interest in the selection of savory items on the tea tray, knowing full well I wasn't hungry.

"Besides, this place—well, it's very hard for her to come here, of all places," Rose said.

I gave her a quizzical look. Why would this place be hard for her of all places? I wanted to ask but Rose's tone was so menacing that I was afraid of her response.

"You did bring swimming costumes for the boys, didn't you?" I asked instead. "I'm very excited about teaching them to swim."

"I had Mrs. Gruder purchase them for the boys, but I'm not sure if I will allow them to swim."

"Mr. Lewis and Mr. Sayles installed a toboggan slide near the boat livery. I'm certain the boys will find it great fun."

Rose looked at the tea tray and again twisted her mouth into a tight rosebud of disapproval.

"You seem displeased," I said.

"All the selections here are so . . . ordinary. I was hoping for something of more substance."

"Should I summon the waiter?" I asked.

She batted my suggestion away with a wave of her pinkish-purple glove.

Nothing seemed to meet Rose's standards these days. I remember when she first married, she fretted and fussed over the household duties, afraid of getting things wrong. She was no longer that timid, young bride. In a few short years, she had transmogrified into a never-to-be-pleased matron.

"Why Dickie! What are you doing here?" Rose asked.

I looked up to see the tall, gangly, and a little-too-old-for-his-Lord-Fauntleroy-suit Dickie approach the table and sit down across from us. "I would like some tea," Dickie demanded.

"You are too young for tea," Rose told him.

"Lemonade, then."

"What is the meaning of this? Why are you here? Where is Mrs. Gruder?"

Dickie shrugged. "I didn't feel like a bath. I was hungry." With that, he picked a lemon tart off the tea tray and popped it into his mouth whole. A dollop of lemon filling squeezed out onto the corner of his mouth. Dickie pushed the dollop into his mouth with his index finger as he struggled to chew the wad of tart in his mouth.

"And Mrs. Gruder allowed you to wander off? By yourself?"

With great effort, Dickie swallowed. "I'm not a baby like Miles," Dickie said, licking a spot of lemon filling from his finger.

Rose stood then and waved for the waiter's attention. "Please bring my son a glass of lemonade. You have lemonade, don't you?"

"Yes, madam."

"And something sweet," Dickie shouted to the waiter.

"There are sweets as well as savories on the tea tray," I pointed out.

"I'd rather have a cookie."

"And bring him chocolate cookies. He's awfully fond of chocolate."

"Yes, madam." The waiter said and hurried off to comply.

"Well, I need to attend to this right away. Mrs. Gruder is getting so lackadaisical in her duties and I won't have it," Rose said. "Stay here with

Dickie until I return. If he wants anything else, please get it for him."

I stood, took Rose's elbow, and moved out of earshot. "Rose," I whispered in her ear. "Am I given to understand that Dickie disobeyed you, disobeyed Mrs. Gruder, and he is rewarded with chocolate and lemonade? And Mrs. Gruder is to be punished?"

Rose wrested her arm from my grip and stepped away from me with an indignant look.

"You know nothing of what it's like to manage staff, run a household, or raise children. I will not take advice from a spi . . . well. . . from someone who does not know the first thing about womanly arts," she hissed.

She turned on her heels, her boots clicking on the veranda as she hurried away.

"Boy! Is Gruder in for it now," Dickie said with a malicious grin. "Getting Gruder in trouble two or three times a day is the most fun I have."

"Really," I said, feigning admiration. "That's the most fun?"

Dickie thought a moment, then amended his answer. "No. Making Miles cry is the most fun. He tries so hard to be brave, but he's no match for me."

"And what does your grandmamma think of all this?"

"What? Me? I'm her firstborn grandchild and a grandson at that! I have Grandmamma twisted around my little finger," Dickie said as he popped another lemon tart into his mouth.

It wasn't until that moment that I realized that Dickie was a condensed version of his father, my brother-in-law Jacob—smug and condescending.

Mentally, I saw the calendar that hung in my room back at Castle Rock. I checked the day off the calendar in my head. ". . . only thirteen more days to go," I murmured to myself.

CHAPTER *twelve*

Rose and the boys had already been served and were eating breakfast when I arrived at the hotel the next morning.

"My little angels were famished and as we had no idea when you would show up—you're late as usual—we decided to start without you," Rose said when I approached the table.

"Good morning," I said and smiled through gritted teeth. I looked at the watch pinned to my bodice. It was two minutes to eight. I was early and not late. I would not start today with an argument. I straightened my spine, raised my chin, breathed in new resolve, and sat down.

"Good morning, Auntie Marguerite," Miles said before he crunched into a piece of bacon.

"Good morning, Miles. Did you sleep well?"

Miles nodded as he chewed, his eyes bright.

"Miles!" Rose said so sharply that I jumped. "Your aunt asked you a question!"

Miles swallowed hard and nearly choked. "S-s-sorry, Maman. Then he turned to me with wide eyes and blinked hard. "S-s-s-sorry, Auntie Marguerite. I slept very well, thank you."

Dickie leaned over toward his brother. "Didn't wet the bed for a change?" he murmured, barely loud enough for me to hear as his mother raised her teacup to take a sip.

Miles' face crinkled into a scowl, and he gave his brother a kick under the table.

"Ow!" Dickie shouted, reaching under the table to rub his shin.

"Dickie, we are in a civilized place. I will not have you shouting out," Rose hissed.

"But Maman, Miles kicked me," Dickie whimpered.

Rose turned her gaze to Miles. "Did you kick your brother?"

Miles stuck out his bottom lip, which quivered slightly.

"Miles! I asked you a question. Did you or did you not kick your brother?"

Miles nodded.

"I will not tolerate that sort of behavior. You are finished with your breakfast. Excuse yourself and report to Mrs. Gruder at once."

"But . . ." Miles said, looking at his plate.

"Immediately," Rose said, her voice hushed but her tone emphatic. She picked up the napkin from her lap and dabbed at the corners of her mouth as she glared at Miles.

Miles stood with tears swimming in his eyes.

"Push in your chair," Rose instructed.

A tear rolled down Miles's chubby cheek as he complied.

"Honestly, I don't know what gets into him," Rose said, turning to me, but my eyes were still on poor little Miles, who hung his head, and turned to leave.

"He is so jealous of his older brother. He lashes out at him for no reason whatsoever."

I turned my face toward Rose, but my eyes slid obliquely toward Dickie.

"Cry baby," I heard Dickie jeer as Miles walked past him.

"Did it leave a scuff mark on your stocking?" Rose asked Dickie as Miles walked dejectedly from the dining room.

Dickie looked under the table and nodded.

"Well! No outdoor activities for Miles. He will remain in the room with Mrs. Gruder for the remainder of the day."

Thankfully, the waiter came to the table and I ordered tea and a soft-boiled egg.

"What would you like to do today?" I asked as soon as the waiter left the table.

I heard Prince bark and looked out the window and could see the golden dog race up and down the dock with Jambo clinging to his back as a steamer approached. Mable and her friends were there clapping their hands and laughing at the antics of the unusual pair.

"I was hoping to teach the boys to fish this year."

"Why spend hours in a boat to obtain a fish when I could send Cook to the market to buy one?" Rose asked.

I smiled. "Father said something very similar when he first visited here. But in the end, he truly enjoyed fishing—once he gave it a try, that is."

Rose raised her eyes to mine and held them in a dull stare. "So you're saying Father *enjoyed* traveling hundreds of miles to retrieve his defiant, wayward daughter? That's how you remember it?" she asked with raised eyebrows.

I shifted uncomfortably. *You weren't here. You don't know.* The words were on the tip of my tongue. I had to press my lips together and bite the inside of my cheek to keep them from coming out.

I turned away from my sister towards Dickie. "Dickie, do you want to go for a walk?" I asked.

"May we go to the store and buy chocolate? I love chocolate," Dickie said. "Can I go, Maman? Please?"

"I suppose," Rose sighed. "There's little else to do here. But you'll need your hat, and you'll need to change your stockings. Come, Dickie, let's prepare for your outing with Aunt Marguerite."

Rose stood, took Dickie by the hand and left the dining room. My egg, toast, and tea arrived, and I found myself alone at the table.

"Mind if I join you?" I looked up to see Miss Caldwell approach the table. She didn't wait for a response but pulled out the chair and sat down next to me.

"Who was that?" she asked and indicated the door that Rose had just disappeared through.

"My sister Rose."

Miss Caldwell planted her elbows on the table, threaded her fingers together, rested her chin on her hands, and gave me a sympathetic look. "You poor thing."

"Whatever do you mean?" I asked as I took my spoon and whacked the top of my soft-boiled egg.

"Sorry, I couldn't help overhearing. I was sitting at the table behind you." She indicated the table with a tilt of her head.

"Overhearing? Do you mean eavesdropping?" I asked, peeling away the top of the eggshell.

"I was sitting right next to you. The only way for me not to hear that conversation would be for me to put my hands over my ears and hum 'Yankee Doodle.'"

"Etiquette suggests feigned deafness in such circumstances," I said.

"Well," she said, rising from the table, "I just wanted to convey my sympathies."

"Whatever for?"

"Your sister is one of *those* women."

"*Those* women?" I asked, dropping my spoon to the table and looking up at her.

"A woman who can only feel good about herself when she is making someone else look or feel bad. Enjoy your breakfast. I'm going to leave before she comes back. I've had as much as I can stand of your thorny Rose."

I felt regret the instant Miss Caldwell walked away. Her intent had been to bring me solace—albeit in a rather sarcastic way—but deep down I think she meant well. I had taken my frustration with Rose out on her. I sighed, then I took the first bite of my soft-boiled egg, which was growing colder by the moment.

By the time I'd finished breakfast, Rose had returned with Dickie in hand.

Today Dickie was wearing a forest green velvet Lord Fauntleroy suit. The ribbons on his broad-brimmed hat had been changed to match.

"You're coming with us, aren't you?" I asked Rose.

"I prefer to stay on this side of the bridge. When Grenell Island Park has proper boardwalks, I might consider taking a stroll on the other side of the bridge. Please take him to the store I can see from the hotel veranda. I don't want him traipsing through cow dung."

"Are you sure you won't change your mind and come with us?"

"Heavens no. I'm still recovering from train-brain."

"We'll be back in about an hour," I told her.

"Have the desk send a message to my room when you return."

As we left the dining room, I asked Dickie what he liked to read and was surprised that I'd happened upon a topic that he enjoyed talking about. Dickie loved dime novels, and his favorite character was Deadwood Dick. He rattled off a list of his favorite Deadwood Dick stories. "I hope to move to Deadwood, South Dakota, someday," he told me.

"Then they could call you Deadwood Dickie," I teased. I wanted to advise that before he moves, he'll need to trade his Little Lord Fauntleroy duds for something a little more rugged or he'd be branded a dandy.

As we walked over the bridge, I asked if he had read *Treasure Island*. He said no, and he asked what the book was about. I told him it was set in the days of sailing ships and pirates and that the young hero of the story, Jim Hawkins, wasn't much older than he was. His eyes grew bigger when I told him that Jim searched for the buried treasure of an evil pirate named Captain Flint.

"Tell me more," Dickie demanded.

"I'll do better than that," I said "I'll lend you a copy of the book, and you can read it for yourself."

By now we had reached E. A. Fox's small store, which was situated in a little bay across the small channel of water that separates the Pullman House on Grenell Island from Grenell Island Park. While Uncle Sam's Grenell Island Store catered to cottagers, Mr. Fox's store catered to the Pullman House crowd. He stocked various sundries that an excursionist might need: hats, toiletries, and fishing gear. His store was also crammed with souvenirs: Indian baskets, viewbooks, souvenir spoons, postcards, and Mrs. J. L. Huntington's popular novel, *Fish Story*. But what hits your eye the moment you walk in the store are the jars and jars of colorful candy.

I heard giggling and wasn't surprised to see Mable and her friends leaving the store, each with a white bag filled with candy. Mable's father, Herbert Worden, was a grocery salesman and sometimes helped Mr. Fox with the store. Mable and Olivia used to spend hours behind the counter collecting the paper lace from the candy boxes to make paper doll dresses.

"Good morning, girls," I said. "This is my nephew, Dickie Tidwell. Dickie. this is Mable Worden. And these are her friends Jennie and Bessie."

"Pleasure to make your acquaintance," the girls replied in flat, dull voices that told me they really didn't give a fig about meeting Dickie. I couldn't see Dickie's face beneath the broad brim of his Little Lord Fauntleroy hat. It wouldn't have surprised me to learn that he was sticking out his tongue at the girls.

I took Mable aside and asked her if she had seen Olivia yet this season.

Mable bit her lip and said that she had waved to her from across the bay but hadn't spoken face-to-face with her. "I have company right now, and my aunt from Illinois is coming soon," she said.

"You know her father died in February," I said.

Mable lowered her head. "Yes. I know."

"She seems a little sad right now. Maybe you and the girls could cheer her up."

"I tried spending time with her last year before her father died. She seems more interested in reading and books than she does talking about . . . well . . . talking about the things we like talking about," Mable said, indicating her friends.

"Mable! Look! Jambo is sitting on Petey's shoulder," Jennie called out.

"I'll let you get back to your friends, but think about giving Olivia a visit. I think she could use some cheering up," I said.

"I'll try," Mable said, then dashed off to join her friends.

"Come on, Dickie. Let's see what Mr. Fox has for us today."

Dickie wasn't interested in the jars of candy sticks or hard candy.

"I want chocolate!" Dickie said, stamping his foot.

Luckily Mr. Fox had tins of Huyler's chocolate. Dickie picked out a rather large tin. I paid Mr. Fox, who handed the tin to Dickie. I told Dickie that he had to share the chocolate with his brother. I could tell by the scowl he made that Dickie wasn't happy with the prospect of sharing chocolate with anyone.

"Bonjour!" I heard from behind me and turned to see Emily Griswold standing in the doorway.

I rushed over to her and gave her a kiss on each cheek in the continental style, though neither of us had ever stepped foot in the Europe. "So glad to see you," I said, holding her at arm's length.

Emily and her sister, Delia, had built a lavish two-story cottage in 1882.

- *Grenell 1893* -

The sisters called their cottage La Roche, French for the rock. Perched high on the back of the female camel hump, they had a commanding view of the shipping channel. Emily had been educated at Holyoke College in Massachusetts and afterward at a French convent in Montreal. Several times a season, Emily and I met to practice our French.

"Comment était ton hiver?" I asked.

"Magnifique!"

Apparently, I thought. I'd never seen Emily Griswold look so radiant.

Dickie tugged at my skirt. "Huh? What does that mean? Why are you talking gibberish?"

"We are speaking French. I asked 'how was your winter' and Miss Griswold replied that it was wonderful."

"Qui est l'enfant?"

"Puis-je présenter mon neveu, Dickie Tidwell. Dickie, this is Mademoiselle Griswold."

"Not for long!" Emily replied, her cheeks turning a bright pink.

"Pardon?"

"I have found *le grand amour*. I've decided to renounce maidenhood. I'm getting married! I'm soon to be Mrs. Gabriel. I'm so happy that I ran into you. I want to invite you to the wedding."

I blinked. Emily Griswold had to be ten, twelve, maybe fifteen years older than I. While we had never discussed her exact age, I knew that Emily was ten years younger than her sister, Delia. Last year at Delia's birthday party, Emily had confided to me that given how sickly her sister had been all her life, she never thought her sister would live past thirty years of age, but here she was still hanging on at age fifty-three.

"I know! I know! Who would have thought that at long last I have found *le grand passion? Les destins m'ont souri.* The fates have smiled on me."

For a brief moment, I was utterly dumbfounded. "Who? How?" I finally managed to stammer.

"Auntie," Dickie whined, tugging at my skirt. "I can't get the tin opened."

"One moment," I told Dickie as Emily continued to gush on about her engagement to Mr. Gabriel.

"I can't get it open!" Dickie said as he shoved the tin toward my face, obscuring my view of Emily.

"Excuse me for a moment, Emily," I said, taking the tin from Dickie and calling to Mr. Fox. "Mr. Fox, could you help my nephew open this?"

I turned my attention back to Emily, who resumed her tale of romance. "My Albert—Prof. Albert Gabriel—his last name is Gabriel, like the angel. Anyway, Albert was born in Marseilles."

"Professor of what?" I asked, noting that now that the tin was open, Dickie was leaving the store. "Wait for me outside," I called after him.

"Languages. He teaches French, Italian and Spanish."

"Did he teach at European universities?"

"No. Not on a collegiate level. Like me, he taught in first-class secondary institutions or tutored wealthy families. He taught in Marseilles and Toulon, and then in Italy until the Franco-Prussian War. He came to the United States after that. He taught in New York City and then finally settled in Watertown where he was engaged to teach language to the family of Allen C. Beach. Mr. Beach is my father's distant cousin, which is how we were introduced. We met on Valentine's Day. Isn't that romantic?"

"I'm so happy for you," I said.

"The wedding is planned for next week," Emily said.

"Next week?" I asked, thinking that seemed rather soon for a man she met only four months ago.

"Soon. Yes, I know but . . ." Emily replied as if she were reading my mind. "But I never thought I would find anyone, and, now that I have, I don't want to waste any time."

I nodded as if I understood.

"Please say you will come to the wedding. It will be a small ceremony, only a handful of family and friends, but I would love to have you and Anne there. We are marrying at sunrise at La Roche next Friday." She reached out and took my hand in hers and gave it a passionate squeeze. "It would mean so much to me if you were there."

"*Mais bien sûr.* But of course. Unfortunately, Anne is in Chicago," I said.

"Oh, at the fair?"

I nodded. "She will be disappointed that she missed it," I said.

"*Merci d'être un ami,*" she said, reaching out for my hands.

We kissed each other's cheeks again, and she left, turning to throw me one more kiss before she approached the counter to ask Mr. Fox about stationery. I went out the door then, expecting to see Dickie sitting on the bench outside.

He was not there.

"Dickie?" I called, looking around.

"Over here," I heard him moan.

He was on the other side of the big oak tree, bent over as if he was studying something in the grass. Perhaps he had found a frog.

"What have you found there?" I asked.

"Oooooo!" he wailed, clutching his stomach.

"Dickie? What is it?" I asked, looking down into the grass.

Dickie turned and looked up at me. His face looked a little green, and there was chocolate smeared around his mouth.

"You have some chocolate on your face," I said, searching in my reticule for my handkerchief. Once I retrieved it, I tried to dab the chocolate away, but only managed to make more of a smear. My actions only made Dickie moan louder.

I stepped back, trying to make sense of the situation. "Dickie, where is the chocolate tin?"

He motioned with a chuck of his head to the other side of the tree. I stepped in that direction, saw the lid and then the tin itself. It was completely empty.

"Dickie! You didn't eat that entire tin of chocolate, did you?"

Dickie said nothing but put his hand to his lips, and I noticed then that his fingers were smudged with chocolate as well. His eyes bulged, he lurched forward and emptied the contents of his stomach all over my shoes.

CHAPTER
thirteen

"Please send a message to Mrs. Tidwell's room that her son is not feeling well," I told the clerk behind the front desk as soon as we arrived back at the Pullman House.

Dickie was as pale and motionless as a china doll. I led him to a settee flanked by two tall potted palms in the grand foyer. We sat, and I nervously waited for Rose to come down, hoping Dickie would not be sick again in the lobby of the hotel. Even though I had cleaned the top of my shoes in the tall grass, the acrid, sour scent still lingered. I felt my stomach churn.

A wave of relief washed over me when I saw Mrs. Gruder coming down the stairs to retrieve Dickie. I explained what had happened. Mrs. Gruder shook her head and whispered to me that this wasn't the first time.

"You think you would have learned from the last time," she said as she led her charge upstairs. "Mrs. Tidwell will be with you momentarily," she called back to me.

The Pullman House had just been repainted inside and out. The outside was now a dazzling white. The inside was bright canary trimmed in bronze. The morning sun glinted off the highly polished wood floor causing me to squint. I settled back on the settee, turned away from the glare and focused on the stairway. Having just finished painting my own tiny cottage, I appraised the details of the painting job as I waited for Rose and was impressed.

Moments later, Rose appeared at the top of the stairs and slowly, regally made her descent. "Mrs. Gruder informed me that Dickie isn't feeling very well. She thinks perhaps it might be something he ate. I have half a mind to speak to the manger. Obviously, his breakfast was not prepared correctly."

I wondered briefly if I should tell Rose about the tin of Huyler's chocolates but before I could decide the clerk at the desk raised his hand and motioned me his way.

"Excuse me, Miss Hartranft?" asked Mr. Lewis, the Pullman House manager.

"Yes?"

"I have a telegram for you."

Surprised, I went to the desk to retrieve it.

"Who is that from?" Rose asked when I returned to the settee.

"Herr Brittlinger. He's invited me to dinner at the Columbian and then to view the comet tonight," I said as I reread the telegram.

Rose looked shocked. "Unescorted? Who is this Herr Brittlinger?"

I folded the telegram and laid it in my lap. "I met him recently through the Kerr family. He is a professor of astronomy at Princeton."

Rose heaved a sigh. "You're not planning on attending, are you?" Rose asked.

"No, of course not. I'm dining with you this evening here at the hotel. But Herr Brittlinger told me that the Columbian Hotel has allowed him to set up a telescope on the tower platform so he could observe a new comet that's just been discovered, and he's invited me to come view the comet tonight. I'm sure Dickie and Miles would love seeing the comet. You might enjoy the viewing as well."

Rose didn't seem excited about the prospect, but I eventually talked her into going. She suggested that perhaps she had a touch of whatever had made Dickie sick and decided that she should lie down so she would be fresh for this evening's adventure. We said our goodbyes and she retired to her room.

After checking the steamer schedule, I sent a reply to Herr Brittlinger that I couldn't accept his dinner invitation because of family obligations but would be happy to accept his offer to view the comet and would be arriving in the lobby around nine that evening with my sister and nephews.

I thanked Mr. Lewis for his help this morning, walked across the foyer through the double doors onto the veranda, and paused at the top of the steps leading down toward the Pullman House dock. I took a deep breath and stared out at the dancing blue waters of the St. Lawrence. My second day with the Tidwells was not going as smoothly as I hoped.

"Yoo-hoo! Miss Hartranft!"

I turned to see Miss Caldwell waving to me from a wicker chair on the far end of the veranda. I threaded my way through the many wicker and rocking chairs. "Good morning again, Miss Caldwell," I said.

She motioned for me to sit next to her. "I'm watching a spirited game of croquet on the croquet lawn. Please, join me."

"I'm glad you called me over," I said as I settled into the deep cushion of the wicker chair next to her. "I must apologize for my behavior this morning. My remarks were unkind."

"Not at all. Clearly you were provoked," Miss Caldwell said as she fished a small silver case from her reticule and opened it. "Would you care for one?" she asked, thrusting the opened case toward me. The interior was gilded and lined with small white cigarettes. "They're Egyptian, a gift from an admirer. I prefer Turkish cigarettes, but the Egyptian ones aren't bad."

I looked around the veranda to see if anyone was watching, then with a small gesture waved away the proffered cigarettes. "No, thank you. I don't smoke."

"I'm not surprised," Miss Caldwell murmured as she took out one of the thin cigarettes and held it between the index and middle finger of her left hand.

My eyes widened. Did she intend to smoke here on the Pullman House veranda?

"Hold your horses. Nothing to get in a kerfuffle about. I've already been told—quite sternly I might add—that I can't smoke here on the veranda nor in the smoking room of the hotel. Men only. But we could go up to my room," she suggested.

"No, thank you," I said again.

"Is everyone in Philadelphia as pious as you are?"

I didn't have a response for that.

"Lots of women in New York City smoke. Not out in public, of course, but in the privacy of their own homes," Miss Caldwell said as she put the cigarette back in the case and clicked it closed.

"I see," I said, not sure if I really believed the daring Miss Caldwell.

She leaned closer to me and I could smell her musky cologne. "You summer here so you know the area well. I've heard there is a lot of smuggling. Canadian rye specifically. Do you know where I could get my hands on a bottle?" She pulled back then and eyed me carefully.

"I–I'm sorry," I stammered. "I'm afraid I can't help you."

"Can't or won't?" she asked, slowly tilting her head to one side as she raised a questioning eyebrow.

"Of course, I've heard that a fair amount of Canadian whiskey is smuggled across the border, but I have no idea how to obtain such contraband."

"Fine," she said as she rose from her chair. "I'll let it go. I wouldn't want to make Sister Mary Marguerite uncomfortable, though we both know that you know." She leaned down close to my ear, and I could smell cigarette smoke on her hat and hair. She then whispered with a slight smile on her lips, "You are a horrible liar. Never play whist, especially here at the Pullman. The ladies here are quite wicked. They'd eat you alive!"

She straightened then to appraise my reaction.

I was speechless. She looked disappointed. Had she hoped to provoke me?

"Well, this has been fun, but I'm going upstairs for a . . ." and she pointed to the cigarette case. "If you change your mind about the you-know-what, you can let me know."

Dickie was feeling much better by the time I returned to the Pullman that evening for dinner. Afterwards, we boarded a steamer, that took us the short distance between the Pullman House dock and the Thousand Island Park dock. A lovely two-story pavilion had been built a few years back. I was happy that there was no longer a gate fee nor a gate. A wide boardwalk connected the dock to the hotel. It was so broad that we could walk four abreast and there was still room for couples to pass by us on either side.

Grenell 1893

The Columbian Hotel occupied the former site of the Thousand Island Park Hotel, which was destroyed by fire some three years ago in the middle of the night taking the chapel, the pavilion, the hotel barn, several stores, and six cottages with it. Luckily, the wind died down and residents were able to extinguish the flames two hours after the fire was discovered. One woman died, a hotel laundress, and a few more obtained slight burns. All in all, the Park was lucky. If the wind had been blowing, every cottage on the Park could have been ashes by daylight.

The trustees of the park had replaced the former hotel with a mammoth, sprawling four-story building that could accommodate four hundred guests. The front was swathed in verandas. Observation platforms perched atop two of the hotel's peaked red roofs. The hotel had opened last year as did the Thousand Island Park electrical plant, which provided electricity to the hotel and the grounds. I hoped the many electric lights surrounding the hotel would not diminish the viewing of the comet.

Herr Brittlinger was waiting for us in the lobby. Tonight he was wearing a black wool gentlemen's evening ensemble with a cutaway, swallow-tail coat. He wore a white shirt with mother-of-pearl dress studs and cufflinks and a white bow tie over a white brocade waistcoat. He clicked the heels of his shiny black, pointy-toed shoes together and bowed from the waist. "Good evening, *Fraulein* Hartranft. You look enchanting this evening," he said with his heavy German accent, rolling his *R*s and over articulating his *T*s. He reached for my gloved hand and kissed the tops of my knuckles. His middle finger again found that spot of bare skin between the cuff of my long-sleeved shirtwaist and my glove, and lingered there. He held this pose longer than felt comfortable, gazing up into my eyes as if he were trying to mesmerize me. His warm breath on my hand smelled of cigars and brandy. I cleared my throat and gently tugged my hand from his grip.

"Thank you. May I say that you are quite dashing yourself this evening? Herr Brittlinger, I'd like to introduce my sister, Mrs. Tidwell," I said, indicating Rose.

"*Frau* Tidwell, it is my great honor to meet you," he said, clicking his heels together again and bowing deeply. He raised her gloved hand to his lips and kissed her knuckles.

Rose seemed taken aback by his European style. She blushed, and then pushed her two boys forward. "Herr Brittlinger, may I present my sons, Master Richard Jacob Tidwell and Master Miles Dickerson Tidwell," she said in a formal voice that sounded as if she were presenting her sons at court.

"What a lucky man I am to be in the presence of two such beautiful women. It is a shame that one of you is married," he said nodding toward Rose, who suppressed a titter of delight. "This way to the telescope," he said, and six flights of stairs later we stepped out onto the platform, and stared out at the night. There was a steamer in the channel; the lights streaming from the square windows of its salons created shimmering stripes in the dark water below. On the other side of the channel, a bright beam of light from the Rock Island Lighthouse sliced through the night.

Herr Brittlinger invited Rose to the telescope first, explaining to her that the comet was the smudge of light in the upper right corner.

"Why is it green? Is it a green rock?"

"No, madam. A comet is made of rock, dust, ice, and frozen gases. The color comes from the type of gas it releases."

Dickie was next. "It's not moving," he complained. "I thought comets were supposed to shoot across the sky."

"You have confused a comet with a meteor or, as you Americans might say, a shooting star. This comet is moving at great speed. Faster than one hundred locomotives combined. It is headed away from us so rapidly that by next week we won't be able to see anything."

"We are very lucky to see it, don't you think, Dickie?" I asked.

Dickie did not seem impressed.

Miles on the other hand oohed and ahhed. "I can't wait to tell Papa!" he said as he stepped away from the telescope.

When it was my turn, Herr Brittlinger stood very close behind me. "Do you see the two tails, *Liebchen*?" he whispered in my ear.

"I do," I said. "One is a yellowish white and the other a faint blue."

"You are very observant." I felt the breath from his forced T on the back of my neck and fought the urge to squirm away from him. "But you know the reason for the two different colors?"

"I do not."

"The white tail is the dust trail. It isn't really glowing; it is only reflecting the light of the sun. The blue tail is caused by the released gas.

A spectacular thing to witness, is it not? A force of nature," he said, lightly leaning into me again.

I straightened and moved sideways away from the telescope. "Thank you, Herr Brittlinger. I'm sure the boys will remember this for a lifetime, as will I." I said, pulling the boys in front of me and resting my hands on their shoulders. "But it is late and well after their bedtime. I'm afraid it is time for us to return to Grenell."

Herr Brittlinger insisted on walking us to the dock. Rose walking ahead of us, holding the boys by their hands, leaving me to follow in their wake with Herr Brittlinger. "Take my arm, lest you stumble and fall in the darkness," he said.

The offer was chivalrous, so I could hardly refuse, but I walked stiffly beside him trying not to let our shoulders touch.

"Please let us repay your kindness by coming to dinner tomorrow night at the Pullman House," Rose said when the steamer pulled to the dock.

Herr Brittlinger clicked his heels and with a stiff bow from the waist intoned in a deep, accented baritone that he would be honored to accept our invitation. I sensed more knuckle-kissing in the offing and picked up Miles who was starting to doze, his head lolling heavily onto my shoulder.

Herr Brittlinger kissed Rose's hand, and she bade him good night.

"Good night, Herr Brittlinger," I said. I readjusted my hold on the sleeping Miles and stepped back before the professor could reach for my hand. "Thank you again."

"Guten Abend, Fraulein."

"Oh, that was not at all what I expected!" Rose whispered to me after the steamer pulled away from the dock.

My sentiments exactly, but I wasn't sure not for the same reason.

"Here I thought your professor would be another loathsome academic with unkempt hair and thread-bare tweeds who uses big words to yammer on about useless information," Rose said.

"That's what you think of professors?" I asked, settling the sleeping Miles onto my lap.

"Professors are not known for dressing well. Look at you. But Herr Brittlinger! My goodness! He looked like a baron or a duke. I think that was a ruby in in his signet ring. A genuine ruby."

I was certain that it was a garnet, but I wasn't going to argue.

Dickie laid his head in Rose's lap and fell instantly asleep. Rose ran a gloved hand over his hair and turned to me excitedly. "If I knew we were meeting someone of Herr Brittlinger's caliber, I would have insisted that you wear one of my dresses. We have a lot of work to do before tomorrow night. Oh, Marguerite, this is most promising."

CHAPTER
fourteen

"Hold still!" Rose insisted as she wound the top section of my hair into a tight bun and secured it with a hairpin. I was sitting in a chair in front of the window so Rose could take advantage of the light. Section by section, she rolled my hair back away from my face and pinned it over the top knot bun, pulling out natural tendrils of curls in the process.

"I'm so jealous," she said, twisting a lock around her finger and letting it fall haphazardly from the pile of hair on my head. "My hair is too fine and straight to accomplish the Gibson Girl style. I suppose if I teased it, I could make it full enough. You, my dear, do not need to tease anything. *Harper's* says this is the romantic hairstyle of the season. Here. I have a pair of tortoiseshell combs that will help secure it in place."

Rose placed fancy, frilly hair combs on either side of my head in hopes of holding the soft, puffed hairstyle in place.

"Here. Come see," she said, pulling me by the hand toward a large full-length mirror in the corner. Rose had called down to the desk midmorning and insisted they bring a full-length mirror to the room. An hour later, the hotel staff carried in a large, oval full-length mirror. Where they had found it, I had no idea. Perhaps they had carried it from the owner's summer home, the Sayles cottage on the cliff at the foot of the island opposite Pullman House. Perhaps they brought it from Thousand Island Park on the last steamer.

I surveyed the room as I approached the mirror. Rose's room was an utter wreck. I'd spent the bulk of the day trying on gowns. Rejected gowns were piled in heaps on the bed. Rose was looking for a very specific gown. First, she dithered over color. She was searching for a gown that would not only set off the pinkish undertone of my skin but also compliment my dark eyes and hair. In addition, the gown had to be simple and not too lavish. "It's only dinner, not a ball," she said to me as if I were the picky one. Dress after dress had been rejected until she finally settled on a cream-colored gown with intricate chocolate brown embroidered details.

While the color was perfect, the gown needed alterations. Originally, it had a fine lightweight netting that edged the top of the low neckline. "I had the dressmaker add this to hide my cleavage," Rose told me. "A mother of four does not need to flaunt. But you, my dear, have a lovely *décolletage* that needs to be accentuated."

My linguistic mind immediately focused on the word. *Décolletage* is from the French and literally means "to expose the neck." When the requested seamstress arrived and removed the netting, more than my neck was exposed.

"Rose, are you sure this isn't revealing too much?" I was used to wearing high-necked shirtwaists day in and day out. I felt positively naked. "What would Mother think?"

"Mother would be thankful that I am here to advise you. At your age, you have to pull out all the stops," Rose said. "Wait!" Rose shouted out before I reached the mirror. Turning me away from the mirror, she smoothed my hair, straightened the bodice, arranged the long, gored skirt just so, and pinched my cheeks to make them pink. She told me to shut my eyes, then at long last, she put her arms on my shoulders and slowly turned me toward the mirror. "Now look!"

I stared at the woman in the mirror. "I don't know what to say!" I saw my mouth move but could hardly believe that my voice was coming out of that image.

Was it true? Was that elegantly dressed woman in the mirror really me? I looked like something on the cover of *Harper's Bazar*, and a little pang in my chest wished that young Edith could be here to see my metamorphosis.

"Don't touch your hair. Don't fidget. Just stand there while I finish getting ready," Rose commanded.

Rose had dressed earlier, donning a cornflower blue gown. The hemline was square in the front and pointed behind. The short sleeves were covered with pleated gauze. Ribbons in a darker shade of blue looped up over the shoulders and were anchored by bows and tufts of pale pink flowers. Rose asked me to tie the wide, darker blue sash around her waist. "Make the bow loops big with two small tails."

"Oh my! Look at the time. We are late," I said when I had finished. "We were to meet Herr Brittlinger five minutes ago."

"No, we are just precisely on time," Rose said authoritatively. "A woman should keep a gentleman waiting to make her entrance more dramatic."

I humphed but didn't say anything as we exited Rose's room and walked down the hall. To my mind, making a late entrance wasn't dramatic, only annoying.

Rose grabbed my wrist before we reached the staircase and whispered in my ear, "Don't rush, don't hurry. Calm. Confident. Regal. And please . . . whatever you do this evening . . . do not speak Latin or Greek, and no quoting men who've been dead for a thousand years."

With those words ringing in my ears, I took hold of the banister and began my descent. I will admit that as Herr Brittlinger's eyes followed me down the staircase, he did not look even a tiny bit annoyed. His weren't the only eyes on me. I noticed several groups of people had stopped to observe as I came down the stairs. Included in this mob was Miss Blond, who was there with her family, also en route to the dining room. Her eyes grew wide, and she scowled and whispered something to the woman I presumed to be her mother. I can't imagine what she had to say about me. Her mother nodded and looked equally shocked. My cheeks reddened, and I wanted to look down and check my low neckline, afraid perhaps that I was exposing too much, but I couldn't do that while everyone was looking at me.

Herr Brittlinger murmured his admiration, then offered his arm to escort me to our table.

The boys and Mrs. Gruder were eating in their room tonight, so it was just the three of us at the table. I let Herr Brittlinger and Rose carry the conversation. I concentrated on sitting up straight, my back never touching the back of the chair that Herr Brittlinger had so carefully pushed in when he seated me.

Throughout the evening, Miss Blond gawked at our table. Every time I caught her staring at me, she would turn to her mother and whisper something. Eventually, I stopped looking at their table but could still feel her eyes on me.

Soon after dessert had been served, I heard my name. "Miss Hartranft! There you are!" I looked up and saw Mr. Quigley come through the dining-room door.

He wove his way through the tables and ended up standing behind the empty chair at our table. "Good evening—or rather—*Guten Abend*, Herr Prof. Brittlinger," Mr. Quigley said, nodding to Herr Brittlinger."

"Mr. Quigley," Herr Brittlinger replied.

"Mr. Quigley, I'd like to introduce you to my sister, Mrs. Tidwell," I said.

"I'm honored," Mr. Quigley said. "Please excuse my interruption. I stopped by to leave a note for you, Miss Hartranft, and was told that you were dining here this evening. You look ravishing by the way, both of you," Mr. Quigley said, nodding toward Rose. "You are a very lucky man, Prof. Brittlinger."

"Won't you join us for tea and dessert," I said, motioning toward the empty chair.

Rose's eyebrows scrunched into a disapproving scowl.

"Thank you, no. I only wanted to ask if you would have time this week to row me to the potholes."

"Actually, I was hoping to take my nephews there sometime this week if you wouldn't mind some youthful companionship. They are ten and eight," I replied.

"Sounds delightful. How about tomorrow? Perhaps nine o'clock?"

"That's fine with me if it meets with Mrs. Tidwell's approval," I asked Rose.

"If you would excuse me," Herr Brittlinger said, rising stiffly from the table. "I see an acquaintance to whom I must give my regards."

"We shall see how everyone is feeling on the morrow," Rose said, trying unsuccessfully to hide her annoyance.

"Nine it is! Good evening, ladies," Mr. Quigley said, and with a salute left the table.

I heard chair legs scrape on the wooden floor as someone pushed back quickly from a table. I saw Miss Blond follow Mr. Quigley from the dining room.

"Marguerite!" Rose whispered across the table. "What in heaven's name are you doing?"

I looked at her, perplexed. "What?"

"After all the preparation I put into this evening. The dress. The hairstyle. Gracious sakes! I even let you wear my best French silk slippers."

"What did I do?"

"After all my careful preparation you dash it all away by flirting with some young man with no prospects at all?"

"I was not flirting."

"Inviting him to join us at the table?"

"I was only trying to be polite."

"Did you see the look on Herr Brittlinger's face?"

"Mr. Quigley asked me to show him the potholes earlier in the week."

"Potholes! What in heaven's name are potholes?"

"They are a geological feature—caused by glaciers I believe—and . . ."

"I don't give a fig about potholes, and neither should you. You should only care about cultivating the interest of Herr Brittlinger. Mr. Quigley can hire a guide to show him the potholes. Shhhh! Here he comes . . . follow my lead. Welcome back, Herr Brittlinger. Would you like more tea?"

"No. I prefer a snifter of brandy after a good meal. Would you join me?" Herr Brittlinger asked.

"Oh, I think not," Rose said, looking uncomfortably around the room.

We had grown up drinking wine with dinner, so I knew it wasn't the alcohol that Rose objected to. Mother had always instructed us that a lady never drinks alcohol in public.

"Do not tell me that Hartranfts—good women of German heritage—are temperance supporters?" He looked aghast at the possibility.

"No, of course not," Rose said.

"Then join me in a toast to our lovely evening together." Herr Brittinger summoned the waiter, with a wave of his hand and whispered the order in his ear. The waiter returned with three empty brandy snifters and a decanter of brandy.

"You have had brandy before, yes?" Herr Brittlinger asked as he poured the brandy into the small globe-shaped snifters.

"No," I said.

A small smile spread from under his waxed mustache. "I know you have an interest in words, *Fraulein* Hartranft, so I will tell you that the word *brandy* originates from the Dutch word *brandewijn* which means *burnt wine*."

"It's made of burnt wine?" Rose asked, inspecting the glass of gold-brown liquid.

"It means not that the wine is burnt, but rather refers to the warm, glowing feeling that grows inside you as you drink it," Herr Brittlinger said, making a circular motion on his chest.

Rose raised the glass to her lips.

"No! You must not drink it yet. First, you must warm the brandy. That is why the glass is shaped this way. Slip the stem of the glass between your fingers, and close your palm around the bottom of the glass. Only a small amount is poured into the glass. The heat of your hand will warm up the brandy, enhancing the flavor and the aroma."

The glass felt cool to my touch. I slid the stem between my ring finger and my middle finger.

"Drinking brandy is an experience." A warm smile spread across Herr Brittlinger's face as he swirled the brandy in his glass. We waited. He watched us intently.

"Now bring the glass chest high and inhale. Not too close! You do not want to overwhelm your senses. Can you smell the floral scents in the brandy?"

I shut my eyes and inhaled deeply. A warm, sharp smell tickled my nose and sent a small shudder down my spine. I opened my eyes to see Herr Brittlinger staring at me intently.

"Bring the snifter to your nose and inhale from both your mouth and nose. Can you smell the spice aromas in the brandy now? It smells differently, does it not?"

I complied. The aroma filled my mouth making me feel warm, giddy.

"Now take a very small sip just to wet your lips." Herr Brittlinger took a sip. The pink tip of his tongue smoothed the brandy over his lips.

I mimicked his actions. The brandy made my lips tingle.

"Drinking brandy or cognac is an art."

- Grenell 1893 -

We sipped in silence for a while, relishing the experience. Herr Brittlinger let out a satisfied sigh. "How nice to finish my evening with brandy. If I had known that the Columbian Hotel, indeed all of Thousand Island Park, has forsaken alcohol entirely due to this temperance nonsense, I would have chosen to stay here at Pullman House. Perhaps I shall dine here every night."

Rose looked at me and smiled. So seldom have I seen a genuine smile on Rose's face. Her smile sent a warm tingling feeling through my body as warm as the brandy.

Eventually, we resumed normal conversation, dominated by Herr Brittlinger's description of what it is like being a professor at Princeton.

When our glasses were empty, Rose turned to Herr Brittlinger and said, "Thank you for a wonderful evening but duty calls. I'm afraid I'm needed upstairs to tuck my darling boys in for the night."

This I knew was a complete fabrication as I was sure that Mrs. Gruder had trundled Dickie and Miles off to bed over an hour ago. But Rose had asked me to follow her lead so I did.

Herr Brittlinger stood and helped pull back Rose's chair. "You are such a gentleman," Rose said putting a hand on the sleeve of his formal evening jacket. "My sister has expressed interest in the stars. Perhaps you can point them out for her?"

"As you wish," Herr Brittlinger said with a click of his heels and a nod of his head. *"Guten Abend, meine Dame."*

I watched Rose glide from the dining room without so much as a glance back in my direction.

Herr Brittlinger turned to me now and pulled my chair out for me. "Shall we go for a walk on the dock? From there we will have a nice view of Mars rising."

"I'm sorry, Herr Brittlinger, but the brandy has made me very sleepy. I'm afraid I must say good night. Thank you for your delightful company."

He reached out to take my hand, but the thought of another kiss and his odd way of fondling my wrist as he leered at me caused me to turn and hurry towards the dining-room door. I had no idea how I would make it home in the dark in this gown and in Rose's ill-fitting silk slippers. I had assumed that after dinner I would change, leave Rose's gown in her room, and walk back to the cottage in my shirtwaist, walking skirt, and sensible shoes. I was nearly through the double lobby doors and out on the veranda when Herr Brittlinger called after me.

"Wait! Wait! Miss Hartranft! How will you make it home without a lantern?" he asked.

He had a point.

"Please, please let me assist you," he said, putting a protective arm around me and ushering me toward the hotel lobby desk.

Once there, I asked the clerk if we might borrow a lantern, promising to return it in the morning.

"Better yet," Herr Brittlinger said when the clerk returned with a lantern for me to use, "I will walk Miss Hartranft home and return the lantern before I catch my steamer back to Thousand Island Park."

I found the night air refreshing as we crossed the bridge from Grenell Island onto Grenell Island Park. It helped soothe the flush I felt from the brandy. I gathered my voluminous skirt in my right hand and raised it slightly so it wouldn't drag along the ground. Herr Brittlinger carefully tucked my left hand into his right elbow and held the lantern before us with his left hand so we could see our way along the unpaved path on the other side of the bridge.

The lights were already out in the Ojibway Inn—the Shiller cottage—but warm lantern light fell in a bright pool outside the open door of Bay Edge. Inside, the Worden family and guests were still active. I heard Mable and her friends laughing as they played Parcheesi at the table. Ahead, the Babcock cottage was dark. We turned from St. James Place and proceeded around the little cove. Both Copenhagen cottages were dark, as was the Pratt cottage ahead of us on Pratt Point. My only neighbors up and awake at this hour were the Pabst brothers. Lights and lively music poured from the Pabst cottage and into the dark, still night.

I babbled nervously as we walked, though I kept my voice low—almost a whisper. "Mr. Babcock manufactures billiard tables in Syracuse. This is the Copenhagen Cottage. It's not named for Copenhagen, Denmark but rather Copenhagen, New York, which is south of Watertown. The cottage is always filled with people from Copenhagen. They all love to fish. Mr. Chickering was just elected U. S. Representative."

As he helped me over the rocky camel's foot, I told Herr Brittlinger that Prof. Pabst was the organist for the Masonic Lodge in Syracuse. "His brothers, Albert and Carl, must have arrived for I hear more than one instrument. They are a very musically talented family."

"I prefer marches to waltzes," was Herr Brittlinger's only response. He had become very quiet as we walked along the uneven path. Perhaps he was concentrating on our footing.

"Shhh," he said as we rounded the Pabst cottage. "We do not want to disturb their music-making."

The lot between the Pabst cottage and my cottage is rife with rocks and roots. I stumbled a bit in Rose's ill-fitting shoes and clung to Herr Brittlinger's arm for fear that I might take a tumble and soil Rose's gown. We edged our way around Sentry Rock and reached the foot of the spiral path that leads to my cottage.

Here, we were away from all the lights and noise, though we could still hear clearly the waltz played by Prof. Pabst and his brothers.

"This is it," I said. "We call it Castle Rock because this rock behind me reminds me of a great turret and . . ." I thought of explaining that Mr. Sharples's Bungalow had been the impetus for the name but thought better of it.

"We?" Herr Brittlinger asked.

"Friend Anne and I own the cottage jointly."

"And yet I have not met her?"

"Anne is in Chicago at the fair."

"So we are alone."

The way he elongated the word *alone* made the tiny hairs at the back of my neck stand up.

"Thank you for a lovely evening. You are such a gentleman for escorting me home. Please be careful on the way back. The path can be treacherous at night. Good night," I said and turned to go up the path.

He caught my hand and stopped me.

"Let me escort you to your door. I can light the way."

"That's so kind, but I know this path like the back of my hand."

"Come. Come. What's the rush?" he asked, pulling me back to the front of the rock. He turned and leaned against the rock next to me and gestured toward the river, Murray Isle, and the sky beyond. "You have a lovely view of the northern sky. Look there. You Americans call it the Big Dipper. In Germany we call it *Großer Wagen*. To us, it looks like a horse pulling a wagon. Astronomers call it Ursa Major. Tonight, it looks close enough to touch.

"The Greek name for it is Big Bear."

"Yes, my dumpling. Big Bear," he said rubbing his thumb across my wrist. "If we wait for a half hour more we will see the rise of Venus to the west. I'm sure you are aware of the importance of Venus in Roman mythology." He bent down and whispered in my ear: "Venus is the goddess of beauty, love, and sex."

"It's been a long evening," I said, edging away from him.

"Let me help you to your cottage."

I stopped and turned to face him, putting my hand on his starched white shirt to emphasize my point. "No, no. You've done enough."

"Not quite yet. Come, *meine Liebchen*. Let me taste the brandy on your lips." He put his hands around my waist and pulled me forward.

With both hands on his chest, I pushed him back. "I'm afraid I might have given you the wrong impression."

He ran his fat index finger along the edge of my bodice caressing the top of my breasts. "Not at all. This dress—cut so low I can see the tops of your bosom—has given me all the impression I need."

"Unhand me, sir," I said through gritted teeth and pushed harder against his chest.

He leaned forward, pressing me against the rock. The lichen-crusted rock pricked my back. The bristles of his mustache poked into my cheeks. His breath, heavy with the scent of brandy, enveloped my senses as the tip of his tongue pushed between my lips. I bit it. He fell back and cried out. I screamed, my voice echoing off the palisades. The music next-door stopped abruptly.

He grabbed my wrists and raised them over my head, holding them with his right hand while he groped my breasts with his left.

"Let me go! Get away from me!" I shouted into the darkness.

He moved his left hand to cover my mouth as his lips began kissing my neck, my ear.

I heard the crunch of heavy footsteps moving quickly through the leaf litter. Prof. Pabst and his two brothers rounded Sentry Rock. Each had an oar raised above their heads and looked prepared to do combat.

"Unhand her, you cad!" Prof. Pabst shouted.

Herr Brittlinger released me and cursed in German under his breath. "There has been a misunderstanding. That is all," he said, spreading his arms wide.

In my struggle to free myself from Herr Brittlinger's grip, my loose hairstyle had been dislodged. Hairpins fell as did a tortoiseshell comb. My dark hair pooled around my white shoulders. I pushed my thick hair back from my face. My chest was heaving from the exertion of trying to escape from Herr Brittlinger's clutches.

"Herr Brittlinger was just leaving," I said. "He must hurry. He has a steamer to catch."

Herr Brittlinger tentatively moved forward, afraid to approach the Pabst brothers who still had their oars raised.

"Wait," I said picking up the lantern and handing it to him. "Don't forget the lantern you were so concerned about returning to the hotel."

Herr Brittlinger snatched the lantern from my hand and stalked off toward Pullman House.

"We'll follow him," Carl said. "We'll make sure he gets on that steamer."

". . . and we'll strongly suggest to him that he never return to Grenell," Albert added.

When they were gone, Prof. Pabst approached me. "Miss Marguerite! Are you alright?"

I gasped for air and only then did I notice there were tears streaming down my face.

"I'm not hurt," I assured Prof. Pabst. "Only frightened. Thank you so much for coming to my rescue."

"May I escort you to your cottage . . . or perhaps you would feel more comfortable staying at our cottage tonight? We have a spare bedroom."

"No! No, that won't be necessary." Spending the night alone in a cottage with three unmarried men would not improve my reputation. "Please. Please, do not speak of this to anyone."

Then, perhaps sensing the reason for declining his offer, Prof. Pabst suggested taking me to Pratt Point. "You can trust Mrs. Pratt to be discreet," he said in a low voice.

I shook my head and wiped away my tears. "I have nothing to be afraid of now. I'll be fine."

"I'll stay at the foot of the path until I see the lantern come on in your main room."

"You're a good neighbor," I said. "Goodnight."

CHAPTER
fifteen

Rose's eyes brightened when she saw me come into the dining room the next morning.

"Good morning!" she sang out. "Hope you slept well. I did. So did my little angels here."

"Good morning, Rose. Good morning, Miles and Dickie," I said as I sat down.

Rose leaned over and said in whispery tones, "That brandy put me right to sleep."

"Did it?" I asked. I had not had a restful night of sleep. I wasn't sure if I slept a wink.

"Well, I'm no longer annoyed at you," she announced.

"Annoyed with me?"

"For inviting that young man to join us for dessert. After all I did! I worked so hard to make sure that last night was perfect! And then you invited some interloper to join us. But this morning, I've come to the realization that it is a brilliant plan."

"Plan?"

"Yes, there's nothing like a little jealousy to light a flame . . . to hurry along a romance. So, tell me! What arrangements did you make with Herr Brittlinger last night?"

"Actually, he hurried off to the steamer without mentioning when I might see him again."

"What?! What did you do? How could you have possibly bungled this?"

I had dithered all night wondering if I should tell Rose precisely what had happened, and now I had my answer. No matter how delicately or indelicately I tried to explain what had transpired, Rose would have her own interpretation of last night's events and it would be my fault.

"Bungled what, exactly?" I asked, feigning a wide-eyed, innocent look.

"A marriage proposal."

"Marriage? What makes you think I would want to marry someone like Herr Brittlinger? I thought you didn't like professors—I seem to recall you referring to professors as 'loathsome academics with unkempt hair in thread-bare tweeds who use big words to yammer on about useless information.'"

Rose's mouth dropped open, and she lowered the bite of food on her fork to her plate. "Well, Herr Brittlinger is more like a duke or a baron—so filled with Old World charm. I found him endearing."

"That's not the word I would use to describe him," I said under my breath. The thought came to me then that perhaps I should tell her about Charles Bartman, though I barely knew him.

"Pardon me, my dear sister, but at age twenty-eight you can't afford to be very picky."

"There you are!" a voice said. "I know I'm early."

I looked over my shoulder and saw Mr. Quigley approaching the table.

Right on time as far as I'm concerned, I thought. "Please join us," I said. I scooted my chair over to make space and Mr. Quigley pulled a chair from the empty table next to us and squeezed in between Miles and me.

"I've already had my breakfast but wouldn't mind another cup of coffee." He motioned to the waiter, then turning to Miles and Dickie asked, "Who are these bright-eyed lads?"

"These are my nephews, Dickie and Miles. Boys, this is Mr. Quigley."

"Very pleased to meet you both," Mr. Quigley said, reaching across the table and shaking their hands. "I rented a skiff and rowed over. I thought it would take much longer than it did. Are you boys ready for an adventure?"

Rose raised her chin and appraised Mr. Quigley with a disapproving eye. "I'm not sure if I want the boys out in a skiff with someone so unpracticed."

"Never fear, my dear sister. I am quite adept at rowing and can step in if Mr. Quigley isn't up to the task."

Mr. Quigley shot me a surprised look. "Indeed! I had no idea."

"Years of experience." I almost said a dozen years but wisely amended my statement before it left my lips.

"But neither of the boys know how to swim," Rose said.

"Well, I do!" Mr. Quigley said, giving Rose a big smile.

"I as well. And, hopefully, by the end of their time here, so will Dickie and Miles." I turned to the boys then and told them that Mrs. Gruder had purchased bathing costumes for them, and I planned to teach them to swim. "In a few days, you'll be as comfortable in the water as little fish. You've seen the toboggan slide, haven't you? Looks like grand fun."

"Truly?" Miles asked.

"Truly!"

Seeing the smiles on the boys' faces, Rose gave up trying to prevent them from going out in the skiff. "The boys need their hats. I don't want their noses freckled or burned by the sun. "

"I'll collect them," Miles volunteered.

"No, Miles, we'll all go together. Come, boys, we must prepare for this . . . outing." She shooed the boys in front of her, then returned to the table and whispered in my ear, "We will continue our conversation later."

I can hardly wait, I thought as she left the dining room.

"So do you really swim, or are you more of a wader?"

"I'm not some Atlantic City summer girl grasping a safety rope and bobbing up and down in the surf. I'm a St. Lawrence river girl who can do the front crawl, breaststroke, and backstroke with the best of them."

Mr. Quigley put his elbow on the table and rested his chin on his hand. "Fascinating," he said in a tone that left me wondering if he were mocking me or admiring me.

Miss Blond entered the dining room with her family, stopped short, and blurted out, "Mr. Quigley, what are you doing here?"

"Miss Hartranft has offered to take me to see the glacial potholes on Wellesley Island this morning."

"Potholes! How utterly delightful. I've always wanted to see glazier potholes!" Miss Blond gushed, raising her hand against her chest to quell her feigned enthusiasm.

I pressed my lips together to suppress a laugh. The thought of what a "glazier"—a person cuts and installs glass—pothole would look like brought a few comical images to mind.

"Not glazier. *Glacier*," Mr. Quigley corrected Miss Blond.

"What's a glacier?" she asked.

"A river of ice," Mr. Quigley started to explain.

"Ice in the river? Now? But it's June!" Miss Blond looked bewildered.

"If you'll excuse me, I need to prepare for our outing. Meet you at the boat livery when you finish your coffee," I told Mr. Quigley and headed toward the livery.

In anticipation of our outing, I had packed a simple picnic basket. I straightened my boater to make sure it was secure on my head and within minutes Mr. Quigley was by my side. He had somehow extricated himself from Miss Blond.

"Is it a far row?" he asked.

"No. We only have to row through the Narrows. I like to pull the skiff ashore near the rocks on the right-hand side of the Narrows and climb up from there.

"Is it a far hike?"

"Not at all."

"Auntie Marguerite! We're ready!" Miles shouted as he broke into a run.

Mr. Quigley gave me an inquisitive look and leaned toward me and said under his breath, "That's what they're wearing?" he asked.

"You've heard of Little Lord Fauntleroy, have you not?" I asked Mr. Quigley. "Don't look so surprised. That's what they were wearing at breakfast."

"I had assumed they would change," Mr. Quigley said with a shake of his head.

Today, the boys were decked out in light-gray velvet Fauntleroy jackets and short pants. Instead of their usual white stockings, the boys were wearing black stockings. For some reason, Rose had chosen to dress them in white silk shirts. The circular lace collars extended nearly to the edge of their shoulders. Huge white loopy bows dominated the fronts of their cropped jackets.

We settled in the skiff. The two boys sat together on the seat in the bow. Mr. Quigley positioned himself to row from the middle seat. I sat in the stern, facing both Mr. Quigley and the boys.

The boat livery proprietor shoved us off. Mr. Quigley dipped the oars in the water.

"Don't get dirty!" Rose called after us.

"Don't get dirty?" Mr. Quigley asked as he checked his pocketwatch. He closed the lid and returned it to his waistcoat pocket then began rowing with confident, deep, quick strokes. He looked over his shoulder after every other stroke to make sure he was on track.

"How am I doing Miss Expert-of-the-St.-Lawrence-River-Skiff? Any tips for this novice?"

I smiled. "Yes, actually. You don't need to dip the oars so deeply into the water."

He was dipping the oars so low and pulling so forcefully that I was afraid he might snap the oars in two.

"Keep your hands at chest level. Dip the oars just beneath the surface with only the blades in the water, then pull, keeping the blades level."

He adjusted his stroke, and I immediately noticed the difference. He wasn't digging into the water but gliding across it.

"Next, by constantly turning around to check direction, you are breaking your rhythm. Pause now and look where you are headed. For right now, aim for the foot of Hub Island, the tiny island closest to us. Are you lined up?"

He looked over his shoulder and checked the position of the skiff. "Yes."

"Now turn and pick a spot on the horizon in front of you, perhaps right above my head. As long as you keep my head lined up with the point on the horizon, you'll know you are going straight and won't have to keep looking over your shoulder."

"Brilliant! Perhaps I can recruit you as the sculling coach for Princeton's rowing team."

"A scull is a whole other matter."

"Hang onto your hats, boys!" I called out as Mr. Quigley picked up the pace and the skiff sliced through the water.

In a matter of minutes, we had passed Hub Island and entered the waters between Murray Isle and Wellesley Island. Tucked back behind a few tiny islands in Escanaba Bay on the Murray Isle side, I could see the new dock and dock house of Palisades Park. From my cottage, I have watched the steamer *Edith May* as she ferried passengers to and from the fledgling park at half-hour intervals. The dock was tucked out of sight from my perspective at my cottage on Castle Rock. With Mr. Quigley manning the oars, I got a better look at it.

Soon we were under the towering palisades of Wellesley Island on the right. We rounded a cluster of offshore rocks on the Eel Bay side of the Narrows, and I directed Mr. Quigley to head for the Wellesley Island shore.

Mr. Quigley checked his pocketwatch as I helped Dickie out of the skiff. "Ten and a half minutes. Not bad. I'll see if I can beat that time on the way back."

"It's not a race," I said as I lifted Miles from the skiff.

"Is for me!" Mr. Quigley said as he helped me pull the front end of the skiff up onto the shore. He turned to me, tucked his chin close to his chest, and intoned in mock seriousness, "Everything is a race. Come on lads! Beat you to the top of the hill!"

Mr. Quigley ran up the path. Miles and Dickie stared blankly at each other for a moment, then scampered after him, giggling and laughing.

"You don't even know where you're going!" I called to the lot of them.

They stopped at the fork in the path at the top of the hill and waited for me to catch up with them. I trudged up the path, wishing my long skirt would have allowed me the freedom of movement the three young men enjoyed.

"So? Where are they?" Dickie asked.

"This way," I said, following the path that went to the left.

Enough people had visited the potholes that the trail from the foot of the Narrows to the potholes had become very pronounced. You only have to know where to land. Hidden behind bushes in a shelf of rock overlooking Eel Bay were two round holes.

"Looks like two wells side by side," Dickie said, peering down at the perfectly round holes.

Both were filled with water, preventing us from seeing to the bottom.

"How deep do you think they are?" Miles asked.

"I've heard that someone measured them and that one is about fifteen feet deep. I'm not sure about the other, and I don't know which is which," I said.

Dickie shrugged, "So what. Two big holes."

"So what! So what! It's a marvel of geology. Think of it, boys! A river of ice, thousands of feet thick, moving slowly—only inches a year—created these potholes," Mr. Quigley said.

The boys' eyes grew round as Mr. Quigley dramatically described with great gesticulation how heavy, how huge, and how slow the glacier was. How it shaped the islands to be long and narrow ridges of rock. How the meltwater created rivers, and within the river were eddies.

"What's an eddy?" Miles asked.

Mr. Quigley fell to his knees before a startled Miles. "Ever pull the plug on the bathtub? And the water goes round and round as it goes down the drain?" Mr. Quigley said, whirling his arms together to dramatize the movement.

Miles nodded.

"That's an eddy. And a rock—maybe the size of this one," Mr. Quigley said, picking up a rock the size of a large apple, "would get caught in this eddy. A rock stuck in an eddy is known as a grinder. That grinder would swirl around and around for months, maybe for years, and as it swirled, it scoured and shaped and made this pothole. Feel how smooth the sides are."

The boys knelt down and rubbed their hands on the inside edge of the pothole.

"Sometimes the grinders are still at the bottom. And as the grinders are shaping the pothole, the pothole is shaping the grinder. Grinders end up to being perfectly round balls."

"Do you think this pothole has a grinder at the bottom?" Dickie asked, peering into the pothole, trying to see through the water to the bottom.

"I can't see through all the green stuff floating on top," Miles said.

"Those tiny circular light-green leaves are called duckweed," I told the boys.

Miles reached toward the duckweed, then jumped back when something moved inside the pothole. Miles let out a little yelp. "W-w-what was that?" Miles asked, pointing to the ripples spreading in the pothole's waters.

Dickie slapped his hand away. "Maman says you're not supposed to point."

Instantly, Miles stuck out his lip and tears swam in his eyes.

"Stop being a baby," Dickie snarled.

"I'm not a baby," Miles sniffed.

"Then stop acting like one. Next, you'll be wetting your pants. Baby!" With that, Dickie gave Miles a shove.

I put my hands on Dickie's shoulder. "Dickie! No pushing! And don't call your brother names."

Dickie squiggled from underneath my hands, whirled to face me, put his hands on his hips, raised a defiant chin to the sky, and looked up at me from beneath the wide brim of his Lord Fauntleroy hat. "I don't have to listen to you! You aren't my mother. My mother says that you don't know anything about children and probably never will because nobody wants to marry you—probably because you'd be a horrible mother."

I was too stunned to reply.

"Look! It was a frog! See his eyes," Miles said, pointing into the duckweed that floated on the surface of the water in the pothole. Both boys dropped to their knees.

By now my face was burning with embarrassment.

"Yikes," Mr. Quigley whispered in my ear. "Now I know why tigers eat their young."

Without hesitation—without seeking permission—Mr. Quigley reached down, grabbed the back of Dickie's jacket, lifted him off the ground, threw him over his shoulder, and walked up the hill. Although upside down, the chin strap held Dickie's broad-brimmed Lord Fauntleroy hat to his head. The matching gray velvet ribbons dangled and bounced with every step Mr. Quigley took. Dickie started kicking and yelling.

Mr. Quigley put his other arm over Dickie's flailing legs. "Don't think you want to do that, little man," he said in a low voice.

Once out of earshot, Mr. Quigley put Dickie down, sat down on rock, pulled Dickie onto his knee, and calmly talked to him. Dickie bit his lip and nodded. After a few moments of talking and nodding, Mr. Quigley set Dickie on his feet, took him by the hand, and they walked down the hill to the potholes.

"I'm sorry I said those things, Auntie Marguerite. That was very rude," Dickie said, not looking at me but looking at his feet.

"Thank you for your apology, Dickie," I said, looking down at him, though I could not see his face. He was completely eclipsed beneath his Lord Fauntleroy hat.

Mr. Quigley patted Dickie's back, then said, "That's a good lad. Now! Let's catch that frog!"

Mr. Quigley stripped off his jacket, shoved up his shirtsleeves, threw himself on the ground, and plunged his arm into the pothole, fishing around for the frog. The boys followed suit. However, the boys had not taken off their jackets or shoved up their sleeves and soon their lacy cuffs were soaking wet and covered in duckweed. It took several minutes and lots of thrashing before Mr. Quigley, at last, caught the little green frog. He gave each boy a turn at holding the frog before they put it down. Both boys squealed with delight when it took its first tentative jump. They then let out a cheer when it leaped back into the deep water of the pothole.

"We weren't supposed to get dirty," Miles said, looking down at his smudged bow. The arms of his velvet jacket were dripping wet and dotted with duckweed. The scramble for the frog had muddied their knees and rent a tiny hole in Mile's black stocking.

"Why does your sister dress them like a pair of dandies?" Mr. Quigley whispered in my ear. "These velvet suits have got to go. Boys can't be boys dressed like this!"

We ambled back down the path and found a nice place for a picnic lunch on the rocks by the river. Mr. Quigley suggested the boys take off their hats and velvet jackets before we ate our cheese sandwiches and spice drop cookies.

"Now, boys, I'm going to tell you a story. It's about a notorious young desperado. He's dressed in jet-black buckskins and wears a broad black hat slouched over his eyes. When we first see our villain, he's wearing a black cloth with eye-holes over his evil, wicked-looking eyes. With gnarled hands he pulls himself up on his thoroughbred steed, which is black as coal. They call him *the Black Rider of the Black Hills*, the Prince of the Road . . ."

"Deadwood Dick!" Dickie shouted out.

"You know about Deadwood Dick?" Mr. Quigley asked.

"Yes! I love Deadwood Dick. I've read all of the novels about him."

"Well, today we're going to re-enact *The Black Rider of the Black Hills*."

"Can I be Fearless Frank?" Dickie asked.

"The strapping youth who saves the damsel in distress? Why of course! Auntie Marguerite will be our damsel in distress."

"Who am I?" Miles asked.

"You can be Charity Joe, the old wagon train leader. I will be the dastardly desperado, Deadwood Dick. The drama unfolds when Deadwood Dick captures the damsel in distress," Mr. Quigley said. He leaped off a rock and scooped me up in his arms. It happened so quickly—so suddenly—that I was quite breathless. Instinctively, I threw my arms around his neck, lest he drop me. With strong, sure strides, Mr. Quigley carried me off to a rock up the path. "Scream for help," he whispered in my ear as he pretended to chain me to a tree.

"Help! Help! Save me!" I shouted to the boys.

"I've chained the fair maiden to the tree and locked her there," he said as he pantomimed snapping a lock closed and locking it with a key. With great ceremony, he put the imaginary key in his waistcoat pocket. "You must retrieve the key in order to set her free. But first, you must catch me! Catch me if you can!" Mr. Quigley took off running and the boys chased him. Mr. Quigley bounced about the rocks, hid behind trees, and occasionally jumped out to scare the boys with a villainous, "Bwah-hah-hah!"

The boys laughed and shouted as they chased after Mr. Quigley, their cheeks rosy with exertion. At last Mr. Quigley—or rather, Deadwood Dick—let the boys catch and wrestle him to the ground. Dickie reached in Mr. Quigley's waistcoat pocket.

"I've got the key!" Dickie said, holding up the imaginary key.

"We'll save you now, Auntie Marguerite!" Miles shouted.

But before they could pretend to unlock my chains, Mr. Quigley jumped up, picked the boys up one in each arm and threw them over his shoulders. He walked toward me with long, confident strides as the boys bounced and giggled. I noticed their backsides, which were sticking up in the air, were soiled. When he set the boys back on their feet in front of me, they were panting so hard from laughter that they collapsed on the ground overcome by another wave of giggles.

"Let me do the honors. The key please," he demanded of Dickie. Dickie complied and pantomimed placing the key in Mr. Quigley's open hand. Mr. Quigley unlocked the lock and took off my imaginary chains.

"Free at last!" I shouted out and wrapped my arms around the two boys at my feet. "Thank you for saving me! You are both so brave!"

"I'm thirsty," Miles said.

"Me, too!"

"To the skiff!" Mr. Quigley shouted as he bounded down the path to the skiff. I was thankful I had packed a few bottles of sarsaparilla.

Before we were all settled in our seats, I made the boys put their still-damp jackets back on. I tried to tie the bows of their lacy, silky shirts which were soaking wet. I made sure their broad-brimmed hats were securely on their heads. Mr. Quigley pushed the skiff from the shore and managed to climb aboard without getting his feet wet. The skiff jostled back and forth as he climbed over the boys and moved to the center of the skiff. The boys thought it great fun.

"Do it again!" Dickie demanded.

"What? Rock the boat?" Mr. Quigley asked, rocking the boat back and forth to the delighted squeals of the boys.

"Again!" Miles said.

Mr. Quigley shook his head. "No. Now it's time for the serious business of rowing back to Pullman House in less time than it took to get us here. Who remembers how long it took us to row here?"

Dickie's hand shot up in the air. "Ten and a half minutes!"

"Who thinks I can beat that time?"

This time everyone's arm went up in the air, including mine.

"Here's my watch, Dickie. You can keep track of the time. Let me know when you are ready."

The boys chanted, "On your mark, get set, go!"

Mr. Quigley dipped the oars in the water and began a furious pace.

"Not too deep. Keep it shallow," I reminded him.

"One minute," Dickie called out as we were halfway through the Narrows. He called three minutes as we cleared the foot of Murray Isle. When Dickie called out, "Six minutes," when we were about halfway from the Narrows to Hub Island. Mr. Quigley picked up the pace. By the time we landed–we were at eight and a half minutes.

"We did it!" The boys shouted, feeling that they had been part of a great race.

"What happened? What's wrong?" Rose asked as she rushed to the skiff with Mrs. Gruder right behind her.

I hadn't expected Rose to greet us at the boat livery. I had hoped for an opportunity to clean the boys up a little before I returned them to her room.

"Where have you been? I expected you back ages ago."

"I'm sorry to have worried you. We had a splendid time. Didn't we, boys?" I asked as I helped them from the skiff.

"Did you let them take their hats off? Look at their noses. They're beet red."

"We caught a frog, Maman!" Miles shouted out.

"What happened to their jackets? They're soaking wet. What is this green slime? Oh, dear, I think I feel a headache coming on," Rose said, raising her hand to her head. "Mrs. Gruder, please bathe the boys and put them into proper attire. Enter through the back door if you can, so the other guests won't see them in such a state of ruination. I'm mortified."

"I'm sorry if the boys aren't as pristine as when we left but we really did have a marvelous time, thanks to you, Mr. Quigley. Thank you again, Mr. Quigley. May I help you shove off," I said.

"Perhaps we can meet again soon?" he asked.

"Yes, perhaps, but now I think it might be a good time for you to leave," I said softly, nodding back toward Rose as I shoved the skiff away from the dock with one good push.

Rose crossed her arms in front of herself as I waved to Mr. Quigley. "What is wrong with you?" she hissed when he was out of earshot.

I apologized again for the boys' soiled clothes.

"Not that."

"Then what?"

"Herr Brittlinger!"

I blinked. "Whatever do you mean?"

"I sent a message to the professor at the Columbian to invite him for dinner tonight and was informed that Herr Brittlinger checked out of the hotel this morning. What did you do?"

"What did *I* do?" My face was flushed with indignation.

"Knowing you, you were probably spouting off about some suffragist nonsense," she hissed.

"Rose, I am not a suffragist. For your information . . ." I looked around and noted our little discussion had attracted an audience. "I wish to talk about this later. Somewhere less . . . public."

"Yes, of course," she said as she turned and walked away from me. "Run away . . .like you always do," she called back over her shoulder.

The words stung. A bitter ending to a sweet outing. *How many days is it before Rose returns to West Philadelphia?* I asked myself as I walked toward the bridge. I was still calculating days when I looked up and noticed Miss Caldwell standing on the bridge.

"Ah, so you have ventured off the veranda," I said.

"But not off the island. I prefer to stay on this side of the bridge. The middle is as far as I'm willing to go."

I joined her at the rail staring through the gap between Grenell Island and Grenell Island Park to the shipping channel beyond. "Lovely view, isn't it?" she asked. We stood there in silence for a while watching the steamer *Bon Voyage* glide past Grenell on its regular route from Brockville to Kingston.

"Nat Hunkerson," I said, breaking the silence.

"Pardon?"

"Nat Hunkerson. He's the boy who works at the Grenell Island Store. He's only twelve but seems to know everything about everything. He's also very discreet—a most capable young man. Tell him I sent you and I'm sure he can tell you who can provide . . . help you find what you're looking for." I suddenly realized that Nat was only two years older than Dickie. I doubted if Dickie would ever be as capable, self-sufficient, or reliable as my dear Nat.

A small smile crept onto Miss Caldwell's face.

"But, regrettably, you may have to venture off the porch and walk down to the store. Although you might be able to catch Nat at the lobby desk. Nat checks for telegrams for the islanders twice a day," I said.

"That won't be necessary. Alas, my days here at the Pullman House are limited. I'll be leaving the day after tomorrow. But how kind of you to share," she said putting her gloved hand on my ungloved hand.

"Leaving so soon?" I asked.

"Yes. Duty calls," she said cryptically.

"Forgive me for asking but . . . well . . . what is your situation?"

"My situation?"

"Are you married? Widowed?"

"No. I never married. Marriage is not for me. One man. Children," she shuddered at the thought. "No, I'm happy with my life. Besides, I've been a little spoiled being in a theater troupe for years."

"A theater troupe?"

"Yes, we're taking the show on the road, as they say. I have several months of traveling from town to town ahead of me. Trains, stagecoaches, occasionally even a buckboard. Last season, we were transported via buckboard from one town to the next and I thought my teeth would be rattled right out of my head! Hence my desire to sit in comfort and stare out at the river and not ever leave the veranda."

"Buckboard? Doesn't sound like being spoiled to me," I said.

"Oh, I meant the freedom I have being an actress. The theater is a relatively equal playing field for men and women. Granted, the women in the troupe get paid a few dollars less, but other than that, we get booed and applauded equally. Of course, we also starve equally between engagements, and managers abscond with our money equally as well. Truly, the biggest challenge for women in the theater that men don't have to face is costuming. Once I was wearing a beautiful, heavy brocade gown on a teeny-tiny stage. In one scene I had to walk back and forth between two male characters, and as I moved, my long heavy train got wrapped around a chair and when I left the stage, the chair went with me." Miss Caldwell threw back her head and laughed at the memory.

"How long have you been an actress?"

"All my life really. I practically grew up in the business. My parents were theater people, so I never had to face the stigma of the 'disapproving family' as many of my fellow troupe members have. I'm sure you know precisely what I'm talking about." Miss Caldwell turned and gave me a pointed look.

I nodded knowingly. Mother and Rose had often whispered about the unsavory lifestyle of traveling acting troupes.

"How about you, Marguerite? May I call you by your Christian name?"

"Certainly."

"What is your . . . situation?"

"Never married," I said.

"Not yet, at least," Miss Caldwell said, taking her cigarette case from her reticule. "But perhaps someday?"

"Perhaps."

She smiled coyly, opened the case and offered a cigarette to me. I shook my head.

"I've been told I cannot smoke on the porch or the grounds. The middle of the bridge would be in compliance with those stipulations, don't you think?"

I shrugged, for I knew she planned to smoke whether I agreed or not. She struck a match against the wooden railing, lit the end of her small white cigarette, inhaled deeply, then let out a long, sinuous stream of smoke. "I heard you say that you studied the classics at Penn?"

"I did."

"And now?"

"I'm a teaching fellow at the University of Pennsylvania Women's School of Graduate Studies."

"*Hmmm*. So you have had *a few* encounters with college men."

"A few," I said with a smile, remembering the first day we met on the Grenell Island Store dock.

"How was your evening with Baron Von Butterfingers?" Miss Caldwell asked before she brought the cigarette to her lips again.

"I think I can now infer the definition of *bounder*."

Miss Caldwell laughed, smoke coming from her mouth in jagged puffs. "I see."

"Miss Caldwell, you know my Christian name; what is yours?"

"I'm Evelyn," she said, offering her gloved hand.

"Evelyn, very nice to have met you. Safe travels," I said.

"Nice to have met you. Good luck with your sister."

"Thank you," I said as I turned to leave. "I think I'm going to need it."

CHAPTER
sixteen

Rose was late. We were to meet for breakfast at eight, but she was not in the dining room. It was nearly eight-thirty when Mrs. Gruder came down to the dining room with the boys.

"Mrs. Tidwell sends her regrets. She's unable to come to breakfast this morning. One of her headaches," Mrs. Gruder said.

Mrs. Gruder situated the boys in their chairs and ordered breakfast for them. We were just finishing up when Mr. Quigley bounded through the door.

"Mr. Quigley!" Miles shouted out. Mrs. Gruder put a calming hand on his arm.

Mr. Quigley headed toward our table; he didn't wait for an invitation, but sat down and motioned for the waiter to bring him a coffee. "Good morning, all! I hoped I would find you here!"

"Mr. Quigley, may I introduce Mrs. Gruder, my nephews' governess."

"A pleasure, madam," Mr. Quigley said, nodding toward Mrs. Gruder as the coffee arrived. He took a quick sip and then let out a satisfied *ahh* of pleasure. "Pullman House makes a far better cup of coffee than the Columbian. Perhaps I should row over for breakfast every morning. Where is your sister, Mrs. Tidwell?"

"She's feeling unwell this morning," I said.

"So sorry to hear that. I was wondering if the boys would like to go to

Thousand Island Park today. Lots of diversions there. They have tennis and croquet like they have here at the Pullman House, but there is also a baseball diamond. Managed to scare up a bat and ball and a couple of other interested baseball enthusiasts and was wondering if you boys wish to join me in playing baseball."

"We don't know how to play baseball," Miles said.

"What! How could that be? What boy doesn't know how to play baseball? Why it's America's pastime! I'm sure Mrs. Gruder wouldn't mind if we took the day and learned to play baseball. What do you say, Mrs. Gruder? Would you like to tag along? Have you been to Thousand Island Park yet?"

Mrs. Gruder didn't seem to know how to respond.

"Do you need to speak to Mrs. Tidwell?" I asked.

"No, she asked not to be disturbed and put me in charge of the boys for the day," Mrs. Gruder said.

"Then come on! Let's go to Thousand Island Park. You want to come too, don't you, Miss Hartranft?"

"I wouldn't miss it."

"We need to brush our teeth, and the boys need their hats. Come along, Dickie, Miles," Mrs. Gruder said, motioning for the boys to get up and follow her.

"Oh, about that, Mrs. Gruder," Mr. Quigley said standing and approaching Mrs. Gruder. He leaned over and said in a low voice, "Could we do something about the Fauntleroy suits? I think it would be very hard to get grass stains out of burgundy velvet. Do you think you can find something the boys could play in?"

"I think I can come up with something," she said.

When Mrs. Gruder brought the boys to the skiff livery, they were dressed in more sensible knickers with sailor shirts, but still wore their large-brimmed Fauntleroy hats, trimmed today with velveteen burgundy ribbon.

"Here you go! I found a couple of baseball caps for you," Mr. Quigley said.

Miles let out a gasp. "Truly? Thank you, Mr. Quigley."

We settled Mrs. Gruder in the bow with Miles while Dickie sat on the stern seat with me. Mrs. Gruder was very nervous when the skiff rocked as Mr. Quigley stepped in. "We're not going to tip over," Mr. Quigley assured her. "We're still tied to the dock."

Mrs. Gruder survived the white-knuckle row from Pullman House to the Thousand Island Park livery. Thankfully it was a calm day or she might have clawed permanent marks into the skiff gunnels. I was grateful for the staff there for helping lift her bulk out of the skiff. Two Princetonians awaited us on the lawn next to the Columbian Hotel.

"We don't have nine for a proper team so here's what we're going to do. Miles and I will be on one team. Dickie and Percy with be on another. Oliver, you're the best pitcher, so you will be the pitcher for both teams. The team in the outfield has to retrieve the ball. If they get the ball back to the pitcher before the batter gets on base, then the batter is out. Now let's play ball! Come on Miles, we'll be at bat first," Mr. Quigley announced.

Mr. Quigley knelt down, handed Miles the bat, then put his hands over Miles's hands. "Come on, Oliver! Throw me one right over home plate," Mr. Quigley called out. The pitch came and Mr. Quigley and Miles hit it together. It bounced into the lawn past Oliver. Dickie and Percy ran for it. Mr. Quigley picked up Miles and ran him to first base. Dickie tried to throw the ball but he ended up throwing it to the ground two feet in front of him.

I hadn't seen baseball played before, so it was hard to say how accurate their play was. I can only say that it was hard for me to discern what the boys enjoyed more—batting or having their teammates pick them up and run them from base to base.

"Miss Hartranft?"

I turned to see Yvette Sawyer standing behind me with her safety bicycle.

"Why, good morning, Yvette," I said.

"I thought that was you!" she said, smiling broadly.

"Thank you for inviting me to your watermelon party. I'm sorry I had to decline; it was the afternoon my sister arrived with my nephews," I said, indicating the two boys running about the lawn.

"As it turns out, we had to postpone it. It's rescheduled for next week. Thursday at two. Feel free to bring your sister and your nephews.

"Off for a morning ride?" I asked Yvette as I noticed Miss Blond and Miss Brunette from Pullman House, standing by the safety bicycles near the dry goods store across the street.

"Yoo-hoo! Mr. Quigley," Miss Blond called out and waved.

"Will the girls from Pullman House be joining you this morning?" I asked Yvette.

Yvette rolled her eyes. "They're not true wheelers. They came here yesterday in their brand-new wheeling costumes and rented safety bicycles, but they don't intend to learn to ride. I overheard their scheme. They love wheeling dresses because the skirts are shorter, so they can show off their ankles. Please notice that they don't wear wheeling boots but low shoes. If you look carefully, you can see Miss Martin, the blonde one, is wearing plaid-checked hose to show off her ankles."

"I see. So they just stand in front of the store all day with their rented safety bicycles?"

"Oh, no. They walk up and down the streets sometimes, leading their safety bicycles. Oh, well," Yvette said, lifting one shoulder and raising her chin, her annoyed look dissolving into a dazzling smile. "They have no idea what they are missing! I love the wind in my face and watching the countryside whiz by. Oh! And I'm planning on a special island-hopping trip—including Grenell. May I send a message to the Pullman House if I need help in organizing it?" she asked as she mounted her safety bicycle.

"Certainly, Nat—he works at the Grenell Island Store—delivers messages to us islanders twice each day."

"Toodles!" Yvette called back as she started peddling away.

The tiny group of baseballers started cheering. Mr. Quigley hoisted Miles on his shoulders.

"What happened?" I asked Mrs. Gruder.

"I have no idea. I wish I could take Mr. Quigley home with us. He certainly has a way with the boys."

"Ice cream time!" Mr. Quigley announced.

"Mr. Quigley, it's still morning, too early for ice cream," Mrs. Gruder objected.

In a swift move, Mr. Quigley swung Miles to the ground, grabbed both the boys' hands and ran over to Mrs. Gruder.

"Oh, but Mrs. Gruder, this is how baseball players celebrate the end of the game. Look at these lads. It's their very first baseball game. Come on. Be the sweetheart I know you are," Mr. Quigley said, tilting his head and flashing a huge boyish grin that melted Mrs. Gruder's resolve. I think I noticed the plump, middle-aged woman blushing as she nodded her agreement.

"I heard there is a fantastic ice cream pavilion at Fineview? Do you know where Fineview is?" Mr. Quigley asked.

"Yes. Not far," I said.

"Walk or row?"

"Row."

"To the skiff!" Dickie, Miles, and Mr. Quigley took off at a dead run toward the boat livery, the boys' sailor collars flapping behind them.

"Wait! Wait for me, Mr. Quigley," Miles called out as he struggled to catch up.

Mr. Quigley ran back, hoisted Miles in the air like he was a sack of potatoes, and threw him over his shoulder. He then trotted to where Dickie stood pouting, scooped him up, and carried him on his hip like he was a rolled-up carpet.

We settled in the skiff, and I directed Mr. Quigley to row downriver. "It's not far. Less than a mile."

As Mr. Quigley rowed swiftly in the direction I indicated, I explained that Fineview sprung up at the boundary of Thousand Island Park a decade or so ago when the latter place restricted Sunday landings. Steamers often landed at Fineview on Sundays, and Thousand Island Park residents walked the mile to Thousand Island Park. Fineview House was built in the mid-1880s and a nice mercantile center developed around the small hotel: meat market, store, millinery and ice cream pavilion.

"I understand there is an Indian camp across the road. It is a summer encampment where they manufacture baskets for the tourist trade. Perhaps the boys might like to see the camp after they finish their ice cream?" I suggested.

Outside the ice cream pavilion sat a man who appeared to be an Indian. He wore a red blanket over one shoulder like a Roman tunic. Two long braids hung down his back. Around his head was wrapped a piece of red cloth. Two large crows perched atop him—one on his head and the other on his shoulder.

"What is that?" Miles asked pointing.

I gently lowered his hand before Dickie noticed.

A young man in an apron had been cleaning tables but jumped forward to explain. "This here is a genuine Choctaw Indian. He goes by Whirling Dog. Mr. Bretsch hired him to tell fortunes. People come from miles around. 'Cept it's the crows that actually do the fortune-telling. A penny a fortune."

"I think I can manage that," Mr. Quigley said as he dug into his pocket and placed a penny in each of the boys' hands. "You first, Miles," Mr. Quigley said, pushing a reluctant Miles toward the table. Miles took the penny and dropped it into the basket.

The crow on Whirling Dog's head jumped down onto the table and stared up at Miles. It took a few jerky steps forward with its large black feet. Whirling Dog put his arm out and the crow flew back. Instead of cawing, the bird spoke in some odd language.

"What's that gibberish?" Dickie asked loudly.

"Choctaw. Both the crows speak that Indian language," the young man said.

"Sounds like gibberish to me," Dick said under his breath.

Whirling Dog nodded gravely, lowered his arm, and the bird flew back to his perch atop Whirling Dog's head. Whirling Dog raised his stoic face to the three adults and said in heavily accented English, "This boy has a kind heart. He will be the father of a great family."

Quigley clapped his hand on Miles's shoulder. "Sounds good, Miles. Your turn, Dickie."

Dickie took a step forward, tossed the penny in the basket, stepped back, and crossed his arms in front of himself.

Again Whirling Dog spoke to the bird. It jumped down on the table, strutted forward, looked into Dickie's eyes, put its head down, and squawked loudly before it took flight. The squawk and flutter of wings startled both the boys who retreated to the safety of Mr. Quigley's side. The crow flew up to a nearby tree and landed on the lowest branch.

"What about my fortune, stupid bird!" Dickie shouted.

Whirling Dog stared at Dickie then called out to the bird. It flew back from the tree and landed on his arm. Whirling Dog said something to the bird in Choctaw, and the bird loudly replied in kind. Whirling Dog lowered his arm, and the bird flapped away, returning to his perch in the tree.

Again Whirling Dog raised his face to the three adults, his expression stonier than before, though I hadn't thought that possible. He spoke briefly, emphatically. I gasped. Mrs. Gruder pressed her hand against her chest. Mr. Quigley suppressed a laugh.

"What did he say?" Miles asked.

"Nothing," Mrs. Gruder said, pushing both boys toward the entrance of the ice cream pavilion.

"He said something," Dickie insisted.

"It was similar to what he said about Miles," I said, sharing a horrified look with Mrs. Gruder. "Come, come! Ice cream time!" I said, hurrying the boys toward the ice cream pavilion.

"I don't think we should mention this to Mrs. Tidwell," I whispered to Mrs. Gruder as the boys were ordering their ice cream.

"Certainly not! What a lot of rubbish and nonsense."

Soon the boys were at tables eating their ice cream, chatting with Mr. Quigley about their baseball adventure. Mrs. Gruder seemed delighted that Mr. Quigley had bought her a dish of ice cream as well. Apparently, she wasn't accustomed to being included.

Mr. Quigley and I finished our ice cream before the boys, so I excused myself, saying I would like to have a look in the millinery shop next-door. Mr. Quigley followed after me like a happy puppy dog.

"Welcome to Burdick's Millinery Shop," a young woman said to me as I entered. "I'm Miss Poppie Burdick at your service. Are you looking for anything in particular?"

"I'm just window-shopping. You have some lovely hats, Miss Burdick," I said with a smile.

"Please call me Poppie!" said the small, slight woman with a breathy voice.

"I particularly like this one," Mr. Quigley said, trying on a small blue velvet hat with a large white silk magnolia blossom and a light-blue ostrich feather circling the crown. It looked absurdly small on his large head.

Miss Poppie smiled and reached for the hat, taking it from Mr. Quigley's head. "A good choice for your lady friend, sir. You have a great eye. I called this one the Gibson Girl hat. I designed it specifically to be worn with a Gibson Girl hairstyle. You have the hair for it, miss. Have you tried a Gibson Girl look?"

"Only once before," I said. Today my hair was styled back and away from my face in a simple French twist. "I'm afraid the Gibson Girl look is not well-suited for a day on the river. It's such a loose style. The wind would dismantle it in an instant."

"True," Miss Poppie mused. She reached up and put the hat on my head, motioning for me to turn to look in the mirror. "But the Gibson Girl hat looks good on the French twist as well, don't you think?" She wasn't asking me; she was asking Mr. Quigley.

I looked in the mirror and could see Mr. Quigley's eyes as he stood behind me and looked at my reflection.

"I have a feeling that all of your hats would look fetching on this lovely lady, Miss Poppie."

I felt my cheeks warm at the compliment.

"I will think about it," I said taking the hat off and handing it back to Miss Poppie. "My nephews have probably finished their ice cream by now. We probably should return to the ice cream pavilion."

We retrieved the boys and walked across the road to the Indian camp, where several dozen Indians were busily making baskets. Men peeled splints from black ash logs, and other men wove large baskets with the black ash splints. The women were engaged in making small baskets of sweetgrass.

"I thought Indians lived in teepees, not the same type of tent you lived in, Auntie Marguerite," Miles said.

"The Plains Indians live in teepees," I said. "These Indians are only summering here in the islands. And you're right, Miles, their tents are very similar to my old tent."

"You tent camped?" Mr. Quigley asked.

"Yes, my first years on the river I tent camped. I still have the tents."

"You are full of surprises, Miss Hartranft," Mr. Quigley said.

I smiled at the memory of feeling closer to nature with only a thin canvas between me and the world outside. What a peaceful, wonderful feeling that was. "Perhaps next year, you and Dickie would like to stay in a tent instead of at Pullman House," I said to Miles.

Miles' face brightened at the suggestion and he nodded his head eagerly.

Dickie pulled a face. "What? So we could live like a couple of dirty

Indians?"

"Dickie," I said, putting my hands on his shoulders. "That's not polite."

Dickie whirled to look at me, put his hands on his hips, and raised his chin defiantly. He opened his mouth to say something. Mr. Quigley crossed his arms in front of himself and glared at Dickie, whose look of indignation withered.

I picked two small sweetgrass baskets with lids and bought them for the boys.

"What am I going to do with this?" Dickie asked.

"I think it would be a perfect place to keep a frog," Mr. Quigley said, then whispered something in Dickie's ear.

"Oh. . . thank you, Auntie Marguerite," he said without much enthusiasm.

"Yes, thank you, Auntie Marguerite. My very own frog basket!" Miles said as we turned to walk back to the Fineview dock.

On the path between the ice cream pavilion and the dock, a young man ran up to Mr. Quigley and clapped his arm about his shoulder in a hearty embrace and said, "Quigley, ol' chap! What brings you to Fineview?"

"Slide Rule!" Mr. Quigley said, returning his embrace.

"What sort of name is Slide Rule?" Dickie muttered to himself.

"I remember you," I said. "You are the poet laureate of Princeton. I'm Miss Hartranft. We met on the Princeton outing last week."

"Indeed," said the tall, gangly lad as he bowed toward me. "Slide Rule, Class of '93, at your service."

"I was very impressed with your poem at Grand View Park. Did you ponder over it during our luncheon? Or was it composed on the spot?" I asked, remembering the many times I had struggled with putting pen to paper to create a poem.

"Rhymes just come to my head fully formed," he said.

"Do you have a poem for Fineview?" I asked.

"I dare say, old Slide Rule always has a poem. Don't you, ol' chap," Mr. Quigley said, slapping a hand on Slide Rule's shoulder.

"Well, let me see. I'll start by finding a pulpit," Slide Rule said, jumping up on a crate. "All good poems need to be recited from a standing position for proper oration and gesticulation."

I smiled, sure my father would have agreed with those sentiments if he were still alive and here with us.

I wondered briefly if the young man had acquired the nickname Slide Rule due to his tall thin appearance or because of his exact and precise measurement of the English language.

"I'm just looking about for a bit of inspiration. Ah . . . here comes my inspiration now." Slide Rule motioned toward the man approaching the dock. "Here comes Mr. Bretsch, the new proprietor of the Fineview House. Sir, this poem is dedicated to you."

> Ah! 'tis so hard to say adieu,
>   Host of Fineview—Host of Fineview;
> In all the world, no host's like you,
>   Host of Fineview—Host of Fineview;
> We're sitting now upon the pier,
>   Into the river drops a tear;
> Our hearts indeed feel very queer,
>   Host of Fineview—Host of Fineview;
>
> The steamer now has hove in sight,
>   Ah, wretched night—most wretched night.
> We're carried quickly from your light,
>   Ah, wretched night—most wretched night.
> We hear and see your last adieu,
>   We feel your hearts are aching too,
> Kind friends, we should be friends most true,
>   After this night, this wretched night.

"You do know that it isn't night," Mr. Quigley said.

"It's called poetic license. *Afternoon* doesn't rhyme with *sight*, I'm afraid."

We thanked Slide Rule for his poem as we lowered the boys into the skiff. I noticed that Mrs. Gruder seemed much more comfortable in the skiff now that it was her third trip.

I explained to Mr. Quigley on the row home that I had once set my sights on being a poetess. "My father instilled in me a love for poetry, but I quickly discovered that reading poetry and writing poetry were two different things."

"Grandfather loved poetry?" Miles asked.

"Yes, when I was your age, your grandfather had a poem for every occasion."

"What would he recite to you if he were rowing in a boat?" Miles asked.

I thought a minute, then decided that Robert Louis Stevenson's poem, "Where Do the Boats Go?" would be perfect for this occasion and recited it as Mr. Quigley rowed steadily toward Grenell.

"You're lying. I remember Grandfather Hartranft, and he never once recited a poem to me."

"Just because you don't remember, doesn't mean that your aunt Marguerite is lying," Mr. Quigley said, looking over his shoulder at Dickie.

"But Maman says that Aunt Marguerite doesn't know the truth because she lies all the time."

My cheeks burned hot. I lifted my head into the fresh southwesterly wind and tried to let it blow the hurt away from me. "You were only four and a half when your grandfather died, Dickie. Perhaps you don't remember."

The boys were both exhausted when we returned to the Pullman House boat livery and Mrs. Gruder, after prodding the boys to thank Mr. Quigley for the baseball game and ice cream, ushered them off to their room.

"May I walk you to your cottage?" Mr. Quigley asked.

Remembering the last escort home, I declined. Not that I feared untoward behavior from Mr. Quigley, but I was concerned the Pabst brothers might be about, and I was too embarrassed for them to see me with yet another man. What might that lead them to think of me?

"You may walk me to the bridge," I said.

Usually in a hurry to get from point A to point B, I was surprised to note Mr. Quigley had adopted a snail's pace.

"So you attend Penn," he said, slowing his pace even more and sticking his hands in his front pockets.

"Yes, I *attended* Penn," I said. After Dickie's comment about lying, I suddenly felt the need for complete honesty.

"Curriculum?"

"The classics."

He nodded as if that made sense. "Are you a New Woman?"

This made me smile as I thought of responding that I would rather be considered a new woman than an old woman. Instead, I said, "That depends on how you define *New Woman*."

"*Hmmm*," he murmured as we reached the base of the bridge. He leaned against the bridge support, crossed his arms in front of him for a moment, then raised a finger to his lips, tapping it there as if to drum out a suitable answer. "I suppose I would define a New Woman as an independent woman who lives on her own and supports herself."

"I live in a house full of other women, but basically my life fits the rest of those parameters."

Mr. Quigley shut his eyes as if pondering something of import, then slowly opened his eyes and stared directly into mine. "Have you thought about traveling the world?"

"I desire to visit Greece. And Rome. Some day."

"My future will take me to mining interests around the world: Africa, Australia, the Orient. Care to tag along?"

"But what about my position?" I asked.

"Which is?"

"I teach classics at Penn."

"My! My! You're an academic. A scholar."

He switched his position then, leaned his back against the bridge support, and crossed his feet in front of him. He looked up to the sky as if he needed to reevaluate the situation and was searching the heavens for insight. Finally, he looked at me again. "Would you reconsider? We could travel the world together. Think of the adventures we will have."

And what about the river? I thought. I would sooner leave teaching—the classics—than I would the river.

"Mr. Quigley, I'm concerned that the disparity in our ages might be an obstacle."

"What difference does that matter?"

"More than you might think. Besides, I love what I do," I told him. And I love the river, I reminded myself. Forget the world. The river is all

I need.

"I never thought I would be interested in a New Woman. They always seemed so obstinate and . . . mannish. But not you. I think you've ruined me forever. After spending time with you, summer girls are . . ."

"Are what?"

"Annoying! I want a woman who is bright. Intelligent. Independent."

"I see," I said. We stood there in silence for a while. Mr. Quigley picked up a few stones and tossed them far into the river, one right after the other.

I watched the rings on the water that the stones caused widen and connect. A thought burst upon me and I turned to Mr. Quigley with a broad smile and an important question. "How do you feel about wheeling Mr. Quigley?"

CHAPTER *seventeen*

Mrs. Gruder sent Nat to Castle Rock with a message reading that Rose was still not feeling well and I should not come to dinner. I was almost relieved. I looked about the little cottage. The lilacs I had arranged the day of Rose's arrival were wilted and brown. Pine pollen covered every surface. It was as if I hadn't cleaned and polished at all. All that work—the painting, the cleaning, the flower arrangement—it had all been for naught. Rose had not stepped foot in our little cottage and had made it very clear that she wouldn't step foot on the other side of the bridge that joined Grenell Island to Grenell Island Park. I pulled my sleeve protectors over my shirtwaist sleeves, opened the jar of furniture polish, and, with a soft rag, set about cleaning the cottage.

Did Rose really think I was someone who could not be trusted to tell the truth? I applied a smear of polish to the kitchen table, then rubbed frantically as if trying to wipe away the thought. What other odious things had Rose told the boys besides that no one would want to marry me because I would be a horrible mother?

I had not lied to Rose, but I had hidden things from her. Charles Bartman, for instance. Perhaps she could ascertain that I was hiding something and construed that as lying. Perhaps Rose had a point.

Once the cottage was tidy again, I rowed out to my little fishing hole and caught a few perch for dinner. I had planned to teach Miles and Dickie to fish. I had hoped to be frying up a skillet of fresh perch with them right now and enjoying a shore dinner at my table. Instead, I ate alone. The cottage was quiet. If Flossie were here, things would be much livelier. Instead, I found myself wishing Friend Anne were here. Anne would know how to counsel me. Not that Anne was one to dole out advice. She was a woman of few words, but her mere presence, the way she looked at me, was often enough to let me know if I was on the right path or not. But Anne was not here, so instead, I sat on the porch and looked out at the river. The last light of the day shimmered on the surface. As the sky darkened and the shadows knit together to wrap me in darkness, the hum of insects intensified and replaced the hum in my head. I closed my eyes and thought of tomorrow. Tomorrow morning, I would teach the boys how to row. Tomorrow afternoon, I would teach them how to swim. Time on the river. Time in the river. The river could and would soothe all the harsh words and unpleasantness away.

I drifted to sleep that night with thoughts of the river running through my dreams. I woke several times when I thought I heard *the Voice* whispering my name. Or was it the wind in the pines? Or the water lapping on the rocks below?

I rowed to Pullman House for breakfast the next morning so that I would be ready to give my nephews rowing lessons as soon as we finished breakfast. I found Rose waiting for me in the dining room at a table in a corner, far away from everyone else. A pot of tea awaited me.

"Where are the boys?" I asked. "They are well, I trust. I was hoping to teach them to row this morning."

"Sit," Rose said, pouring me a cup of tea. "The boys are having breakfast with Mrs. Gruder in their room. I requested a secluded table as we have things to talk about this morning."

"Is Mother alright?"

"You're concerned about Mother? Really? Truly? When have you ever thought of anyone but yourself? You spent yesterday gallivanting around with a young man half your age and then pretend you are concerned about Mother?"

Instantly, I knew my instinct not to introduce Rose to Charles Bartman—or even tell her about my interest in him—had been a good one.

"Half my age? Are you referring to Mr. Quigley? He's more than half your age, and you are older than I am."

Rose reddened and screwed her lips into a disapproving knot. "Let's not quibble over sums, shall we?" she said, clearly flustered. "You know precisely what I mean. Spending time with that Mr. Quigley while dashing away the only clear prospect that you've had in a year or more is precisely what we need to discuss."

"This clear prospect you speak of—are you referring to the *one* dinner we had with Herr Brittlinger? It was one dinner. I would hardly construe that as courting."

"There, there," Rose said, reaching across the table and patting my hand as if she were soothing a small child. "You clearly don't understand how any of this works. If you did, you would have been married ages ago, so you simply have to trust me."

I wanted to inform Rose that Herr Brittlinger was a bounder. A masher! But then she would want to know where I had learned those words. Instead, a took a breath and said, "I appreciate your concern for my welfare and my future, but I found Herr Brittlinger's attention a little too forward."

"Don't be daft. He was nothing but a gentleman."

"But you weren't on our walk home from the Pullman House, were you?"

"What happened? Whatever it was, I'm sure you only imagined some slight. For someone who is supposed to be so schooled, you are lacking knowledge of etiquette and decorum," Rose said in a huff. She picked up her teacup and took a sip. "Mother's right," she mumbled, more to herself than to me, as she returned the cup to the saucer. "Two years at finishing school would have served you so much better than that loathsome academy."

"Naïve or not, I no longer desire any interaction with Herr Brittlinger."

"You told him that?"

"Not in so many words."

"Oh, Marguerite! What have you done? Do you see what you are doing to your family?"

"What has this to do with my family?"

"Everything! Please, please forget this ridiculousness about Greek and

Latin, and concentrate on your duty as a daughter."

I blinked. Unsure of her meaning. I waited, patiently, for her to explain.

"Mr. Tidwell does very well, despite this wretched Panic affecting the rest of the country. We have a suite of rooms on the third floor, a bedroom with an attached salon. Mother and I can teach you the womanly arts—etiquette, decorum, how to take care of a household. Perhaps if you spend more time around your nephews, you can learn to be a good mother. You can—no, you must—come live with us before it is too late."

I looked down and watched my tea slosh gently against the sides of the delicate china teacup as I raised it to my lips, trying to keep my face neutral and unaffected by the horror of Rose's proposal. I took a sip, returned the cup to the saucer, swallowed hard, and gathered my resolve before I raised my eyes to Rose's intense glare. I forced the corners of my mouth into a wan smile. "You've certainly given me a lot to think about."

Rose continued to elaborate on her plan, which included dance classes, a new wardrobe, and perhaps a ball given in my honor, the coming out debut that I never had. "After a season of attending the social events in West Philadelphia, I'm sure we can have you married off by next spring and delivered safely into the hands of a husband who can properly look after you."

Rose reached across the table, took my hand, and looked at me with a curious mix of pity and concern. For the first time since she had arrived on Grenell, I felt that Rose was genuine and loving—that she really cared for me and wanted the best for me, though I wasn't sure I could ever be happily shoehorned into the world she described.

"It seems you've given this a lot of thought. I will need time to ruminate," I said placidly.

"Thinking has always been your downfall. There is nothing to think about. Just say yes."

I glanced down at the watch pinned to my bodice. "Oh, look at the time! I had hoped to teach the boys to row this morning and swim this afternoon. I rowed over this morning in my lady's skiff. It will be much easier for the boys to manage. It's much smaller than the skiff that we were in the other day with—the last few days." I decided at the last moment that I should not refer to Mr. Quigley.

Grenell 1893

"And what of my proposal?"

"I will give you my answer on the morrow."

Disappointed, Rose scowled and left to retrieve the boys.

"I'm first," Dickie said, scrambling into the skiff and sitting on the middle seat.

"Why do you have to be first all the time? Why can't I be first sometimes?" Miles pouted.

"Because I'm the oldest! That's why! The oldest always goes first!" Dickie said defiantly, crossing his arms across his cropped, dark-blue velvet Lord Fauntleroy jacket.

"Not fair!" Miles sulked.

I knelt down and whispered in Miles's ear. "I completely understand your point of view, Miles. I was the second daughter. Your mother was the first daughter, and she always went first, but I was able to learn by watching your mother's mistakes. Life was easier for me. Don't think of it as a slight. Think of it as an advantage."

"Maman always went first?"

"She was the firstborn," I said as I stood. "Dickie, you're facing the wrong way. You won't be able to reach the oars. Turn around."

Miles tugged at my skirt and motioned for me to bend down. "I won't make that mistake when it's my turn, Auntie Marguerite!"

"Very good, Miles," I said, chucking his chin. "A great man once said, 'It's not what happens to you, but how you react to it that matters.'"

I repeated Epictetus's quote to myself in Greek. The ring of the words in my ear made me smile. I thought of the bust of Epictetus that stood in a line of other busts of Greek philosophers in the lecture hall at Penn. Epictetus's teachings had been embraced by Marcus Aurelius, perhaps the greatest of all Roman emperors. I recited the quote over in my head, as I settled Miles in the bow, and climbed into the skiff, and waved to a dockhand to help cast us off: *It's not what happens to you, but how you react to it that matters.* I wasn't sure yet how that applied to my discussion with Rose this morning.

It was a still morning, hardly a ripple on the water. It would be an outstanding morning to teach the boys to row as we wouldn't have to battle wind or waves.

"Come on! Hurry up, you clod. We're waiting," Dickie shouted to the dockhand.

"Dickie! Do not be so impolite!" My cheeks reddened at Dickie's impudent behavior as the dock boy approached. "Good morning. Petey, is it?"

He nodded.

"We're out for our first lesson in a skiff and could use a hand casting off. If you could untie the lines and give us a big shove, I'd appreciate it."

"Certainly, miss," Petey said and hurried to comply.

"Thank you, Petey," I called back as we glided away from the dock after a nice push from Petey.

Petey said nothing but tipped his hat and sauntered off.

"Dickie, that was rude to call Petey a clod." I kept my voice low, as I knew how easily voices carry over water.

"But he's dressed like a clod. And who cares if I was rude? He's only a servant."

"He is not a servant. He is a dockhand for the Pullman House, a young man at work to help put food on the table. He deserves your respect."

"Respect?" Dickie spat the word out and scowled as if the idea of respecting someone dressed in less than velvet and lace was the most preposterous thing he had ever heard. He dipped the oars deeply into the water and strained to pull the oar handles toward him.

"Dickie, try to keep your strokes shallow. Dip the blades just beneath the surface of the water," I reminded him.

"I know. I know. I heard you tell Mr. Quigley that."

At his second attempt, his stroke was more shallow and easier to pull back. The skiff slid effortlessly across the smooth surface of the water.

"Ah, much, much better," I said. "See the difference?"

"You didn't help me, you know," Dickie said. "I knew how to do that all along."

Miles waved to me from the bow, and he mouthed the words, "I won't make that mistake."

I smiled. I let Dickie's prickliness evaporate in the fresh morning river air. I breathed in deeply. The morning sun made the skiff's varnished cedar glisten. The river rolled in front of us like an unfurled bolt of blue satin. I loved watching the droplets of water from the raised oars make a chain of ringlets in the water.

"How do I turn this thing?" Dickie groused.

"Pull a few times on your right oar only," I said, keeping my directions short, succinct.

Miles was watching Dickie intently and mimicking his actions, likely practicing in his head for when it would be his turn.

Actually, Dickie did better than I had expected and I relaxed, enjoying the morning row as Dickie rowed upriver past the front of Grenell with all her pretty cottages perched atop the tall cliffs of the yacht basin. Several boats were moored in the deep basin below the high cliffs. The largest of the sailing yachts, *Tiger*, belonged to the Kerrs. There was also the steam yacht, *Otsego*, which belonged to Mr. Burditt. As we passed the Curtis place, a cottage called Edgewater, at the most southern tip of Grenell, I noted that a new seawall had been built around the point, and a fine new lawn extended down to the water's edge.

We rowed past Grenell Island Park's south bay, and I waved to Uncle Sam on his porch, then to the Reeves enjoying the morning sun from their porch, and finally saw George and Herb in hot debate in front of the store.

"Should we go through there?" Miles asked, pointing to the thin strip of water that separated Grenell from Wilson Island.

"No, let's go around Wilson Island," I said. "Too many rocks to navigate between Wilson and Grenell."

After we rounded the head of Wilson Island, the boys switched positions, and Miles had his turn at rowing. On the backside of Wilson Island, we encountered the sailing yacht *Allie*, moored in the lee of the wind.

Looking up at the tall mast as he rowed past, Miles then read the name painted on the bow. "*Albie*? Who names a boat *Albie*?"

"It's *Allie*," I corrected him. "*Allie* is owned by Mr. Wilson, from Watertown. He summers here on Wilson Island. See the small wooden cottage up there beneath the trees? And oh my! What a large number of tents. Mr. Wilson loves to entertain. Looks like he has a large group rusticating on the island this week. Mr. Wilson hosts a clam bake each season with dozens of guests. He's also quite a sailor. *Allie* has won several pennants in yacht races this last season."

"Do you sail, Auntie Marguerite?" Miles asked.

"No. But I hope to learn someday. You are doing quite well rowing, Miles."

"Please do learn, Auntie Marguerite. I would love to learn to sail. If you learn, then you can teach me."

"That is a lovely idea, Miles." I said.

Miles rowed in silence, as he needed little direction from me.

"Is that your cottage, Auntie?" Dickie asked, pointing to our little cottage, which was just coming into view.

"Why, yes. That's our cottage. We call it Castle Rock."

Dickie let out a dismissive puff of air. "Why would you call that little shed a castle?"

"Well, I have always thought that the rock looks like a castle turret, especially the way the path curls up around the outside of it."

"What happened to that tree?" Miles asked, pausing from his rowing to look up at the splintered white pine on the shoreline.

"Dickie, do you remember?" I asked, for I had told the boys the story before.

"It blew over in a storm or something," Dickie said, then shrugged.

"Not exactly. It was struck by lightning." I told the story of that night: the wind howled, the tent pole snapped, the hair on the back of my neck stood straight up, and then a lightning bolt, with blinding white light, struck the tree, sending splinters everywhere, and severed the tree in half. The east half of the tree fell, and the ground shook.

"It's ugly. If it were near our house, Papa would have the gardener chop it down," Dickie said.

"But it's still alive," I explained. I hadn't been sure if it would live. The tree had split in two in a blink of an eye. The center of the tree had a deep-red core for the first year or two, which has since weathered to dark gray. A denuded snag pointed skyward, and inside there was a deep, dark cavity. I had no idea how deep it was. Despite the loss, the western half of the tree lived on, growing greener and fuller each year. I liked to run my hands over the scar where the lightning bolt had blasted the bark from the trunk from the top of the cavity to the ground and along a root that protruded above ground.

I shut my eyes remembering that night, lying facedown on the rock, my arms outstretched, embracing the cold wet rock as the menacing storm whirled around me.

"It doesn't look like it will live much longer. Papa would say it should be cut down," Dickie insisted.

I wanted to point out that each spring a pair of wood ducks made their nest in the cavity of the great tree, a family of squirrels had a summer drey in the higher branches, and occasionally a bald eagle would perch atop the snag early in the morning or late in the evening. The tree, despite its splintered look, was teaming with life. I said nothing of this. Instead, I praised Miles for his rowing.

My comment made Dickie scowl, fold his arms across his chest, and look away in disgust. Apparently, Dickie took my compliment to Miles as a slight. He was silent as we rowed around Pratt Point, but then sat up, pointed to Hub Island, and finally shaking himself from his sour mood asked, "Why is there a cookstove in the middle of that island?"

"There used to be a grand hotel there called Hub House. It burned down ten years ago. All that remained after the conflagration were charred timbers, the cookstove, and the docks."

"Look! There's a tent," Dickie said. "Are there Indians on the island so close to Pullman House?"

"No. A group of people from Kingston, Ontario is camping there this week. It's not unusual for people to camp there or for fishing guides to use the island and the cookstove for shore dinners."

As Miles rowed on, I thought of that afternoon my first year on Grenell when I met the Good Gray Poet, Walt Whitman, on the porch of the Hub House. It was still one of the most thrilling moments of my life. Mr. Whitman died last year. And even though I had met the man face-to-face only one time, it was as if I had lost a dear, dear friend.

I was still deep in memory about my audience with Mr. Whitman when I noticed a woman frantically waving to us from the Pullman House livery dock. As Miles rowed closer, I was surprised to realize that the frantic woman was Rose. Mrs. Gruder stood beside her like a black cloud. "There they are," Rose called out. "This way! Yoo-hoo! This way! Hurry!"

Miles looked back and tried to row faster at his mother's frantic urging, missed the water all together, and nearly fell off his seat to the bottom of the skiff as he fanned air instead of water.

"Oh, do be careful! You mustn't tip over. You mustn't!" Rose cried out as she wrung her hands.

I could see the panic in Miles's eyes. "Miles," I said, keeping my voice serene. "Calm down. Put the oars in the water, and line the stern up like I taught you. Face me."

"Quickly! Quickly! Get to shore," Rose shouted.

Dickie turned to face his mother kneeling on the seat and leaning out over the water.

"Dickie! Dickie! Do not dangle over the water! Get to the bottom of the boat! Hide! Hide!" Rose looked as if she might swoon.

"Dickie," I said, "turn around and sit down. Miles, you are doing fine. Keep rowing slowly and steadily."

Two dockhands were there to reach out and pull the skiff into the dock as soon as we were within arm's reach, when Miles—flustered by his mother's panicked tone—was having a hard time maneuvering the boat to the dock.

"Get the boys out of the boat!" Rose ordered and the dockhands quickly complied.

Rose dropped to her knees and gathered the boys to her in a loving embrace with tears streaming down her face.

"Rose?" I asked, climbing from the skiff onto the livery boat dock. "What is it? Has something happened?"

Rose stood, her tearful countenance hardening to a glare. She snapped her fingers above her head. "Mrs. Gruder!" she shrieked. Mrs. Gruder raced over and gathered up the boys. "Take them upstairs and start packing immediately. We're leaving on the next steamship. Go! Hurry!"

"Rose! What has happened? Is it Mother?"

"I can't believe you would put my boys in this sort of danger!"

"What sort of danger?"

Rose took out the newspaper tucked under her arm, unfolded it, and pointed at a headline which read, "The Sea Serpent Again"

"Sea serpents? All this hysteria is about sea serpents?"

"*Again*. The entire Pullman House is atwitter. I'm told there have been sightings not just this season but for the *past twenty years*."

I rolled my eyes. "Mysterious sightings, yes. But no one has ever been hurt or injured."

"I will not have my boys be the first. And to think that you wanted to teach them to swim here with monsters lurking about!"

"Rose. Just last week there was a story about a crow delivering a newspaper to Castle Francis. It's easy to see that the story was made up to sell papers. You can't believe everything you read!"

"You must leave this horrible place. Come with us now. Today! Leave your horrid suffragist clothing here. We will start afresh. New clothes. New accessories. New life."

"Rose," I said, stepping forward and taking her hand, "I can't just drop everything and leave. I have responsibilities here."

Rose pushed my hands away and stepped back. "Responsibilities!" she spat out. "You know nothing of responsibilities. And if I remember correctly, dropping everything and leaving your responsibility to our family is exactly what brought you here. Come with us now before it's too late."

She turned on her heels and dashed toward the Pullman House. "Running away. That's all you know how to do," she called back to me.

I felt rooted to the spot. I stood staring at the empty walk long after Rose disappeared inside. A feeling of sadness and dread sifted through me. My stomach churned uncomfortably. The world around me came to a standstill. Then the wind tugged at my skirt and pulled a few wispy curls free from my tight updo. I opened my mouth and gasped for air. Only then did I realize that I had been holding my breath. My limbs were heavy as I slowly moved toward Pullman House. I checked the steamer schedule that was posted on a chalkboard on the veranda. The next steamer from Grenell to Clayton was in thirty-five minutes. I paused and looked at life on the veranda. Guests drank tea and talked pleasantly with each other. On the lawn, a trio of young ladies was playing croquet. The day looked the same, but everything felt different.

I went inside and wrote a telegram to Lily saying only that the visit had not gone well and that Rose was leaving early. I asked if she could visit Mother and let her know that there were no sea monsters in the river and that I was very sad she had not come. I knew Lily would convey my sentiments accurately. I wasn't sure what stories Rose would weave.

After I sent the telegram, I asked for stationery and a fountain pen, found a quiet spot on the veranda, and wrote a long and detailed letter to

Lily about how frantic and sad I felt. After Lily's letter, I wrote a note to Mother to tell her how disappointed I was that she had not come to visit and hoped that she was well.

I watched the 10:55 steamer come and go but still saw no sign of the Rose and the boys.

I asked for yet more stationery, refilled the fountain pen, and continued writing letters. My note to Anne said only that Rose had left early, and the visit had not gone well.

Two more steamers arrived and departed, but my sister and nephews had not come down from their rooms. I continued writing. I wrote a spirited letter to Nora about recent events, then as an afterthought scribbled a note to Mr. Bartman. With Rose leaving early, I might have an opportunity to see him sooner than I had told him I'd be available—perhaps at the watermelon party on Thursday. The thought brought a brief smile to my lips. "There is always a silver lining," I whispered to myself.

By the time I had folded my note to Mr. Bartman, stuffed it into an envelope, and addressed it, I heard porters chatting as they rolled a trolley heaped with four steamer trunks and lots of hatboxes from the service stairs at the back of the hotel. I turned expectantly toward the main staircase.

The boys were the first down the stairs, and I rushed to say goodbye to them.

"I'm sorry, miss," Mrs. Gruder said. Her eyes were sympathetic. "Mrs. Tidwell was very explicit that I was to take the boys immediately to the dock and not *dillydally* on the veranda."

Not wishing to compromise Mrs. Gruder's position, I stepped aside so she could usher the boys down the veranda stairs, across the lawn, then to the pile of trunks waiting for the steamer.

I turned to see Rose descending the stairs. I met her at the door to the veranda. "Rose, won't you reconsider?" I asked.

"Me? You are the one who needs to reconsider. Tell me that you have decided to leave this place and come and live with Mother and me."

"Thank you for your kind offer. It's most generous. I need time to . . ."

"Time? You have had more than a decade to rectify your mistake," Rose said as she walked around me, across the veranda, and down the steps.

"My mistake?" I called after her, then followed her down the stairs.

She whirled and faced me when she heard my footsteps on the boardwalk behind her. "I should have known better to have returned to this place. This evil, evil place. It was the beginning of it all. Your wanton, willful ways and . . ." Rose paused. A look of distress displaced her disapproving scowl. "And Father's demise . . ." she whispered. She raised a gloved hand to her face and choked back a sob. "Your wanton ways killed Father. You do realize that, don't you?"

The whistle of the steamer *St. Lawrence* screamed as it approached the dock. Or did the scream come from me? Prince ran up and down the length of the dock barking. Jambo clung to his back. On the steamer above, a group of children laughed and pointed at the dog and the little monkey that rode on its back. I stood stupefied, unable to move as life whirled around me.

"Why do we have to leave?" I heard Miles asked Rose. "Auntie Marguerite promised to teach us to swim."

The disapproving scowl returned. Rose turned Miles away from me and toward the steamer. "Auntie Marguerite can not be trusted to keep her promises. Auntie Marguerite has always run away from her responsibilities and the truth." Rose gave Miles a little push toward the gangway. "Go. Go! Do not look back."

"She promised to loan me a book about pirates, but she didn't," Dickie grumbled.

"Mrs. Gruder, please take the boys aboard and no standing at the railing. Keep them in the salon." Rose paused then. I thought she would turn and talk to me. But she didn't. Instead, Rose paused to straighten her posture, gave each glove a tug, and adjusted her hat before she stepped on the gangway, boarded the steamer, and disappeared into the steamer's salon. She did not look back.

Rose's words echoed in my ears as I searched the salon windows hoping to catch a glimpse of her and the boys. *Run away. Responsibilities. Truth. Father's demise. Your wanton ways killed Father.* I searched the windows hoping to be able to wave goodbye to my nephews, but could not see them.

Eventually, the lines were cast off, the whistle blew, and the steamer chugged from the dock.

I stood at the edge of the dock watching until I could no longer see the steamer itself but only the coil of dark smoke it left in the sky.

"Miss Marguerite?" Nat was there at my elbow.

"Yes, Nat?"

"The clerk asked if I could retrieve the pen from you."

Only then did I notice that I was still clutching the pen in my hand. "Oh! Yes, of course! Thank him for me, will you?"

"Are you alright, Miss Marguerite? You look a bit dazed. May I walk you home?"

"I have my skiff. I can row."

"Your letters? At least let me take the letters to the post office for you."

"Yes. Thank you, Nat."

Nat walked me to the skiff livery, helped me into the skiff, and cast me off.

I started rowing with no destination in mind. I breathed in the silky river air and gave myself over to the rhythm of the oars. I rowed and rowed and rowed. I had no idea how long I had been rowing or what route had eventually taken me to a small cluster of islands that were only vaguely familiar. Eventually, I caught sight of an island that I knew and realized that I had rowed across the boundary and was in the queen's domain, surrounded by a delightful cluster of islands near the Ontario mainland known as the Navy Fleet Islands.

I turned the skiff south, crossed back over the border, spied Grand View Park, and began rowing toward the little enclave. Once at the livery, I let the dockhand help me secure the skiff and climbed onto the dock, and moved toward the Grand View Park Hotel. As if she knew I were coming, I saw Flossie watch my approach from the veranda. Suddenly, she flew down the steps, ran across the lawn, threw her arms around me, and wrapped me in a protective hug. Only then, did I allow myself to sob.

CHAPTER
eighteen

"Miss Hartranft! Miss Hartranft! Did you hear?"

Flossie and I turned to see Mable Worden and her two friends hurrying toward us as we walked on the wagon path through the Grenell farm.

"Mable, what is it?"

"Miss Griswold asked us to be her bridesmaids!" Mable's cheeks seemed extra pink this morning with the news.

"Mable, this is my friend, Miss Bixby. Flossie, may I introduce Miss Mable Worden who lives in the second cottage this side of the bridge to Pullman House. These are her friends, Jennie and Bessie."

"Pleasure to meet you, miss," the girls murmured in unison before continuing on with the news of the wedding.

"It's to be a simple wedding, to be sure, but Miss Griswold said our fresh young faces would enliven the proceedings," Mable said.

"We're to wear white dresses," Jennie added.

"We each have a white summer dress that will do," Bessie reported.

"We're thinking of going to Burdick's Millinery Shop in Fineview to see if we can buy wide satin ribbons for our sashes," Jennie said. "Miss Griswold said there is no need for tiaras and veils like in a traditional church wedding. They're to be married on the rock in front of their cottage overlooking the American channel. Isn't it romantic?"

"We're taking the steamer this afternoon over to Fineview. Would you like to come?" Mable asked.

"I think that's a lovely idea. Thank you for inviting us," Flossie said. "I've been wanting to meet the Choctaw Indian there with his fortune-telling crows. Shall I meet you at the Grenell Island Store dock?"

Agreeing to the time and place, the girls darted off down the sidewalk to spread their good news as I raised an eyebrow at Flossie. "Since when are you so interested in fashion?"

"Never!" Flossie said defiantly, meeting my eye. "The girls' enthusiasm is contagious. Besides, I've been wanting to meet that Choctaw Indian you told me about. What did you say were his fortunes for the boys?"

"That Miles will be the father of a great family," I said as we resumed our walk toward the store at a leisurely pace.

"And Dickie? His fortune was not so glowing?"

I shuddered visibly. "He said 'Many clouds here. Darkness in the heart of this one. The end will not be kind.'"

Flossie put a gloved hand over her mouth to suppress a laugh.

"It's not funny!" I told her. "Mrs. Gruder and I had to quickly usher the boys away to gloss over the horrid prediction."

This was the first time Flossie had made any reference to my sister or nephews in the three days since she had rowed me back to Grenell from Grand View Park.

Like a cyclone, Rose had whirled into my world, stirred things up, uprooted a piece of my heart, and left a gaping hole after her sudden departure. But with Flossie by my side, the last three days had been spent in quiet happiness. Flossie made sure I was up early, helping her collect specimens for her botanical project. In the evenings, as Flossie glued and labeled her specimens in the herbarium, I wrote letters. I can't remember when I have written so many letters. Writing both morning and night, I sent two letters a day to Lily, who responded to each one in kind. Normally, correspondence to Nora might go unanswered for a week or more before she would apologetically pen a reply that she had been too busy with social duties, childrearing, and household management to respond in a timely manner. But then again, my letters to Nora this past week had been perhaps more interesting than my usual drivel about class lectures and grading papers. Nora had lots of questions about Mr. Bartman, Mr. Quigley, and Herr Brittlinger. I reveled in our renewed friendship.

 I'd also written more matter-of-fact and less titillating notes to Friend Anne and Keiko about how Flossie and I had been spending our days. Both Flossie and I had written to other members from the 1881 Grenell Island Symposium. We had stayed in touch over the years.

 We lost the first of our seven sisters in 1885—only four years after our symposium. But then Susan Warner had been much older than the rest of us. Anna B. Warner, her younger sister by ten years, still lived on Constitution Island, where she has continued to write novels, children's hymns, and hold Sunday school classes for cadets at West Point across the river. We always referred to the younger Warner sister as Anna B. to distinguish her from Friend Anne. A writer at heart, Anna B. had been the most ardent correspondent through the years.

 Next was Sophie Mills who, when I met her in 1881, was working at a settlement house in New York City. She was now Mrs. Dixon having married nearly ten years ago. Like Nora, since her nuptials, her correspondence had become sporadic.

 Ruth Clements lived in Philadelphia and was the headmistress of the Friends Central School. Though we did not see her every week, we saw her often enough that lengthy correspondence was unnecessary. It was not unusual for Ruth to spend most of her summer here with us on Grenell. This summer, however, Ruth was spending the bulk of her time in Chicago visiting her friend Della Wentworth, who was at the Columbian Exposition with her class of deaf students, demonstrating the Bell method of speech and lip-reading for deaf and hard-of-hearing children.

 That left Dr. Elizabet DuPont—the only one of the ladies of the symposium with whom I have never corresponded. But then, I had never considered Elizabet to be my friend. Flossie had written to Elizabet earlier in the week, but, like Sophie, she had yet to respond.

 On our morning and afternoon walks to and from the post office, Flossie attracted followers like the pied piper. Though only a guest, Flossie had been embraced by the islanders as one of our island family as she spent a month or more on the island each year.

 This morning, as we approached the post office, a woman stuck her head out the second floor living quarters of the Grenell Island store and bellowed, "George! Do you know where Charlie is?"

George grunted as he hefted a crate onto a handcart. He took a red handkerchief from his pocket and wiped his brow before he looked up and said, "How the blazes would I know where Charlie is, woman? Can't you see I'm working? Send Grace to find him."

"What? Grace is only six. Our five-year-old is already missing! Do you want Grace to go missing as well?"

George sighed, and picked up another crate, and put it on top of the first one. "Can't you see I'm busy? I have a delivery to make to Murray. You'll have to deal with the kids."

Flossie and I did not wait for the woman's response but hurried around to the front of the store.

"Who was that?" Flossie asked.

"George Grenell's wife, I suppose," I replied.

We ran into Mr. Burditt coming out of the store. Flossie engaged him in a lively discussion about the upcoming American Canoe Association annual meet and regatta. Mr. Burditt was the president of the Susquehanna Club and had been on the island since 1878. When the Carthage Band decided to sell their clubhouse, which sits on the same peninsula as the three-story Susquehanna Club, Mr. Burditt purchased it, renaming it Grove Cottage. Now instead of his allotted few weeks a year, he spends the entire season on Grenell, overseeing the comings and goings of the twenty-some Susquehanna Club members as they take turns staying at the club. Fascinated by Flossie's tales about the Mohawk canoe, he promised to bring a group of Grenellians to watch the canoe races next month in his steam yacht, *Otsego*.

I slipped away during their discourse to post our mail in time to be processed and dispatched on the morning mailboat. By the time I returned, Mr. Burditt had moved on, so Flossie and I sat on a bench on the dock. Soon Lois Kerr arrived to wait for this morning's mail delivery. We chatted as we waited. From Lois, we learned that Mr. Carlisle's doctor had given him permission to travel to the island. His boatman, John Gardiner, was busily getting the cottage in order. The Carlisles would arrive from Newark early next month.

Lois Kerr regaled us with a colorful account of yesterday's fishing adventure. She'd caught a nice stringer of perch, but, more importantly, she had witnessed a muskellunge catch. "We were rowing back when a boat near us raised a white flag, which signifies a muskellunge catch. We were quickly surrounded by skiffs with curious, enquiring visitors. Everyone wanted a peek at the monster. It was a beauty! A marvel to see. It weighed thirty pounds and measured four feet and three-and-one-half inches."

"How exciting," Flossie said, her silver and gold curls shimmering in the sunlight around her head. Flossie nodded toward a skiff not far from shore and asked Lois, "Who is that rowing Mary Mason?"

Lois told us it was Seward Prosser and confided she thought there might be a marriage proposal before next spring.

The mailboat arrived and tied up. No one came from the store to meet the mailboat, so the skipper brought the mailbag inside, the rest of us trailing behind him. Once inside the door, I heard the heated voices of Uncle Sam's two nephews rising from the backroom. The cousins were arguing yet again. Herb peeked his head around the doorjamb and saw the mailboat skipper and the crowd of islanders who followed him. Herb waved George away and growled, "Off with you now! I have work to attend to." George murmured some expletive and stormed out the back, slamming the door behind him as he exited. Embarrassed, Herb apologized to the mailboat skipper, raised a hand to the stunned islanders, and promised to have the mail sorted as soon as possible.

"There is another delivery—a crate for Mrs. Grenell still in the boat," the skipper said and Herb called for Nat to retrieve the crate.

As we waited for the mail to be sorted, Emily Griswold arrived and was delighted to add Flossie to the guest list in Friend Anne's stead. After this, we gathered our mail. But before we had a chance to sort through it, Nat called for us to come over and see what had been delivered for Mrs. Grenell.

Loaded atop a cart was a pen filled with a dozen or more tiny chicks, peep, peep, peeping away.

"They're adorable," Flossie said, sticking her finger into the crate and brushing the fluffy little birds. "I want to hold one."

We followed Nat and his precious cargo down the boardwalk toward the Grenell cottage.

Unable to contain herself, Flossie skipped ahead, reaching the Grenell porch long before Nat and I arrived. "Aunt Lucy! Aunt Lucy," she called out. "Come see what someone sent you. Hurry. Hurry!"

"Here now," Uncle Sam said, peering over the top of his newspaper, "what's all the fuss about?"

Aunt Lucy came out the door drying her hands on her apron. She gasped. "My stars! Who sent me such a wonderful present? Chicks! And such an odd color. I wonder what breed they are."

"There's an envelope tied to the top of the crate, ma'am," Nat said, taking a pocketknife from his pocket and cutting it free.

Aunt Lucy pulled her spectacles from her apron pocket, and instead of putting them on, she held them to her eyes and quickly read the note. "These little beauties are from my son, Myron. He's a Columbian Guard at the World's Fair. Quite an honor, you know," she explained to Flossie. "They are Columbian Wyandotte chickens."

Flossie dropped to her knees so she could be eye-to-eye with the chicks. "What a long name for such tiny creatures."

"These chickens were bred to be showcased at the fair,'" Aunt Lucy announced after reading Myron's note. "Believe it or not, they were hatched under electric lights. Can you imagine that? Myron says they'll be great beauties someday and great layers. He says that each hen will produce about two hundred eggs a year! Think of it! Two hundred eggs a year! But he also says that I should be careful as Columbian Wyandottes tend to be a bit broody."

Nat had the crate open, and Flossie had picked up one of the peeping balls of fluff and was holding it to her face. The little chicks weren't yellow but were black-and-gray with huge orange feet. "So soft! Broody? What does that mean?" Flossie asked.

"A broody hen is intent on hatching out eggs. She'll hide hers, steal eggs from other hens, and sometimes gets feisty with you when you're a'gatherin'. But don't you worry your pretty little head, Miss Flossie. I've dealt with more than one broody hen in my day. I'm sure it's nothing I can't handle. Oh my! Look at them. That son of mine is a treasure!" Aunt Lucy blinked away a tear or two, momentarily overwhelmed with emotion, then snapped back into no-nonsense reality. "Nat! I need a bucket of water. Poor little things have traveled hundreds of miles. We need to get them settled. Thanks for escorting them to their new home. I've got my hands full."

Lucy disappeared inside the cottage as we oohed and aahed over the chicks until Nat returned with the bucket of water and more news. Mrs. Sharples—or Friend Helen, Friend Anne's childhood classmate—had just checked into the Pullman Hotel and was looking forward to seeing us as soon as possible.

I looked at Nat and blinked. Nat had only walked to the end of the dock in front of the Grenell cottage and hauled a bucket full of river water back. How had he heard the news in that short time? I shook my head, amazed. Nat—like his father, Hunk, before him—always had his ear to the ground and knew the news before anyone else. "Tell her we'll be there in time for afternoon tea."

We were about to leave the porch when the woman who had been hanging out the store window approached with two children in tow.

"Well, lookie here. Who's comin' to visit us now?" Sam said, peering over the top of his paper.

The little boy broke free from his mother, rushed up the stairs, moved Sam's newspaper aside, climbed onto Sam's lap, and proclaimed, "It's me! Charlie Grenell."

"And who's that cutie with the blonde braids?" Sam asked, pointing to the girl who hid her face in her mother's skirt.

"You know who that is!" Charlie said, shaking his finger at Sam. "That's my big sister, Grace."

"Uncle Sam, I was hoping the children might stay here for a few hours. Lots of coming and going at the store, and the two of them are underfoot. Not having children of his own, Herb is . . . well, I think it's better if these two stay here for a while."

Mrs. Grenell was at the door now. "Certainly, Anna, I can put Charlie to good use. Got a mess of green beans that need to be snapped."

"Thanks! You're a lifesaver!" Anna said, turned on her heels, and rushed off.

"Grace, would you like to practice sewing on buttons?" Aunt Lucy asked.

Grace nodded but didn't say anything as she gazed at her toes.

"You go inside and get the sewing basket. You know where it is," Lucy said.

Biting her lip, Grace looked up at Lucy before she edged past her, opened the screendoor, and slipped inside the cottage.

"Sakes alive," Lucy whispered to Flossie and me. "The girl is six-years-old and hasn't learned to thread a needle yet. I've been teaching her hand-stitching. We'll start with buttons and move onto a simple running stitch. There's a girl," Lucy said as Grace appeared at the door with the sewing basket in hand.

"Hopefully, this winter Grace can start on her first sampler," Lucy said as Grace settled into a big wicker chair.

Sam sat back in his chair and raised his newspaper again.

"Sam! What are you doing? Put that paper down."

"What?" Sam asked, looking very perplexed as he peered over the top of the paper.

"Get the bucket of green beans and the tin bowls," Lucy told him.

Sam flinched. It was as if he'd been smacked with the newspaper right between the eyes. He dropped the newspaper to his lap and sputtered, "You expect me to snap beans? Why that's . . ."

"My lord Sam if you say 'woman's work' I'm going to fetch a rolling pin, and you'll never utter that phrase again. Besides, I'm not asking you to snap the beans, just supervise the snappin' of the beans. If I recall, supervisin' is your strong suit. I got these chicks to settle in. Make yourself useful!" With that, Lucy retreated into the cottage, letting the screen door slam shut behind her.

Sam stood, took Charlie by the hand, and said, "Come on, youngin', let's go fetch that bucket of green beans." From his hangdog look, it was clear that Sam would rather be reading the newspaper.

We said our goodbyes and hurried back to Castle Rock. It wasn't until we returned to the cottage that I found a letter in our stack of mail from Mr. Bartman. The Clarks were going on an outing to Carleton Island tomorrow morning, and he asked if I were able to come.

A smile spread over my face. *Mr. Charles Bartman is my silver lining,* I thought to myself. The bright spot of hope after Rose's departure.

I read the note to Flossie. A week ago, my dear friend would have probably teased me for wanting to spend time with "this Mr. Bartman" but I think she sensed that my time with Rose had left me feeling vulnerable and confused, especially when it came to finding a suitable match. Instead, she said nothing but gave me a tender hug.

CHAPTER
nineteen

Friend Helen had arrived at Pullman House yesterday, and we had called on her for tea. She had news. "I'm with child again," she said, blushing. Helen and Philip already had a daughter and two sons. "My doctor advises against traveling back and forth between West Chester and here. I'll have to trust Mr. Caswell and Arnie to carry out the construction without me."

After sharing her good news, Helen had taken Flossie and me to the building site and met with Arnie to assess progress on Bungalow. On the way back to our cottage, I told Helen about the Princeton outing and my budding acquaintance with the Clarks of Chicago and their guest for the season, Charles Bartman. Friend Helen had been more than happy to loan me a lovely dress and hat for today's outing.

Wearing a frilly white day dress with a small-brimmed hat fitted out with colorful silk flowers, I reached for Charles's hand as he helped me aboard the *Mamie C.* for a day trip to Carleton Island. The soft morning breeze caressed my face as I stood in the bow as the *Mamie C.* steamed upriver past Clayton. Mr. Bartman stood to my left. Mr. Clark and his three sons stood to my right. I raised my chin, feeling like an intrepid adventurer out to explore a new world. "I've never been this far upriver," I said as we passed the cut between Wolfe and Grindstone Islands. Have you, Mr. Clark?"

I gripped the railing as the engineer slowed the little steamer and turned the *Mamie C.* into the oncoming wake of a larger steamer that had just passed us en route downriver. *Mamie C.* was lacquered white with gleaming brass rails and portholes which twinkled in the early morning sun.

"Several times, Miss Hartranft," Mr. Clark said. He adopted a wide stance and stood confidently with his hands behind his back as the *Mamie C.* dipped into and then rose up and over the wake.

The three Clark boys gripped the railing and laughed. The youngest, Edwin, threw his arm in the air and let out a *waaa-hooo*, as if he were riding a bucking bronco at a rodeo.

I turned back to Mr. Clark. "Uncle Sam—I mean Mr. Grenell—told me that Carleton Island once belonged to the French, then the British, but now, of course, is an American island."

"Indeed, it's a very historic island. No one knows exactly when the first fort was built here. Charlevoix, the French Jesuit priest and historian, made mention of the beautiful harbors at the head of Carleton Island in 1721 and reported there were soldiers placed there to guard the mouth of the St. Lawrence. Some say the French called it Fort Frontenac."

"Is that the way you heard it, Father? I thought the British built the fort in 1778," the youngest of the three, Edwin, said. "I read it was built in an octagon shape and named Fort Haldimand for British General Frederick Haldimand."

"I read the fort was never really completed," added Mancel, the oldest of the three boys.

"That's because the War of Independence came to an end, and the island fell into American hands," Edwin explained.

"That didn't officially happen until after the War of 1812," Mancel countered.

"I'm encouraged that you boys have been reading up on the fort," Mr. Clark said.

"I hope to see the well. It's drilled into the Trenton Limestone and goes very deep. Some say there is treasure at the bottom left there by the retreating British army," Edwin said.

"That's a pile of horse hooey! There are rumors of treasure everywhere in the Thousand Islands. If I had a nickel for every story about treasure, I'd be as rich as Father," Mancel replied.

"Mancel! Do watch your language, especially in the presence of a lady."

The debate over the islands, its history, and the prospect of treasure continued between the three boys as Mr. Bartman and I stared out at the water and listened to their banter. In our notes to each other this past week, we had both written that we were eager to continue our discussion of Aristotle versus Plato, but in the hour and a half that it took for us to reach Carleton Island, the river occupied my interest. As the *Mamie C.* chugged along, my eyes caught sight of so many birds: a pair of kingfishers, an osprey, and a heron wading in the shallows. Here and there, I saw cottages dotting the shoreline—some modest and some grand—but overall, I noted that the eleven miles between Clayton and the head of Carleton Island were not as populated as the section of the river between Clayton and Alexandria Bay. As we rounded the head of Carleton Island, I saw enormous chimneys, void of any sort of structure, rising from a grand precipice, relicts of an age gone by.

"So much history!" I said, marveling at the chimneys as we passed them.

"And just a scratch in time compared to the Greeks and Romans. Wait until you see the Greek and Roman ruins in Europe," Charles said. These were the first complete sentences he'd uttered since we had left Grenell.

"Have you traveled to the ancient world?" I asked.

"Yes! Athens, Crete, Olympus, Naples and Rome."

A shiver of excitement traveled through me.

Charles looked down as if examining his feet, then finally said in a voice so low I could barely hear it above the wind, "I would love to share my travel journal with you sometime. That is—if you have any interest in looking at it."

"Of course. I would be honored," I said.

A meek smile turned up the corners of his tiny mouth.

The *Mamie C.* slowed and rounded the head of the island. The ruins of the fort stood high above a quiet bay.

"Imagine," Edwin said, "this bay was once filled with His Majesty's tall ships—square-riggers—with the guns of the fort protecting them from the bluff above."

"It is a wonderful natural harbor, isn't it?" Mancel noted. "And there is another matching harbor on the other side of this strip of land. Looking at the map, the head of Carleton looks like a mushroom stuck on the top of the island. Two natural protected harbors behind the mushroom cap and narrow peninsula, or stem, connected the cap to the main island."

"Our host, Mr. Wyckoff owns the 'mushroom cap', as you put it, and is building a grand villa there. He owns a bit more of the island as well," Mr. Clark informed us.

As we cruised around the head of the island, I gazed in wonder at the grand summer home under construction. The tower behind it had already been completed.

"Is that Mr. Wyckoff's tower?" Edwin asked. "Why, it must be a hundred feet tall or more."

Mr. Clark clapped a hand on his son's back. "Good eye, young Edwin. The tower is one hundred and eleven feet tall, to be precise. It houses two water tanks that will provide ample water for the villa once it's completed. Mr. Wyckoff plans to call it Carleton Villa and hopes it will be ready for use before 1895."

"Would that be William Wyckoff of Remington typewriter fame?" Mr. Bartman asked tentatively.

"Quite right. As you can see," Mr. Clark said, gesturing toward the mansion under construction, "the typewriter business is quite lucrative."

By now Mrs. Clark had joined us on the bow. "I apologize for my absence. I was using our travel time to catch up on some much-needed correspondence," she said. "Oh my! The villa is coming along quite nicely. I hope the Wyckoffs will delight us with a tour." Mrs. Clark turned to me and put a white-gloved hand on my arm. "You will love Mrs. Wyckoff. Francis is a true river woman, an avid angler. The Wyckoffs came to the island maybe five or six years ago. Mr. Wyckoff was in poor health. They stayed at one of the clubs; there are several clubs at the foot of the island."

"Four, I think," Mr. Clark interjected. "Let's see, there is the Utica Club and Ithaca Club."

Charles and I shared a glance and smiled, as they were both names of cities in ancient Greece.

"And the White Hat Fishing Club and the Carleton Club," Mr. Clark continued.

"Right. I'm not sure where he stayed, but within a few weeks, he had returned to robust health," Mrs. Clark said.

"Hale and hearty! It's the salubrious air, you know," Mr. Clark said.

I smiled. Many feel the river has healing aspects for both mind and spirit. A notion I agreed with whole-heartedly.

"Well, after his remarkable return to health," Mrs. Clark continued, "he decided to build a permanent home here."

"His new project is not a summer home, mind you, but a permanent home," Mr. Clark added.

"He'll leave during the bitterest part of winter, of course," Mrs. Clark assured me. "But they plan to be here nine months out of the year."

"He will run his business from here?" Charles asked, seeming more comfortable talking now that Mrs. Clark was present.

Mr. Clark nodded. "Yes. He will have his stenographer live here full time, of course, for his correspondence."

"Now that I think of it, didn't Mr. Wyckoff start his career as a stenographer?" Mrs. Clark asked.

Mr. Clark nodded. "Indeed he did. The villa is only three miles from Cape Vincent, so he will be able to get daily posts. And if need be, he can catch a sleeper car in Cape Vincent in the afternoon and be in New York City to conduct business by the next morning," Mr. Clark said, placing his hands behind his back again as the *Mamie C.* slowly approached the dock.

"What a marvelous age we live in," I said.

Once docked, Mr. Wyckoff—tall, barrel-chested, and sporting a prodigious white walrus mustache—approached our small group. Introductions were made.

"This is Mr. Bartman, a neighbor of ours from Chicago. He hoped to escape the madness of the fair and find a quiet spot to work on a book about Greek and Roman art," Mr. Clark said to Mr. Wyckoff.

"Oh! Do say! Wait until I show you the Corinthian columns we have in Carleton Villa. Mind you, it is still under construction, only a shell of what it will one day be."

"But a beautiful shell," Mrs. Clark said as she looked up at the villa. "What sort of marble is that?"

Mr. Wyckoff explained that the lower floor was constructed of

Gouverneur marble, a grayish-bluish marble that seemed to glow white in the late-morning light.

"The quarry is only fifty or so miles from here as the crow flies," Mr. Wyckoff explained to the younger Clarks, pointing toward the New York mainland.

As we walked toward the villa, I immediately noticed it was much, much larger than Bungalow. Turrets, dormers, massive chimneys, and decorative finials protruded from the steep roof. Corbeled turrets clung to each corner of the villa.

We climbed the broad marble steps that lead to a wide veranda and passed through a carved, basket-handle, marble archway that served as an entrance. "This will be the grand hall," Mr. Wyckoff said, indicating the huge room before us with a wave of his arm.

Grand indeed! The room was two stories high and long enough that two Castle Rocks—my modest cottage—would have fit inside the grand hall.

Charles bent down and whispered in my ear, "Look at the coupled Corinthian columns on the second-story gallery." My eyes followed his finger as it swept around the gallery overlooking the grand hall. "It isn't just a grand home; it's a work of art," he whispered in my ear.

Charles's breath on my ear sent a small electric current of delight through my being. Recovering, I turned my attention to Mr. Wyckoff, who was explaining that a great cellar extended underneath the entire structure and housed a gas room, a laundry, a huge refrigerator that could store more than a ton of ice, a furnace room, an iron shop, a carpenter shop, a coal room, a canned goods storeroom, and a vegetable cellar.

Mr. Clark let out a long low whistle of admiration.

"We plan to live here all year, you know," Mr. Wyckoff said. "Come! Come! Let me show you the library."

A red brick fireplace stood in the center of the wall opposite the entrance to the library. A huge, expansive window covered the entire wall to my left so that soft north country light flooded the library and afforded spectacular views of the river. What a wonderful nook to enjoy a book. The mahogany crown molding gleamed in the light. I imagined how the library would look decked out with shelves and books. We stood at the window, and Mr. Clark pointed out Tibbett's Point, Wolfe Island, and Lake Ontario the horizon.

Our tour was limited to only these two rooms. Mr. Wyckoff said that the rest of the first floor and the upper floors were cluttered with too much workmen's debris for the ladies to safely traverse. The grand hall alone was enough to give me a general impression of how magnificent the home would be.

"But you must be hungry! Come! Come! The grand barbecue and clam bake awaits. Harry Savage, the esteemed caterer of the Utica Club, has prepared an ox. It's been roasting for the last twenty-four hours. Smells heavenly. He's also prepared a clam bake: clams, bluefish, lobster, and trout. Plenty of side dishes as well."

I was overwhelmed by the number of people at the barbecue. Every table seemed filled. Mrs. Wyckoff bade us to follow her to a table reserved just for the Wyckoffs and their guests. Instead of waiting in a buffet line like the others, waiters brought to our table platters piled high with slices of meat, clams, fish, and lobster. The variety of side dishes was overwhelming: minced cabbage, creamed tomatoes, sweet potato croquettes, mayonnaise of beets, stewed celery, and creamed onions. The food was delicious. I was careful to eat slowly and in tiny portions so I wouldn't strain my corset.

Nearly two thousand people had accepted the invitation by Messrs. Folger and Hance to Carleton Island. Most were ferried to the island from Cape Vincent aboard a steamer. After they toured the property and feasted on Mr. Savage's outstanding fare, the group gathered near a large map for the auction. From what I overheard, the owners of the property were hoping to sell upward of a thousand lots today. The Clarks had been invited to explore the possibility of investing in a hotel that was proposed for the project.

Not interested in watching the auction, the three Clark boys, Charles, and I opted to explore the fort ruins instead. Mr. Clark instructed Charles to have the group back to the dock by five.

The flat-top bluff stands sixty feet above the surface of the river. A path wove through the high grass making for easy walking. A half dozen or so towering chimneys stood in a circle. "They look like giants gathered around a campfire," I said, my head tilted back staring at their crumbling tops.

"How poetic," Charles said, and his mouth turned up into a small tight-lipped smile.

I smiled, too, remembering my failed attempt at being a poetess years ago. Perhaps I would share that story with Charles sometime. That is, if we continued to renew our acquaintance.

The boys ran willy-nilly around the ruins as Charles and I walked. The wind off Lake Ontario was strong as it ruffled through the grass and whistled through the chimneys, giving the site a haunting air. Occasionally I put my hand to the hat on my head, even though I had secured it with not one but two hatpins. I dared not lose it as it did not belong to me.

We never did find the well that was reportedly full of treasure. After thoroughly exploring the site and gazing out at the views of both river and lake, Charles checked his pocketwatch, clicked the cover shut, whistled, then motioned for the boys. They bounded toward us like long-legged puppies content at first to follow us as we walked back toward the dock, but they soon found our gait too plodding and galloped ahead. By the time we reached the dock, my ears pricked at the sound of angry voices. A group of vexed men stood around Mr. Wyckoff and Mr. Clark, venting their concerns.

"They are even talking about changing the name of the island from Carleton to Carrolton," a man with a massive beard said.

"Who?" Mr. Wyckoff asked.

"The blasted papists!" a small, animated man with a trim imperial beard replied.

"What's a papist?" Edwin whispered to his mother who had retreated with Mrs. Wyckoff away from the throng of men towards the boys, Charles, and me.

"It's what some people—not us—call Catholics," Mrs. Clark whispered in an authoritative, matter-of-fact tone.

"Change the name? Whatever for?" a tall gentleman asked.

"I don't know. Some blasted saint or something," the bearded man spat out.

"I believe Charles Carroll of Carrollton was the sole Catholic signer of the Declaration of Independence," Mr. Wyckoff replied.

"Be that as it may . . ." the small man blustered, "our fair island was overrun by Catholics last week. Must have been a hundred or more. Brought over on the steamer *Maud*. Claimed they were looking for a place to found a Catholic Chautauqua or some such nonsense. According to yesterday's paper, it's rumored they took a year's option on Carleton Island."

"No wonder there was such poor participation in the auction," Mr. Wyckoff mused.

"I tried to keep it out of the papers," the small man explained, gesticulating wildly.

"But from what I hear," Mr. Clark interjected, "it's not a chautauqua exactly—like the Methodists organized—but more of a summer school. Talk is they expect to spend nearly five hundred thousand dollars to fund a Catholic institution here on Carleton. The sessions will be held in July and August. They are inviting Catholic businessmen to take stock in the enterprise. It could mean a boon for the area."

The small man whirled and fastened an angry gaze on Mr. Clark. "Are you mad! A boon? It will send a flood of papists to the area."

The tall man nodded, stroking his beard thoughtfully. "It will draw Catholics from all over the United States. French Canada as well," he murmured.

"Every diocese in the United States is asked to support this enterprise," came a voice from somewhere.

"I heard the pope himself is behind the project," another man offered.

"Of course he is! Damn papists don't do anything without the pope's stamp of approval," the small man complained.

Now more voices joined in, everyone talking at once. Above the din, I heard, "Once they get a toehold in our islands, there'll be no stopping them."

"You know they call the Freemasons a satanic cult," another angry voice called out.

"Papist Irish and Italians are flooding our borders. We can't keep them out of the country but we can keep them out of here," the small man promised.

At this, Mrs. Clark turned to Mrs. Wyckoff and put a hand on her arm. "Perhaps we should wait on the *Mamie C.* Thank you for a lovely afternoon, Frances. We must be leaving. We hope to get Miss Hartranft back to Grenell Island before dark. Please thank your husband for a lovely barbecue and tour of the villa."

As we boarded the *Mamie C.*, Mrs. Clark turned to me with concern creasing her face. "I'm sorry for all that unpleasantness. I'm not sure how your parents feel about Catholics, but I was raised a Quaker and we believe in accepting all religions."

For a brief moment, I considered sharing with Mrs. Clark that I was indeed Catholic but thought better of it, and only nodded politely in acceptance of her apology.

CHAPTER
twenty

𝒥 don't know what I expected, but when I realized that the debonair man in the pearl-gray morning suit and black top hat was the groom and not some younger relative, my eyes widened in surprise. He was rakishly handsome.

I quickly reined in my surprise, regained a neutral countenance, and blushed slightly as I glanced around at the small group of wedding guests, hoping no one had noted my reaction. He was much younger than I had expected. I had envisioned a man perhaps closer to Herr Brittlinger's age.

Surrounded by a small cluster of guests, Emily Griswold and Albert Gabriel were married shortly after sunrise in a simple ceremony on the rock overlooking the American channel. Mable, Bessie, and Jennie wore white summer dresses full of lace and frills. Each had a different colored satin sash. After the ceremony, the girls excitedly shared the meanings behind their color choices. Mable's sash was white, which meant "chose right." Bessie's was blue, which she explained meant "love will be true." Jennie wore pink and blushed a matching shade when she told me it stood for "of you he'll always think."

Emily looked radiant in her wedding gown. Ever since the wedding of Queen Victoria in 1840, white had been the traditional color of wedding dresses and bouquets. Beneath the fitted bodice of Emily's gown, a full skirt made of organdy and lace billowed out. A long gauze veil was attached to a tiara of orange blossoms, infusing the early morning breeze with a lush, sweet scent.

When I was introduced to Prof. Gabriel after the ceremony, I was amazed to discover he was even more good-looking face-to-face than he had appeared from afar. I looked up into his pale blue eyes and admired his long, aquiline nose and his impeccably trimmed Van Dyke beard. *"Enchanté de vous rencontrer,"* I said when we were introduced.

His eyes twinkled. "Ah," he said, then smiled, taking my hand in his, and kissing my gloved knuckles. His eyes held mine as he gazed at me from beneath dramatic eyebrows. I couldn't help but note the periwinkle flecks in his eyes. He was certainly charming. Then, in a burst of flawless French, he told me that he was enchanted to meet me as he had heard much about the beautiful Miss Hartranft who had a gift for languages.

As I offered my congratulations to him in halting French, I inwardly admonished myself for not practicing my French before today's ceremony. My accent seemed so feeble by comparison and I was struggling to find the right words. I reminded myself that Prof. Gabriel was "the real McCoy"—a well-traveled, well-educated French man. Of course, his French would be flawless.

Throughout the wedding breakfast, I couldn't help stealing glances at the groom. Prof. Gabriel had to be at least a decade younger than Emily. And while Emily looked ravishing today, together the two looked so . . . so . . . *so what*? What adjective was I searching for? I felt uneasy as I tried to put my finger on what made me feel so troubled about this match. I felt my cheeks redden at my line of thinking. Who was I to be critical of Miss Emily? After all, hadn't I entertained thoughts of . . . well, a possible match with Charles Bartman who was no doubt younger than I? Must a woman always marry a man her senior? Why couldn't two people with a passion for the same sensibilities not spend their lives together even if the woman were slightly older? Or even a decade older?

Shortly after the plates were cleared from the sumptuous breakfast, the cake was served, and the bridal couple disappeared to change for their wedding trip. The cake was a spiced fruitcake slathered with white icing, which was decorated with ornate scrolled designs and topped, of course, with orange blossoms. After cake and tea, the wedding couple appeared in their traveling suits, waved goodbye to their guests and were whisked away in Captain El's large sailboat, *Cora*.

The destination was a secret but before she left, Emily had taken me aside and told me she would have loved to have honeymooned on Grenell but didn't want to displace Delia. "My marriage has been hard for my sister to accept. Promise me you will look in on her while I am away." Emily shared that they would only be away from the island for a few weeks so I was certain they were not going abroad.

Flossie and I stopped to praise Delia for the elegant wedding breakfast, perfect in every way. Delia asked if we would do her a favor and take a basket of leftover food to the Pratts. We were more than happy to oblige.

We'd learned last week that Alice, Edith, and Olivia had been invited. Alice had declined the invitation, feeling her presence as a new widow at a wedding was not suitable, but had urged the girls to attend. Olivia was not keen on the idea from the start, but once she found out that Mable and her friends would be flower girls, she decided to remain at home with her mother. Alice wouldn't permit Edith to attend without her sister. Alice confided that Edith was heartbroken and had spent an entire afternoon crying.

"So what did you think of Emily's angel?" Flossie asked after we left La Roche with a basket full of food. "That's how she described him to you, did she not?"

"He seems quite charming," I said, biting my lip.

"A little too charming, don't you think?" Flossie asked, looking at me with raised eyebrows.

"What do you mean?" I asked.

Flossie sighed deeply and shook her head as if to clear it. "I don't know. I've never trusted outrageously handsome men, especially if they appear to know how good-looking they are. Good looks can cripple other aspects of their personality. An overtly handsome man sometimes depends on his good looks to get him through life . . . like a crutch."

"Hmmm," I said, pondering Flossie's hypothesis. "Is it the same for women, do you think? Can beauty cripple a woman?"

"Only if the woman knows she's breathtakingly beautiful. Don't worry! You don't fall into that category."

I stopped on the path and waited for Flossie to turn and look at me.

"What do you mean by that?"

"I've known you since you were sixteen. You're one of the rare ones. You have no idea how beautiful you are nor how men stare at you when you walk by. . . even at your advanced age."

"Advanced age? Now you're starting to sound like . . . R—," I cut short. I had not mentioned Rose's name since her departure.

"Rose? Really? Well, Rose and I are the same age, and we are both older than you. But that's where any similarities end, I hope! Come now," she said, linking arms with me, "let's not ruin a perfectly beautiful day by talking or even thinking about Rose."

We had a lovely visit with Alice. Edith eventually came out onto the porch, shedding her sulkiness to ask questions about the wedding gown. "We could hear the violins from here," she said. Olivia, however, remained very sullen and quiet. A question about *The Iliad* eventually coaxed her into the conversation.

Bored with our conversation on *The Iliad*, Edith changed the subject. "Who arrived at Castle Rock this morning?"

"This morning? No new arrivals today. Anne and Dr. Okami aren't arriving until tomorrow afternoon," I said.

"Well, looks like there is a whole group of people arriving, or they're already here. There are piles and piles of luggage just off the dock. I've seen Nat rowing over with steamer trunk after steamer trunk," Edith reported.

"Perhaps Anne sent her luggage ahead," Flossie proposed.

"There were lots and lots of hatboxes. I've never seen so many hatboxes in Nat's skiff at one time," Edith said.

Flossie and I shared a look. Neither Anne nor Keiko owned more than a handful of hats between them.

We stood then, said our goodbyes, and headed back to Castle Rock eager to investigate our recent deliveries.

"May I come too?" Edith asked.

"Of course," Flossie said.

"Would you like to come, Olivia?" I offered but she declined, saying she hoped to finish reading *The Iliad* today.

Even though Edith had warned us what we would find, I was still stunned to see the pile of trunks, crates, and hat boxes when we rounded

Sentry Rock. Where did they come from? Who were they for? And how would we fit those trunks and boxes in our tiny cottage?

Flossie immediately went to the luggage tags reading one after the other. "They are all from West Chester from Mrs. Sharples," she reported.

"Ahoy!" Nat called out. I looked up to see Nat rowing this way with yet another skiff's load of things.

"My stars, Nat! There's more?"

"I brought the tents out of storage from Hunk's barn. Hope you don't mind, but I know you don't have room to store all these things in the cottage."

"That was smart thinking!" Flossie said.

"Oh, and I brought the morning mail. There's a letter from Mrs. Sharples. Perhaps it explains about the delivery," Nat said, handing over a stack of mail after he had secured the skiff to the dock.

Flossie, Edith, and Nat undertook the task of assembling the tent while I opened the letter. As I read through it, tears filled my eyes. *Dearest Marguerite. . . the letter started. Rubbing elbows with the moneyed set this summer means you need an expanded wardrobe, As I'm with child and won't be socializing this summer, I'm happy to lend you my wardrobe which I'm quickly outgrowing. As I can't be at the river this season, I'm most interested in the day-to-day events on and around Grenell. Please keep me posted.*

I was so happy that young Edith was here to help us unpack my borrowed wardrobe. Edith knew what everything was and what it was for. There were costumes for a wide range of activities: wheeling, tennis, croquet, bathing. There were dresses for informal parties and gowns for galas. Edith disappeared for a while but returned with her stack of *Harper's Bazar* magazines. Nat left and returned with two stepladders and a pole to run between them. We hung the dresses on the pole, then covered them with a spare bedsheet to keep dust and spiders from them.

My new wardrobe arrived just in time, because later in the afternoon mail was an invitation from the Sawyer girls to a polka dot party on July 5th.

"A polka dot party? What in heaven's name is that?" Flossie asked.

"Oh, they're quite popular this season. The invitations usually arrive on polka-dotted paper," Edith said.

I held up the invitation to verify that this was true.

Edith took the invitation and examined it closely before she continued. "There'll be polka dots everywhere. The decorations, dance cards, and programs will be done up in the polka-dotted style. Everyone is requested to wear something with polka dots, but for those who don't have polka-dotted attired, a polka dot ribbon or badge will probably be supplied to them at the door and pinned to their lapel."

Flossie and I shared a look.

"Am I given to understand that the whole reason for the party is the celebration of . . . polka dots?" an incredulous Flossie asked.

"I suppose. Let me see," Edith said, taking a peek under the sheet protecting my gowns. "Mrs. Sharples is evidently up-to-date on the latest trends." Edith held up a lovely two-piece day dress made of soft ivory silk and covered with small polka dots stitched with metallic gold thread that twinkled and winked in the afternoon sun. The bodice was fitted and boned, trimmed with glass buttons and ivory velvet rosettes. "Wait! I think there was a hat to match this." Edith rummaged through several hatboxes before she found a small hat with a curved brim and upturned back edge, covered with the same ivory silk and gold metallic polka-dots, and festooned with an ostrich plume.

"What? No, matching gloves and parasol?" Flossie chided.

"Let me check," Edith said, "It's quite possible there might be matching gloves and perhaps a parasol. Wouldn't that be fantastic?"

Flossie rolled her eyes, let out an exasperated huff, and left the tent.

CHAPTER
twenty-one

The very next morning, on our way back from the post office with the morning mail, we took a detour to La Roche to fulfill our promise to Emily to visit her sister. Delia was on a wicker chaise on the porch with a colorful quilt tucked around her legs even though the morning was already warm. Her head was tilted back, her mouth agape, and an open book—spine up—was splayed across her chest. A small snort escaped Delia's mouth as Flossie put her foot on the porch step, and we froze.

We shared a look, wondering if we should tiptoe off and not disturb Delia's morning nap.

"Here's your tea, miss," Delia's maid, Biddy, called out as she set down a tray on a nearby table. "How lovely!" Biddy said in her heavy Irish brogue when she noticed us. "I'll bring more cups. Miss Delia, look alive! You've got company."

Delia's eyes fluttered open. She raised a bit, closed the book, and put it on the chaise next to her. "Excuse me. I'm afraid the last few days have taken quite a lot out of me. Weddings are endless planning, you know."

"We were just checking in on you," Flossie offered.

"Perhaps we should come back at another time," I suggested.

"Nonsense. I'd love to have the company. So quiet without Emily around." Delia raised her handkerchief to her mouth then and coughed slightly, more out of habit than necessity. Delia—short for Adelia—had always been described as sickly, though I had never known the nature of her malaise, which seemed to include shortness of breath, fainting spells, and a pale countenance. But these maladies describe any woman of our era who stayed out of the sun and wore her corset too tight.

Biddy arrived with a larger tray, which held another pot of tea, two more cups, and three dessert plates heaped with generous portions of leftover wedding cake. "Here now, miss. Let's get you sitting up," Biddy said as she helped Delia to a more upright position, tucking a pair of fat pillows behind her.

"Thank you, Biddy," Delia said.

Biddy, short for Bridgett, had been the Griswold maid for nearly five decades now. She'd come off the boat from Ireland at the age of fourteen, went straight to the Griswold household, and had remained there ever since. Biddy was not the simpering type who hung back and waited to be told what to do. Whenever I had visited La Roche in the past, I always found Biddy to be brusque and busy, quick to wrest control of day-to-day affairs of the household. She fit into the family more like an elderly aunt than a paid servant.

"Please excuse my reclining pose," Delia said as Biddy departed.

"It's very Grecian," I said, thinking of the many illustrations on Greek vases and vessels Charles had shown me that depicted Greeks in repose as they ate and drank.

Delia chuckled at that. "This is not my ordinary practice, I assure you. I spent so much time on my feet last week. My ankles are so swollen. They feel much better when they are elevated."

"After planning such a wonderful wedding, you deserve a rest," Flossie said before we each took a sip from our teacups.

"It's so quiet this morning," Delia said, dabbing at her nose with her handkerchief.

"Yes, though there is still a lot of birdsong in the morning," I noted. As we sipped, I could hear warblers, sparrows, kingbirds, and robins.

"Yes. But very quiet when compared with a morning with my Emily—my little magpie. She chatters all day long, any season. I'd resigned myself decades ago that the two of us would live out our lives as maiden sisters. This has been a most jarring life detour."

Not sure how to respond, Flossie and I each took another sip of tea and let the silence settle around us as we watched the steamer *St. Lawrence* approach the Pullman House dock, a coil of black smoke trailing behind it.

"You know, Emily almost married once before," Delia said absently as she settled her teacup back onto the saucer.

"No, I didn't," I said.

"Decades ago now. A local boy with some ridiculous first name that sounded like a last name. Robinson? Flanders?" she batted the notion away with her hand. "Father put an end to that before it went too far. Oh my." She tsk-tsked softly before she took another sip of her tea. "If only Father were around now. Emily. My dear, sweet, naïve Emily. She always seems to choose men who are . . ."

Flossie and I both sat up a little straighter and leaned a tad bit closer to our hostess almost breathless as we waited for her to complete the sentence.

"Whatever is that hubbub?" Delia asked turning her attention toward Pullman House. "I hear it nearly every time a steamer docks at Pullman House."

I heard Prince barking. I couldn't see him, but I imagined he was running up and down the dock with Jambo clinging tightly to his back. A roar of laughter arose from the hurricane deck of the steamer.

"There it goes again! Such an uproar every time a steamer lands."

I explained about Prince and Jambo.

Delia nodded. "A monkey? You don't say. Well, anything is better than that confounded cannon. What was Mr. Sayles thinking? I'm surprised Mrs. Sayles allowed it. After all, their lovely cottage is even closer to the hotel than ours, situated as it is on the bluff overlooking Pullman House. I'm lucky to be so close to the Sayles cottage as I can hear their children practicing their instruments. You've met the Sayles children I'm sure, Miss Hartranft, but have you had the pleasure, Miss Bixby?"

"I'm afraid I haven't," Flossie replied.

"Oh well," Delia said, sitting up a little and leaning forward, anxious to share what she knew about the Sayles children. "Their oldest, Miss Josie, is quite accomplished on both the piano and the violin. And Master General Sayles—can't remember his given name; they've called him General since he was a knee-high to a grasshopper—the General plays the violin as well. Together the two produce the most wonderful duets. Mrs. Sayles let me in on a little secret at the wedding yesterday. Josie and the General plan on performing at Pullman House in the coming weeks. Midweek entertainment, you know. If you hear about it, you should definitely attend. Perhaps I will get off this porch and make a trip over there myself."

"What's this?" Biddy asked as she approached to clear the tea table.

"I was thinking we could wander over to the Pullman House to hear the General and Josie."

"Now, now Miss Delia . . . get that silly notion straight out of your head. You shouldn't be goin' anywheres until the swellin' in your ankles subsides. Besides, you know perfectly well you can hear the music from Pullman House from the comfort of your own porch. And you can hear all their practicin', too. Right lucky, you are. Can I be gettin' you ladies anything else?" Biddy asked as she lifted the tray from the table.

The steam whistle from the *St. Lawrence* shrieked as it drifted slowly from the dock and chugged toward Thousand Island Park. The whistle seemed to signal the end of our visit as well.

"Is there anything we can get for you until your ankles are better?" I asked.

"We'd be happy to retrieve your mail for you," Flossie offered.

"Thank you, but Biddy loves the chance to get away from La Roche—and no doubt away from me as well—for a half hour or more each day. Besides, she needs to put in the grocery order for the week and pick up whatever she needs for meals."

"Well, don't hesitate to send a message via Nat if you need anything, even if it's only a bit of company," I said, rising from my seat.

"I'm fine. I have my books and the river. Really, who needs any more than that?"

"Indeed, that sounds like heaven to me," I said. I reached out and took Delia's hand in mine and gave it a reassuring squeeze. "Thank you for the tea. Do feel better."

We left the porch and walked down the long stairway behind the cottage that put us on St. Marks Place.

"May we stop by and see how the chicks are doing?" Flossie asked as we descended the porch.

"Certainly," I said.

Flossie and I were unnaturally quiet as we walked toward the South Boulevard. I wanted to ask Flossie what she thought of Delia's truncated comment about the match between Emily and Prof. Gabriel but my upbringing prevented me from uttering a sound. Mother preached endlessly about the evils of gossip when I was a girl. Even today, she reminds my sisters and me that "Gossip dies when it hits a wise person's ears." Yet despite her constant instruction, I suddenly realized, Mother—and now Rose—were the first to employ gossip when we were together as a family. They always bolstered their revelations with the phrase, "I don't mean to gossip, but . . ." before sharing some outrage or dismay over another's faux pas. Mother and Rose always end by saying, "I only tell you this to instruct you as to what not to do, and this tidbit of information should not leave this table."

I smiled as I noted that gossip usually didn't leave my mother's tea table, but any one of her friends who came to our house for tea was likely to hear the same salacious gossip bracketed by the same justifications. Mother's tea table was a wellspring of tittle-tattle. Evidently, Mother felt her friends needed instruction as well.

St. Marks Place was always well-shaded with the female camel hump on one side and the heavily wooded baby's camel hump on the other. As we walked along in the cool shade, I looked up at the back of the great cottages, La Roche, Jersey Heights, and Glimpses and thought about Friend Anne's stance toward gossip. Each new student who came to live in her house received the same orientation. I remembered her "Three Gate Speech" from that first day I came to live in her large two-story home near the University of Pennsylvania. I've heard it oft-repeated to each and every new housemate who came after me. "Before a thought leaves your mouth in the form of conversation, it should go through three gates," was how she always started. The first gate was the gate of truth. Was it true? We must never offer forth a comment that we weren't certain of its veracity. The next gate was kindness. Was our comment unkind in any way? If so, it must remain behind the gate. The last gate was the necessity. Did our comment add anything of worth to the conversation?

Pondering the Three Gate Speech now, I realized that pausing to think before speaking might explain why Friend Anne spoke so slowly, almost haltingly. Friend Anne wasn't just against gossip; she was also against frivolous musings, vapid compliments, effusive praise, etc. It was her staunch belief that nothing but genuine sentiments should pass through the three gates. Therefore, Friend Anne was not one to blurt something out, but by the same token, she could be very direct at times. She never seemed afraid to say something negative to a member of the household if she felt that it was true and necessary. More than once, I was the recipient of a blunt comment. It may not have sounded kind at the time, but in the end, I could always see that her intent was to improve my character.

When we first met, Friend Anne's speech was sprinkled with "thee", "thou", and "thy" But as the Woman's Medical College of Pennsylvania was the first of its kind in the world, it began attracting women from across the seas. As more and more foreign students applied to the university, Anne noted that those not well-acquainted with English found her Quaker pronouns confusing. Over time, she amended her speech and now a "thee" or "thou" only slip out when she was very tired, flustered, or distressed, which was rarely.

Flossie walked ahead of me, her silver-and-gold curls shimmering in the light filtering through the tree canopy. Flossie Bixby, I noted with a smirk, did not adhere to the three-gate method of speaking. Flossie gossiped, chided, reprimanded, praised, and prevaricated but all in a most delightful way. I was frankly stunned that she had been silent about our conversation with Delia for so long. Oh, how I wished she would turn and share her thoughts.

Perhaps she had forgotten about Delia's comment and was now more focused on stopping to check in on Lucy's new chicks.

We nodded to the Mr. Hudson as we passed his cottage, Breezy Bay, on the corner of South Boulevard and St. James Place. He was reading the paper on the porch. I was stunned to see a tent standing on the lot between Breezy Bay and the Grenell cottage. In front of the tent was a buckboard wagon with lumber that George and his wife, Anna, were unloading.

"Morning, ladies," Sam called from his porch when he saw us.

"Good morning, Uncle Sam," Flossie cried out, waving at our island founder as he rocked on the porch. "We were hoping to peek in on the chicks."

Sam said nothing but motioned us toward the porch steps. "Lucy is back yonder helping Mavis with Alma Mae. Chicks are in here."

Sam creaked open the screen door and we followed him to the back of the house.

"George looks like he has a big project next-door," I said, hoping Sam would fill in the details.

Sam shook his head. "George and Herb are like oil and water. They've been bickering since George arrived. Finally came to a boiling point a few days back. George quit! Bought the lot next-door, rented a tent, and is intent on building a store of his own."

"Three stores on Grenell?" Flossie asked.

Sam grimaced, shook his head, and batted the notion away with his hand. "The chicks are back there," he said, indicating a wooden crate, "tucked back in the corner behind the cookstove."

"She keeps the chickens in the kitchen? Whatever for?" Flossie asked.

"Chicks need to be kept warm. Lucy had Arnie build a brooding box nearly the moment the chicks arrived. More like a throne, really, on a little pedestal to keep them birds off the floor and out of drafts. That woman is always complaining about her rheumatism, whenever I need this or that brung to me. But for them birds, she gets on her hands and knees a dozen times a day—some times just to check to make sure there's no draft."

Flossie lifted the muslin cover of the brooding box. "But where are they? All I see is some jug in the corner with flannel over it."

"That's a water bottle. Lift up the flannel flaps on either side."

Flossie lifted up a flap, and the sound of cheeps and peeping filled the room. "How ingenious! The flaps are like the wings of a mother hen, and the chicks all flock beneath them to be near her warm body."

"Sumptin' like that," Sam said. "I dare say Lucy thinks she's the mother hen. She'd have them nestled under her arms if she could. I tell you one thing, I got half a mind to wring Myron's neck for sending them birds."

"Oh, you don't mean that," I chided Sam.

"You don't know the half of it. Lucy's gone batty over these birds. Gets up in the middle of the night to refill the water bottles with boiled water. *Woo heee!* There's a new peckin' order in this house since these dang nab birds arrived. Birds are up here," Sam said, holding his hand way above his head. "Lucy's here," he indicated a cut lower. "Then George's young 'uns—Grace and Charlie. And me? I'm down here around the boots somewhere. Just wait until I get my hands on that son of mine. Columbian Guard or no, I'm ready to take him to the woodshed."

As Flossie clucked and cooed over the little chicks, I tried to soothe Sam's ruffled feathers as best I could. Finally, Flossie put the chicks back in the box, covered it with the muslin and we said our goodbyes to Uncle Sam.

"So what did you think of our visit to Delia this morning?" Flossie asked casually as we headed back to Castle Rock.

"She looked very tired. I hoped the swelling in her ankles goes down soon," I said.

"Not that!"

"Whatever do you mean?"

But Flossie shot me a knowing look. "Don't play coy with me. You know perfectly well what I mean! That comment about Emily almost marrying before, then clucking over poor naïve Emily and then . . ."

"And then what?"

Flossie rolled her eyes.

"Oh! You mean the unfinished statement," I said.

"Of course!"

I shrugged, feigning disinterest. To be honest, I wasn't sure what I thought, but I was dying to know what Flossie thought. "What do you think?" I asked, trying to sound dispassionate.

Flossie stopped and looked me straight in the eye, pursed her lips in a self-satisfied smirk, and said, "I told you so."

CHAPTER
twenty-two

"When are they due to arrive?" Flossie asked as she scoured out the farmer's sink in the kitchen.

I opened the screen door and carried in the empty drip pan and slid it back under the icebox. "They're arriving on the afternoon train. I'll be gone by then, so please make my apologies. Nat has finished setting up our sleeping tent. I'll make up the cots."

"I'll change the linens on both beds so they're ready for Anne and Keiko. I've already removed all my personal items from Anne's room," Flossie said, drying her hands on a dishtowel.

"Oh! Thanks for reminding me. I need to do the same," I said as I grabbed an empty crate and went to my room. I first cleared the toiletries from the washstand and then carefully placed them in the crate. Next, I looked around the room to see what else I might need. My gaze fell on the great yellow book, *Leaves of Grass*. I would only be in the tent for the week that Keiko was here. Would I have time to read? That wasn't the point, I decided. Even if I didn't have time to read, having the great yellow book nearby was a must. I looked at the other books on the shelf above the bed to see if there was anything else that I might like to read in the next week. When I pulled a book on Aristotle from the shelf, a photograph fell from between the pages and landed face down on the floor. I turned it over to find my brother-in-law, Edwin Dillworth staring at me. The photo had been presented to me twelve years ago when the Dillworths suggested a possible match between Edwin and me. Photographs were exchanged, but we never met. I went off to Penn, and Edwin Dillworth married my younger sister, Lily, instead. I'd forgotten that I had the photograph. Was it odd for me to possess a photograph of my sister's husband? What if someone else found it? Would they think I was pining away for my brother-in-law? Perhaps I should give it to Lily. But I brushed all those thoughts away. I hadn't time to think of that now, so I returned the book to the shelf but placed the photograph safely in the pages of *Leaves of Grass*, and hurried down the spiral path to the lower camp.

I had just finished making up the cot in the sleeping tent when I heard a familiar voice. "It's like I've stepped back in time."

Was that Anne? I peeked out of the tent opening and saw that my ears weren't playing tricks on me. "Anne, you're early! We weren't expecting you until this afternoon."

"We took an earlier train." Anne's eyes met mine and a rare smile turned up the corners of her mouth. "My first thought was that Nat had rowed back in time and it was 1881. Seeing the tents like this made me think of the symposium. Then I thought perhaps our cottage had burned down and we needed to revert to tenting again. But I see our cottage is still intact and has been recently painted. Marguerite, you did well."

Anne helped Keiko out of the skiff and onto the dock. Nat placed their valises and a few boxes onto the dock.

"Keiko! Welcome to Grenell Island. Welcome to Castle Rock." I bowed to Keiko who bowed in return.

"Why have you put up the tents?" Anne asked as she stepped off the dock and peeked inside the first tent.

"Flossie is still here and instead of sleeping on cots in the main room, I thought Flossie and I could sleep down here in the tent. You and Keiko may have the bedrooms."

"I see," Anne said. Then she looked over my shoulder and nodded to the second tent. "But you each need your own tent?"

My cheeks reddened. "No. One tent is for sleeping and . . ." I paused, unsure of how to continue. "The other tent is to house things Helen sent to me."

"Things?" Anne prompted. She walked around to the second tent, untied the flap, peeked in, and let out a small gasp.

I felt a hot flush spread across my cheeks.

"Helen sent you all this? But why?"

Suddenly, I saw the wardrobe tent as Anne might see it. Having lived in a Quaker home surrounded by Quaker simplicity for nearly a decade, the tent with all of the gowns, dresses, hats, and myriad accessories seemed ostentatious. I opened my mouth, but no explanation came forth. Instead, I offered tea. "You must be weary after your long journey. Come, let's show Keiko our cottage," I said.

By now, Flossie was bounding down the spiral path. "Anne! Keiko! Welcome! Welcome! I've already put the kettle on for tea. Come! Come! I can't wait to hear about your trip. How was the fair?"

But before we could ascend the spiral path, I heard a yoo-hoo and saw Edith emerge from behind Sentry Rock. "I've come to help you pack," she called out.

"Edith, I'd like to introduce you to our guest, Dr. Okami."

Introductions were made, and we taught Edith the proper way to bow and how to say *konnichiwa* or "good day" in Japanese.

"Did you say you've come to help Marguerite pack?" Anne asked.

"Yes," Edith responded.

Anne turned to me then. She said nothing but waited for an answer as if she had asked a question.

"Well, actually, I'm leaving later this afternoon," I said.

"Leaving?" Anne inclined her head toward me as if she weren't sure if she had heard me correctly. Her face remained placid, showing no flicker of surprise or annoyance on her face.

"I've been invited to spend the Glorious Fourth with the Clark family," I said.

"The Clark family?" she asked.

"A prominent family from Chicago who summer on Comfort Island near Alexandria Bay. I met a guest of theirs on the Princeton outing."

"A guest?"

"A gentleman by the name of Charles Bartman. He's an art historian for the Chicago Institute of Art, an expert in Greek and Roman art. I did mention him in my letters to you, didn't I?"

"No. You didn't," Anne said, her face and voice matter-of-fact.

"I'm sorry. I was certain that I had," I said as I felt my cheeks redden again.

"Marguerite, you seem very flustered. Almost embarrassed. Is there something you're not telling me? Do you have designs on this gentleman?"

Now even the tops of my ears felt ablaze. "Oh, nothing like that! He is in need of a translator—he has lots of documents written in ancient Greek—and I'm assisting him. I only know that I enjoy talking with him about his current project."

"So will you be working all weekend translating Greek into English?"

"Well . . . not exactly. Although I am taking my Greek dictionary with me, I'm not sure how much translating we'll be able to squeeze in. The invitation was issued by the Clarks. They're concerned about Mr. Bartman. Well, Mrs. Clark is. Thinking him too shy and bookish. Mrs. Clark feels I can help bring him out of his shell. I'm so glad you arrived early or . . ."

"You wouldn't have seen us until after the Fourth?"

There was a loud crunch.

Keiko stepped back, then squatted down and searched through the grass for the source of the sound. "It seems I have broken something here in the grass. Oh my. It is—was—a beautiful tortoiseshell comb."

Edith dropped to her knees to help Keiko search. "Here," Edith said offering Keiko her handkerchief. "Place the pieces in this."

A faceted oval of amethyst glass winked at me in the morning light. I remembered with a sickening stir of my stomach the night Herr Brittlinger had kissed me against my will, disheveling my Gibson Girl hairstyle. The hair comb—Rose's elegant tortoiseshell hair comb— must have dropped from my hair that night.

Keiko wrapped the pieces in the handkerchief, rose from her kneeling position, and approached me. The anguished look on my face must have made her think I was heartbroken. "My apologies, Marguerite," Keiko said as she bowed. "I can see you are gravely affected. Was the comb precious to you? A gift perhaps from an admirer?"

"Not at all, Keiko," I said, blinking away my memories of that night. "The comb didn't belong to me. It was one of a pair my sister Rose lent to me. I was dismayed because I only now remember that I've forgotten to return them to her."

I gazed down at the comb, broken into three pieces. The amethyst glass was surrounded by small rhinestones. A gilded vine with leaves decorated the center of the comb. Small rhinestones, many of which were missing, had studded the vine.

"Perhaps I can fix it," Keiko suggested.

"It was one of two," I said, "so it's not a total loss. I will send the remaining comb back to Rose."

"I must see the original," Keiko said.

"Is it in your room?" Edith asked. "I would be happy to retrieve it."

"Yes, in the top drawer of the washstand."

Edith trotted up the path and soon returned with its match.

"In Japan we have ways of mending things. I will repair it for you. Again, forgive me for my clumsiness," Keiko said, bowing deeply.

"I can get a magnifying glass and help you find the missing rhinestones," Edith offered.

"No, please, Edith. I fear it is beyond repair. And, Keiko, please don't apologize. It is not your fault. How could you have known there was a tortoiseshell comb in the grass? It is my fault. The comb was in my care and ruined due to my negligence. Just throw it away. I'll buy Rose a new set of combs."

"You might be surprised at how it looks. At least let me try," Keiko said as we walked up the spiral path.

Flossie had ascended before us and had the tea table set.

"No," I said, taking the broken pieces in my hand. *It is all ruined*, I thought, my eyes swimming in tears. I blinked and my throat felt thick with unexpressed emotion.

Flossie set the teapot on the table.

"Please rest from your journey and enjoy your tea. I must pack for my weekend at the Clarks. Anne. Keiko. I wish to hear about your trip. I do. You must tell me about it when I return from Comfort Island."

CHAPTER
twenty-three

Four hours later, I was standing on the wharf at Alexandria Bay surrounded by two trunks, five hatboxes, and two valises for a four-day stay at the Clarks' beautiful summer home on Comfort Island. It took a half hour, but Edith and I finally decided that the walking costume with leg-of-mutton sleeves was the perfect dress for my arrival. Edith felt pigeon-green and beige were perfect for my coloring. A matching straw hat and parasol helped round out the ensemble. I was grateful that Edith had made sketches of outfit combinations for me, matching accessories with dresses, as I was overwhelmed by the wardrobe choices and would be without her sartorial tutelage for the rest of my time at Comfort Island.

I re-puffed the leg-of-mutton sleeves, then smoothed the front of my skirt as I saw the *Mamie C.* approach with Charles and Mr. Clark standing in the bow. I grasped my parasol handle with both hands and held it directly over my head, not wanting to appear like a parasol-twirling summer girl.

"Have you been waiting long?" Mr. Clark asked as the dock attendants caught the line from the *Mamie C.*

"No, not at all," I said, closing my parasol.

"Come, let's get you aboard and out of the sun while we load your trunks," Mr. Clark said as he handed me aboard. No one seemed surprised at the pile of luggage.

The stretch of water from Alexandria Bay to Comfort Island was known as Millionaires' Row, summer home to the rich and famous. Palatial homes studded the islands. I could tell Charles had put great effort into being able to identify each island, grand structure, and owner. First he pointed out Island Imperial, owned by G. T. Rafferty of Pittsburgh, known as the coke king. Next was a tall cottage with a prominent bell tower and a white pennant flying from a staff at the top of the tower. "That's Linlithgow, owned by the Honorable Robert Livingston from New York City. The owner of the next island is Mr. Chandler, also from New York City. He named his island for his wife, Florence. And next . . ." Charles paused and pressed his fist to his mouth as he tried to remember particulars of the next island. It had a rocky base atop which was perched a tall, but compact house with towers soaring skyward. At the foot of the island was a boathouse with a matching tower. "I know they are from Brooklyn and . . . that's right . . . the Hunts. St. Elmo! That's what it's called. Coming up on our right is Friendly Isle, summer home of E. W. Dewey also of New York City. Though I suppose these days he prefers to call it Dewey Island. This stately stone house is called Normandie Lodge on Nobby Island and serves as a retreat for Henry R. Heath of Brooklyn. Castle Rest, belonging to George N. Pullman of Pullman Palace Car fame; and Hopewell Hall, owned by W. C. Browning, who owns a chain of men's clothing stores." Stonework walls and gardens encircled the base of the island. A massive house stood atop the island like some Rhineland fortress. A smaller turret building, either a boathouse or gatehouse, was built over the water. And I could see a large yacht house with a gaping door large enough to admit the tall mast of a sailing yacht.

"Oh, on the left side here this is Cherry Island," Charles said, ushering me to the port side. "On Cherry Island, there are several large summer homes: Melrose Lodge, Ingleside, and Styvesant Lodge. Melrose Lodge belongs to another Pullman brother. Ingleside belongs to a Mrs. March. The Marches, like the Pullmans, are from Chicago and great friends of my parents," he confided. Charles apologized for not remembering who owned the other cottages on Cherry Island before motioning me back to the starboard side in time to point out a Red Cross flag flying above a lovely summer cottage on the Wellesley Island shore on the other side of the channel. "Mr. Clark tells me the flag indicates that Clara Barton of

Washington, D. C., the mother of the Red Cross, is currently staying at Camp Royal, which is owned by the Rev. Royal H. Pullman, brother to George Pullman. The reverend is a great supporter of Miss Barton's work. She has spent many summers visiting in the Thousand Islands."

I smiled when Charles pointed out the small island on the left called Devil's Oven. I remembered Captain Visger pointing out this unique island on my first tour of the islands back in 1881. Now, more than a decade later, a tiny gazebo crowned the small but towering island. "Sometimes the Clarks picnic up there. They know the owners, a mister . . ." he paused. "It will come to me," he said, biting his bottom lip. But before he could think of the name of the owner of Devil's Oven, Charles waved a hand as if erasing any thought about it and instead went on to describe the island we were approaching. "The long narrow island is Cuba, owned by Mr. Chauncey of Brooklyn. And we're coming up on Wau-Winet which is owned by C. E. Hill. He's from Chicago, too. In fact, it is Mr. Hill who introduced the Clarks to the islands," Charles said as we passed a long, narrow island with a large cottage, equally large boathouse, and several outbuildings. The buildings seemed to overwhelm the long narrow island, that pointed downriver like a bony finger. "The Clarks visited the Hills at Wau-Winet in 1882 and subsequently purchased nearby Pratt Island, which the Clarks renamed Comfort Island."

I opened my mouth to say that they had arrived in the islands only a year after I first visited Grenell Island in 1881 but thought better of the comment and instead asked the name of the island to our left. We were so close that, I felt I could jump from the *Mamie C.* and land on the island. "Warner Island, which belongs to H. H. Warner of medicine fame. He's from Rochester. I'm sure you've heard of Warner's Safe Kidney and Liver Cure."

I nodded but did not share that Friend Anne was not fond of the "cure," thinking it a lot of humbug.

Eddies of swift current whirled around us as we approached a long, narrow log cabin on what I would call a shoal as it didn't have a tree. The cabin stood in the middle of a long, narrow outcrop of rock.

"Mr. Clark built a log cabin on this little island last year," Charles informed me. "Their cottage doesn't have a ballroom or a large banquet room, so the Clarks often entertain large groups of people in the log cabin.

We'll be going there tonight for an informal hop. The Clarks have invited people from neighboring islands."

A hop? My mind instantly began inventorying my wardrobe. How many hops would there be and which dress should I choose for tonight? These thoughts crowded my mind as we approached the Comfort Island dock.

Mr. Clark was the first off the *Mamie C.* as soon as she was securely tied to the dock. He immediately turned to help me disembark. "Welcome to Comfort Island," Mr. Clark said to me then turned toward Charles. "Charles, I trust you to give Miss Hartranft a tour of the grounds and cottage."

Charles nodded his compliance, and Mr. Clark excused himself and walked up the curving sidewalk to the cottage. From the dock, I could see a massive four-story tower rising above the canopy of trees. Beneath the canopy, I saw a covered porch edged by a beautiful lawn.

Charles froze then. It was the first time we had been truly alone since that day on the shore of Grand View Park. He shifted his weight back and forth between his feet and wrung his hands. "Where would you like to go first?"

"A walk around the grounds would be nice," I said.

"Certainly." Charles motioned for me to walk ahead of him up the sidewalk.

We paused when we reached a place where the sidewalk swung left to the front steps of the cottage porch. "The island has a nice beach," Charles said, pointing away from the cottage and toward the eastern shore. He motioned with his hand toward a flagstaff. A light breeze tugged at the flag, which unfurled and rippled in the southeasterly wind as we approached. Below it a white pennant proclaimed the name of the island—Comfort— in big red block letters.

"Looking downriver, you can see Warner Island, Wau-Winet, Devil's Oven and in the distance, you can see Hart Island and Sunken Rock Lighthouse."

Indeed, if I squinted, I could see the gabled roofline of the Hart summer home sticking up through the canopy of trees. Everywhere I looked I saw turrets and towers of grand stone summer homes. It was easy to see why this section of the river was referred to as Millionaires' Row.

"You said this island was originally called Pratt Island? I know of a Pratt family who has a cottage on Grenell, but I suppose Pratt is a very common name in this region of the country. But I am curious. Why didn't they name the island Clark Island? Why Comfort?"

"They used to have a summer home in Old Point Comfort, Virginia, but in 1881 their daughter, their eldest child, died while they were summering there. Mrs. Clark was so heartbroken that she didn't think she could return. They came to the islands the year after her death. They named the island Comfort for Old Point Comfort, Virginia."

And *perhaps*, I thought, *for the comfort they felt being on the river.* I turned to the scene before me—so serene and comforting.

"She was the oldest of their four children and the only girl. I believe her name was Mary, but they always called her Mamie."

I gasped and brought my hand to my chest. "The *Mamie C.* Their steamer is named for her?"

Charles nodded, said nothing, then looked out at the river. "Such a lovely natural beach. The boys love swimming here."

A small crest of sand glistened in the sun in a protective cove on the shoreline below the flagstaff. "I brought my swim costume," I said. "Perhaps we'll swim one day?"

Charles raised startled eyebrows above his small dark eyes. "Do you swim or wade?"

"Swim! One should not live on an island and not know how to swim. You do know how to swim, don't you?"

Charles looked sheepish. "No. I haven't learned as of yet, but then I have never stayed on an island before."

After an awkward moment, during which Charles spent a lot of time looking at his feet, he finally suggested we move along the sidewalk on the channel side of the island. We walked along in silence, admiring the trees and the river views. Eventually, the sidewalk ended and we found ourselves on a dirt path that swung toward the middle of the island and into a thickly wooded area. Ahead I could see through the trees another grand estate. A small channel, similar to the one that separated Pratt Point from the rest of Grenell proved to be the dividing line between the Clarks' estate and the one I could see through the trees beyond.

"There are two cottages on the island," Charles said, pointing to a grand stone summer home now coming into sight through the trees. "The Clarks' cottage is at the foot of the island, but the Oliphants of Brooklyn own Neh Mahbin at the head of the island. The original cottage burned down in 1890—something about a log in the fireplace that rolled out onto the carpet in the middle of the night. The Oliphants and their guests escaped in their bedclothes. I heard they were able to save a dresser and—oh, yes—the piano. Mr. Clark said if the wind had been from the west, the Clark cottage would have burned down as well. Luckily, it was spared."

"Do the Clarks socialize with the Oliphants?" I asked.

"Yes. I've been to Neh Mahbin several times during my stay. We're invited there for a lawn party on the night of the Fourth."

"Neh Mahbin! That's quite a mouthful. Sounds Turkish! Or, perhaps Persian. Whatever does it mean?"

Charles mused and scratched his head. "I have no idea. We'll have to ask. Come along. Let's walk back to the Clark cottage. I'll show you the inside."

Once back at the front of the cottage, Charles took me up the broad staircase to the wide wraparound veranda. The Clarks, Charles informed me, considered the porch one of the most important "rooms" of the cottage as it often served as morning room, tea room, dining room, and reading room. There were a half dozen rocking chairs on the side that faced downriver. On the channel side of the porch, there was a long dining table, which probably served as both breakfast and tea table. At the end of the channel-side porch, a hammock was strung at an angle, and I could imagine swaying in the river breeze while relaxing with a book. As we stepped through double doors, I found myself in a most inviting front parlor—not stuffy and pretentious but homey. The room was bathed in light as sunlight streamed through four floor-to-ceiling windows to our left. A grand staircase on our right led up to the second floor. A square grand piano dominated the room. There was a fireplace on the far wall. In the center of the room, a long Louis XV style sofa faced the fireplace, the perfect blend of elegance and comfort. The dark mahogany cabriole legs and intricately carved curving frame gleamed in the morning light. The plush deep-red velvet damask cushions looked terribly inviting. Behind the sofa were two tables pushed together. In the middle of the table was a book rack filled with a dozen leather-bound tomes. Next to the bookrack were packs of playing cards, a score pad and pencil, and an unfinished puzzle about halfway completed. It was an image of a sailing ship on rough seas. In front of the fireplace stood several club chairs, in which one could settle in and read a book. I ran my hand over the top of the couch drinking in all the details. The Clark cottage, it seemed, housed an active, fun-loving family.

"Come," Charles gestured. "I'll show you the second floor." The stairway wrapped around the right side of the room. At the top of the stairs, Charles gestured down the hall that ran the length of the second floor and told me there were eight bedrooms. "I'll let Mrs. Clark escort you to your room later," he said, looking somewhat embarrassed. We continued up the stairs to the tower, where a door opened out onto a narrow walkway encircling the tower. It felt as if I were stepping onto a magic carpet floating in the wind. I gripped the railing.

The cottage was built on the highest point of the island and the tower was four stories above that. We were up above the treetops surrounded by the wind. Looking over the water downriver, I saw large steamers and private yachts crisscrossing the waters in front of Alexandria Bay.

Our perch seemed so precarious, but the view helped quell the flutter of butterflies in my stomach. I saw miles downriver past Sunken Rock Lighthouse.

Charles stood far back from the railing, never stepping onto the walkway but remaining in the doorway. "I'm not fond of heights, but the view is so remarkable. You should see this view at night. Everyone on this end of the river displays grand illuminations. Watching the Glorious Fourth pyrotechnics displays from the tower should be spectacular."

"Miss Hartranft," Mrs. Clark called out as I descended the stairs. When I reached the landing she held out both her hands, reached for mine, and squeezed my hands tightly. "You look splendid. I love your hat, your gloves. You are so nattily put together."

I blushed and immediately wanted to explain about Helen and Edith, but lowered my head in a demure bow and said thank you, instead.

"So happy you could join us this weekend. Thank you, Charles. I'll show Miss Hartranft to her room," Mrs. Clark said, linking her arm through mine. "I trust Charles showed you around the grounds?" she said as we left him behind.

"Yes. Your home is lovely. The grounds are breath-taking."

We walked down the wide hall arm in arm until we reached the third door on the right.

"I thought I'd give you a channel-side room so you could watch the steamers on the river at night. The steamer *St. Lawrence* has installed electric lights this year. It's quite lit up as it cuts through the night. Have you seen it?"

"Yes, it's beautiful! Especially on windless nights when it plies the calm waters between Grenell and Murray Isle. It's as if there are two steamers, the lively one above and the silent watery mirror image below."

Mrs. Clark turned the gleaming ornate brass doorknob, and pushed the door open. "Please come in. You'll find your trunks and other bags on the other side of the room."

I gasped as I entered the room. The walls were painted a lovely coral pink. The oriental carpet was mostly green with scrolls of pink, rose, and white flowers. "I don't think I've ever seen a room that was so bright, so cheery, so . . ."

"Pink?" Mrs. Clark chuckled then. "I know. But I have all boys and I wanted a room for a girl."

"Charles told me about Mary. I'm so sorry for your loss," I said, laying a comforting hand on Mrs. Clark's forearm.

"Thank you for your kind words, but that was long ago. I've grieved and moved on," she said.

I turned and admired the room. It certainly was a room for a girl with its pink walls, pink French toile quilt with matching curtains, and scalloped valances. The large mahogany bed with elaborately carved posts and headboard faced the windows. Across from the bed on the wall between the windows was a marble-top vanity with a trifold mirror. A matching wardrobe and armoire stood on either side of the room.

"I'll send Katie to help you unpack," Mrs. Clark said.

"Thank you," I said. It had been years now since I had lived in my father's house and had staff to unpack for me. "I was wondering. Charles mentioned a hop tonight. What is the recommended dress for this evening?"

"It's not much of a hop, really. We'll have a harp band. It's mostly for background music, though people do dance. Oh, you may wear what you have on if you like," she said, then reconsidered and put her hand on mine. "But oh, my dear, please feel free to wear something else if you'd like. With a house full of young men, I'm out of touch with what young girls do today. I know many of them change clothes three or four times a day. An outfit for every activity, every mood. So do as you wish. It's just not my custom," she said, gesturing toward the huge pile of trunks and bags piled by the armoire.

"And I can send my lady's maid, Katie, to help you dress. She would be more than happy to help with your coiffure. We're rather informal here. What you're wearing will be fine for most evenings. But on the night of the Glorious Fourth, we will be going to Neh Mahbin. It's the only day you may wish to wear a gown. The Oliphants do it up right for the Fourth. The crème de la crème from the surrounding islands will be there, decked out in their finest. I'll be wearing a gown."

"I was wondering about Neh Mahbin. Do you know what the name means?"

"Neh Mahbin means 'Twin Island' in Algonquin, the language of the Ojibwa. When the Oliphants purchased the island, Mr. Oliphant immediately had a channel dug at the property line so he could say he owned his own island, though technically I suppose Neh Mahbin is part of Comfort. If we are twins, clearly we're the larger of the two twins." Mrs. Clark paused, gazed at me for a moment, then stepped forward and took my hands in hers again. "I'm so delighted you are here. I miss having a woman around sometimes. The boys are great—all bluster and rough and tumble. So much energy. Mamie was eleven when she died; that was twelve years ago. I've been so nostalgic since Charles arrived. Mamie was born the same year as Charles. So every time I look at him, I think of her and wonder what she would look like now. Or what would her life be like? Then Charles introduced me to you." She paused, spreading my arms wide and looking at me from head to toe. She brought my hands together, leaned in, and, in a low voice, almost a whisper, she said, "I'd like to think she would be very much like you, attending Penn or some other enlightened college and getting a degree in something."

I opened my mouth to correct her. After all, I was not *attending* Penn; I was *teaching* at Penn. Then the numbers started tumbling in my head, and I realized that Charles was a bit younger than I had hoped: a full five years my junior. It was at that moment that Mrs. Clark saw the consternation on my face and mistook it for discomfort.

"I'm sorry if I've made you feel uncomfortable," she said, releasing my hands and stepping away.

I reached forward and grabbed Mrs. Clark's hands before they fell to her side, pulling her closer to me.

"Not at all! I'm happy. No! I'm honored that I can give you a little female companionship. I look forward to getting to know you better this weekend."

CHAPTER
twenty-four

Thankfully, the hop was an informal one, as I had not been to a dance since the Walton House in Clayton back in 1881. Mostly, it was about refreshments and mingling. Mrs. Clark took great pleasure in introducing me to the millionaires of Millionaires' Row. Her introductions always started the same way: "You remember our houseguest, Mr. Bartman? His lovely companion for the weekend is Miss Hartranft from West Philadelphia." Then before they could ask my relation to the former governor, she surged on to tell them I was studying classics at Penn and had a gift for languages—French, Greek, and Latin. That tidbit of information usually startled but sometimes intrigued the millionaire of the moment.

Charles asked Mrs. Clark if he could introduce me to Mr. and Mrs. Hill as they were acquaintances of his parents. Mrs. Hill was a slight woman with a sparkling glint in her eyes; she smiled at me after Charles had introduced us.

"It's my pleasure to meet you, my darling. Mrs. Clark shared that you are newly acquainted with our Charles," she said, laying a proprietary hand on his forearm. "I'm pleased to see that he is spending time with such a lovely young creature that apparently is as intelligent as she is beautiful. Well done, Charles." She turned, winked at Charles before rising on tiptoe to plant a soft motherly kiss on his cheek before leaving, her taffeta skirt rustling softly at her departure. Two bright red patches appeared on Charles's cheeks. He swallowed hard, and his Adam's apple bobbed up and down. He was apparently struck mute, by such a display of sentiment from Mrs. Hill. He opened his mouth but no words came forth. He motioned me toward the refreshment table.

After the round of introductions, Charles and I were happy to find an isolated corner away from judging and perplexed stares and simply dissolve into rapt conversation about all things classic.

The harp music was beautiful but not so loud that we could not hear each other's views of Aristotle, Socrates, and Plato. A few couples danced, but the millionaires and their spouses mostly mingled and enjoyed the fine array of sweets at the refreshment table. Occasionally, Mrs. Clark would drop by to see if we needed more refreshments. We would smile, shake our heads, and tell her we were fine. She would smile at us, lingering a moment as Charles shifted his weight from foot to foot. As soon as she retreated, we instantly picked up where we had left off in our discussion.

We spent the next day on their houseboat, *Comfort*, which they had acquired three years ago. "Oh, how our neighbors teased us about our homely little boat," Mrs. Clark told us. "They couldn't make heads nor tails of it. Called it a queer duck-bottom craft."

"The Hills said it resembled an awkward sailing sloop," Mr. Clark reported.

"I didn't care what they thought. I loved the idea of having a houseboat. I got the idea when we were in England. The English have long narrow houseboats on the canals. The boys were younger then and always hungry. Now that I think of it, they still are. I thought how wonderful it would be to have a kitchen and all the comforts of home wherever we went on the river," Mrs. Clark said.

"So Mother was the first to introduce houseboating to the Thousand Islands," Mancel said.

Alson patted his mother on the back. "Seems it's become quite the craze. Did you see John Payne's elegant houseboat, *Pleasure*, last evening, Mother?"

"I did. It is gigantic."

"It doesn't compare to Dewey's houseboat. It's palatial. There was an article about it in *Daily on the St. Lawrence*. It has a huge salon with heavy

Persian rugs and a piano. Six staterooms, three on each side, neatly fitted with folding berths, chiffonier, and a toilet compartment. There's also a large dining room in the aft with huge windows. It's furnished with wine, silver, and china closets to host galas or banquets. I heard the interior is extensively gilded," Mancel reported.

"What's he calling it?" Mr. Clark asked.

"He christened it the *Idler*. You can't miss the name! He had the name neatly carved and gilded. Mancel's right. It's prodigious, seventy-five feet long and almost nineteen feet at the beam," Alson said.

"The new houseboats are large but with the same spoon bow and stern. Most don't have their own engines but need to be towed from place to place by a steamer yacht or tug," Mr. Clark noted.

"I'm glad our little *Comfort* can go wherever she wishes all on her own," Mrs. Clark said. "My aim isn't to have the biggest or the most gilded. *Comfort* is just that—comfortable."

We found an uninhabited island somewhere on the Canadian side of the river. The Clarks' cook came along, and while she happily prepared a feast in *Comfort*'s galley, the boys explored the island. Charles and I relaxed by the shore on a blanket with Mr. and Mrs. Clark as the two-man crew of the *Comfort* carried out tables and chairs onto the island.

The feast was announced and Mrs. Clark handed each of us a souvenir menu card with a large American flag at the top and our menu listed in embossed gold letters below: lobster à la Grover, spring chicken à la Mrs. Cleveland, artichokes à la Washington, soufflé au chocolade à la Jefferson, patisserie à la Yankee Doodle.

The lobster was sweet and tender, but the desserts stole the show. I expressed my amazement that a soufflé could be prepared in the tiny *Comfort* galley. Mr. Clark called the cook forth, and we all gave her a well-deserved round of applause.

"Dining al fresco on an island is the best sauce of all," Mancel said.

"Hear! Hear!" Alson acknowledged and raised his glass.

We all raised our glasses in agreement. I took a sip from the crystal stemware as I looked out at the sparkling blue St. Lawrence glimmering in the midafternoon light. Several rocky islands dotted the vista in front of me. As I placed my glass down, my eyes ran the length of the table: linen tablecloth and napkins, a centerpiece of red roses, white daisies, and blue bachelor buttons in a footed silver flower vase, crystal stemware, silver flatware, and silver salt cellars with matching silver pepper mill. Such opulence! This was perhaps the poshest picnic I'd ever attended. Yet, as I looked at the faces of the boys and their adoring parents, I was mesmerized by the Clark's familial love.

"What a brilliant day," Mancel said as if reading my thoughts. He took a sip of his wine, then leaned forward on the table. "Though, I find it odd that we had to cross over into the Dominion of Canada in order to celebrate the Glorious Fourth."

Mr. Clark chuckled and nodded in agreement. "Finding an uninhabited island on the American side is nearly impossible. If only our neighbors to the north would allow us to buy on the other side of our watery divide."

"From what I understand, a large number of islands on the Canadian side are owned by the Mississauga Indians and are being held in trust for them by the Canadian government," Mancel said.

"Didn't they talk of opening the islands up for sale a few years back?" Mrs. Clark asked.

"Quite right, my dear, but only just recently they have rescinded that proposal," Mr. Clark said as the cook and her kitchen girl started clearing the table. "There was quite an uproar about it. It seems the Canadian people are quite fond of picnic outings and were fearful that they may not be able to find a spot if they open the sale of islands to Americans. Like us, they would have rows and rows of fine summer homes instead of undeveloped islands."

"Perhaps they have a point," Alson interjected. "The American side is getting so populated that it's hard for fishing guides to find uninhabited islands for their shore dinners."

"I hear there is talk of making a few parks expressly for that purpose. The Anglers' Association has come up with a list of suggestions and passed it along to the New York State Forest, Fish and Game Commission," Mancel said.

"Bully idea. They should get on with it. If they don't hurry, every inch of the American side will be developed."

The next two days were a blur of non-stop activity blissfully spent on Comfort Island. The boys went fishing every morning. The rest of the day was filled with rowing, sailing, and sports—mostly croquet and badminton. I was pleased that—like me—Charles was not much of a sportsman. We watched as others played. The boys were quite competitive. Some afternoons I swam. The boys were impressed with the variety of strokes I knew. Charles put on his bathing costume but did not swim. He waded into the river but only up to his knees. I don't know if he ever got his bathing costume totally wet.

On Sunday night, we boarded *Mamie C.* for a sunset cruise. "It's become a Sunday evening tradition for us," Mrs. Clark said as we settled into the salon. "About a month before her death, Mrs. Dewey, who summered on Friendly Island, requested that we and several other islanders honor the Sabbath and her memory by erecting every Sunday evening a cross of white lanterns in place of our usual display of lights. She died four years ago, and every Sunday evening since then colorful displays are muted and replaced with the crosses of white lights. You'll see them at Comfort, Nobby, Friendly, St. Elmo, and other prominent points. The white crosses are simple but endearing."

The sky was blush orange. The sunset colors grew more vibrant as the sun dipped lower in the sky and eventually the brilliant colors faded and melted into soft darkness. Used to seeing the bright colorful lights at night, I found the white crosses were quite striking. Instead of a splash of colorful lights, each island lit a singular white cross, radiant in the growing darkness. Knowing that the river community did this once a week in remembrance of their dear friend was poignant.

We rose early the morning of the Fourth, aroused from our beds with a sunrise cannon salute from Alexandria Bay. Midmorning, at the urging of Edwin, we piled into the *Mamie C.* and headed to the waters off the Alexandria Bay wharf to watch a balloon ascension made by G. P. Grant of O'Connerville. The mammoth balloon was perfectly decorated for the Glorious Fourth. The top half was striped red and white. The dark blue bottom half was dotted with gold stars. The balloon was tethered. Soon after we arrived, we found a spot between the many skiffs and steam yachts full of onlookers who had gathered to watch the spectacle. The balloon rose slowly in the blue sky, and, once tethered high in the air above us, the daring Mr. Grant climbed out of the basket and, quick as a cat, shimmied down a rope and climbed onto a horizontal bar that hung beneath the basket. There, he dazzled the crowd with trapeze turns and twists that had the crowd gasping. When Mr. Grant climbed back into the basket, the air was filled with cheers and the toots of appreciative steam whistles.

The sight of the balloon rekindled my memory of the aero-machine I saw from Point Breeze on my first day on the island. It seemed so long ago now. I recounted the story of the aero-machine as we steamed back to Comfort Island. The boys were enthralled with my description and asked lots of questions—many of which I could not answer.

In the afternoon, Alexandria Bay organized races and contests. The boys took the skiff to watch, while Charles and I stayed on the island. Charles showed me his travel journal of the Greek Isles. I had expected him to read to me about his days in Greece, so I was surprised to see that his travel journal was a sketch journal. I'm not sure why I was so taken aback. He is an art historian, so why wouldn't he capture the lovely vistas in pen and ink?

Late in the afternoon, I began dressing for the gala lawn party at Neh Mahbin. Mrs. Clark's lady's maid, Katie, split her time between Mrs. Clark's room and mine. She helped me into the dress that Edith suggested I wear for the gala tonight, the cerulean blue gown appliqued with dark blue panne velvet swirls. The scoop neckline seemed even more daring than the gown Rose had chosen for me that night with Herr Brittlinger. The bodice and short capped sleeves were made of ivory Brussels lace. Edith had included some lovely delft blue silk slippers.

When Katie asked how I would like my hair styled, I told her the simpler the better. She skillfully combed my hair into a simple upswept style with tiny curls cascading from the top. "Would you be a wantin' to wear an aigrette?" she asked, holding up a small headdress of white egret feathers. I grimaced. Women festooned with feathers always made me uncomfortable for some reason. Ticklish perhaps.

"No? Well, I think I have just the thing," Katie said. She left the room and returned moments later with a large bronze comb with a beautiful matte white onyx stone surrounded by a delicate filigree scroll. "This will look lovely in your dark hair."

"Where did you get that?" I asked.

"It belongs to Mrs. Clark," she said.

I thought of the night with Herr Brittlinger and Rose's crushed tortoiseshell comb. "No. I couldn't impose."

"Mrs. Clark won't mind, I assure you. She instructed me to make sure you have everything you need for the lawn party tonight."

"But what if I lose it?"

"Fret not, miss. 'Tis not a costly comb. Just a bauble really. When she sees it in your hair—oh, my—the delight it will bring to her. She's always wishin' she had a daughter to share her things with. Believe me, wearin' this comb will be the greatest compliment you could give 'er. There," Katie said, holding a mirror behind me so I could see the back of my hair in the tri-fold vanity mirror.

"Do you have a necklace or a choker?" Katie asked.

"I'm afraid I don't have any jewelry," I said.

Katie opened her mouth, but before she could suggest it, I told her I definitely wouldn't be borrowing any jewelry from Mrs. Clark.

"Iffin' you don't mind me saying, miss—I think simple is best. Mrs. Clark dresses simply for the most part. Exceptin' perhaps the midsummer ball at the Frontenac. That's the one time of the year she goes all out."

"Thank you so much for all your help, Katie," I said

Katie bobbed a curtsy. "It was my pleasure, Miss Hartranft," she said before she left my room.

It was approaching sunset as we walked the trail to Neh Mahbin. The staff had placed lanterns along the path on our way through the wooded area to the little bridge. It was still pretty light out now, but within the next hour, the lamplight would be most helpful. I could hear the lively music over an undercurrent of chatter. Through the leaves, I could see the colorful electric lights strung everywhere. Their glow was almost fairylike. A scene from Shakespeare's *A Midsummer's Night Dream* came to mind. The night felt magical and marvelous.

Neh Mabin's lawn was filled with flowers. The scent of roses and jasmine filled the air. Many of the same people I had met the night of the hop were present but in their finest apparel. But there were also many more that I had yet to meet.

The table inside was laden with delicacies I wasn't acquainted with. Of course, some were instantly recognizable as mounds of small lobsters, platters of clams, and oysters on the half shell. But others were a puzzle.

"What's that?" I asked Charles.

The exotic dishes seemed conventional to him. When I asked what was piped into pastries, he told me it was foie gras—goose liver—served with dollops of olive oil and shaved truffles. Next, he explained that the cooked oysters covered with breadcrumbs, laced with herbs and slathered in a rich butter sauce were called Oysters Rockefeller. The lovely silver tureen held stewed eels with nutmeg, garlic, onion, and anchovy paste. And, finally, on a large silver platter were croquettes of fowl with a piquant sauce, which was a fancy way of saying seasoned cold chicken rolled in a pastry and fried with a spicy sauce. What I thought was an unattractive flower arrangement was, in reality, a fashionable food among the moneyed set. The flowerless green stalks in a tall, tulip-shaped vase, were celery stalks. While I had eaten stewed celery earlier at Carlton Island, I had no idea that some eat the vegetable raw. It was very crunchy, yet moist.

"My mother always makes sure to have a celery vase on the table for all her gala dinners. According to her, anyone who is anyone has a celery vase on their table," Charles informed me.

For dessert, there were sugar cookies piped with red, white, and blue icing. A chef at the end of the buffet prepared cherries jubilee by lighting the brandied cherries with a flame. With a whoosh, the flame glowed blue and orange over the chafing dish. The chef dramatically spooned flaming brandied cherries over bowls of vanilla ice cream.

Charles's nonchalant attitude toward the sumptuous sideboard was my first clue that Charles Bartman from Chicago was indeed one of the moneyed set—or at least his parents were. I had not grown up in poverty—not by any stretch of the imagination—but even my mother, who considered herself well-to-do, would have been wide-eyed at the opulence of the evening.

After partaking of some of the foodstuffs, we ventured out into the garden. Mrs. Clark waved us over, eager to introduce us to other gala guests. I dutifully followed Mrs. Clark as she made introduction after introduction. I recognized many names from the newspapers: captains of industry, financiers, and politicians.

"Oh, I see the Pullmans," Charles said to Mrs. Clark. He was pointing, but exactly who he was pointing to was lost on me. "I'd like to introduce Miss Hartranft to the Pullmans," Charles told Mrs. Clark as he took my hand and tucked it into his elbow.

Mrs. Clark beamed at the suggestion. "Have a lovely evening," she said before she turned and retreated back to the house.

We wove through the crowd of people toward a tall man in his sixties with a healthy tuft of white hair. He had no mustache but sported a prodigious white goatee. He heartily shook Charles's hand and patted him on the back. I was somewhat taken aback at the familiarity between the king of the Pullman car company and the reticent Mr. Bartman. After introducing me, Mr. Pullman and Charles exchanged news of family and neighbors back in Chicago. Mr. Pullman motioned for a balding man with a full but meticulously groomed white beard to join us. "Miss Hartranft, I would like you to meet my brother, Reverend Royal Pullman, and his guest Miss Clara Barton."

I knew the woman must be in her seventies, so I was surprised to see that her wavy brown hair showed no signs of gray. She had an expressive face with kind brown eyes and a wide mouth, which broke into an easy smile upon our introduction. Her touch was warm and genuine, devoid of pretense or affectation, as she took my hand.

A tingle of excitement shuddered through me. The woman was brimming with charisma. "It's a pleasure to meet you, Miss Barton," I said.

"Oh, please! Call me Clara," she insisted. "Miss Hartranft, is it? I met General Hartranft during the War Between the States. Any relation?"

"A distant cousin of my father," I replied.

"A gallant man, a true gentleman," she told me. We spoke briefly about her relief efforts during the Russian famine last year.

"Reverend and Mr. Pullman were very instrumental in shipping Iowa corn from the Mississippi to the east coast free of charge. It was a gallant gesture."

Suddenly, she caught sight of someone in the throng of people. "Excuse me," she said to me as she waved her hand, motioning a gentleman to join us. "Oh, Mr. Heath, do come over. There is someone here whom I would like you to meet."

"My dear, Clara! You are looking well," a tall, lean gentleman with a pronounced widow's peak and closely-shorn full beard said as he approached. He bowed deeply toward Miss Barton then turned toward me. "And who do we have here?"

"This is Miss Hartranft from West Philadelphia."

Mr. Heath's eyebrows raised at my name.

"A distant relation to General Hartranft," Miss Barton said as if sensing his next question.

"Well, this is an honor. While I never met your relation face-to-face, his reputation precedes him."

After our introduction, the Pullman brothers greeted Mr. Heath with vigorous handshakes and pats on the back.

"When are you leaving for Europe?" the Rev. Pullman asked.

"Early next month. We sail for Edinburgh on the steamer *New York* on the ninth," Mr. Heath said.

"Mr. Heath, please divulge the reason for your trip to Miss Hartranft," Miss Barton implored.

Mr. Heath told me that last summer he had invited Mr. Wallace Bruce, the United States Consul at Edinburgh, to stay with him at Nobby Island. During their time together, Mr. Heath learned that the brave Scotsmen who fought for the liberation of slaves during the War Between the States were lying in a potter's field in unmarked graves. Mr. Heath and Mr. Bruce decided right then that these brave lads needed a suitable resting place and memorial. He is traveling to Edinburgh to attend the unveiling of the Lincoln monument.

"It will be the first statue of Lincoln ever erected outside of the United States. It's a life-size bronze figure of Lincoln with one hand behind him and the other extended grasping a scroll." Mr. Heath adopted the pose so we could properly envision what the statue looked like. "The statue will be placed on a nine-foot square base of polished Aberdeen granite, making the entire monument fifteen feet in height. The names and regiment of each Scotsman are carved into the granite base. The sculptor was a soldier in the War Between the States."

"We thank you for your efforts in this endeavor," Miss Barton said.

Mr. Heath bowed low to the tall Miss Barton. "You are too kind, Miss Barton."

"Is it true that you were the first to build a castle here in the islands?"

Charles asked.

Mr. Heath chuckled. "Normandie Lodge is hardly a castle."

"It's hardly a log cabin!" Mr. Pullman retorted.

Elizur K. Hart, the former congressman from our fair state of New York, had much to do at what you see before you now—Millionaires' Row and all.

"Yes! Hart is from Albion, where I spent my formative years," Mr. Pullman said.

"Wasn't it Hart who introduced you to the islands?"

"Indirectly. At his urging, Mother and Royal first came here during the war. Mother fell in love with the area. Returned year after year. Insisted I buy an island. That was back in 1864. I bought two, Sweet Island, which I renamed Pullman Island," Mr. Pullman raised his arms in an apologetic gesture, "and Nobby Island, so named because it looked like a doorknob."

"George invited me to camp in the summer of 1870," Mr. Heath said. "Back then he had a small modest cottage surrounded by guest tents. I was still recovering from my experiences during the war, and George thought a few weeks of this salubrious air would restore my health. He was right. Wasn't too long after that, I purchased Nobby Island from him. I built Normandie Lodge the very next year. Not to be outdone, Hart, who'd been visiting the islands for decades to fish, decided to buy Hemlock Island and rename it Hart Island. He constructed an eighty-room cottage that towered four stories into the sky."

Mr. Pullman leaned closer to me and said in a conspiratorial whisper, "So you see, I was the Johnny-come-lately when it came to grand castlelike structures on the river. My little cottage looked a tad anemic compared with the giants on either side. I tore down the original small wooden cottage and built Castle Rest in 1888."

I smiled a little to myself thinking of my tiny Castle Rock and the grand Castle Rest downriver from here. "The main tower looks rather like a Pullman car standing on end. Was that the intention?" I asked.

Mr. Pullman cast a surprised gaze my way. "That is a rather clever analogy, Miss Hartranft. I've never really thought of it before, but you are right, my dear. It was not intentional, I assure you. But perhaps I now know why that tower seems so special to me." Mr. Pullman turned toward Mr. Heath, "I was greatly saddened when I heard of Hart's passing. Any news on what his son plans to do with the place?"

Mr. Heath took a sip of champagne and nodded. "Everyone is wondering. I have it on good authority that his son, Charles, plans on making repairs and occupying the cottage next spring. Hart knew what he was doing when he picked that island. I still think it is one of the most desirable locations in the area. I especially like that most of the island has been left in its natural state, although the cottage appears to be going to rack and ruin—on the outside at least. I'm told the interior is in good condition. The younger Hart insists that the island is not for sale at any price, or so it was reported in the papers."

Pullman tapped his walking stick on the ground as if to solidify the point. "Indeed! Well, that should put the rumors to rest."

"Miss Hartranft it was a pleasure," he said saluting me as if I were the general he was saying good-bye to.

Our hostess Mrs. Oliphant beckoned us inside then and gave us a tour of the house. Later when the orchestra took a break, she surprised us by playing a song on the banjo. The crowd clapped and laughed as they sang along.

When the orchestra returned, many gathered to dance under the moonlit sky on the dance floor constructed in front of the veranda.

I secretly hoped that Charles would not ask me to dance. The delft-blue slippers Helen had sent were about a size too small. I worried that blisters were forming. There was no quiet corner where Charles and I could retreat. We stood instead near the dance floor and watched couples whirl around the floor, the ladies in colorful silk and satin gowns, and the gentleman quite dapper in their cutaway jackets and crisp white shirts. Suddenly I felt a little woozy, even though neither Charles nor I had partaken of the champagne that was flowing freely. The waltz ended and the dancers and observers applauded.

As the applause died down, Charles looked at me sheepishly. "Did you want to go back inside?"

I admitted that I didn't. It was too hot and stuffy inside.

"Well, I hope you don't mind if we return to the Clark cottage," he said.

"Not at all," I replied somewhat relieved.

We thanked our host and hostess, and then Charles informed Mrs.

Clark he was escorting me back to the Clark cottage. I thanked Mrs. Clark for another lovely day. We turned away just as another dance ended. The crowd rippled with laughter and applause. The orchestra started up again with a livelier tune, a polka perhaps. The music and lively banter of the guests grew fainter as we walked toward the Clark estate.

As soon as we crossed the little bridge that connected the two parts of the island, the lanterns that lined the woodland path sent our looming shadows wavering against the backdrop of the woods on either side of the path. I stumbled in my ill-fitting shoes and leaned heavily on Charles's arm. Each step took us further away from the sounds of the lawn party. As the music diminished, the sound of our footfalls crunching through the leaf litter became more prominent. Charles and I were quiet. After the noisy, jostling crowd, it was nice to let the still of the night close in around us. When we reached the sidewalk on the channel side of the island, a steamer passed. Studded with electric lights, the steamer cast a reflection that glimmered and winked in the dark waters. Once past the cottage, we turned toward the porch steps. Charles paused on the front walk to turn and look out at the scene downriver. I'm not sure which was more dazzling: the magnificent dwellings illuminated with colorful, electric lights or the moonlight. The waning moon floated high in the sky and lit up the water below, which glistened like polished silver. The dark-silhouetted islands were suspended between the moon-bright sky and the silvery moonlit waters below. We didn't talk but drank in the scene before us. Occasionally a bottle rocket would explode like an exclamation point in the sky. A roar of laughter and applause erupted as the orchestra finished another number on the lawn of Neh Mahbin.

"I'm sorry I didn't ask you to dance," Charles said.

I grimaced a little at the thought of dancing and tried to wiggle my toes. They were numb.

"It's not that I didn't want to dance with you," he said as if he took my silence as a reproach. "It's just that I . . . well . . . I learned to dance back when I was a boy in short pants but have not danced since then. I'm afraid I've forgotten all I learned."

"To be honest, I was somewhat relieved. It's been ages since I attended a dance. I'm afraid I'm hopelessly out of practice as well," I told him. The last dance I had attended was twelve years ago at the Walton

House in Clayton, but I left that unsaid. "Think nothing of it," I told him with a reassuring pat on his arm. "My shoes this evening are a little tight. Walking is painful enough. Dancing would have been agony."

Charles exhaled then as if he had been holding his breath after a long time underwater.

We turned then, content to let the moon and the moonlit water carry the conversation.

We were standing in rapt contemplation when an explosion shook our world. The suddenness of the noise made me jump. We turned our backs on the moon and watched the heavens above the trees between Comfort Cottage and Neh Mahbin as swift rockets pierced the starry sky and exploded, illuminating the sky in a kaleidoscope of color. The applause from the delighted Neh Mahbin guests and the shrill whistles of passing steamers tooting their appreciation filled the intervals between pyrotechnic delights.

In one such interval, Charles turned to me. "Mrs. Clark has offered to give me a refresher course. I hear there's a hop at the Columbian this Friday. I would love to take you. You could wear more comfortable shoes."

"That sounds lovely. So the Columbian on Friday?"

"Yes, but I hope to see you before then. To help with translation."

"To help with translation," I said. "Of course."

A whistle of a rocket drew our attention back toward Neh Mahbin. The dazzling white light shot skyward like an arrow high above the treetops then exploded into a brilliant red firework that glimmered in the night sky and bathed the island below with a rich, ruby light.

"To the tower?" Charles asked. "Can you manage the stairs in your slippers?"

I bent and removed my slippers, and holding them in my hand, ran at a most undignified gait up the porch steps with Charles close on my heels. We were both panting and laughing as we arrived at the top of the tower stairs. This time, Charles stepped out onto the narrow walkway without hesitation We were above the treetops now and we had an unobstructed view of the fireworks. From our vantage point, we could see fireworks displays downriver at Westminster and a few other skyrockets on either side of the river. The night was alive with color and sound.

Grenell 1893

As I stood gripping the railing, marveling at the spectacle in front of me, Charles stood behind me. He put his hands on the rail on either side of me. He was still panting from our rapid ascent. His warm breath on my neck sent cold shivers down my spine.

CHAPTER
twenty-five

"Where are Anne and Keiko? Where is the skiff?"

Flossie put a hand on her hip, tilted her head to one side, and gave me a pointed look.

"Oh right. I guess I could put one and one together and deduce they've gone for a row. Do you know when they'll be back? I'm due to meet Charles at the Columbian in an hour. We're hoping to get a few things translated this morning. We have the Columbian Hop this evening. He's changing for the dance at the Kerr cottage. Oh, and if you have time, would you be a dear and brush my gown for this evening? I won't have much time as I've decided to do my hair in a high updo, and you know how long that takes me. But if you have time to help me, that would be—"

The expression on Flossie's face made me stop mid-sentence. Flossie put both hands on her hips and inclined her head toward me, her usual impish features hardened into an impertinent glare.

"What?" I asked.

"I'm not your lady's maid," she said. "I'm busy trying to finish my herbarium. I hope to complete it before I leave for the American Canoe Association rendezvous next week."

"Yes, so sorry," I said as I searched for my Greek-English dictionary. "It's just that clothes and hair take so much time and energy. I'm struggling to keep up. I'll ask Edith if she can brush out my gown and help me with my hair. Oh bother! Have you seen my Greek-English dictionary?"

Flossie walked to my small camp table next to my cot, picked up the dictionary and brought it back to me. "If you're not careful, your newborn appetite for fashion and style will eat away everything you learned at Penn."

I watched Flossie walk away. What did she mean by that comment? Then I glanced at my bodice watch and realized I didn't have time to disentangle her meaning if I were going to chat with Edith before I caught the next steamer to Thousand Island Park.

The last four days had been a whirlwind of activities. The Sawyer sisters of Thousand Island Park had included us in their circle of friends. In the afternoons we played croquet, bean bags, and all manner of little games. We'd even rented safety bikes and gone wheeling with Yvette and Mr. Quigley one afternoon. In the evenings, there were card parties and walks to the ice cream pavilion and, oh yes, the polka dot party. I'd worn the ivory dress with metallic dots that Helen had sent. Charles had secured a polka-dot bow tie from Mr. Clark. Mr. Quigley had engaged the proprietress of the millinery shop at Fineview to sew large white muslin dots on his frock coat and trousers. Yvette had done the same with a pearl-gray dress. The two made a fetching couple, and I was happy that I had introduced them. That must be the feeling my mother's matchmaking friends are striving for when they introduce me to some available widower.

But the best part of our days were our mornings, which we spent in a secluded corner of the Columbian reading parlor. Charles usually arrived first, and by the time I arrived, he would have the table spread out with sketches and papers. I've learned so much about Greek pottery in the past week—so many vessels for so many different purposes. While Charles knew the names, he didn't know the etymology behind them. He told me that the double-handled drinking cups had two different names—the larger one called *kantharos* and the smaller one *mastoid*—and he was often confused trying to remember which was which. I explained that *mastoid* was modern Latin but from ancient Greek *mastoides*, meaning "breast-shaped." I'd been focused on the words and not on the anatomical reference and hadn't realized the impropriety of my statement until I saw two red patches on Charles cheeks, which caused me to blush as well. But I'm certain he will never forget the name of the smaller vessel now.

I was amazed when I discovered how well Charles could sketch. His sketches of the Institute's pottery collection were so realistic that I felt I could pick them up and hold them in my hand. I especially loved his sketch of a pottery piece portraying a symposium. One afternoon, while I was translating a passage from a book on Greek pottery, I caught him making a sketch of me. He claims I have a classic face.

The two evenings we did not have an activity, I received dance instruction from the Kerrs. Mary Mason was more than happy to help me improve my dancing skills. She pressed John into service as my dance partner. Lois kept the music box wound. It played strains of Strauss's "The Emperor Waltz" over and over again. John didn't grumble too much but commented absently to me, "I never thought I would see such beauty on Black Bart's—I mean Charles Bartman's arm."

I blushed at that, misstepped and trod upon his toe. "I'm sorry," I said flustered.

"Not at all. You are doing swimmingly. You're quite graceful," John assured me.

"When I'm not stepping on your toes, I suppose," I said, feeling color rise into my cheeks.

When the music ended, Mary Mason pointed out that the waltz, in particular, wasn't only about getting the steps right but more about the attitude. "Above all, strive to look like you are having the time of your life. The more nervous you are, the more likely you are to misstep. Keep your head up, your chin up, the elbow on the gentleman's shoulder up, and most importantly your thoughts and attitude up. Remember: up, up, up!"

"You'll do fine," John said.

All week, as thoughts of the upcoming dance waltzed through my head, rumblings of outrage concerning the hop rippled through the Park. Thousand Island Park was founded as a Methodist camp. Its bylaws positively forbid dancing, card playing, and other modern vices within its sacred precincts. I remember the days when the Park employed rappers to knock on the windows to enforce the nine o'clock lights-out rule. Through the past decade, rules had relaxed. Still in all that time, never had there been a dance at the Park. Many of the Park Methodists raised their hands in holy horror at the very idea of a hop and shouted, "And planned on a prayer meeting night, no less!" A prominent Park official said that the

Columbian had gone too far and that the trustees were meeting to decide if they would demand that the Columbian cancel the event.

A small part of me hoped that it might be canceled. I hadn't danced in over a decade and was very nervous. There would be other dances, balls, hops, and Germans up and down the river. One could dance every night if that were what one so desired. If not this night, there would be another, giving me more time to practice. Or, as Flossie pointed out, more time to fret.

Edith helped me coil my hair into a tight updo. Despite my protestations, she secured an aigrette, a tuft of ostrich plumes dyed in complementary shades, to the right side of my head.

"I feel silly—like a feathered fool," I said. "What if my feather tickles Mr. Bartman's face while we're dancing?"

Edith said, "It isn't silly. It's stylish." She showed me a sketch in *Harper's Bazar* and then held a mirror for me to look in. So this was what being stylish looked like. I wasn't sure I liked the notion. I sighed, I gathered my opera-length gloves and a lantern, and thanked Edith for her help.

I left the lantern at the base of the bridge and hurried to meet Charles at the Pullman House dock to catch the 8:05 steamer to Thousand Island Park. It was still light when we entered the Columbian. At 8:30, the Guntzman Orchestra entered the hotel parlor, which had been cleared for the evening's ball. The festivities started with a concert of three songs. The air was electric as guests arrived and sat in rapt attention, waiting nervously for the dance to begin. Everyone was whispering, "Will the trustees interfere?"

When the last notes of "Chanticlers" died away, the programs were passed out. I was thrilled. The first dance was a waltz, and there were four waltzes altogether, by far my favorite dance. When the sweet strains of *"Du and Du"* by Strauss floated through the air, couples tentatively took to the dance floor, no doubt wondering if some official was going to rush in and put a stop to the whole affair. Soon beautifully dressed couples whirled in giddy mazes. Charles and I looked at the door to the parlor, and, once certain no one was going to run in and stop the dance, he offered me his arm, and we joined the gay throng. Round and round the dance floor we moved, rising and falling with the beat of the music. I tried hard to remember Mary Mason's advice. I raised my chin and smiled so broadly that my cheeks hurt. I pivoted my head, looking over first Charles's left shoulder and then his right as we swirled with the music. I did not look at Charles because he looked so nervous. His arms were so stiff. When I did glance at him, I could see his lips move as he counted: one, two, three.

When the last notes of the *"Du and Du"* resounded, a huge smile burst across his face. The sweet waltz yielded to a more upbeat song named "Pretty Maiden," a polka. Charles and I looked at each other, laughed, and moved to the edge of the room. Neither of us was up to the challenge of the polka. I wanted to relish our successful waltz.

We stood for a while watching the dancers before Charles asked if I would like some punch. He indicated the direction of the refreshment table with an open palm. I nodded and we moved across the room.

As we approached the refreshment table, the orchestra struck up a schottische. I looked out and saw Mr. Quigley —Thomas—and Yvette take the dance floor. Thomas held Yvette's right hand in his right hand at the top of her right shoulder. Yvette reached a long slender arm in front of Thomas, and he took her left hand in his left hand. Cradled beneath his arm and standing shoulder to shoulder, they took to the dance floor with quick step-hops, first to the left and then to the right.

Yvette looked quite fetching in a yellow gown. I noticed that Mr. Quigley's cowlick stuck up from the crown of his head like a little ducktail.

Thomas released Yvette's left hand and twirled her like a ballerina atop a music box, around and around and around, then caught her arm and spun her in his arms before returning to the side-by-side step-hop promenade around the dance floor.

I couldn't take my eyes off them. They were perfectly matched. Even though they were dancing in time with the music, they seemed to spin faster and make a revolution around the dance floor faster than anyone else.

"Look," I said nodding to couple when Charles handed me a glass of punch, "it's Yvette and Thomas."

"Who?" Charles asked, panning the crowd.

"Mr. Quigley. A schoolmate of yours from Princeton. I met him on the Princeton outing. You were there. It was when we were in the bow of the *Nightingale*."

Charles shrugged and took a sip of punch.

"You don't remember? The group of them almost came to fisticuffs."

Charles downed the rest of his punch, turned, and took two steps toward the refreshment table. "Need a refill?" he asked.

I'd yet to take a sip. "No, thank you," I said. "You really don't remember?"

"I wasn't paying much attention. This Quigley fellow is still in college, right? And a footballer?"

I nodded.

"I didn't pay much attention to those types when I was in school. Why would I pay attention to them now?" At that he walked toward the corner of the room as a way of ending the conversation.

I blinked as I remembered that morning on the bow of the *Nightingale*. Charles had been listening. He had turned around when I talked about the etymology of the word lithography. I took a sip of the punch. Then another. Perhaps he had only been listening to me. I set down my glass of punch and followed Charles to the opposite corner of the room.

After a schottische was another waltz, and we took to the floor again.

I paused, remembering my dance etiquette from long ago. "Mother always said it wasn't proper to dance with only one partner."

Charles said that Mrs. Clark had spoken to him about the same thing. "But who will really notice?" he said, looking around. "I doubt anyone even notices the two of us."

I was glad Charles felt the same way as I did. Because I was still unsure of my dancing abilities, I didn't trust them to another partner. Besides, I hadn't bothered to take a dance card, and no one else seemed eager to dance with me.

We took to the floor for dance seven and dance nine, both waltzes by Waldteufel. The last dance was a polka. Charles nodded toward the door, and we stepped outside onto the veranda. After the warm parlor, the fresh St. Lawrence breeze was a relief.

We started walking with no destination in mind, wandering down St. Lawrence Avenue. As the music from the Columbian faded, we could hear hymns coming from the Tabernacle, where the weekly prayer meeting was being held. We then turned onto Park Avenue and moved from one pool of streetlight to another until we found ourselves at the base of the South Bay bridge.

"Where does this bridge lead?" Charles asked, squinting into the darkness. "It does have an ending, doesn't it? It seems to disappear into the night."

"It's nearly a third of a mile long," I said. "The Park officials staked out about eight hundred lots on the other side of South Bay. There had been a road that looped around the backside of the bay but they built this bridge to attract buyers. You can't see all the architectural details in the dark, but it is quite ornate. It was built at some expense."

"Were there ever any cottages built? I don't see any lights."

"Yes. In fact, Mr. Hinds whose uncle has a cottage on Grenell Island, has a cottage near the entrance of the Narrows."

"When was the bridge built?"

"Oh, some time ago." I was hesitant to say that I knew precisely when it was built. It was 1886, only five years after I first arrived on Grenell Island, nearly seven years ago. "They're talking about tearing the bridge down."

"What a shame. It's a wonderful place to watch the moonrise," Charles said, pointing out at the moon hanging low in the sky.

"Moonset," I corrected him. "The moon rises in the east, but sets in the west." The moon, a waxing crescent, hung low in the sky, framed perfectly between the dark shapes of Grenell Island to our left and Murray Isle to our right. Normally, I would have let this comment pass. Mother and Rose had hammered into my head that I was never to correct a gentleman as they didn't appreciate being corrected by the weaker sex.

"Look, Anne and Keiko are awake. You can see the light in our cottage," I said pointing toward Grenell. "Flossie is still up and working on her herbarium in the tent in the lower camp."

I loved how the tent glowed from the lantern light within. It looked like a dollop of sweet honey. We stood there staring at the moon as a soft breeze rippled through my aigrette and the ringlets of hair that framed my face.

I could see the bridge from our cottage during daylight but not at night. How many times had I looked out into the night sky and at the dark shape of Wellesley Island, not knowing there was a young couple on the South Bay Bridge looking back at me?

"I've never found girls very interesting, especially pretty girls. They seem so empty-headed. You're not either of those things."

I wasn't sure what he was trying to say. Did he mean I was not pretty and I'm not empty-headed? He struggled to find the right words and I waited.

"I never know what to say to pretty girls, much less beautiful girls, so I usually just ignore them. But I can always find something to talk about with you. Meeting you has changed my whole summer," he said. Then he bent down and gave me a quick kiss. His upper lip was dotted with cold, clammy sweat.

I smiled nervously at him as he pulled away, but he wasn't looking at me he was looking away.

"Since the Princeton outing, I've wanted to spend all my time with you," he said more to the setting moon than he did to me. "And while I enjoy working with you at translations, I haven't gotten much accomplished on my book. I . . . I can't think much when you're sitting next to me. I'm afraid I'm horribly behind schedule, but I can't seem to help myself."

I fought the urge to ask questions. Was he saying he didn't want to spend as much time with me? Was he telling me that he needed to spend more time working on his book?

"Time seems to fly when I'm with you," he said.

Again, I was unsure if this was a compliment or a complaint. Time, I thought, lingering on his last thought. "Oh my! The time! The last steamer from Thousand Island Park to Grenell Island leaves soon. I fear if we don't hurry, we won't make it."

From there we made a mad dash from the bridge through the now quiet streets as the Tabernacle was dark and silent. The pious crowd gathered there had left and gone back to their cottages or tents. There wasn't any music pouring from the Columbian. The large windows spilled out patches of light that fell across the lawn. Here and there we saw people walking away from the hotel toward their cottages.

We made it to the dock just as the steamer was preparing to push away from the dock. The purser gave me his hand and urged me to leap the short space between the steamer and the dock as the gangway had already been pulled. Once aboard, I turned to watch Charles leap over the ever-widening gap. We laughed nervously as the whistle blew, grateful that we had made the last steamer of the evening. We could have found someone to row us to the Pullman House, I suppose, but it would have made our arrival at Grenell much later and set a few tongues wagging. We walked to the rail and watched as the steamer chugged steadily toward Grenell. We were quiet, still breathing hard from our dash to the dock.

"You remind me of Minerva or Athena; I can't decide which." He thought a moment, then announced. "I prefer Minerva to Athena."

"You choose the Roman Minerva rather than the Greek Athena?" I asked as we neared the Pullman House dock.

"Athena was also the goddess of war. I do not see you as a warrior. The Romans didn't stress Minerva's relation to battle."

"True," I said as the gangway was attached to the steamer. We disembarked onto the silent, dark dock. There was no Prince or Jambo to greet us.

"But wait," he said, looking up into the night sky. "There is this wonderful painting of Athena, but I can't remember the artist." He hit his forehead with the heel of his hand. "Oh, how dismal. I'm an art historian and I can't remember the name of the artist. But perhaps it is an ancient unknown work."

"Go on."

"I know it is Athena because she has an owl. Her hair is dark and flowing. I imagine it looks much like yours when your hair is unbound." He slowly lowered his eyes to me then, perhaps imagining my hair loose and flowing around my shoulders.

The corners of his small mouth turned up. "Yes. I mean no. I was wrong. About Minerva, I mean. When I think of that painting, you remind me more of Athena, goddess of wisdom and learning. I wouldn't be surprised to learn you have a pet owl."

We were quiet as we left the dock and walked past Pullman House to the base of the bridge that linked Grenell Island to Grenell Island Park. I retrieved my lantern and lit it from the box of matches I had left alongside it. Charles insisted on walking me home. We were silent as he crossed the bridge and passed the dark cottages that lined the little bay at the foot of Grenell. When we reached the Pabst cottage, Charles continued on straight toward Pratt Point.

"No! Not that way," I said in a loud whisper. "It's this way to Castle Rock," I said, pointing. "We need to go around the Pabst cottage."

"Sorry," he said. "It's very dark now that the moon has set."

"Are you sure you will be able to find your way back to Glimpses?" I asked, thinking perhaps instead of Charles walking me home, I should walk him back to Glimpses. I stopped then, and as quietly as I could, so to not wake up the Pabst brothers, I described how he should return.

He nodded, but I wasn't sure if he wouldn't be wandering about Grenell Island Park for the rest of the night.

At the base of the spiral path he paused, and I thought he might kiss me again, but, instead, he shifted nervously from foot to foot and said he had had a wonderful time and hoped he would be able to escort me to another dance soon. I handed back the light and told him I would retrieve the lantern from the Kerrs at Glimpses tomorrow. He paused. The lantern light hissed and lit up his long narrow face and his small, dark eyes. Charles opened his mouth as if he hoped to say more, but inspiration fled him. He turned, then took a step and turned back quickly.

The light in the cottage was extinguished but Flossie had left the light on low in the tent.

"Well," Flossie said. I had thought she might be asleep but was grateful she was awake. How would I have gotten out of the gown with the long row of tiny buttons down the back if she hadn't been? I sat on the edge of her cot and handed her a buttonhook. She sighed, but sat up and started unbuttoning my gown. "I could hear the snatches of music and sometimes singing. I swore I heard a throng of people singing, 'O Lord, Be With Us When We Sail.'" I thought that was an odd song for a hop."

I laughed. "There was a prayer meeting at the Tabernacle tonight. I think they were probably singing and praying extra hard to counteract the evil vice of dancing on their sacred confines."

Once unbuttoned, I thanked Flossie, took the buttonhook from her, and slipped out of the gown. Flossie asked about the decorations and if there had been any uproar or an attempt to stop the hop.

As I described the gala decorations at the Columbian and the collective nervousness at the start of the evening and that first dance, I removed layer after layer of undergarments, sighing with relief when my corset was finally removed. At last, I slipped on my sleeping gown.

"Do you know that my sister Lily sleeps in a corset. She says she feels uncomfortable when she's not wearing it."

"Egad!"

I sat on the cot, pulled the pins from my hair, and began brushing it out as Flossie lay back on her pillow and pulled the light quilt up to her chin. Suddenly, Flossie flopped on her side rested her head on the hand that was propped up by her elbow. She watched me for a while before she inhaled deeply and asked, "Well, did he kiss you?"

"Flossie!" I said. I dropped the brush to my lap and glared at her. "What an impertinent question!"

"That would be a yes, for why else would you be turning that shade of red?"

"Never you mind whether he kissed me or not," I said, resuming my brushing. "You made me lose count," I said, then continued counting my brush strokes in my head, starting over with one.

Flossie giggled, then thankfully changed the subject. I thought about the kiss as Flossie burbled on about her herbarium project. It had not been an ardent kiss. More like a quick kiss that a father or grandmother would drop upon my forehead—only closer to my mouth. Not exactly on my mouth, as he had misjudged a bit and kissed my upper lip. His upper lip had been so sweaty. I felt my face flush at the thought of the kiss—my first kiss with Charles. Would there be more? Would they become more practiced? More passionate?

My thought went back to that night with Herr Brittlinger and my embarrassment devolved into shame. I should never have allowed Herr Brittlinger to walk me home. Miss Caldwell had warned me. Then my shame flamed to anger as I realized that Herr Brittlinger had stolen my first kiss. I brushed the thought away with a shake of my head. I would not mar this evening by thinking of that unworthy bounder. Besides, with any luck, I would never see Herr Brittlinger again.

"You're not even listening to me, are you," Flossie challenged.

"Sorry," I said placing my hairbrush on the night table between us. "I think I'm tired from the excitement of the evening. Forgive me, dear Flossie, but I'm off to sleep."

CHAPTER twenty-six

Nat appeared the next morning as I was finishing a well thought out note to Rose. Nat returned the lantern I had loaned to Charles and placed a note written in Charles's elegant handwriting on the table next to me. I reluctantly opened it and read it while Nat watched, not knowing if it was romantic in nature, but perhaps it needed a prompt response that I was to send back with Nat.

The note mentioned nothing of moonlight or waltzes; it only requested that I meet him at the Columbian an hour earlier than we had decided last night. "Does he need a response?" I asked Nat.

"No, miss," Nat said as he turned to leave. "Mr. Bartman had business to attend to at the Park. He left on a steamer about the time he gave me the note."

"Nat, could you wait?" I called after the boy. I quickly folded the letter I'd been writing to Rose, stuffed it in an envelope, and addressed it. "Do you think you can post this letter in time for the morning mail?"

Nat gave me a doubtful look and shrugged. "I'll try my best."

I knew then that it was probably too late to go out in the morning mail, but the sooner Rose received this note, the better I would feel.

"Another letter to Rose?" Flossie asked as Nat scurried off.

I had sent more than a dozen letters to Rose since she'd left, and she had not responded to one. The fact that I had not heard from Mother either only caused me to worry more. "It occurred to me when I woke this morning that perhaps Rose hasn't responded to my letters because I never returned her haircombs. I wrote an apology note, told her I broke one, and promised I would send her a new pair as soon as I found suitable replacements."

I checked my bodice watch and gasped, "I barely have time to change!" I left the sleeping tent and headed for the wardrobe tent with Flossie on my heels.

"Change? Why would you need to change? What's wrong with what you're wearing?"

"This? It's great for reading a book here at camp, but I feel I need to be a little more nattily dressed and have a hat if I'm going to the Columbian."

I turned just in time to see Flossie roll her eyes. She waved that thought away and put her hands on her hips. "Back to Rose. Do you really think that she would stop communicating with you because of unreturned haircombs?"

"Yes," I said as I searched through the rack of dresses looking for something suitable for today's outing. "She's stopped talking to me before for lesser infractions."

"But why wouldn't she simply ask you to return the combs? Wouldn't that be easier?"

I turned and gave Flossie a look. Nothing about Rose was easy. I couldn't fathom how Rose thought or why she did the things she did. "What do you think of this?" I asked, holding up a blue-striped day dress. I think there is a hat that matches this one."

"Marguerite," Anne called from the top of the spiral path.

I stepped outside the wardrobe tent and looked up at her. "Yes?"

"Do come and have a late breakfast with Keiko and me."

"So sorry, but I'm due at the Columbian shortly, and I need to dress. Please breakfast without me," I said and dashed back into the tent. Flossie helped me unbutton the day dress I was wearing and put the blue-striped dress over my head. As Flossie buttoned up the long row of tiny buttons that lined the back of my dress, I pinned the hat to my head.

I rummaged through the box of jewelry as I impatiently waited for Flossie to finish. I fished out a Limoges bracelet and laid it across my wrist.

The colors seemed to coordinate with the dress and especially the hat, but was it too much for daytime wear? "I can't remember what Edith said about daytime jewelry," I said to Flossie as she finished fastening the last button. "No, I think this is better suited for evening wear. Besides, can you imagine how it will clink and clank against my wrist as I'm rowing over?" I placed the bracelet back into the box and closed the lid, then pinned my bodice watch to my dress.

"Look at the time! I can make it if I row hard! Flossie, would you mind covering the dresses and tying the tent flaps after I leave? You're an angel."

I spread open the tent flap to exit and stopped short as Friend Anne was standing just on the other side. Her face looked stern. "Marguerite. Might I have a word with thee?"

"Yes, of course!" I said.

"Wilt thou follow me to the other side of Sentry Rock so we do not disturb Keiko or Flossie?"

"Thee?" "Wilt thou?" Her use of her old Quaker pronouns snapped me to attention. I exchanged a glance with Flossie, who looked away, and I knew then that something was amiss.

Anne turned, and I followed her around the sleeping tent and Sentry Rock. She walked another ten feet before she turned to face me.

"I'm very disappointed in you." Her words were lacking emotion, as bland as if she had just asked me to pass the salt, please.

"Thy absence from our fair camp has had an impact on all of us."

My mouth dropped open, but before I could reply, Anne held up her hand to stop me.

"Please let me finish before thee responds."

I closed my mouth and bit the inside of my lip to stop the tears I felt flooding my eyes.

"Keiko is leaving in a week. Not just leaving our cottage, but our country. Perhaps we will see her one day, but perhaps not. She has been thy housemate for four years. The two of you have been close. Yet neither of us has had more than a few minutes of distracted time to speak with thee since our arrival."

I gulped, my throat thick with emotion.

"I understand thou hast made a commitment today, but tomorrow thou must plan to spend time with Keiko and me."

"I am so ashamed," I said, batting my eyes to blink away the tears that were threatening to spill from my eyes. "I deeply apologize."

I opened my mouth to say more, but no words found their way to my lips. Anne reached forward then and put her hand on mine. I looked at her through the tears swimming in front of my eyes.

"No need to say more. You have apologized. You should know that Flossie told us last night that there was some tension while your sister was here."

My head fell back at this comment, and a ragged laugh escaped my throat. I squeezed my eyes shut dislodging my tears that streamed down the side of my face into my ears.

"Tension. Oh my, yes. There was tension," I whispered.

"Flossie reports that you have not spoken of those events and that she has not pressured you to share."

I tipped my head forward and I looked at Anne, causing the tears to flow down the front of my face now.

Anne handed me the handkerchief she'd pulled from her sleeve. I dabbed at my eyes and then at my nose.

"I have always felt somewhat responsible for the rift between you and your family and if there is anything I can do . . . even if it is just to offer you comfort, please let me know."

Family. I wished to express to Anne that despite her well-earned title—Friend Anne—she felt like more than a friend to me. Anne was an odd combination of an older sister and an aunt. Deep down inside of me—even though she was far too young—she felt more like a mother to me than my own mother. But despite the closeness I felt toward Anne, we rarely touched. The calming hand she had placed on my hand now was far more than we usually shared. Still, I felt the need for an embrace. I hugged Anne tightly, resting my head on her shoulder, feeling my tears dampen her dress. She did not return the hug. Her arms remained stiffly at her side, her arms and shoulders tense beneath my embrace. I pushed back, fearing I had made her uncomfortable.

I looked down at my feet afraid to meet her eyes. "Rose left with an ultimatum. I am to move out of your house to her house."

"Or else?"

My eyes were focused on Anne's feet, which were motionless. I shook my head. I hadn't dared to imagine what the consequences might be. Slowly I looked up and let my eyes meet Anne's. She stood stoically, her face a blank slate. Finally, she nodded, as if acknowledging that she had heard what I said, though her face did not betray how she felt about this statement.

"We must talk about this sometime," she said after a long silence. She reached forward and took my hand in hers again. "Now is not the time. I understand you need to go, but before you leave, I must ask . . . is this gentleman you are meeting, is he . . ." Anne fumbled for the words. ". . . a serious attachment?"

"We are only acquaintances." As I said this, I felt my cheeks grow warm. It wasn't a lie. The truth was that I didn't know. "I only know I enjoy speaking to him about Greece and Rome. We share similar sensibilities."

She nodded then and let go of my hand.

"I promise we will spend the day together tomorrow," I said as I turned and rushed to the dock. I stopped short when I saw that Flossie was already in the skiff. She had untied the skiff and was holding onto the dock.

"Hurry! Let's go! You don't want to be late. I'll row. I don't want you to arrive hot and sweaty."

"Oh, Flossie, thank you," I said as I climbed into the skiff.

Flossie pushed us away from the dock and began rowing. "Certainly! Truth be told, I was hoping to see how Charles organizes his work. Perhaps I can garner a few tips for labeling and categorizing baskets and other artifacts."

As always, being out on the water calmed me down. The soft breeze dried the tears from my face. I trailed a hand in the river as Flossie rowed in strong sure strokes. The coolness of the water soothed and refreshed me. "Does it look like I've been crying?" I asked Flossie as we pulled up to the Thousand Island Park skiff livery.

"A little . . . but . . ."

"But what?"

"I'm sorry, but Charles doesn't seem the sort who notices things like that, especially when he is working on his project."

I stepped out of the skiff as soon as it reached the dock.

"Run ahead," Flossie told me. "I'll secure the skiff and meet you at the Columbian. You'll be in the reading parlor, right?"

"Yes," I called back. I hurried along the boardwalk as quickly as decorum would allow and ascended the stairs to the veranda. Before I entered the wide double doors of the hotel, I stopped to run a hand up the back of my hair to tuck errant curls back into my tight updo twist. Next, I straightened my hat and smoothed the front of my dress. I took a deep breath to soothe away the worry that plagued me this morning and entered the hotel.

I saw Charles in our favorite far corner of the reading parlor and was about to raise my hand to wave so he would know that I was there when I heard someone utter his name. "Is that Charles Bartman from Chicago sitting over there in the corner?"

The mention of his name made me stop abruptly. I took a step back so that I was screened by a tall palm.

The woman's voice was scratchy with age. I peeked through the fronds of the palm to see if I could discern who was speaking but only could see the back of a rather large hat.

"Do you mean Clarence and Etta's son? Oh yes. I do believe you're right. I didn't know he was staying at the hotel," said a silky-voiced woman in whispery tones. She was totally eclipsed by the older woman's hat, which I realized was fortuitous or she may have caught sight of me skulking behind the palm. As long as I could not see her, I knew that she could not see me.

"He isn't. I heard that he's staying downriver on Comfort Island with the Clarks," the older woman said with a dismissive air.

I heard the younger woman's teacup settle into the saucer. "Do tell. So what is he doing here at the Columbian?"

"That is a very good question. I've seen him here often and with a young woman."

"Who is she?"

"Another good question," the older woman paused and took a sip of her tea. After her teacup clinked back into the saucer, she continued. "The two have been spending lots of time in that corner over there discussing who knows what with no chaperone around to monitor the conversation."

"Ghastly," the silky-voiced woman replied just as Flossie came through the Columbian door. I put a finger to my lips as she joined me by my side.

"What's more, they attended that grand hop the other night. I saw them leave together and walk toward the Tabernacle under the cover of darkness. Alone. Unchaperoned. She was wearing a low-cut gown. I have no doubts that they were not on the way to the Tabernacle for the prayer meeting. I never saw them return," the older woman said, her ominous tone making her voice huskier.

"Oh my! Scandalous!"

"Etta would be horrified if she knew," the older woman continued.

"Charles is the second son, correct?"

"Indeed. He's quite bookish and perhaps a little socially unsavvy." The woman with the big hat clucked her tongue then and let out a sigh. "These summer girls are quite brazen these days. The Park was so much better when the Methodists had more of a firm grip on affairs."

"Do we know who her people are?"

"That's just it! We do not."

I wondered briefly who she meant by "we." Were others gossiping about my discussions with Charles?

The woman with the big hat reached for a scone on the tea tray. "Perhaps someone should put pen to paper and enlighten Mrs. Bartman. She has a right to know that her dear, sweet Charles may be in grave moral peril."

"I agree. I think a well-worded letter is in order. I could hardly scandalize the woman, but since you know Mrs. Bartman better than I, perhaps you should be the one to write her," the woman with the silky voice suggested.

I raised a hand to my mouth and placed the other over my stomach. I didn't wait for the answer. I turned and fled. I was halfway to the dock before Flossie caught up with me.

"Marguerite, what is it?"

I turned to face Flossie unable to respond. I felt panicked. My hands shook.

Suddenly, Flossie's eyes widened. "That was you they were talking about?" she asked. "They think you're leading Charles Bartman *astray*?"

Placing him in *grave moral peril*. You don't take their comments seriously, do you, Marguerite? The very idea is idiotic! Ludicrous!"

"Flossie, what am I doing? I'm out of my depth."

"Oh, Marguerite. Who cares what two women at the Columbian Hotel think? These women are so empty-headed! Their lives are devoid of anything of substance. They can only prattle on about imagined misdeeds. Only equally vapid women would pay attention to any of their gossip. Who cares what they think?"

"Flossie, you don't understand! I grew up with women like that. Rose and Mother are of the same ilk. To them, a woman's reputation is the only thing she has and it is at the mercy of people like the woman with the big hat. One misstep can ruin a woman's chances for marriage forever. Not only that, such gossip could damage Charles's reputation. They're right! He is socially unsavvy. I'm socially unsavvy. What if news makes it back to Mother or Rose? If it has, I'll never be able to mend my rift with either of them. Meanwhile, I've disappointed Anne. And what must Keiko think of me? I've been a discourteous, inattentive hostess. I must return to Grenell at once," I said, heading for the skiff.

Flossie chased after me and put her hand on my shoulder to stop me. "Wait, Marguerite! You can't leave Charles sitting there in the Columbian wondering what happened to you. Come, let's make our excuses. Then, if you still feel like leaving, I'll row you back to Castle Rock."

"No. NO!" I said, shrinking back from her touch. "I can't go back there. I can't let those women see me with Charles ever again."

"Perhaps you can ask him to meet you at Pullman House?"

"No more hotels. Anywhere public is out of the question!"

"And I don't suppose you want him to come to Castle Rock, either."

I couldn't answer. I imagined how tongues would wag if women like Mrs. Big Hat saw Charles enter our cottage. I shook my head at the thought.

Flossie was quiet then. She enveloped me in a tender hug and patted my back like she was soothing a small child. She took a deep breath and then held me at arm's length. "There, there, Marguerite. You are overwrought. I shall deliver your regrets to Charles. I really want to see his sketches. Tomorrow, Anne and Keiko want to come to the Park to meet some swami. May I ask Charles to join us? Would that be acceptable to you?"

"A swami—as in someone who teaches Hindu religion? Where?"

"Somewhere here at Thousand Island Park. Will it be alright if you meet Charles in the company of three other women? Older women? You and Charles will be properly chaperoned then."

My first impulse was to say no. No to seeing Charles anywhere at any time where those tongue waggers might see us. Seeing me with Charles again might somehow add credence to their story that I was a corruptor of morals. Perhaps Flossie saw these thoughts stirring inside me for she held her hand up, causing me to stop and think. I finally nodded my assent.

"You don't think Friend Anne or Keiko will be offended if Charles accompanies us, do you?" I asked.

"Not at all! Besides, Anne and Keiko are interested in meeting the young man who has been occupying all your time since their arrival."

CHAPTER
twenty-seven

𝒫rince barked as our steamer departed. "Look, Anne and Keiko, there is Prince and his little simian friend, Jambo." We watched Jambo cling to Prince as he ran up and down the dock as the steamer pulled away from the Pullman House landing.

We had decided that our lady's skiff was too small for the four of us and arrived at the dock just in time to take a steamer from Grenell to Thousand Island Park. It was a short trip across the water. I spotted Charles waiting for us near the two-story Thousand Island Park Pavilion as we approached the dock.

"Mr. Bartman," I called out, waving at him as the lines were thrown to the dockhands. Charles looked up and gave me a rare smile.

"It's a pleasure to see you again, Mr. Bartman," Flossie said as she bounced off the gangway.

"Miss Bixby," Charles said, nodding toward Flossie and sounding unusually formal this morning.

"Mr. Bartman, how kind of you to greet us," I said, feeling a flush of embarrassment after failing to meet with him yesterday.

"Not at all. My steamer arrived from Alexandria Bay about fifteen minutes ago. I'm looking forward to today's outing and meeting your friends."

Anne and Keiko joined Flossie and me. I introduced Charles first to

Anne.

Charles stood rigid with his hands clasped behind his back but made a slight nod of deference toward Anne. "Ah, Dr. Ashbridge, Marguerite has told me much about you. Happy to make your acquaintance."

"And this is our housemate, Dr. Okami. Keiko, this is my new friend, Mr. Bartman." I informed Charles that in Japan it is proper to bow at introductions—all greetings and farewells for that matter. Charles dutifully brought his arms from behind his back, held them to his side and mimicked the bow I made.

"*O-me ni kakarete ureshī desu*, which means: 'it's an honor to be seen by you' or 'it is an honor to meet you,'" Keiko replied.

I noted that our introductions had attracted a few stares. "Dr. Okami is the first Japanese woman to receive a degree in Western medicine," I announced a little louder than I needed to, but it had the desired effect. The comment sent a wave of whispers rippling through the crowd.

"Shall we?" Anne asked, gesturing toward the wide boardwalk that led from the Thousand Island Park dock to the Columbian Hotel.

"After you," Charles replied.

Anne, Keiko, and Flossie walked ahead with Charles and me following directly behind them.

"I trust you are feeling better," Charles said. "Flossie reported that you were feeling unwell yesterday."

"Yes. Much better today," I said. "My apologies for not meeting with you. I hope that didn't put you too far behind schedule."

"No. I was able to get a fair amount of work done, though it would have gone much quicker with an expert translator at my side."

As people passed the trio in front of us, heads turned to gawk at Keiko. She is doll-like, a full head shorter than Anne and quite petite. Her dark, almond-shaped eyes seemed darker still because of her light complexion. Keiko wore her black hair pulled back in a tight bun with a small-brimmed hat pinned to her head.

"I've forgotten how foreigners attract stares," I said. "Anne has a big house near the university—and having a big heart—Anne often takes in foreign medical students."

"Foreign medical students other than Dr. Okami?"

"Yes. So far there has been Anandibai Joshi from India. You'll hear more about her today I am certain. She was the first. Then there was Sabat Islambouli from Persia. Let's see—Keiko, of course, and— oh yes!—Susan La Flesche from Nebraska."

Charles chuckled, and I wondered briefly if I had ever heard him laugh in the few weeks I had known him. "You do realize that Nebraska is hardly a foreign country. It's been a state for over twenty-five years now."

"Of course, but Susan is the daughter of Iron Eye, the last chief of the Omaha, and her grandmother was Nikuma, princess of the Iowa. So even though she isn't a foreigner, her dark skin attracted looks even in tolerant Philadelphia. I once saw a mother grip her child's hand tightly and dash across the street to avoid coming in close contact with her."

"I suppose it is common to avoid what is unfamiliar to us," Charles said.

"True, but how will those unfamiliar to us ever be familiar if we avoid all contact? I guess I should consider myself lucky that I've had the opportunity of meeting women from all corners of the globe," I said.

By now we had passed the Columbian Hotel and swung onto St. Lawrence Avenue.

Immediately, I recalled how it looked the night of the hop and how we walked from one pool of streetlight to the next. This is the business section of Thousand Island Park. The storefronts were dark that night, and the street had been empty. Today under the bright July sun, there were lots of islanders patronized the many shops that lined the street. I looked around at the many women milling about from shop to shop. Was one of them the nosy Mrs. Big Hat? Were there others watching Charles and me? I quickened my pace to catch up with Anne, Flossie, and Keiko who had slowed to look at a storefront.

"Look! There is a Japanese bazaar. Here at Thousand Island Park," Flossie said. "Is it new this year?"

"Yes," Charles said. "I heard the Clarks speaking of it. Mr. Tetsuka is a friend of theirs. He's had a Japanese bazaar near the Crossman in Alexandria Bay for several years. Just last week I went with them to look at an Oni statue they are thinking of purchasing. I had occasion to speak with Mr. Tetsuka and he said that he opened a branch bazaar in Thousand Island Park this year."

Keiko turned and looked up at Anne. "I would be interested in meeting this Mr. Tetsuka," she said.

"Certainly, perhaps on the way back. I promised Miss Dutcher that we would be at her cottage by ten."

Keiko bowed solemnly, and we continued on toward the large Tabernacle looming before us at the end of the street.

I was thankful that Anne told the group about the huge, circus-like tents that served as the main gathering place for the Park in the early years. The tent had been replaced by a wooden structure called the Tabernacle. Behind the wooden facade, the Tabernacle was open on three sides to let in cooling river breezes.

The three blocks between the stores and the Tabernacle were filled with colorful cottages and a few tents sprinkled between them. The domiciles, whether wooden or canvas, were evenly spaced in neat rows along the street.

St. Lawrence Avenue came to a T in front of the Tabernacle where we turned left and headed up Park Avenue. Tucked beneath a thick canopy of trees to our right was a lively cottage with a very unique sign.

Keiko giggled at the sign hanging in front of Mosquito Lodge. A large sign, shaped like a man's face, hung on a tree in front of the cottage. A three-dimensional mosquito crafted from wire sat on his forehead, its needle-like proboscis stabbing him between the eyes. "Mosquito" was written above his grimacing mouth and "Lodge" on his chin. I remember almost a decade ago when Mosquito Lodge was only a tent camp, but like us, after tent camping for a number of years, the owners finally built a nice cottage, although theirs was quite a bit larger than ours.

About the time we passed Mosquito Lodge, I heard a buzzing, an odd ethereal noise that rose from the trees beyond us, and couldn't help wondering if the mosquitoes from Mosquito Lodge had escaped and were having a soiree somewhere in the trees above. After a few more steps, I could hear the noise more distinctly. The buzzing was some sort of drum. Above that, I heard tinkling, something bright and silvery-sounding. A few steps closer I could make out low, resonate human humming. Not singing exactly, more like droning.

Around the next bend, we saw the sign for Observatory Avenue. There was only one cottage at the end of this steep street.

"There's Miss Dutcher's cottage," Anne said, pointing up.

On the night of the hop, I had not noticed the yellow cottage with white gingerbread trim perched on a rock surrounded by woods as we walked to the South Bay bridge. At that late hour, the lights mostly had been out. In the bright morning light, the cottage looked like a sentinel overlooking the rest of the cottages on the streets below crowded together in neat rows, side by side, cheek to jowl.

"Who is Miss Dutcher again?" Flossie asked.

"Ruth met her at a normal school," Anne said.

"Ruth?" Charles whispered in my ear. The shapre smell of his shaving soap sent a tingle of delight coursing through me.

"Ruth Clements. Anne and Ruth were schoolmates at a Friends school in West Philadelphia. Ruth went on to normal school, while Anne studied medicine," I whispered back.

"Libbie—Miss Dutcher—taught school at Somerset, New York, for many years. She's retired from teaching now and has taken up art. Watercolor, I believe," Anne continued. "Ruth will be very disappointed about missing this visit. She's still at the fair attending an educational conference."

The mingled sounds of chanting, drumming, and silvery tinkling grew steadily louder, wafting down to us from some magical spot on the ridge beyond the cottage. We were afraid to disturb the worshipers, so we stood on the porch and waited. The porch of the little cottage rose above the top of the surrounding young trees, affording us a commanding view of the river—South Bay to our right and the American channel to the left with Rock Island Lighthouse and the New York mainland beyond. From here, we could look down at the hotel. The cottages and tents of the park looked like a child's playthings lined up on a green carpet and peeking up at us from under the green canopy of trees.

We heard the screen door creak open. Miss Dutcher tip-toed out and welcomed us to her cottage in hushed tones. She was a short, compact woman in a shirtwaist and brown skirt. Her hair was pulled away from her face in two coils. She apologized to us, saying that the Swami's morning session with his devotees had gone longer than expected. She disappeared into the cottage and returned with a pitcher of lemonade and cups. As we sipped, she whispered how she had met Swami Vivekananda at the Parliament of Religions earlier this year at the Chicago Exposition. She had been so taken with him that she had offered him a few weeks of respite from his endless touring here at her cottage at Thousand Island Park. He agreed. She returned from the fair and immediately began construction on an addition to her cottage to accommodate the Swami. It was finished only the day before he arrived. "Mr. Mitchell and his crew were indefatigable in their efforts to finish the project," she said. "They worked day and night to complete the addition before his arrival."

Soon, a stream of people descended from the rise behind the cottage. They nodded and waved to Miss Dutcher, calling back that the Swami would ring when he was ready for his audience with the good doctors.

"He does realize that we aren't all doctors, doesn't he?" Charles asked.

Before I could ask Miss Dutcher, she stood and disappeared into the cottage again, returning with large cushions in blue-striped ticking. "Newcomers sometimes find the rock difficult to sit on," she said passing a cushion to each of us. "Ah! He is ready!" Miss Dutcher said pointing to the sky and tilting her head as if listening to a small bird.

We all stopped chattering and tilted our heads to listen. Mingled with the chittering of birds, we heard the tinkling of a small bell.

"Please, leave the cups on the porch. I will clear them later. Come now. Bring your cushions and follow me," Miss Dutcher said as she descended the porch steps.

We followed Miss Dutcher as she wound around the north side of the cottage and up a well-worn path, each of us carrying our cushion in front of us. The path dipped down into a shady dell with a tiny stream then rose again out to a bald area devoid of trees and swimming in bright sunlight. We came across an area of flat rocks, in the middle of which stood a magnificent oak with spreading limbs and welcoming shade. Beneath the tree, sitting in a crossed-legged pose, was the Swami Vivekananda.

I stopped before I entered the circle of shade beneath the tree and stared at him.

Swami Vivekananda looked almost a part of the rock: his spine poker-straight, his hands resting palms up, one on each knee. His heavy-lidded eyes were shut against the daylight. He sat so still that I thought he might be asleep except that his posture was erect. It was as if every part of him was focused on something I could not see or hear. I glanced at Miss

Dutcher to see if she would rouse him from his reverie, but she stood quiet and still. We waited.

At last, his eyes fluttered open, and he rose. I suppressed a gasp. I was taken aback by his height. He was as tall as Charles, but his shoulders were broader. When I had heard there was a swami staying at the Park, I had envisioned a wizened, bald man with ashen features. Swami Vivekananda was young, perhaps in his late twenties. He was wearing a panju, a light-colored tunic that came to his knees, belted at the waist with a narrow cloth belt. Underneath the tunic, I could see baggy trousers made of the same cloth, and leather slippers on his feet. His head was wrapped with a long white expanse of cloth, the end of which dangled over his shoulder nearly to his waist.

"Greetings, brother and sisters of America," he said in a soft, melodic voice that sounded part wind and part birdsong. "Please, please—be seated."

We stepped into the shadow of the great oak, forming a half-moon arc around him, placing our cushions on the ground before we sat. "Miss Dutcher tells me you wish to learn of the gifts of India." His eyes were large and doe-like, his features dark. His skin was far darker than I had expected. Anandibai had been petite, even shorter than Keiko, with light skin.

All I currently knew of India was what I had learned from Anandibai Joshi. When she arrived in America, she wore the garb of an upper-caste Brahmin. Most days at the Woman's Medical School of Pennsylvania, of course, she wore a shirtwaist and dark skirt, the same as the other female medical students. But on festive occasions, she would don her sari and wear her *nath* nose ring and her *bindi*, a vermillion colored dot in the center of her forehead. She had lent me her copy of the *Bhagavat-Gita*. I still remember her admission statement almost verbatim, so moving was it in its conviction: "In this I must not fail. My soul is moved to help the many who cannot help themselves." Despite the opposition of friends and family, she had made the arduous journey to America to help the poor, suffering women of her country.

After she came to live with us, I'd slowly learned how daring her actions were. To the Brahmins, the caste to which she belonged, it was prohibited to travel across the ocean and eat food prepared by people of a different caste. But she had come here to America in direct violation of their customs and faced rejection from her community, family, and friends. She did this before she had been accepted to a medical school. Even now, I marvel at the fortitude and self-conviction it took to leave everything she knew to come to this foreign land against all odds and hope to gain entry into a medical school.

I looked up when I heard Swami Vivekananda say something about the Greeks. As I had been caught in my own musings, I had missed much of what he had said. He was speaking of an Emperor Oshoka of India who visited the west in 300 B. C. He claimed Oshoka met many a Grecian king and imported to them the principles of Hindu religion which later flourished into Christianity. "Thus it is explained, why you have the doctrine of the trinity, of the incarnation of God, and of our ethics."

I looked around at the faces of my companions, the ladies all sitting to my left and Mr. Bartman sitting to my right. Flossie was the most engaged, she seemed to be hanging on each of the Swami's melodious words.

The Swami ended his talk, lowering his eyes, bringing his hands in front of him in a prayer position then bowing slightly to us. He sat then eyes closed in a meditative state.

Miss Dutcher motioned for us to stand and follow her. "I'm sorry to hurry you along," Miss Dutcher said when we were a few paces away, ". . . but the Swami likes time for writing in the afternoon. This is his favorite spot—his favorite tree. He feels more spiritual here than other places."

"It's a beautiful tree, so well proportioned and shaped," Flossie whispered as she looked back at the oak.

Miss Dutcher stepped closer to Flossie, and bent her head towards her and said in low tones, "Swami Vivekananda says that in India near his home temple they have a similar tree—not an oak of course—but the Swami speaks of hugging the tree to let it absorb your cares and worries, sending the pain you feel down into the ground through the roots to be cleansed by the Earth and sending your prayers for relief up through its limbs to the heavens."

Flossie's eyes widened and I witnessed a shiver of delight slither down her spine.

Miss Dutcher motioned for us to follow her, and we turned toward the path to her cottage. I'd taken several dozen steps down the path when

I turned to make a comment to Flossie and was surprised not to find her directly behind me. I stopped then and gazed back up the path to locate her. She was standing on the other side of the tree, her arms wrapped around the trunk, her cheek pressed against it, her eyes squeezed shut, and an angelic smile across her face. I left her there, unsure how long she would stay hugging the tree.

We piled the cushions on the porch and thanked Miss Dutcher for her hospitality, and our introduction to the Swami. By then, Flossie had caught up with us. She babbled incessantly about the Swami. "He's a wonderful orator. Electrifying! Mesmerizing!" she proclaimed as we walked back down Park Avenue toward the Japanese bazaar.

"Did you speak often of religion with your housemate from India?" Charles asked.

"Sometimes," I said. "She was a vegetarian. Once a week, she would cook a meal for us. Lots of spice. Mostly she spoke of poverty."

"I was most fascinated with her *nath*, her nose ring. It was gorgeous," Flossie said.

"A nose ring? Like a bull might wear?" Charles asked. "

"No. It was a lovely piece of jewelry," I said "A ring about the size of a silver dollar, but gold. The bottom half was ringed with small pearls on the inside of the ring, small diamonds lined the outside of the ring, and a teardrop pearl dangled from the bottom. It was attached by a chain to a piercing in her ear. It was quite impressive. It is traditional for a woman to wear a *nath* at her wedding and thereafter for formal occasions."

"But why?" Charles asked.

Flossie was eager to contribute. "As an anthropologist, I think there are multiple reasons. One is that in Ayurvedic medicine, a pierced nose on the left side is said to relieve pain during childbirth. But on a deeper level, there is a belief that women should not directly exhale air through her nostrils near her husband as in doing so, it may have an ill-effect on his health. The *nath* acts as both a reminder and an obstruction."

"So Dr. Joshi was married?" Charles asked. "Isn't it unusual for a woman doctor from any country to be married?"

The four of us shared a glance as we walked down St. Lawrence Avenue.

Anne literally stepped forward and walked alongside Charles in order to fill in the details of Anandibai's story. "Dr. Joshi was from a very well-to-do family who afforded her an education, rarer in their country than it is in ours. When her teacher moved to another province, it was decided that she would marry him so she could continue her education. Her teacher was twenty-nine and she was only nine."

Charles stopped in the middle of the road. The rest of us took a couple of steps beyond before turning to see the astonished look on his face. "She married at nine? To a man twenty years her senior?"

"According to Anandibai, to be married that young is not an oddity in her country. But for her to move away from home and live away from her parents, she had to be married."

"A long-standing belief that still prevails in our country," Flossie said.

"She had her first and only child at age fourteen," Anne said. "She nearly died during the delivery. The baby did not live long. It was then she decided to become a doctor to help the women of her country. She did this at great personal expense as she was shunned by friends, family and the people of her village."

"Did they accept her once she returned?" Charles asked as we continued down the avenue.

"I don't know. She died soon after her return. Her ashes were sent here to the United States for burial. She's buried in Poughkeepsie, New York," Anne said.

I'll never forget that day. Anne read the words from one of Anandibai's letters at her gravesite: "Though I cannot teach courage, I must not learn cowardice, nor at least leave undone what I so long since determined to do. I am not discouraged."

By now we had reached the Japanese Bazaar. The others turned and ascended the steps into the shop, but I lingered behind. The brave words of Anandibai Joshi echoed in my head.

Flossie stuck her head out the door and motioned for me to join the group. I stepped inside the door just as Keiko and Mr. Tetsuka bowed formally to each other then began conversing in Japanese. The short, clipped words were sparse at first then came in a deluge. Keiko turned to us and bowed in apology for their insensitivity in speaking in a foreign tongue and leaving us out of the conversation.

"Not at all," I said. "It is a delight to hear your native tongue."

Mr. Tetsuka took us on a tour of his shop then, which was crammed with Japanese paper lanterns, oilpaper umbrellas, all styles and colors of folding fans, as well as clothing—silk, woolen and cotton wrappers. There were humming tops and other small toys for children. The abundance of artwork was astounding: brasses, ivories, embroidery, paintings on silk. There were cigar cases, match safes, porcelain figures, and wood carvings. In the back, there was a lacquered Japanese folding screen with a cherry blossom motif, and rows of Japanese bamboo stacking tables. Charles was mesmerized by the fluid motion of Shodo, Japanese calligraphy. Keiko offered to teach him Shodo if he were interested. By the time the two finished talking, we had scheduled a visit to Comfort Island. Charles was sure that Alson would be interested in Shodo.

"Do you have time for a few translations this afternoon?" Charles asked after we bowed goodbye to Mr. Tetsuka and stepped back out onto St. Lawrence Avenue. We paused then, Flossie, Anne, and Keiko waiting for my response, knowing the cause of my hesitation.

I thought of dear Anandibai and the words that Friend Anne had read at her gravesite. She had faced a more severe censor than a few wagging tongues. My cheeks reddened, shamed at my cowardice yesterday. I raised my chin, straightened my spine, and replied that I could spare a few hours to help him with translation.

Flossie blinked and shared a surprised look with Anne and Keiko. "Would you like us to join you?" she asked.

"Of course, you are more than welcome," I said as we exited the Japanese bazaar and headed toward the Columbian Hotel. "But I think we will do just fine on our own."

CHAPTER
twenty-eight

"Welcome to Comfort Island," Charles said as we stepped out onto the dock.

"They're here," young Edwin shouted as he bounded down the path followed by his two brothers. Alson and Mancel adopted a more dignified gait.

"Good to see you again Miss Hartranft," Mancel said as he helped me from the gangway onto the dock.

"And you as well. May I introduce my campmates? This is Miss Bixby, Dr. Ashbridge, and Dr. Okami."

Obviously schooled by Charles, the three boys put their hands at their side and bowed. Mrs. Clark joined us then, greeting us with a slight bow of her head and a warm smile.

"We have the parlor set up for the magic lantern show," Mancel said. "We darkened the windows and hung a sheet for viewing the slides."

"May I carry those boxes for you?" Alson asked taking a box of slides from Keiko's hands. Mancel took the box containing the magic lantern from Flossie.

"We can't wait to see it," Edwin said, running ahead of the group.

"We went to the Japanese Exhibition at the fair of course, but it will be better having it narrated by Dr. Okami," Alson said.

Heavy velvet curtains had been hung over each window, and once the door was shut it was indeed very dark in the Clarks' front parlor. The table had been cleared of games and books and was ready for the magic lantern. While my eyes were still adjusting to the sudden darkness, Keiko set up the magic lantern.

This would be my fourth viewing of the Chicago Columbian Exposition slides in the past three days. Keiko had showed the slides to Flossie and me one evening a few days ago. The next night, we went to Glimpses to show the Kerrs. Last night, Mr. Tetsuka had rowed over for a viewing. Each time, I saw the slides I noticed something new and learned something different. I trusted that today would be the same.

Mr. Clark lit the tiny kerosene light inside the magic lantern, and light flooded through the lens, bounced off the white sheet, and made me blink. Keiko carefully unwrapped the glass slides, selected one, and slid it into the opening at the front. A blob of shapes appeared on the sheet. Keiko adjusted the lens, and the shapes slowly sharpened: and the Chicago World's Fair came into focus there on the Clarks' parlor wall. I instantly recognized the bridge that led to the island in the central lagoon. Located on the lush treed island were the Japanese tea house and the Ho-o-den, or Hall of the Phoenix.

Most of the slides were black-and-white, but my favorites were the interior shots of the Ho-o-den that had been colorized. They were brilliant gold with the branches of trees above and the feathers of the two phoenixes in blues, greens, and white. The slides that Keiko had purchased showed many of the other buildings that other countries had built, but to me, the Japanese buildings on the wooded island seemed the most enchanting.

Anne spoke up, "I only wish the slides could convey the feeling of being on this enchanting island in the evening." The Clarks murmured agreement before Anne continued. "As the sun sets, the island is lit by fairy lights of colored glass along the paths. Such a contrast to the bright lights of electricity. The fairy lights are small, brilliantly colored oil lanterns. So soft. So inviting. Day or night, the Wooded Island was the place fairgoers could relax and be in nature."

Keiko nodded. "In Japan, we strive to live in harmony with nature rather than dominate nature. We have many festivals that celebrate the changing of the seasons and the beauty of nature."

As soon as we saw the last glass slide, Mancel flung open the heavy velvet curtains and blinked at the brightness of the day. Mrs. Clark invited us out onto the porch where we found lunch waiting for us. As we ate, the boys had lots of questions about Japan and its art and customs.

After lunch, Anne, Flossie and I helped Keiko change into her yukata kimono, carefully tying the inner belt and placing the *obi* belt over it. The Clarks applauded when Keiko entered the parlor. The kimono was dark blue silk with light blue, orange, and white flowers embroidered on the fabric. Keiko is reed-thin. Her raven black hair was styled in an elegant chignon decorated with matching silk flowers.

Alson had an easel set up in the corner. He asked Keiko to stand near the window for good light and immediately started sketching.

"So lovely!" Mrs. Clark said.

"It was my wedding kimono," Keiko said, careful to remain motionless as she spoke.

"You were married?" Charles asked.

"I am married," Keiko said. "My husband, Okami Senkichiro and I were both teachers at the Sakurai Girls' School."

Flossie's face brightened. "I didn't know you were a teacher."

"Yes, I taught English."

"What does your husband teach?"

"My husband teaches art."

"Your husband allowed you to come across the ocean to a foreign country? To be away from him for . . . a couple of years?" Mr. Clark asked.

"Love is more than holding on to someone. Sometimes love means releasing the one you love to be the person they are meant to be," Keiko said, never moving from her pose.

"The kimono is so tight. How do you move? Isn't it difficult to walk in a kimono?" Edwin asked.

"Our western clothes hobble women as well, only in different ways," Flossie told Edwin.

"Hence," Anne said, "the reason for the dress reform movement."

"Egad!" Mancel declared. "Are we in the middle of a bloomer revolution?"

"I've worn bloomers," Flossie confessed. "They are perfect for wheeling. Better than getting my skirt tangled in the spokes of my safety bicycle."

"For wheeling, fine. But soon if we're not careful, ladies will be wearing trousers and dressing like men," Mr. Clark said.

"As a doctor, I'm most concerned about corsets and the weight of undergarments. The average woman wears about thirteen pounds of undergarments," Anne said.

"Thirteen pounds?" Edwin asked, astounded.

"Yes, that sounds about right. There's the chemise, petticoats—sometimes four or five petticoats—bustles, hoops and a corset," Mrs. Clark said, counting off the undergarments on her fingers.

Edwin put his hands over his ears. "I don't need to hear about ladies' undergarments," he muttered.

"The corset is what concerns me the most," Anne continued. "It displaces the inner organs, restricts breathing and—in my educated opinion—is harmful to women's health."

"Shhh!" Alson demanded from behind the easel. "All this talk is very distracting!"

Flossie moved across the room to stand behind Alson so she could watch him work at the easel. "Ahhh! Marguerite! You must come see: only a few lines on the sketch pad and he's already caught Keiko's lithe poise in a few graceful strokes."

Alson's eyebrows scrunched together in vexation.

"Ladies, please. This way," Mrs. Clark offered, motioning us toward the door. "Why don't we leave Alson to his sketching. Let's enjoy the view downriver."

Once we were outside, Charles motioned me toward the porch steps. "I'm more in a mood for a walk. Will you join me, Marguerite?" Charles asked. "Alson does not like people looking over his shoulder while he draws. He's still self-conscious about the creative process," Charles confided as we left the ladies on the porch and moved toward the channel-side path. We adopted a slow meandering gait. A wake from a passing steamer washed up on the rocky shoreline in a rhythm akin to our strides. At the far corner of the island, before the path veered inland through the woods and crossed the small bridge over the channel to the Oliphant side of the island, there was a small stone bench. "Would you like to sit?"

Charles asked, gesturing toward the bench.

We sat in the deep shade of a towering cedar and stared out at the river. It was quiet, save for the twittering of birds and the lapping of the water on the shoreline. An ant crawled across my foot. I watched him scuttle first left, then right in a hurry to go somewhere, but I wasn't certain it knew where it was off to at such a rapid pace. I picked up a stick and laid it in front of the ant. Undeterred, the ant scrambled over it.

I looked up at Charles. He was staring out over the water. In that instant, I realized that we were alone for the first time since the night on the bridge in the moonlight. The thought made me a little nervous. A squirrel jumped through the leaf litter behind us. The sudden noise startled Charles. I thought he might jump out of his skin. I noticed a small line of beaded sweat on his upper lip. He reached up and dabbed it away with his handkerchief, which he hastily shoved back into his right pocket. He then wrested carefully from his left pocket another handkerchief.

"I have something to show you," he said as he unwound the something that had been carefully wrapped in a handkerchief. He slid his hand forward. I could see a brooch lying face down in his cupped hand.

"What is it?" I asked.

"Turn it over," he said.

I did and there was a classic cameo set in a lovely gold baroque oval. The woman carved into the surface had her head inclined upward as if looking up to the heavens. I had the feeling that if I stared at it long enough, I would actually see the woman's hair rippling in the river air.

"This is quite beautiful. Does it belong to the museum?" I asked.

Charles jerked his hand back and looked alarmed. "No! Of course not! My superiors would never allow me to take a piece from the museum. Nor would I ever dream of taking something from the museum to my home in Chicago let alone on an excursion far from Chicago."

"Oh," I said, surprised by his indignant response.

His posture and tone softened then. "No, this was my grandmother's," he said looking down at the brooch.

"Oh," I said, looking at the brooch with renewed interest.

"I bought it for her as a thank-you gift. She sent me to Italy and Greece after my graduation. I bought it for her in Naples."

I looked at him and waited, for I felt there was more to the story.

In the short time I'd known Charles, I knew that questions sometimes flustered him, so I waited for him to find the words to tell me what he wanted to say.

"She died last year," he said. His Adam's apple bobbed up and down with emotion before he continued. "Before she died, she gave the brooch back to me and said that someday I must give it to a woman I love."

He placed the cameo—handkerchief and all—into my hand and closed my fingers around it.

It took a moment for me to realize what he was telling me without saying the words.

"I'm . . . I'm very honored. I'm not sure what to say."

An awkward pause followed. Had he more to say? We seemed suspended in the moment. There was no wind, no air, no sound nor movement.

He reached for the cameo, turned it facedown, and pointed to the bail on the back. "You can wear it as a necklace by threading it onto a chain, or wear it as a brooch."

He placed the cameo back into my hand, closed my fingers around it again, squeezed my hand, and jumped nervously to his feet. "We should be making our way back to the cottage. Dr. Okami said she would give a calligraphy demonstration, and I don't want to miss that."

Our walk to the bench had been slow and leisurely, but the pace back was brisk, almost frenzied. Charles walked a few steps ahead of me, looking over his shoulder to make sure I was keeping up. He did pause at the base of the porch steps and gestured for me to precede him up the steps, as etiquette dictates. He rushed ahead of me across the porch and opened the door, ushering me inside.

When we entered, we found Keiko sitting on the floor, a low table in front of her. "Like many of our practices, it is the process as much as the end result that is an art form."

"Good," Charles whispered in my ear, "she is just starting."

"Calligraphy starts by making the ink using a grinding stone, a few drops of water, and a *sumi* stick."

"What is the *sumi* stick made from?" Edwin asked.

Keiko held up the black *sumi* stick, which was about the same length and girth as my index finger. "It is made from pine tree soot."

"Wouldn't it be easier to have the ink made ahead of time than to make ink each time you want to write or draw?" Mancel asked.

"Ah! It is not about ease; it is about ritual. There is a reason behind this process. The making of the ink helps put the calligrapher into a meditative state, while at the same time warming the shoulder and loosening both the shoulder and elbow joints."

"How long does it take to make the ink?" Alson asked.

"The process takes about twenty minutes. Shorter if one rushes, but rushing is never encouraged. It is always wise to honor the passing of time." Keiko motioned for Alson to kneel next to her.

Alson took his turn making *sumi* ink. Once the ink was made, Keiko taught Alson how to make the symbol for happiness. Keiko explained that the white brush was made of goat's hair, which produced rounded forms and fleshy brushstrokes. The brown brush was made of wolf's hair and was perfect for making sharp, bony strokes.

Varied emotions flickered across Alson's face as he worked: concentration, frustration, and joy. He was totally enthralled with the process. Gone was his self-consciousness at the rest of us looking over his shoulder.

Keiko spoke of other Japanese art forms like ikebana, the art of Japanese flower arranging, and haiku, Japanese poetry.

My ears pricked at the mention of poetry and I asked her to tell us about haiku.

"A Japanese haiku is only three lines and seventeen syllables. The first line is composed of five syllables, the second of seven, and the last of five. The poems are usually about nature, but always about change. There is no rhyme. My teacher stressed the importance of pairing two distinct images—often very divergent images. I love haiku as it captures a beautiful morsel of the day. Haiku is beauty and emotion condensed into a few words."

Mrs. Clark passed out paper and pencils. The room was silent then as the group of us tried to construct our own haikus.

I looked out the window letting the scene outside inspire me. After writing down a few keywords here and there, and silently counting the syllables on my hand, I came up with a poem.

"Did you finish?" Charles asked.

"I did. And you?"

He nodded. We exchanged sheets of paper, each eager to read the other's poem. He read mine:

one bright sun above
shines on calm water causing
many suns below

I read his:

clouds on horizon
connect blue sky to water
white between two blues

At last! I'm a poet, I thought to myself. I told Charles about my failed attempts at poetry, but all that disappointment seemed unimportant now. While he had never thought of himself as a poet, he liked the visual aspect of haiku and thought perhaps he would add a haiku a day to his sketch journal.

"Promise me you'll send me a haiku tomorrow in the mail," Charles said.

I smiled. I liked the thought of sharing a cherished moment with Charles each day. "Only if you promise to do the same," I said.

CHAPTER
twenty-nine

By the time Keiko, Anne, and I arrived at Pullman House dock, there were over a dozen people there waiting for the steamer *St. Lawrence* to pick them up for the Wednesday evening searchlight excursion. There was a young couple standing alone near the corner of the dock and three families, all with daughters. The older girls were running about giggling and the two youngest girls were held by their mothers.

"Where is the boy with the dog and monkey?" asked a girl dressed in a lovely blue gown with amethyst trim. She appeared to be the eldest of the trio. Her hemline was lower than her two sisters, but she still wore her hair down so I guessed she was younger than fourteen-year-old Olivia but older than eleven-year-old Edith. From the hemlines, I guessed the girls to be thirteen, eleven, and seven.

"Why? Do you want to make sheep's eyes at him?" the middle sister asked. She was wearing a dress of brown-and-green stripes. Her hair flowed down her back in attractive curls, and a large bow adorned the right side of her head.

"Kissy! Kissy!" the youngest sister taunted, and the two younger sisters made kissy faces at their older sister and giggled.

The older and younger sister had light-colored hair. But, like me, the middle sister had darker hair. Instantly, I thought of my own sisters.

"I only wanted to buy a biscuit for the dog and monkey," the oldest-sister insisted.

"Or play kissy kissy with their owner?" the middle-sister teased.

"Stop," the oldest sister said. She retreated to a bench and sat down, reaching into her reticule and pulling out a small white bag of candy.

"Hey! Isn't that my bag of candy? I left it on the washstand in our room," the middle sister asked.

"Certainly not! It's mine," the oldest sister insisted.

Hands on hips, the middle sister advanced. "I don't think so! Come on Lisa, give it back! You're always stealing my candy."

Their mother's head turned toward the girls, sensing a quarrel brewing. "Tressa!" she called and motioned the middle-sister over. She lifted the youngest of the girls from her mother's arms and placed her on the dock, then did the same with the other young girl. "Entertain Paige and Autumn. You girls can play a game with them while we wait."

With her two younger charges in tow, Tressa returned to the bench and her two sisters. Within seconds the sisters were singing a rousing clapping song called, "A Sailor Went to Sea." The younger girls watched and Autumn tried to clap along but the pace was too fast for her to keep up.

As the giggles between the girls grew, Keiko turned to me and asked how long the tour would be.

"Perhaps three hours. It varies," I told Keiko.

I turned away from the girls, though their chanting still rang in my ears. I fingered the outline of the cameo pinned on my high stand-up collar. Even though I wore crocheted gloves, I could feel the profile of the woman carved in the shell. The wind tugged on the ends of my hair as I felt the wind-tossed strands of the woman on the shell. Did Charles really think I looked like a Greek goddess?

"Is that our steamer?" Keiko asked, pointing to an approaching steamer.

I knew instantly that the steamer heading downriver was too small to be the *St. Lawrence*. I squinted to bring the steamer into sharper focus and could see the distinctive pilothouse atop that looked like an octagonal birdcage and knew it was the steamer *Maud*. "No, but perhaps the next one after that," I said. Round Island is two miles upriver, but I could see two large steamers at the dock and the black smoke rising from their stacks.

One of the steamers had just pulled away from the Frontenac dock and I figured it was probably the *St. Lawrence*, although it could have been the steamer *Empire State*.

The girls had reached a fevered pace with the clapping rhyme, and finally unable to keep pace, they had dissolved into giggles. They seemed so carefree. So happy. Had Rose, Lily and I ever been so carefree? It seemed so long ago.

The older sisters took the little girls on their laps and played patty cake.

Maud was passing us now, and I could see that the steamer that had pulled away from the Frontenac dock could not be the *St. Lawrence* for it was too large. It was probably the steamer *Empire State*.

The mother of the three girls approached and introduced herself as Mrs. Tingley. She introduced us to her husband and the other adults of the group, Mr. and Mrs. Steiding, and Mr. and Mrs. Morley. She called over her girls in order to introduce them. The older blonde was Lisa, the younger blonde Dresden, and the pert middle child with the dark hair was Tressa.

"And this little sprite is Autumn Lily," Tressa said, jostling the three-year-old up and down on her hip. The movement made Autumn titter with laughter.

Lisa held the other girl, who appeared to be about five. She had dark, straight hair and large knowing eyes. "This is Miss Steiding," Lisa said, her formalness befitting of the child's calm dignity.

"Good evening," I said bowing to the serious Miss Steiding, a pleasure to make your acquaintance.

"We arrived last Saturday," Mrs. Tingley informed us, "we were so weary from our trip we decided not to go on the excursion that night. The girls have asked every day if this was the night of the searchlight excursion. Have you been before?"

We replied that Anne and I had been on the searchlight excursion many times but this was Keiko's first.

"We've heard so much about it. One can't come to the islands without going on a searchlight excursion," Mrs. Tingley said. Immediately, both adults and the girls poured out a continuous stream of questions: "Do you always take the steamer *St. Lawrence*? What about the *Empire State*? Did you hear about the race between the *Empire State* and *St. Lawrence* last night? It was in all the papers this morning. Do you think there will be another race this evening?"

We responded that the steamer *St. Lawrence* was the only excursion we had ever taken as the *Empire State* doesn't stop at the Pullman House and that we doubted there would be another race between the *Empire State* and the *St. Lawrence*. "At least I hope not," I added. "I prefer a slow cruise."

"Look! Here comes a steamer now! Is that the *St. Lawrence* or the *Empire State*?" Dresden asked. Like her older sister, Lisa, her hair was more golden, she wore a white dress with a brilliant red sash and a matching ribbon in her hair.

"It's not the *St. Lawrence*," I said, "The *St. Lawrence* is a sidewheeler. It must be the *Empire State*."

It wasn't quite dark yet, though the sun had dipped below the trees long ago. Another steamer was coming upriver in the wake of the *Empire State*, discharging a long sinuous coil of black smoke. The western sky still held a blush of the day. As the steamer neared the dock, I squinted into the growing darkness wondering if Charles was on the upper deck. I wondered if he were peering toward the Pullman House dock, trying to find me in the crowd below.

The three young families boarded before we did and I was surprised to find Charles waiting for me by the gangway. "Would you like to go to the hurricane deck?" he asked after greeting the three of us and wishing us a good evening. "Or would you rather remain in the salon."

We all agreed the lights would be easier to see from the hurricane deck. As we went up the broad back staircase, well-lit with electric lights, Charles told me about the lights on Emery Island. "It was positively girdled in light." Above, near the building site, were the letters C. G. E. written in dazzling light.

"Charles Goodwin Emery," I said.

"And besides the initials, there was a cross, a heart, and an anchor of gold."

"Was the Frontenac lit when you stopped?" I asked.

"Oh my, yes! It was a pyramid of light."

By now we were on the hurricane deck and found a spot along the railing on the starboard side of the steamer.

Grenell 1893

I noticed that the Steidings, Morleys, and Tingleys had split-up, each finding a spot on the port side.

As the *St. Lawrence* docked at Thousand Island Park, Charles and I stared out at Castle Francis, which had a fine display of lights. The beacon of Rock Island Lighthouse was lit and began revolving. The brilliant eye of light swept around and around directly across from us.

"I wonder how long it takes to make a complete revolution?" I asked.

Feeling challenged by my question, Charles started counting, but soon we broke into laughter as he realized he was counting too quickly. The light swept by again, blinding me for an instant but revealing that Charles was looking at me with a tight-lipped smile on his face. When my eyes met his, he looked away and fumbled in his vest pocket for his pocketwatch. He was looking forward when the light swept across our faces and, with renewed seriousness, he began counting. His eyes were fixed to the second hand of his pocketwatch, and, after timing several of the revolutions, he determined that it took fifteen seconds for the light to make a full revolution.

By now, the passengers at Thousand Island Park were aboard, and the steamer *St. Lawrence* glided downriver as the skies darkened and the stars came forth. The slender new moon lay low on the horizon's rim. Next to it, Venus shone bright and vibrant. Soon, the islands were in repose, hiding behind a veil of darkness until a dazzling shaft of light shot from the top of the wheelhouse, revealing pines and rock. The illuminated water mirrored the islands. It truly looked as if the islands were suspended between heaven and Earth.

The cottages, rocks, boats, and trees that I'd seen a hundred times now appeared in sharp focus, materializing magically, brilliantly out of the darkness. Charles explained that the searchlight utilized ten-thousand candle power to turn night into day. Whatever the light touched seemed somehow enhanced. Rocks appeared more formidable, the trees more beautiful, and the cottages and summer homes like something out of a fairy tale. Here we saw a barking dog running along the shore. There we saw a fisherman rowing home. All would have been invisible under the cover of darkness. On the port side, we saw the lights of Fineview and a group waving to us from the dock.

The Mandolin Orchestra in the salon had started playing when we left Thousand Island Park, and it seemed we were floating through the darkness buoyed by music. Central Park on the mainland, or starboard side was well illuminated. The name of the small enclave was spelled out in scarlet, green, and amber lights.

Neh Mahbin sparkled ahead of us in the darkness. When we neared the shores of Comfort Island, the searchlight revealed Neh Mahbin's elegant stone staircase. The veranda that was so crowded on the Glorious Fourth was now empty. The tower of the Clarks' cottage had two giant globes of light. I tingled as I remembered standing on the tower that night and watching the fireworks at Neh Mahbin.

Warners Island looked like it was wearing a scarf studded with tri-colored jewels: diamonds, rubies, and amethyst. I gasped when I saw the electric fountain in front of Casa Blanca on Cherry Island. It was outfitted with colored lights beneath, making it appear like a fountain of liquid color splashing and changing before my eyes. "Simply mesmerizing," I sighed and leaned toward Charles, my shoulder briefly brushing against his.

We saw the lights of Hopewell Hall over the heads of those lining the port side. At Castle Rest, George Pullman's place, a cascade of light fell from the top of his tower clear to the ground. Strings of fairy lights cast rays of light that outlined the switchback paths leading from the dock to the grand summer home in the center of the island, which was lit with dazzling twinkling lights and looked more like Aladdin's palace than a summer cottage in northern New York. Friendly Island's paths were so thick with lights that they looked like rivers of fire. As others crowded to the port side, Charles whispered in my ear, "We'll get a better view of these islands on the way back." The smell of his shaving soap tickled my nose. Gooseflesh erupted on my arms.

Ahead we could see a red heart on Hart's Island, and, off the starboard side, the electric lights of Alexandria Bay shone steadily in white splendor. As we turned around when we reached the Crossman Hotel in Alexandria Bay, the Mandolin Orchestra in the salon took a break and we could hear the music of the twenty-two-piece orchestra from the Crossman wafting across the water until we were well past Cherry Island.

As the searchlight swung to the islands on the mainland side, the crowd lining the port side of the hurricane deck roared with laughter.

Grenell 1893

We let go of the starboard railing and drifted to port, craning our necks over the crowd to see what was causing the commotion. The searchlight was fixed on a couple in a skiff out for a moonlight row. The illuminated couple turned their backs to the light and the young man put his arm around the young lady to shield her from prying eyes. The crowd on the *St. Lawrence* whooped and hooted. Charles and I shared a sheepish glance, then returned to the starboard railing.

Charles and I had not seen each other in two days. Commitments with the Clarks and my renewed commitment to spend time with Keiko had prevented him from traveling upriver to meet me at the Columbian, but we had traded haikus in the mail, posting them twice a day. I have a small, handcarved wooden box I purchased at Mr. Tetsuka's store, where I kept our haikus. Looking through the collection of haikus in the box, I could see that Charles often wrote haikus about clouds while I was more apt to write of trees or flowers—but then again, I had been working with Flossie on her herbarium for a few weeks. Perhaps I would write a haiku about the searchlight. I vowed to start carrying a small notebook and pencil in my reticule for noting images and phrases that flitted into my head.

The Mandolin Orchestra started playing again. Many had descended from the open hurricane deck to the salon below to spend the return trip dancing. Among the throng that went below were the three couples from Pullman House, leaving the two smaller girls in the care of the older Tingley girls.

While their parents no doubt danced below, the girls danced around the center of the hurricane deck. Autumn Lily, the youngest of the group, danced in her smocked frock unaware and uncaring if anyone was watching or not. Her ability to lose herself to dance, uncaring of who observed, made her a delight to watch.

When we reached Thousand Island Park, the steamer turned to starboard and steamed along the Park's westernmost shore. Last week the Park Herald had encouraged cottagers whose residences border the coast or the open plaza surrounding the hotel to take special pains for the remainder of the season to illuminate their properties every Wednesday and Saturday evening for the searchlight excursions. The cottagers along Coast Avenue had taken this suggestion to heart. The street looked like something from a fairy village. One cottage facade was decorated with red, white, and blue lanterns.

I looked across the water and saw a campfire ablaze on Hub Island where the Kingstonians were camping. We heard them yell and cheer and could see orbs of light swinging to and fro. The searchlight swung in their direction, and we could see five fellows swinging lanterns and waving as we slid by.

We crossed in front of South Bay then. The steamer's brilliant searchlight swung its brilliance and fastened on the South Bay bridge starting at Prospect Point and slowly illuminating its expanse over the water. I imagined with searing embarrassment how I would have felt if the spotlight had fallen on Charles and me the night we stood on the South Bay bridge. My breath caught wondering if we might find a couple there, but the light swept the entire length of the bridge without catching a couple in an embrace.

As we crossed the entrance to the Narrows, the searchlight highlighted the palisades on the Wellesley Island side. Starting with a tiny pinpoint spotlight, the beam rose from the base to the craggy top, then widened to take in the whole lovely rock in at once. It was a sight I'd taken in a thousand times, but watching the light peel back the night to focus in on such a grandiose rock was truly dazzling.

The steamer slowed, and many of the dancers from the salon below made their way up to the hurricane deck as we were approaching the abandoned Cliff House. As the railing became more crowded, we made room for the Tingley sisters and their two small charges. Tressa held Autumn Lily while Lisa held Paige.

"Is that the haunted hotel?" Dresden asked, clutching to the railing and standing on tiptoe.

"Some say that it is," I told her. Perched high on the rocks and once a dazzling white, the Cliff House had been abandoned and left to the elements nearly a decade ago. The searchlight swung its penetrating glare onto the dilapidated structure. The windows were dark and empty; shutters hung from odd angles, and others were gone, ripped away by vandals or wind.

"A group of young people rowed over to the Cliff House the other night, but mother and father wouldn't let me go with them," Lisa lamented.

Our tour guide raised the megaphone to his mouth and let out a low, mournful wail. Some of the summer girls in the crowd let out a titter of nervous giggles. The guide told of the ghosts of murdered souls, babies who had been thrown down a well in the back of the hotel, and the most vivid, the tale of a handyman who broke into the storehouse, stole two watermelons, and ate them both. He'd developed colic and died. On stormy nights his form floats in and out of the storeroom. The light from the searchlight shot across the rock to the little storeroom up and behind the hotel.

I whispered in Charles's ear that Arnie had told me there never was a well behind the Cliff House, so the story was no doubt apocryphal.

"On nights when a full moon shines bright and moon rays shine on the Narrows side of the old house, something eerie happens. When a moonbeam shines directly into that window," the guide said and paused as the searchlight swung to shine on the center of three windows on the east side of the hotel, ". . . and casts its magical light down the central hall of the hotel. For the space of some ten minutes, a ghostly procession can be seen by any person bold enough and daring enough to take a position on the stairs."

The guide paused dramatically once again. I turned to scan the crowd. Most had their eyes fixed on the Cliff House before them, including the Tingley girls.

"First comes the handyman who stole the watermelons. He marches along with a heavy tread, balancing an immense melon on his head, his face buried in the half of another melon, and at intervals, as he grinds at the melon, uttering most unearthly groans. He is followed by a beautiful young lady who sobs as if her heart will break, and constantly wrings her hands, with a large glistening diamond on the thumb of her left hand. Then come three little children leading each other, their auburn locks dripping with water and moss."

The guide was silent then, and the steamer engaged her engines and turned slightly back toward the Park. The crowded shifted away from the starboard rail although we stayed, as did the Tingley girls and their young charges. The guide let out a loud, booming Boo ha ha and again nervous giggles rippled through the crowd.

Lisa giggled, but her charge did not. Paige stared unblinkingly at the

Cliff House. "Lisa, the people aren't in the hotel like the man said. They are down there below in a big skiff."

Lisa, Charles, and I craned our necks to look at the rickety dock below the hotel.

"Where?" Lisa asked. "I don't see a skiff. I don't see anyone."

"Right there," Paige said matter-of-factly. "There are two mothers, two fathers, and four small children. Children smaller than me. Smaller than Dresden. But why are they all wearing big winter coats? It's too hot for that."

"Oh, my, Little Miss Steiding! You sure have a vivid imagination. Come, let's find your parents." Lisa turned then, walking away from the starboard railing. Paige turned her head and peered back over Lisa's shoulder, her eyes never leaving the shoreline below the Cliff House.

Knowing the story of the Eel Bay catastrophe, I turned and searched the shoreline thinking I would see the skiff Paige had described. For it was on a blustery November day back in the fall of 1880, that two families—each with two small children—left the Cliff House for Gananoque, but never made it. They were found drowned in Eel Bay the next day. Two families. "Two mothers, two fathers, and four small children. Children smaller than me." Thinking of Paige's words sent a shiver down my spine. It was the first time I ever truly considered that the Cliff House might be haunted.

"That's quite a story. Have you ever seen the Cliff House before?" Charles asked.

I looked at him and blinked.

"Of course," I said. "I can see it from my cottage."

"Really? Where is it from your cottage?"

I blinked again. I pointed to our cottage. I could almost make out the white paint in the night but I knew what I was looking for. "That is Grenell Island," I said.

"Oh, I thought we were almost to Clayton."

"I hope not! We're to disembark at Pullman House."

It was obvious Charles had no idea where he was. I reminded myself that he had only been in the islands a few weeks and it was dark. Easy to be confused. But hadn't we pointed out Hub Island? The Narrows? The bridge where we had shared our first kiss?

By now we were passing between Hub Island and Pratt Point. I looked to see a light on in the main room and wondered if Alice was still awake or if it was Edith at the dining room table sketching.

We heard a cheer and looked over to see that the Kingstonians had added some chemical to their campfire that made it blaze red, the flames growing larger, embers rising like fireflies into the night. Moments later we were landing at the Pullman House dock. I turned to stay goodnight to Charles and was surprised when he said he was catching a later steamer back to Alexandria Bay. I thought Charles had planned to return to Clayton as more steamers are in and out of Clayton at this late hour. "Are you sure there is another steamer coming to Grenell tonight?"

"Yes, I checked the schedule. There is another steamer coming through in about twenty minutes."

"Would you like me to wait with you?"

"That's not necessary. Besides, it's proper for a gentleman to walk a lady home."

We gathered the two lanterns that we had left at the base of the bridge and lit them. Anne and Keiko walked ahead, and Charles and I walked behind. Charles seemed to be moving so slowly, especially for someone who had to board a steamer in twenty minutes.

When we reached the Pabst cottage, Charles headed for the Pratt bridge. I stopped him from crossing and motioned that we needed to turn here. Castle Rock was to the left.

"Why don't we say good night here? Thank you again for the lovely evening. You must hurry back to the dock to catch that steamer." I worried that Charles would miss the last steamer of the evening and be marooned on Grenell for the night.

"But I need to escort you home," he insisted. "I can't leave you unescorted in the dark without a lantern."

I took in a sharp breath. It was clear I knew where I was going, and he didn't. I'd walked this way alone a hundred times before and was perfectly capable of walking the rest of the way on my own with or without a lantern. I pushed away my exasperation. "Anne," I called in my loudest whisper. The lantern stopped and her dark figure turned toward me, the lantern barely lighting her face.

"See. I have a lantern and I'm not alone. I'm afraid if you don't hurry, you will be marooned on Grenell."

He seemed baffled at my sense of urgency, but I turned him toward the Pullman House.

He took two steps and then turned back toward me.

"Marguerite?"

"Yes?"

"I'm looking forward to the midsummer ball at the Frontenac."

He turned then and walked up over the camel foot. I wasn't sure if he would be able to see the lights of Pullman House when he reached St. James Place. My instincts told me that I should wait to make certain, but I didn't want to inconvenience Keiko and Anne by making them wait any longer for me. I turned and moved toward the lantern Anne was holding at the end of Prof. Pabst's property, hoping Charles would make it back to the Pullman House dock in time.

CHAPTER
thirty

Nat pushed away from the dock, gripped the oars, and pulled hard. The skiff sat heavy in the water, weighed down with tent, trunk, and all of the gear for Flossie's herbarium project. Flossie gave Keiko a hug farewell, then pushed back and bowed solemnly. "It was an honor to have known you," Flossie said. "Safe journeys back to your homeland."

Keiko bowed. "Best of luck to you in the canoe races in the week ahead."

Flossie climbed into her canoe and knelt in the center. She grabbed the paddle and pushed away from the dock. "Goodbye, everyone," she called. She waved then, threw a kiss, dipped her paddle in the water, and, with short strokes, slowly pivoted her canoe until it pointed north towards the Narrows. She took a few strokes forward, then stopped. "Marguerite. Marguerite!" she called back over her shoulder as her canoe continuing drifting north. "Promise me you'll check on the chicks!" As soon as she saw me nod and wave an acknowledgment to her request, she turned back and, with swift, sure strokes, quickly caught up with Nat who was nearly halfway to Murray Isle.

The three of us stood for a moment and watched her as she paddled, the sunlight highlighting her silver-and-gold curls. At last, Anne turned to Keiko and said, "It's time. Do you want to check the cottage one more time? If you leave something, it may be months before you will be reunited with what you left behind."

"No. I'm certain I have everything," Keiko assured her.

Nat had already rowed Keiko's steamer trunk and valise to the Grenell Island Store dock earlier this morning.

"Shall we go?"

"Wait!" I said. "I have a letter to mail!"

Last night, after I had changed into my sleeping gown, performed my ablutions, dutifully brushed my long curls one hundred strokes, and plaited my hair into one long braid, I'd penned a few moonlight haikus. I ducked inside my tent now, retrieved the envelope addressed to Charles, and tucked it into my skirt pocket.

We took the north shore path and arrived at the dock just after the mailboat left. My moonlight haikus would not go out until this afternoon. Charles would not receive them until the morrow. I chastised myself for not rising early and stealing away to the post office before now. I peeked into the store and saw Herb busily sorting the mail. I wondered if Charles had posted a note to me last night before he returned to Comfort Island. He'd been known to stop in at the Crossman, pen a haiku, and slip it in an envelope to me.

Anne must have noted my glance toward the post boxes, for she suggested we pick up our mail on the return trip.

No one spoke as we walked along the North Boulevard path. The ringing of hammer falls punctuating our silence. Work was in full swing on the two-story boathouse across from us on Murray Isle. It would house all the boats for the hotel and the entire second floor would be a large ballroom for hops and galas. As we turned onto Park Avenue, I thought of our adventures. Anne and I had made a list of things Keiko must see and do before she left the islands. We had hiked to the potholes, climbed to the top of the cliff at the foot of Bluff Island, and sang "America the Beautiful"—even though it wasn't the Glorious Fourth—and told her the mystery of Maple Island as we rowed home. We went fishing, and Keiko caught a bass and taught us a new way to prepare fish. We went to Fineview for ice cream, visited the Indian camp there, played cards on a rainy day, and sat in awe of the sunset each evening.

We were silent as we waited for the steamer and silent as we steamed toward Clayton. The day was bright. A storm had rumbled through last night long after I'd extinguished my lantern. The passing storm had swept the air clean of all humidity and haze. As we stepped aboard the steamer, I breathed in the freshness of the river air.

Anne remained stoic at the Clayton railroad station. She leaned forward and whispered something in Keiko's ear, then bowed to her. With tears swimming in my eyes, I said my farewells. Keiko had told us many times that goodbyes in Japan are long-drawn-out affairs which was why we took such an early steamer from Grenell. Keiko explained that the reluctance to leave or say goodbye is important for strengthening and preserving relationships. "It is how we show appreciation and respect for someone, especially our superiors." We bowed, and she bowed. She bowed, and we bowed. It was evident that Keiko did not want to turn and board the train, that doing so first would have been some slight to us. Eventually, Anne bowed, then took one step back. With each bow, we began taking a step back. It was as if the invisible connection of caring between us was being stretched thin enough that it could finally be broken.

"Board!" the conductor bellowed. Even this did not induce Keiko to leave. She bowed again.

Steam whooshed from the side of the great locomotive, and the engine nudged ahead on the track, causing the car to lurch forward a few inches. The conductor rang his bell and called out, "All aboard!" Some days the conductor's "all aboard" came as a question: "All aboard?" Sometimes as it sounded like a warning: "All Aboard! You best be! You're about to miss your train." But today it came as a blunt statement. Keiko finally boarded the train. We watched through the car windows as she found her seat.

Then the wheels creaked into motion, and the train rolled forward. Suddenly, tears spilled from my eyes. Anne looked at me quizzically. She didn't need to say the words aloud. I knew she was perplexed by my tears. I didn't explain. I couldn't explain. I took a breath and searched inside for the source of my tears as I pulled my handkerchief from my sleeve and waved it at the train before I dabbed my eyes. From inside the Pullman car, I saw Keiko return my wave. I took a ragged breath.

It was then I realized I wasn't crying for Keiko as much as I was for Anandibai. When she had left from the West Philadelphia railway station, I had assumed I would never see her again, but I was looking forward to a life-long epistolary relationship. She was dead before the year was out. We watched the train until it rounded the bend and was blocked by buildings on Water Street. There seemed to be an endless well of tears inside me for new tears appeared the moment I dabbed old ones away. We stood silently and watched the black smoke from the stack rise above Clayton's skyline. He could hear the *chuff chuff* of the escaping steam and the long whistle warning of its approach. Most of the people had left the station, and the whistle now was faint in the distance. I dashed away my tears, took a deep breath, and turned to Anne. "Before we take a steamer back to Grenell, I need to find something for Alma—Arnie and Mavis's baby girl. I've been here over a month now and haven't been to visit the baby."

"Good," she said and she linked her arm through mine and we left to explore the shops along Water Street.

—

I was disappointed upon our return to find that there was no envelope for me from Charles. In fact, there wasn't a letter to me from anyone. I ticked back the days in my head. Rose had left weeks ago and still not one letter. Not one note.

We stopped to visit Mavis and baby Alma. I'd found a Mother Goose book, and Anne had purchased a set of soakers, perhaps a more practical gift than mine as Mavis seemed somewhat taken aback by the book I presented to her.

"Miss Marguerite, thank you but Alma can't read, ya know. More likely to gnaw the corners right off the cover," Mavis said. Although Mavis had lived on this side of the Atlantic for most of her life, she still carried a Scottish lilt in her voice.

"Of course she doesn't read yet, but you and Arnie can read to her until she is able to read. She needn't handle the book until she's old enough to do so."

Mavis took the book from me and nodded.

"Babies love rhymes," I explained, remembering reciting Mother Goose rhymes to my nieces and nephews. I took Alma Mae on my knee and recited the "Pease Porridge Hot" ditty as I bounced her to the rhythm of the words. A huge smile spread across the moppet's face. She clapped her chubby hands and dissolved into a cascade of giggles.

Mavis nodded again but her wide eyes indicated that she regarded me as a little daft.

 Anne presented the soakers and Mavis threw her hands up in joy. "I've been knitting wool soakers day and night since Alma was born. Never seem to have enough. And just the right size for my wee one's bum. Thick, too! These'll keep furniture and laps dry."

 We played with Alma till she rubbed her eyes and stuck out her lower lip. Mavis picked up the exhausted tike, jostled her on her hip, and soothed her by stroking her short curls. We said our farewells and left so Alma could nap. "Though I don't know how she can sleep through all that hammerin' out there, but she does. I'll be happy when it's finished. Arnie helps George sometimes when he's finished working on the Sharples' place. Many hands make light work."

 We looked over to George Grenell's new structure—rising up between Sam and Lucy's place and Breezy Bay. George was astraddle a beam. He took a nail from his mouth, carefully positioned it in front of him, and hammered it in place. I paused for a moment hoping to catch his eye and wave a greeting, but George seemed so focused and intent on his project that he didn't notice our presence. We walked past the barn to St. James Place.

 A rare smile sprung to Anne's face as we left the Hunkerson cottage and headed back to Castle Rock. She was amused by Mavis's reaction to my gift. "Mavis was taken aback by your Mother Goose," she said. "But don't worry, Arnie will love the book. It will mean more to him than Mavis as you were the one who taught him to read. It was the perfect gift."

 Castle Rock seemed exceedingly quiet upon our return. Without Keiko and Flossie, the camp seemed lifeless. As I often do when feeling uncomfortable or out of sorts, I suggested a row to Grand View Park to pick up a loaf of rye bread. I rowed there, and the rhythm of the oars and the sound of the river around me washed away any lingering sadness. Eel Bay was silky, calm and the most loyal blue. As I gazed across the water, it seemed to twinkle back at me and buoyed my spirits. When we arrived at Grand View Park bakery, I suggested we buy a loaf for the Pratts. Anne liked that idea. She had yet to see Alice since her arrival. Anne rowed back. I loved watching the droplets from the oars form patterns across the smooth water.

 As we approached the Pratt dock, I saw that there was a woman sitting in a rocking chair on the dock reading a book. "Ahoy," I called out as we rowed closer, so that we wouldn't startle the woman.

The woman looked up then and I realized that it wasn't a woman: it was young Olivia who at that moment looked mature beyond her years. "Greetings," she called back, but the response was subdued. She rose at our approach, put the book on the rocking chair, and grabbed the bowline that I offered her. Olivia's countenance was devoid of cheer.

As soon as we landed, I heard the giggle of a young child and was bewildered. Was Mavis visiting the Pratts with Alma?

I caught sight of Edith holding a young child, perhaps a year older than Alma. Edith twirled around in a circle, and the little girl erupted in giggles. "Look! Look!" Edith told the child when she caught sight of us. "We have visitors! Let's go greet them! Wanna horsey ride?" The little girl nodded and Edith galloped down the incline to the dock, jostling her young ward up and down. Edith galloped across the dock and whinnied as we were climbing out of our skiff. "Meet our newest cousin. This is Mabelle. Mabelle, meet our dear friends, Miss Anne and Miss Marguerite. Mabelle's mother, my aunt Harriet and Mabelle's older sister, Jessie, are up on the porch. Do you wanna walk? Mabelle's just learned to walk." Edith put Mabelle gently on the dock. Anne took one hand, and Edith took the other. Anne and Edith started slowly toward the cottage with little Mabelle toddling between them.

I turned to see if Olivia was going to join us on the porch, but she was already settled back in the rocking chair, her head bent over an open book.

"I thought you finished *The Iliad*," I said, recognizing the book.

Olivia pushed the dock with her toe and set the rocker in motion. "I did. I was just revisiting some of its themes. I was so consumed in the language that I didn't realize that essentially it is a poem about fatherlessness." The last word was said softly, yet slowly and precisely.

"Fatherlessness," I repeated as softly and precisely as she had. "Yes. Diomedes is fatherless."

"The book starts with the poet lamenting how hard life will be now that he is fatherless," Olivia said not looking at me, but the book.

"Speaking of your father," I said, "we just returned from the Grand View Park. We went to stop at the bakery, but I stepped inside the hotel.

Do you know whose muskellunge is hanging in the lobby?"

Olivia's eyes looked up at mine inquisitively, and she shook her head.

"Your father's. He caught it back in 1881, the first year I came to Grenell, the year I met you. Your mother lost you one day. She was frantic. Found you sleeping under a cot in the tent."

A small smile crept onto Olivia's face and she nodded. "I've heard the story many times."

"Olivia? Have you been fishing yet this season?"

She looked at me and blinked. "No," she said, as if surprised by her response.

"You used to love fishing with your father."

"I did," she said, nodding as she slowly rocked. She looked out at the river as if pondering this new line of thinking. "Father's skiff is so big, so unwieldy. It's hard for me to row any great distance."

"I know of a fishing hole not too far from here. I think you could manage the short row."

Olivia looked pensive. "I have not seen anyone there yet this season."

"So the fish are there just waiting for you." I stood and laid a hand on her shoulder and leaned close, whispering in her ear, "You must fish for two now."

I wandered up to the cottage then. Alice introduced us to her sister, Harriet Roberts, and her daughter Jessie, who looked to be about four. Alice was delighted with the bread, and we promised to meet again soon.

Later that evening, I looked out to see that Olivia was in her father's boat in his fishing spot. I penned yet another letter to Rose, a second letter to Mother, and finally a few haikus to send to Charles in the morning mail.

Charles' note had arrived in the afternoon mail. Unlike me, he had it posted in the morning mail. I shouldn't have been surprised that his haiku was about clouds. He had written his haiku about the clouds across the moon, just as I had. A shiver of pleasure rippled through me as I thought of the two of us at different points on the river looking up at the same moon. The poem somehow reminded me of the warm feeling I had had standing next to Charles at the railing on the steamer. That feeling faded as I thought of our awkward goodbye later.

I heard a splash and looked up in time to see that Olivia had landed a big fish. She struggled with it from inside the skiff, then raised it high enough for me to see. It was hard for her to lift, so it must have been heavy. I pulled my handkerchief from inside my sleeve and waved it wildly.

Long after Olivia had pulled up her anchor and rowed home with her catch, I sat on the porch and watched the sky. The sun was now below the trees that crown Murray Isle, and the light of the setting sun was reflected up onto the bank of clouds above which glowed orange, yellow, and lavender. I heard the dip of oars and looked out to see a skiff approaching our dock in the darkening water below. Anne must have seen the approaching skiff, too, for she came out of the cottage, and together we descended the spiral path to the skiff and its lone occupant at the dock.

"Good evening, Miss Hartranft, Miss Doctor Ashbridge," Mr. Tetsuka said as he stepped out onto the dock. He bowed solemnly, and we returned his bow.

"Keikosan asked that I perform a *toro nagashi* on the night of her departure," he said.

"A *toro nagashi*?" Anne asked. "I'm unfamiliar with that term."

"You will see. It is a twist on our common custom. *Nagashi* means flow. The word toro is usually used to represent the spirit of the dead but for you Keiko wants the *toro* to represent the spirit of your friendship. Not dead, but connected always. The *toro nagashi* lanterns will float down the river to symbolize how you are on an island here and she is on an island on the other side of the world, but the spirit of your friendship will always be connected through the water."

He bowed then, and we returned his bow. He returned to his skiff. "I will release the lanterns from the head of the island. You watch from above."

He rowed away from the dock, and we climbed to the porch above. We watched him row to the west. The brilliant sunset colors softened as light drained from the sky. When Murray Isle cast a long black shadow across the water, Mr. Tetsuka lit the paper lanterns and set them afloat in the water.

It was a still evening without much wind. The three floating lanterns drifted eastward between Murray and Grenell. The lights glowed, surrounded by ripples of reflected light. We watched the lanterns until they bobbed out of sight, rounding Pratt Point. I looked at Anne, she looked at me, and we took the path behind the cottage up the hill towards the outhouse but climbed higher until we reached the top of the bald at the crest of the camel hump. From there we watched the three lights that stayed clustered together as they moved slowly and steadily down the river and towards the sea.

CHAPTER
thirty-one

Two days later, Castle Rock was alive with a different sort of energy. My sister, Lily, arrived with her twin seven-year-old daughters, Iris and Ivy. I anxiously awaited their arrival on the dock. Prince and Jambo raced up and down the length of the wharf as the steamer eased its way to the dock.

"Ivy! Iris!" I said when I saw them at the railing. Lily stood behind them waving her hankie. The twins blew kisses.

Dressed in white dresses with matching bright yellow satin sashes, the two girls stepped off the gangway and flew into my arms. I bent down on one knee so that I could bury my head in their honey-brown locks. They smelled like sunshine.

"My goodness," I said, looking directly into their periwinkle eyes. "It's only been a month but I do believe that Ivy has grown! She's a hair taller than you, Iris."

Iris shrugged. "I'll catch up with her tonight. Ivy was born first, but I'm just minutes behind."

The two reached for each other's hand and clasped the other's tightly.

"How do you know I'm not Iris?" Ivy asked. Then the two leaned forward and whispered in unison, one into each of my ears. "Mummy can't always tell us apart."

"Sometimes even our governess is befuddled," Iris said.

"But you always know, don't you, Aunt Marguerite?" Ivy asked.

I nodded, but did not share with the girls that I wasn't always sure. But I'd learned years ago that when the girls stood side by side and held hands, which they did often, Ivy always stood on the left and Iris on the right.

The girls looked at each other and laughed, then whispered to each other.

"Girls, no whispering, and speak English please," Lily patiently reminded them.

"Twin language?" I asked.

The girls nodded. "Mummy gets annoyed when we speak twin language," said Iris.

"We don't want to annoy Mummy. Not when she was kind enough to bring you by train and steamer all the way to Grenell Island."

Lily had become alarmed when, around the age of two, the girls began babbling some strange tongue. It didn't help that they did this in front of their grandmamma, our mother, who was convinced that their strange utterances had something to do with Quakers and were the result of time the girls spent with me.

After doing a little research, I learned that the condition was not unusual among twins and went by either one of two lovely names derived from Greek: idioglossia (Greek for "personal tongue") or by the name cryptophasia (Greek for "secret speech"). Mother, however, could not be convinced they had not been somehow influenced by Quakers—who are sometimes known to speak in tongues—and the girls were no longer allowed to visit me at the home I shared with Anne.

"Would you like to feed the monkey?" I asked. "His name is Jambo. His four-legged friend is Prince. They are the best of friends. Inseparable. Just like the two of you. Here. A penny for each of you! Petey will explain how to feed them."

The girls closed their fingers over the shiny pennies in their palms and, still holding hands ran off through the crowd on the dock to the small throng of children knotted around Petey, Prince, and Jambo.

Nat was busily loading Lily's trunks, hat boxes, and valise onto his skiff so he could row their luggage to Castle Rock.

"Oh, Lily, I'm so happy you are here," I said. "I have so many plans for the girls this year. They already know how to swim, and I hoped this year I could teach them to row and fish. See, look," I said as we rounded the hotel on our way to the bridge. "There's a new toboggan slide this year. I think the girls will love it."

By now the girls had fed biscuits to Jambo and Prince and were running back to tell us all about it. The girls chattered about Jambo and Prince the entire walk to Castle Rock.

The girls loved animals and the out of doors, although, Ivy was afraid of spiders and Iris was afraid of snakes. The two comforted each other and tried to allay the other's fears. Iris checked under Ivy's pillow each night to assure Ivy there were no spiders hiding there. Then, Ivy would check under Iris's pillow to reassure Iris there wasn't a snake coiled beneath it.

"I thought the girls might want to sleep in the tent with me, and you may have my room all to yourself, Lily," I said.

The girls jumped up and down, hugged each other, then hugged me.

"I'll send Nat for another cot as soon as he arrives with your luggage," I said.

"Don't bother," Lily said. "Despite the fact that the girls had two beds in their room at home, I always find them in the same bed, sleeping there with their arms around each other."

The screen door creaked open, and Anne popped her head out. "Did I hear giggling? Is it true? Could it be? Are the Giggle Twins here on Grenell? Come here and give me a hug!"

The usually reserved Anne melted whenever she was around the twins, which unfortunately was only when they came to visit here on Grenell as their grandmamma insisted that they should never set foot in Anne's West Philadelphia home.

The twins skipped up the path, giggling all the way, and into the welcoming arms of Friend Anne. "My goodness! What is your mother feeding you? You have shot up like beanstalks. These tall twins couldn't possibly be the same twins who visited Castle Rock last year."

"But we are!" the twins insisted.

While the girls bantered with Anne, Nat arrived in the skiff with their baggage. The Dillworth family arrived with four trunks, a pile of hatboxes, and several valises. Lily and I directed which trunks stayed in the lower camp and which needed to be carried to the upper camp. We asked Nat to put the girls' things in the wardrobe tent, which would soon be bursting at the seams.

"Wardrobe tent?" Lily asked, then gasped when she looked inside.

"Friend Helen is with child and has lent me her wardrobe for the summer as I've been attending all sorts of events this season that require—more than a shirtwaist and walking skirt. I'm glad you are here. While beautiful, these dresses take so much time to maintain, and some are impossible for me to wear unless someone is here to help me dress. Flossie had been standing in as lady's maid—reluctantly, I might add. But you've arrived just in time to help me prepare for the midsummer ball at the Frontenac tomorrow night. It's supposed to be the most elegant of the season."

"So when will I meet this Mr. Bartman from Chicago?"

"Later this afternoon. We're meeting at Fineview Park."

"And what's at Fineview besides the dashing Mr. Bartman? Is he dashing?" Lily asked

"Dashing? I'd describe him as scholarly. Academic."

Lily's eyebrows knitted together in consternation. "Marguerite. 'Academic' is not a word that describes how someone looks."

"Well, it is for me. But then I spend all my time surrounded by academics. I guess that's my way of saying he looks smart and . . . introspective."

"Smart. Introspective. Hmm," Lily said. "Just tell me . . . for comparison's sake . . . does my Edwin look smart and introspective?"

I pressed my lips together in deep thought as I pondered Lily's question. I had never thought of it before, but Edwin did look smart. Indeed, Edwin was very smart, with a rapier-sharp wit. Introspective? No. Edwin was not the brooding type. I thought of the photo of Edwin that was tucked into *Leaves of Grass*. I remembered the first time I saw it. 'Dashing' was the first word that had come to mind.

"Marguerite? You drifted off there for a moment. My question was purely rhetorical. You were speaking of Fineview?"

I looked up to see an amused smirk on Lily's face.

"Yes, yes! Of course. Fineview. There's a lovely ice cream pavilion there. And I thought the girls might enjoy visiting the Indian village across the road. I'd love to buy a sweetgrass basket for *each* of them."

"*When* will we learn to row?" Ivy asked.

"Soon," I said, taking long, sure strokes.

"May I take a turn now?" Iris asked.

I shook my head. "No, not now. The water in front of Thousand Island Park is full of boats. Steamers coming to dock. Other skiffs leaving the skiff livery for fishing grounds. Not a good place for beginners. We'll find a nice quiet secluded spot for your first lesson."

Charles was on the dock waiting at Fineview for us. He did not come to help secure the boat or help us onto the dock but stepped back and allowed the dockhand to help us instead. Once out of the boat, I ran a hand up the back of my tight French twist to ensure there were no lose pins, and ran my hands down the front of my dress to smooth out any wrinkles, then checked the cameo pinned to my high-collared blouse to ensure it was on straight. I took the twins by the hand and walked to the end of the dock where Charles was waiting for us with his hands behind his back.

"Charles! How lovely to see you! I hope you haven't been waiting long," I said.

Charles pressed his lips together and shuffled uncomfortably from foot to foot. I wondered for a moment if he'd been struck mute.

I opened my mouth to say something, but I wasn't quite sure how to phrase the puzzlement I felt. Finally, I simply asked, "Charles?"

"Not long, I suppose," he said tentatively as if he really weren't sure how long he'd been waiting.

"Charles, I'm happy to introduce you to my sister, Mrs. Lily Dillworth and her adorable girls, Iris and Ivy. Lily, this is Mr. Charles Bartman of Chicago."

"It's so nice to finally meet you, Mr. Bartman," she said.

"It's a pleasure to meet you, Mrs. Dillworth," Charles said, then pressed his lips together as if afraid to say anything else. He stood with his hands behind his back as if he were hiding something. But what? A bouquet of flowers? A weapon of some sort?

"Marguerite has told me so much about you," Lily said.

Charles did not respond. In fact, I think he might have edged away a bit.

Perplexed, I turned to the girls. "Who wants ice cream?"

They erupted in a chorus of "I do! I do!"

I took them by the hand and walked toward the ice cream pavilion trusting that Charles would follow.

"Aunt Marguerite, look! That nice Indian man has two very big birds."

"Yes. They are crows."

The girls let go of my hands at the same time and rushed ahead, clasping hands together again as they approached the crows.

The crows flapped and cawed slightly as the girls approached.

The girls whispered to each other in their twin language. The crows flapped and erupted in Choctaw. One flew down to the table in front of the old Indian and strutted to the end of the table, tilting its head first left and then right as it appraised the girls.

The girls whispered again to each other in twin language.

The bird babbled back. I noted that the twin language sounded much like Choctaw.

"What language are they speaking?" Charles asked in a low tone. I waved my hand, hoping to delay answering that question.

"A penny for a fortune, correct?" I asked, digging in my reticule for my change purse.

The stoic Indian raised his hand and waved me off. "No need for pennies. These girls are kindred spirits of my crows. Full of sunshine and cherry pie."

Lily and I shared a look.

"Thank you," I said to the Indian as I put my hands on the girls' backs. "Say good-bye to the crows, girls," I said, gently pushing them toward the pavilion.

When we were seated and eating our ice cream, Lily once again tried to engage Charles in conversation. "Marguerite, tells me you are an art historian. I'm afraid I'm not sure what that means. Could you enlighten me?"

Charles stared at the ice cream in his dish, then said rather dispassionately, "I study the history of art, especially Greek and Roman art." He paused as if thinking, raised a spoonful to his mouth, and slowly put it in his mouth.

I thought perhaps he was thinking of what more to say, but he continued silently eating. Embarrassed by his silence, I spoke a bit about the project we'd been working on, hoping Charles would add a few comments. But he didn't.

After we finished our ice cream, Lily took the girls by the hand and went across the road to the Indian camp. Charles and I followed along.

The girls both inhaled deeply. "Ahhhh!" they said in unison.

"What a fresh smell."

"Smells like comfort."

"Like home."

"Mmmmm! Almost like vanilla!"

"Mummy, look at their beautiful braids! May we wear our hair in braids tomorrow? Not the kind that falls behind our back but the kind that are on the sides and fall forward. I want to look like an Indian princess, too."

The girls oohed and ahhed over the baskets, and each chose a basket with a lid.

"What will you put in your baskets, girls?" I asked as we left the Indian camp. Their response made me smile as it seemed to be one thought expressed through both of their voices.

"Something very special . . ."

". . . but only something from Grenell Island . . ."

". . . to remind us of our time here . . ."

"We'll keep it on our bedside table," they concluded in unison.

Lily took the girls by the hand and asked if they could stop and look in the millinery shop.

"Of course," I said. "Charles and I will meet you on the dock. Take as much time as you like."

The girls skipped ahead with their mother following at a more dignified pace.

There was no need to rush, so I slowed my pace and once Lily and the girls had ducked into the store, I turned an appraising eye to Charles and asked if everything was alright.

His Adam's apple bobbed up and down and his head fell forward as if he hoped to study his belt buckle.

"Charles? Are you unwell?"

He shook his head. "No. I . . . I'm . . . it's just that . . . I'm so terribly nervous about meeting new people."

"But, Charles, at the Olphiants' lawn party you didn't seem so nervous in front of some very famous men—Mr. Pullman, Mr. Heath, and all the rest."

"That was different. They're men. Besides, I've known the Pullmans my entire life. Being the lone man in the company of four lovely ladies left me tongue-tied."

I smiled at that—Charles thinking of Ivy and Iris as lovely ladies.

"I see," I said.

"I'm sure you do," he said. I noted an irritated tone in his voice.

"What does that mean?" I asked.

"Now, you know why everyone calls me Black Bart," he said, more to his shoes than to me.

"Whatever do you mean?"

"Don't deny it. I heard John Kerr call me that in front of you."

"It matters not what other people think." My cheeks flamed red with that statement, because had it not been only weeks earlier that I had been afraid to meet with Charles because of what Mrs. Big Hat thought? "That's not totally true. I understand your turmoil. But I've been fortunate to be influenced by very strong women like Anandibai and Keiko. Perhaps you can be inspired by them as well."

We continued to walk on in silence, the only sound being the crunching of small gravel beneath our feet. We stopped at the edge of the dock, and I raised my hand to feel the cameo pin. Through the thin tip of my glove, I could feel the profile of the figure carved there. "I'm very excited about tomorrow night."

"I am too. I hope I have not ruined your sister's impression of me. Another reason for my nervousness today. It's so important that your family likes me. I know without a doubt that my mother will adore you as Mrs. Clark does."

We heard the chatter and giggling of the girls as they walked ahead of Lily, who was carrying a tower of hat boxes.

Charles turned to me then and looked me straight in the eye. "Marguerite," he said earnestly, "I promise that I will make up for my sullenness today at the ball tomorrow night. Mrs. Clark promises that tomorrow night will be magical—the event of the season. I decided that tomorrow night will be the perfect night, too. . ."

"Sorry to keep you waiting!" Lily called out. The girls skipped ahead and were hugging me now.

"Not at all. My goodness. Did you buy out the store? You each found a hat?"

"And one for you, too."

"For me! Lily, Helen has lent me quite enough hats."

"Nonsense. One can never have too many hats. Wouldn't you agree, Mr. Bartman?" Lily didn't give Charles a chance to respond. "Besides, look how lovely this looks on her." Lily stopped, opened the largest of the hatboxes, and pulled out a large-brimmed white fabric hat festooned on one side with a large white bow from which sprang a whimsical array of coque feathers stripped to the tip and dyed in a rainbow of colors. It was a very simple, yet very unusual, very elegant hat.

"You must try it on."

"Lily," I resisted.

"I will not take no for an answer."

"I can't wait to see this on you, Marguerite." Then, turning to Charles, "I promise you will be amazed."

Lily pulled the two hatpins from my now rather sedate-looking boater and put the large white hat upon my head.

"Look at how the feathers dip and dance in the wind," one of the twins exclaimed.

I raised my head to peer up at Charles from beneath under the wide brim of the hat. His eyes were wide. He looked utterly dumbfounded.

"Mrs. Dillworth, I don't know how you did it. How could you make the loveliest woman I've ever had the pleasure of spending time with even more enchanting? I'm mesmerized," Charles murmured as if in a trance. His eyes locked on mine.

Lily laughed. "Thank you, Mr. Bartman, but this is nothing. Wait until you see Marguerite tomorrow night."

"I can hardly wait."

CHAPTER
thirty-two

It wasn't a pumpkin turned into a gilded coach with a team of six white horses that bore me to the ball, but rather the *Mamie C.* And I did not go alone as the little cinderwench had.

Charles was only afforded a glimpse of me from the bow as Mr. Clark greeted me at the dock and quickly whisked me up the gangway and into the salon. "I will leave you ladies to prepare yourselves for the ball. Charles and I will remain on the bow," he said before closing the door.

The balloon sleeves of my gown stuck out so far that I had to turn sideways to fit through the salon door. Mrs. Clark who stood when I entered. "My heavens, Miss Hartranft! You look like a princess."

"Thank you," I said, as I dropped a curtsy, "but it is you who looks like royalty."

Mrs. Clark was wearing a light gold gown that seemed to glow with light. Clusters of diamonds ringed her neck, and a dainty tiara shone from her elaborately styled hair.

Inwardly, I chuckled to myself as this is how I imagined she might be dressed for our outing to Carleton Island. "I've never seen fabric glow like that," I said.

"It's a Worth gown made of *peau de soie* silk."

"*Peau de soie*—French for 'skin of silk.' An apt description." I reached out but didn't touch the fabric. It looked so lightweight, almost liquid.

Her gown, like mine, had a lily-shaped skirt, which nipped in at the waist, skimmed over the hips, and angled out into a wide hem. I wondered briefly if the hem of her skirt was reinforced with eight inches of canvas as my hem was. Lily assured me that the stiff hem coupled with abundant fabric would cause the dress to swing out gracefully when I danced.

Also like my dress, Mrs. Clark's gown had stylish puffy sleeves. Mine were the size of watermelons. Though not quite as large as my sleeves, Mrs. Clark's sleeves were artfully decorated with ribbon loops and gauze puffs. Her dress had a low, rounded neckline, while my V neckline plunged dangerously deep in both the front and back.

"You, my dear, look positively radiant in that ruby-red gown," Mrs. Clark said, seating herself as the boat moved away from the dock.

I carefully sat, hoping not to wrinkle my gown on the short trip from Grenell to Round Island. "It's quite a departure from my usual drab attire. At Penn, I usually wear a white shirtwaist with a brown or green skirt, but, then again at the university, I try to blend in and, if all possible, make my male colleagues forget that I am a woman."

"No one will make that mistake this evening, I assure you."

"Do you think my gown clashes with the cameo? My sister Lily had a nice pearl choker she wanted me to wear, but as the cameo was a gift from Charles, I thought I should wear it." I raised my hand instinctively to the cameo at my throat. I could barely make out the details of the woman carved in profile through the thick black satin opera-length gloves I wore.

"It looks lovely," Mrs. Clark assured me. "The black velvet ribbon is perfect. It accentuates your flawless skin better than a pearl choker would. But, my dear, I have a feeling you could wear a gunny sack and look as enchanting. So *that's* the cameo he gave you."

"Yes. He told you?" I asked tentatively, thinking this a good sign—of what, I wasn't quite sure.

"He told me that he had sent for it. He anxiously awaited its arrival. He was over the moon when it arrived the morning that you came to visit with Dr. Okami. Let me see the back of your hair."

I grasped the arm of the club chair and turned my head.

Mrs. Clark gasped. "Katie, take note of how Miss Hartranft's hair is arranged."

"My sister calls it a Dutch-braided bun."

"I love how the headpiece of crystal and pearl leaves accentuates your dark hair."

"Lily has always been gifted at coiffure."

Mrs. Clark looked out the window. "Oh my, look at all the yachts. I'm afraid there is a line for dropping people off at the dock. Katie, I need my opera gloves." Katie retrieved the gloves from a satchel she carried. The gloves were made form the same *peau de soie* silk. Mrs. Clark tugged them on and pulled them over the tops of her elbows. "Katie, are the bows straight?" Katie dutifully straightened the tiny bows at the tops of the gloves.

"Did you bring a fan?" Mrs. Clark asked. "Thankfully, the Frontenac has electric lighting, which will help keep the ballroom cooler. But unfortunately, electric lighting glares so. Lamplight is much kinder to an aging face like mine. Still, a nice fan is a necessity."

"I'm afraid I didn't," I said.

"Not to worry. Katie brought extras of everything. Katie, I think the black ostrich-feather fan would be perfect."

Katie brought the fan to me. I opened my mouth to protest, but Katie raised her eyebrows and tilted her head forward. I remembered her speech about how sharing her things with me would make Mrs. Clark happy, I gladly accepted the fan.

"Katie is bringing a bag of necessities: sewing kit, smelling salts, powder. We've secured a room for the evening in case we need to repair our gowns. Please feel free to use the room even if you just want to retire for a while. The ball is sometimes so overwhelming. So many people! And sometimes the ballroom is unbearably hot—all those bodies dancing on a July night! Be assured you will have a quiet place to retreat."

There were a number of yachts waiting their turn to discharge their passengers at the Frontenac dock. The Clarks' boatmen decided to while away our wait time by taking a counterclockwise trip around Round Island.

As I gazed out the porthole at the beautiful cottages that dotted the Round Island shoreline, I thought of last night with the twins. After we were all dressed and ready for bed, they snuggled against me in my cot as I read to them from Andrew Lang's *The Blue Fairy Book*. Of all the stories therein, the girls loved "Cinderella, or The Little Glass Slipper" the best. Most of the day was consumed with preparing me for the ball tonight. The girls delighted in helping their own "Cinderella" get ready for the ball. Lily pampered me all day. First, she massaged my face with a sugar scrub. After she wiped away the gritty scrub, she slathered on Galen cream. It was cool to the touch and so soft and smelled heavenly—like roses. She ordered me to rest with cucumber slices on my eyes while she gave me a manicure, buffing my nails until they shone. It took nearly an hour for her to arrange my hair into the Dutch-braid bun. The girls stood silently by, handing hairpins to Lily as she coiffed my hair into the elegant braid. Lily fussed over every detail, from my hair down to the dark black slippers.

"They'll show every speck of dust. Are you sure you don't want to wear the red slippers?" she asked, holding the slippers up. "They match your gown perfectly."

"No. the black slippers are the most comfortable," I decided. "Besides they go with the black gloves and the black velvet ribbon at my neck."

"A cameo is so staid," Lily said. "I'll gladly lend you my pearl choker."

"But Charles gave me the cameo." I wanted to add that he gave it to me as a symbol of his love, but he hadn't exactly said that. Still, I was certain that that was what he had meant.

Finally, when I was ready, Lily and the twins followed me out of the tent and the few steps to the dock, where Nat was waiting to row me to the store dock so I didn't have to walk. The girls stood in awe at the dock. "You look just like Cinderella," Ivy said as Nat helped me into the skiff.

By the time we circumnavigated Round Island, space had opened up for the *Mamie C.* at the Frontenac dock. Once secured to the dock, Mr. Clark rapped on the door before he opened it. "Ladies, you both look beautiful tonight," he said as he offered his hand to Mrs. Clark. As soon as Mr. Clark had escorted Mrs. Clark down the gangway, Charles stepped to the doorway. He put his left hand behind his back and offered me his gloved right hand. "Marguerite," he said, kissing my knuckles lightly, "you look radiant tonight."

Charles was wearing a jacket with tails, a dark vest. Beneath his white stand-up collar was a perfectly knotted white ascot tie. His hair was parted in the middle and slicked down with pomade. It gave him a polished, sophisticated look that would have probably stunned his Princeton classmates.

The sun had dipped behind Grindstone Island, and the sky glowed peachy around us. The grounds of the Frontenac were illuminated with strings of white electric lights. The flower gardens on either side of the broad, flat stairway that led to the hotel were in full bloom.

My mind briefly drifted back to the night I first came to Round Island. The hotel had then been called Round Island House. It was much smaller but still elegant. I had walked the broad stairs from the dock to the hotel in rapt conversation with Mr. Sharples. Things had changed forever for me that night. My whole body tingled with anticipation. I had this feeling that I would be able to say the same about this night.

When we reached the top of the walk, I watched the Clarks climb the grand staircase of the entrance portico that leads to the expansive veranda surrounding the Frontenac. The music had started already. I paused for a moment, wanting to take in the spectacular scene. I looked down the staircase, admiring the scalloped flower beds on either side of the grand walkway, and looking out across the water, which was has now a deep apricot.

Over the music spilling from the grand hotel, I heard a familiar voice, but I couldn't quite place it. I turned to look for the source and was startled to see Dr. Elizabet DuPont walking my way. I hadn't seen her in twelve years. Surely, my mind was playing tricks on me, I thought as we moved toward the grand staircase. But she spoke again. I will never forget that voice. Then, squinting through the gathering darkness, I caught sight of her face. It was indeed Elizabet and she was coming my way, but I didn't think she had caught sight of me. Quickly, I bent down to adjust the strap of my slipper. Elizabet and I had never had a kind exchange of words that entire summer we were together back in 1881. Hopefully, she would not recognize me.

"Is everything alright?" Charles asked.

"Yes. My slipper strap came loose. It will only take me a minute to tighten it up," I told Charles as softly as I could, not wanting to draw attention to myself.

I stood as soon as Elizabet passed. And just as I breathed a sigh of relief, she turned around.

"Miss Hartranft? Is that you?"

"Why, yes. Good evening. Is that you, Dr. DuPont? I didn't recognize you in the twilight." I felt a tinny taste in my mouth at the lie.

"My goodness. This is most unexpected," she said, smiling broadly. She approached me and reached for my gloved hands. "You look positively radiant this evening." She gave me a soft kiss on each cheek.

"You look lovely as well," I replied tentatively.

"It has been so long. Too long," she said.

"Yes," I said, unsure what to say and fearing what direction this encounter was taking. I blinked.

"I have someone to introduce to you, Darling," she said raising her hand over her head and motioning to a man at the top of the stairs. "Do come down and meet my dearest friend." Dutifully, the man responded. "This is Miss Hartranft of West Philadelphia," she said, looping her arm through the gentleman's arm. She leaned forward then and whispered in my ear, "Or do you prefer doctor or perhaps professor these days?"

"Miss is just fine," I said, wondering if Charles had overheard.

"This is my betrothed, my fiancé, Dr. Lehmer. We're to be married next month." A proud smile spreading across her lips.

"Best wishes on your impending nuptials," I dutifully said.

"And this is?" Elizabet asked, nodding to Charles.

"This is Mr. Charles Bartman of Chicago. He's an art historian for The Chicago Art Institute. Curator of the Greek and Roman classics wing."

"Ah," Elizabet said, pointing her unopened fan in my direction as she turned to her fiancé. "Miss Hartranft speaks ancient Greek as easily as she breathes. And several other languages besides."

"Impressive," her fiancé said, giving me a nod of recognition.

"Charles, this is Dr. Elizabet DuPont—at least until next month," I said.

"Oh, there are the Bastables," Elizabet said. With her fan, she indicated a couple approaching from the dock below. She turned back to me. "So sorry, Miss Hartranft, but we really must run. Please come for tea next week. I'm staying here at the Frontenac for the month."

"I'm sorry. My sister and nieces are here. Perhaps another time," I politely declined.

"Nonsense! There's a lawn party for children next Thursday. It's perfect! You must join us. I'll send the details. Bring Anne, your sister, and your nieces. We simply must catch up. Thursday. I do insist."

"Thursday," I repeated.

"I thought you said the friend who is staying at the Frontenac was Nora somebody," Charles said after Elizabet left.

"Nora Huffington Withers. And that was not Nora. Nora and I are dear, dear friends. I don't see her as often as I'd like. I saw her fleetingly in West Philadelphia last month before I left for the island. I haven't seen Elizabet—Dr. Dupont—well in a very long time."

"Do you still need to fix the strap on your slipper?"

"No. It's all fine now," I assured him.

With that, Charles tucked my hand into his elbow, and we slowly ascended the grand staircase. The orchestra started a waltz as we entered the ballroom.

"Shall we?" Charles asked, proffering his gloved hand my way.

I took his hand, and moments later we were swirling around the dance floor. Lily was correct. The weighted hem made my skirt swing and sway as we twirled in a giant circle around the dance floor. This was only the second time I had attended a dance with Charles and I felt like we had been dancing together forever.

We mingled with the Pullmans during the polka and the schottische but were back on the dance floor for the next waltz and the third and fourth one as well. I had looked about the ballroom for Nora but had not seen her.

We had finished yet another waltz when I finally caught sight of Nora near the ballroom entrance. "There she is," I whispered in Charles's ear and beckoned him to follow me as I wove through the throng of dancers exiting the dance floor. "I've been looking for you all evening. I was starting to get worried," I said to Nora rushing to her and giving her light kisses on each cheek. "You look lovely! The green brings out the green in your eyes."

Nora was dressed in a Nile-green silk gown. Antique ivory lace hung from the low neckline of her dress, and large, and wide swathes of the same antique lace veiled her large, droopy balloon-sleeves. Tiny ringlets of curls hung about her face which had filled out a bit since the birth of her boys. Her hair was poofed slightly and drawn up in a high, loose bun on the top of her head with a small aigrette of green feathers sticking out of it.

"You look lovely as well. Though I must admit I never took you for a scarlet lady, such a departure from your drab academic duds. The cameo is an interesting choice. I would have thought pearls more suitable for a gala such as this. But I digress. We've only just arrived. We were delayed. But I suppose you've heard about our excitement," Nora said.

"No. What has happened?"

"You haven't heard? Really? It's the talk of the island. Well, as you know, we're staying with the Myers family. They have children about the same age as mine. Lovely cottage: indoor plumbing, all the latest amenities. Can you imagine getting ready for a ball using a basin and pitcher? But I digress. Well, the Myers family has a lovely St. Bernard, named Oscar. Quite valuable, you know, and so well-trained. Last year, they bought a most adorable dog cart. The children positively adore Oscar. He pulls the children around the island in the dog cart. Well, it seems sometime early this morning, Oscar strayed onto the *New Island Wanderer*. No one on the steamer seemed to notice that this mammoth dog was unescorted by his master, which only points to how well-behaved the animal is. Who knows how long he rode about the river on the steamer before disembarking in Alexandria Bay! The children, of course, were frantic, not to mention Mr. Myers. They did not have a clue where Oscar disappeared to. I did mention that Oscar is quite a costly pet. The cottage was in an uproar all day. After scouring the island and not finding him, Mr. Myers finally surmised that the keen animal must have boarded a steamer. Mr. Myers finally tracked him down in Alexandria Bay, where he was wandering about town. He's quite a friendly dog. Everyone loves him. Hence the reason for our late arrival. Mr. Withers—Rupert—is around somewhere. But mercy me! Listen to me prattle on! And shame on you, Marguerite, for allowing me to do so," she said hitting me lightly on the arm with her folded fan. "You should have stopped me immediately and introduced me to your man of the moment."

Man of the moment? The words hit me like a pie in the face. I brushed the comment away and opened my mouth to make proper introductions, but Nora pushed me out of the way and approached Charles, taking his gloved hand in her own.

"Well, well, well, what have we have here? You must be the Mr. Bartman of Chicago I've been hearing so much about," Nora said, eyeing him up and down.

"Charles, this is Mrs. Nora Withers," I said to Charles, who was looking over Nora's shoulder. "We've been friends since we were school girls."

"It's a pleasure to make your acquaintance, Mrs. Withers," Charles said with a nod of deference. "Marguerite speaks of you often."

"Does she now?" Nora said coyly. "There is so much about our past together to share. I expect you've found our escapades quite enlightening."

Charles, a bit perplexed, looked at me and then back to Nora.

Nora either didn't notice or didn't care about the startled look on Charles's face. She turned back toward me and looped her arm through mine. "Yes, we're all so happy that Marguerite has finally captured the attention of a younger man. A bit unconventional—but that's our Marguerite, a bit unconventional. Everyone in our class has been married with children for ages now. Oh, Marguerite did you hear Mary Pendleton just had her seventh child? Seven! And here's our dear Marguerite--not yet married. We've all but given up hope on her."

"No. I did not hear about Mary Pendleton," I said, blushing a bit. "I'll have to drop her a note of congratulations."

"And I hear you are from Chicago? It's no surprise that Marguerite needed to find a man far away from the staid, straightlaced sensibilities of West Philadelphia. Chicago! What a rough-and-tumble city that is. Well, it will take a rough-and-tumble man to handle our daring Miss Marguerite. Are you up to the task?" Nora asked, tapping Charles's chest with her folded fan.

There was a pause as Nora eyed Charles again as if assessing him for spunk or failings. My cheeks flushed warm. The air seemed slightly electric, sizzling around me. "Oh, come now, Nora, you make it sound like I'm incorrigible," I said with a forced smile.

Nora put a splayed hand to her chest, threw her head back, and laughed. I noticed for the first time that Nora's teeth were like kitten teeth, tiny but sharp. She put a hand on my arm and leaned in, saying in a low voice that was loud enough for Charles to hear, "Marguerite, my dear, you are the very definition of incorrigible." She turned swiftly to Charles then, placed a hand on his arm, and intimated in a low voice, "Did you know that Marguerite ran away from home when she was only sixteen?"

Charles's head swiveled my way. "You—you ran away from home?" he stammered.

"Not really. Nora exaggerates. I told my parents I was on an excursion with Nora's family while I was really attending a Walt Whitman symposium here in the Thousand Islands," I explained.

"Oh, that was the *first* time. Marguerite got me in so much trouble! My parents were furious. So when she ran away the *second* time, it was without my help. She did that all on her own in the middle of a dark, stormy night." Nora turned to me, smiled pleasantly, and waited. Her eyes seemed to challenge me to deny her revelation.

Charles's eyes were large now. He looked at me beseechingly, as if he wanted me to explain.

"It was all a misunderstanding," I said, looking at Charles.

"Oh, yes that's right! I forgot. You were afraid your parents were going to imprison you in a convent," Nora said, patting my arm as if to placate me. Nora turned back to Charles. "Her parents were desperate. They thought the convent was the only hope for their wayward Catholic daughter."

I opened my mouth to defend myself but realized the more heartily I objected to her claims, the more they sounded true.

"You—you're Catholic?" Charles stammered.

"Charles, please take Nora's comments with a grain of salt. At school, Nora was notorious for making a trip to the library sound like a scandalous adventure. She's prone to hyperbole."

This comment prompted another wave of laughter from Nora. "Me? I may embellish adventures here and there, but at least I don't concoct hoaxes."

"Whatever are you talking about?" I asked, my bewilderment edging on fear now.

"Do you remember the moon-bright night you dressed in a white sleeping gown, climbed to the top of the hill behind your cottage, and moaned and cried like a ghost? Caught the attention of all those staying at the Hub House." Nora turned to Charles then and gripped his arm before she continued. "I venture to say you had no idea that your companion this evening is the source of all those Cliff House ghost stories. Not that she doesn't hear a ghostly voice of her own. She thinks it is the voice of her brother-in-law, the one who offered to marry her first, then married her younger sister when she turned him down so she could attend the University of Pennsylvania and get her doctorate degree and become a professor there."

The orchestra had started again, but I couldn't hear anything else but the conspiratorial whisper coming from Nora's mouth as she leaned in close and said in his ear, "She keeps his portrait in a book on her bedside table. Perhaps she is regretting choosing academics over her brother-in-law."

I was positively stupefied.

Charles looked at me as if he wasn't quite sure who I was and blinked hard. "I . . . uh . . ." I think I need some refreshments," he said as he backed away from us. I was about to say that I would join him, but before I could, he turned and walked in long, swift strides across the ballroom floor in the opposite direction of the refreshment table.

"Have you tried the punch?" Nora asked, fanning herself as I watched Charles slip out the ballroom doors and into the night.

I turned to face Nora, every fiber of my body seething with embarrassment and indignation.

"The punch is far too sweet for me," she said, scrunching her face into a grimace.

If I had a glass of punch, I might have thrown it in Nora's face. My head was swimming. "Wh-what? Wh-why? Why did you say those things?" I finally managed to stammer.

"What?" Nora asked, batting her eyes at me in feigned innocence.

"That little litany of 'What's wrong with Marguerite?' Here, let me count the ways."

"Stop. You're being over-sensitive. Besides, I didn't say anything that wasn't true," she said as she snapped her fan open and rapidly set about fanning herself.

"Some were marginally true at best, but all were totally inappropriate. Let's see, you started by suggesting that I am almost too old to marry. Then that I ran away from home, that my parents thought I was so out of control they wanted to imprison me in a convent, and that I start hoaxes. By the way, I wasn't moaning. I screamed because I accidentally picked up a snake not because I was trying to imitate a ghost! And worst of all—that I keep my brother-in-law's portrait by my bedside and dream that I hear him calling my name." Each of these declarations felt like a needle jabbed straight into my heart.

Nora rolled her eyes. "I thought things were serious between the two of you? I assumed you told him all those things. You weren't hiding those things from Mr. Bartman, were you?"

"Of course, I wasn't hiding them from him but I hadn't had time to tell him every foible in my life. I've only known him for a few weeks."

Nora tsk-tsked. "You should never start a marriage on a foundation of misrepresentations. I did you a favor."

"You made me sound like a raving lunatic," I said, trying to keep my voice low so no one around me would hear.

"Calm down. No reason to be concerned about a few stray comments about your past. If things are as serious as you say, he won't just run off into the night, never to return."

I stepped forward, grasped Nora's elbow, and pulled her close to me so that I could whisper in her ear. "Of course, I'm concerned about Charles's reaction to your . . . outburst. But I'm also hurt. I feel betrayed. Nora, I told you those things in confidence, as my friend. Those things were not to be twisted into salacious tidbits for you to blurt out at a ball."

Nora wrested out of my grip, opened her fan, and leered at me over the top of it with a menacing look. "My dear, Marguerite," she snarled, "you always thought you were so smart. You live in your erudite world of Latin and Greek. You have no idea how the real world works."

I was starting to understand.

CHAPTER
thirty-three

"Aunt Marguerite, are you awake?"

My eyes fluttered open to see two pairs of eyes staring at me. The girls were kneeling on the straw mat of the tent with their little chins resting on the straw-tick mattress.

"May we cuddle with you?" they asked in unison.

The request made me smile and set my heart pattering. I sighed deeply, rubbed the sleep from my eyes, sat up, and held the quilt up so the twins could burrow underneath. I readjusted the quilt tucking it around the two girls, each snuggled into my side. I kissed the tops of their heads. I had no idea which twin was which and didn't care.

"Tell us about the ball," the twin on my left said.

"Did you feel like Cinderella?" the twin on my right asked.

"Yes," I said, remembering how I felt stepping off the gangway on Charles's arm and walking the grand walk up to the Hotel Frontenac. "I felt exactly like Cinderella!"

"Did you dance?" a twin asked.

"Yes, we waltzed around and around the grand ballroom. And the hem of my dress flared out gracefully as we danced, just as your mother said it would," I said. I shut my eyes and heard "The Emperor Waltz" playing in my head. I could see Charles's face with a hint of a smile on his face as he whirled me around the dance floor.

"Aunt Marguerite, why is your hair wet?" a twin asked.

It all came back to me then how everything had turned topsy-turvy: that the prince—not Cinderella—had run out into the night, never to return.

After Nora and I went our separate ways, part of me wanted to retreat, run upstairs to the Clarks's reserved room, and spend the rest of the evening with Katie. But a harassing thought prevented me: what if Charles returned to look for me? If I had retreated, I might have burst into tears, but because I had remained, I had to put a smile on my face and pretend that everything was alright.

I slowly made my way around the perimeter of the ballroom, nodding to those I didn't know and speaking briefly to those whom I had recently met. It was odd that most didn't even inquire as to Charles's whereabouts. To those who, did I told the truth: "He told me he was going for refreshments."

The truth. Rose said I didn't know what the truth was. Perhaps she was right.

A half hour before we were to meet the Clarks back at the dock, Mrs. Clark found me. "So sorry to hear that Charles had to rush off for an emergency. I've only just received his note. He asked that we return you to Grenell safely. Have you been alone long?"

"Not long," I said, trying to remember what time it had been when Charles fled into the night.

"Did he tell you what the nature of the emergency was?" Mrs. Clark asked as we moved toward the ballroom door.

"No, he didn't," I said.

"Well, don't worry. Mr. Clark and I will make sure you make it back to Grenell. If you're ready, we can leave now."

Nat was snoozing on the dock, waiting to row me back to Castle Rock. I untied the flaps of the tent and found two cherubs snuggled together in the second cot. I didn't want to wake them, so I didn't light the lamp. It took forever for me to unbutton my gown without a buttonhook. Thankfully, the row of tiny buttons was on the side and not the back. Once free of my gown, I stepped out of it, draped it over the chair, and piled layer after layer of undergarments on top of it. I pulled my sleeping gown over my head, then unpinned my hair. I stood there in the dark staring at my cot, knowing I would never be able to sleep, so I untied the tent flap and walked outside to the end of the dock. I sat down and put my feet in the water, wondering why the water always seemed warmer and silkier at night than it did in the day. I slipped out of my sleeping gown and into the water. As silently as I could, I moved forward in the water, and, once free of the dock, I turned onto my back, spreading my hair out behind me.

Anne's words came back to me: "Relax in the arms of the river, and trust that and island will catch thee." I shut my eyes. I felt my hair floating on the surface of the water behind me. I spread my arms. I let the river wash over me, rinsing away my confusion and purifying my thoughts. I opened my eyes and looked up at the dark sky and marveled at the multitude of stars above. The stars didn't care about what happened in the Frontenac Ballroom tonight. They glittered and shimmered and shone down on the world the same as they had last night.

"Relax in the arms of the river, and trust that an island will catch thee." I let that thought roll over in my head again and again as I floated in the welcoming arms of the river.

"Aunt Marguerite?" the twins asked in unison.

I opened my eyes, roused from my reverie. "Yes?"

"Could you read to us?"

I picked up The Blue Fairy Book from the night table, paged it open to where we had left off and began: "Once upon a time, in a very far-off country, there lived a merchant who had been so fortunate in all his undertakings that he was enormously rich." That sentence seemed to describe the world I had just visited.

We were in the middle of "Beauty and the Beast" when Lily untied the tent flap and stuck her head into the tent. "Hey, sleepyheads. You weren't supposed to wake your aunt Marguerite, remember? She was out late last night and you were supposed to let her sleep."

"Sorry, Mummy," the twins sang out in unison as Lily entered the tent, closing the flaps behind her.

"Don't apologize to me. Apologize to Aunt Marguerite."

"Sorry, Aunt Marguerite," they said, each giving me a good hug.

"I loved our cuddles," I said, kissing the tops of their heads.

"Come along. Let's get dressed," Lily said, motioning for the girls to follow her. The girls scrambled from the cot and followed their mother to the wardrobe tent.

Luckily, I had remembered to lay out today's clothes on the valet before I left for the ball. As I dressed for the day, I listened to the girls laugh and talk as Lily dressed them.

I retrieved the pins from where I'd dropped them on the camp desk late last night and twisted my hair into a sensible bun. I smiled when I heard the girls ask their mother if she could plait their hair so that they looked like Indian princesses. It would take some time for Lily to brush and plait their golden-brown hair, so I knew I had time then to write a quick note to Charles. I sat on the chair draped with undergarments and last night's gown and dipped my pen into the inkwell and thought. I started with a haiku that had been rolling around in my head after my midnight swim. This past week we had been either opening or closing our notes with a haiku, and I shouldn't break with habit. But what else should I say? Short and simple I decided. I should ask if he was well and suggest we meet soon to talk about what had happened at the ball. I signed the note, stuffed it into an envelope, quickly addressed it, and slipped it into my pocket.

I was just making up the cots when Lily, whispering for the girls to be quiet, sent them up to the cottage. Lily stayed behind and quietly peeked into the tent to check on me. "I thought you might have gone back to sleep. It's just after dawn."

"I'm wide awake. It looks like a wonderful day. Mornings are the best part. Besides, it smells as if Anne has prepared breakfast." I inhaled deeply. "*Mmmm*. Bacon."

I came out of the tent and tied the flaps open to air it out.

"So, did you have a wonderful time?" Lily asked as we started up the spiral path.

"To a point," I hedged.

"Did something happen?" Lily asked as I opened the screen door.

"We thought you were asleep, Aunt Marguerite," the twins cried out when we came into the cottage.

"I'll get another plate for you," Anne said.

Lily eyed me carefully as we ate breakfast but didn't query me again until we had left the breakfast table. "Did something happen last night?" she asked in a low voice.

I looked at the girls then and said, "I have a letter to mail, perhaps you could walk me to the post office."

"We want to go, too," the girls said, jumping up and down.

"I'm sorry, girls, but this morning is your morning to help Friend Anne with the dishes," Lily said.

Anne opened her mouth to protest, but I gave her a pointed look and shook my head slightly.

"You can go to the post office this afternoon," I told the girls.

With that, we were out the door. We walked slowly along the north shore as I recounted only the events of the evening starting from the time we talked to Nora until I met up with Mrs. Clark.

When we reached the crossroads of Park Avenue and Highland Avenue, I stopped and turned to Lily. "I don't understand," I said. Tears filled my eyes and threatened to spill over. "I'm not sure which distressed me more, Nora's diatribe or Charles disappearance. Nora is my friend. Why would she do this to me?"

Lily took my hand in hers, pressed her lips together, then took her handkerchief and dabbed at my eyes. "Oh, Marguerite. I don't know how to tell you this, but Nora was never your friend. Nora is a horrible gossip. She's quite adept at ferreting out peccadillos and then retelling them in a way that makes things sound like licentious acts of debauchery. She doesn't forget a thing."

Lily hugged me, saying, "Of all the people to share those things with."

"But now I've dragged you into this morass by telling her about Edwin's portrait. I do hear a voice. I do have his portrait. But I've never thought *the Voice* was Edwin. You must believe me, Lily."

"Don't worry," Lily said, patting my hand and giving me another hug, "the people who listen and believe Nora Huffington Withers are not the people I prefer to associate with."

"But Nora aside, what of Charles? To leave me alone like that and send a note to the Clarks and not to me. That can't be good. I'm sending him a note asking that if we can meet."

"Well, as you said—and I observed first hand—Charles is sometimes awkward around people. I'm sure Nora made him extremely uncomfortable. Perhaps he truly had an emergency. Perhaps he was ill and too embarrassed to disclose the particulars of his illness. Maybe the emergency was clothing related. He might have ripped his pants or spilled something on his shirt. You told me that he is very self-conscious."

"Perhaps," I said.

"Try not to think the worst. I'm sure he will try to contact you as soon as possible to get all this straightened out," Lily said, patting my hand again.

By the time we returned to Castle Rock, the girls had finished the dishes. Anne had rolled back the oriental carpet and was playing a rousing game of jacks on the floor with the twins. The girls were laughing and giggling. Soon we were all on the floor. Lily taught the girls how to play variations of jacks: double bouncies, cherries in a basket, pigs in a pen, over the fence, around the world.

"When did you learn these? I only remember 'over the fence'," I said.

"Rose was married, and you were away at boarding school," she said. "I had no one else to play with, so jacks was a perfect game for a little girl left all alone by her two big sisters." Lily feigned a pout.

It was the left-handed version of jacks that had all of us laughing and hooting so loudly that we didn't hear Nat knocking at the door. Eventually, he gave up and opened the door and came in. We turned and saw the telegram envelope in his hand. Lily looked at me and smiled.

"See! I knew it. It will be alright," she said.

Alas, the telegram was not from Charles. The telegram was for Lily, not for me.

CHAPTER
thirty-four

"Miss Hartranft!" a female voice called out.

I turned to see Mary Mason and Lois coming down the path from Point Breeze.

We had just visited Aunt Lucy to check up on the Columbian Wyandotte chickens for Flossie. If she asked, I'd be able to report that they were now twice the size as when they had arrived, losing their fluff, and spouting stiff-looking feathers. They weren't that cute anymore—at least not to me. But Aunt Lucy thought they were the most beautiful chickens she'd ever seen.

The twins were fascinated with the birds, which were still in a box in the kitchen, tucked in the corner behind the cookstove. Aunt Lucy had added roosting pegs to the box and was proud as punch that all had survived without getting "spraddle leg," whatever that is. She let the girls hold the chicks. "It's good for laying chickens to get used to bein' handled. That way they grow into gentle, people-friendly hens," Aunt Lucy told me.

After the birds were put safely back in their brooding box, Aunt Lucy gave the girls' hands a thorough scrubbing. "There! All clean and right suitable for handling one of these here gingerbread cookies. Just baked a batch. New recipe. I was hoping you could try 'em out for me." She handed each girl a cookie. I didn't need to prompt them to thank her, which they did with an affectionate hug, making the tough old woman choke up a little.

The girls were still eating their cookies as we walked to the store when the Kerr sisters caught up with us.

"How good to see you, Marguerite! Who are these lovely angels?" Mary Mason asked.

"Theses are my nieces, Ivy and Iris," I said. "Ivy and Iris, these are the Kerr sisters, Miss Mary Mason and Miss Lois."

"Pleasure to meet you," the girls said as they dropped a curtsy.

"However can you tell them apart?" Lois asked.

"Aunt Marguerite always knows," one of the twins said.

I was standing behind the girls. I shook my head over their little heads and put a finger to my lips.

Lois and Mary Mason smirked.

"We're so happy that we ran into you," Mary Mason said. "Were you on the way to the store? We are as well."

"We were going to walk over to Castle Rock this afternoon," Lois said as we all turned and walked toward the store. "We have exciting news."

"Rev. Stoddard of the First Baptist Church of Amsterdam is staying on the island this summer," Mary Mason said. "Perhaps you've met him."

"I don't believe I have," I said. The girls, now finished with their cookies, grabbed my hands and swung them back and forth in happy arcs as we walked.

"The reverend is staying at the Rogers' camp, directly across the little bay at the head of the island from the Gardner cottage. Due to the proximity of their camps, Mrs. Gardner has been well acquainted with the reverend. She's often talked to us about the one thing missing on this delightful island and that is the ability to worship on Sunday. Eunice—Mrs. Gardner, that is—has invited Rev. Stoddard to conduct a religious service on Gardner Point next Sunday. Prof. Pabst has agreed to play the Gardner organ for the service. We're inviting all on the island to attend."

"Mary Mason and I will be holding a Sunday school inside the Gardner cottage. We do hope Ivy and Iris can attend," Lois said.

"Please! Oh please, Aunt Marguerite, might we go? We love school," Ivy implored.

"Perhaps you could ask the girls' mother for us," Mary Mason suggested.

"Mummy's not here," Iris said.

"She had to go help Mimi, our other grandmother, who broke her leg," Ivy explained.

"We're staying with Aunt Marguerite and Friend Anne," they said in unison.

"Auntie Marguerite is teaching us to fish."

"And row."

"We already know how to swim."

"We love the toboggan slide," they said together.

"Some of the boys are too afraid to go down."

"But not us."

"It sounds like you are having a lovely time on Grenell," Lois said to the girls as we reached the store.

"We hope you and Dr. Anne will come to the service," Mary Mason said.

"I can't speak for Anne but I don't see why not," I said as I opened the door for the Kerr sisters. After the Kerrs had collected their mail, the twins dashed to the post office window and stood on tiptoe so they could peer in at Mr. Kilborn. Ivy asked in a loud, clear voice if she might have the mail for Aunt Marguerite and Friend Anne.

"That's not how to ask for it," Iris said. "It's Miss Hartranft and Miss Ashbridge."

"Hartranft is Grandmamma's name."

"That's because Aunt Marguerite is Grandmamma's daughter."

"Here you go, girls. You have quite a stack of mail," Mr. Kilborn said, handing a stack into Ivy's waiting hands.

"But why don't you have a different name from Grandmamma like Aunt Rose and Mummy?" Ivy asked as she handed the mail to me.

We walked outside to the store porch where I sat on a bench and sorted through the mail, stacked it neatly, and placed it inside this week's edition of the *Friends' Intelligencer* before I replied. "Aunt Rose and your mother changed their names to their husbands' names when they were married. You get a new name when you get married."

"What new name will we get?" Iris asked.

"That all depends on who you marry or if you marry," I said.

Ivy let out a gasp. "Does that mean we might end up with different last names like Aunt Rose and Mummy?"

"Indeed . . . unless, of course, you marry brothers."

Iris reached across and grasped her sister's hand. "We simply must marry brothers then, for I want the same last name as you."

"And I you."

"Why, Marguerite! *Bonjour*," I looked up and saw Emily, the new Mrs. Gabriel, approaching on the arm of Mr. Gabriel.

I stood to welcome them. "You're back from your wedding trip."

They both greeted me by kissing each cheek.

"Yes. And thank you for dropping in on Delia as I had asked," Emily said.

"It was our pleasure," I said.

"Who are these lovely moppets? Oh my! They are a matched set!"

"These are my nieces, Ivy and Iris. Girls, this is Mr. and Mrs. Gabriel."

Mr. Gabriel released the hand of his bride, which had been safely tucked in his elbow, gave the girls a gallant bow, and said, *"Enchante."*

He reached forward, took one twin's hand and then the other's, and kissed each softly while whispering to them in French what lovely young girls they were.

The girls seemed awe-struck by this action and then somewhat embarrassed as the looked to me for the correct response.

"He said that you are very beautiful young girls and he is enchanted to meet you. Say *merci*," I told the girls.

"*Merci*," they said in compliance.

"That means 'thank you' in French."

The twins nodded as if they knew.

After chatting with the Gabriels for a few moments, I tucked my bundle of mail under my arm, took the girls by the hands, and started walking back to Castle Rock, this time via the north side of the island.

I thought of telling the girls that Emily and her sister, Delia, had had the same last name for about four decades and now their surnames were different: Griswold and Gabriel. At least they both started with a G. But I thought perhaps this thought might be more distressing to them than comforting to them. I wondered briefly if the thought was distressing to Delia. Emily had said that the marriage had been hard for her sister to accept.

Three steps later, Iris let out a bloodcurdling shriek. We all stopped in our tracks.

"What?" I asked as her scream echoed off the water and then the palisades of the Narrows beyond.

Iris pointed.

"Oh, Iris, it's only a little garden snake," Ivy said, patting her sister's hand.

"It's called a garter snake, like the garters that hold up your stockings," I corrected her.

"I wouldn't want a snake to hold up my stocking," Iris said and cringed slightly, brushing at the skirt of her dress as if there might be snakes underneath holding up her stockings now.

Ivy crouched down to get a better look at the snake. "Look! It has a red tongue! Aunt Marguerite, will you pick it up as Miss Bixby does so that I can get a closer look at its tongue?"

Iris clutched my leg and buried her face in my skirt. I patted her head. "I don't know the proper way to pick up snakes as Miss Bixby does, so as not to hurt them," I told Iris. "Besides, I think it would frighten your sister. Perhaps we can write a haiku about the snake instead."

The girls had been fascinated with the tiny poems I wrote on small scraps of paper. Every morning and every evening I wrote a haiku and put it in the small rosewood box I kept on my writing table. Charles and I had shared haikus twice a day in the last couple of weeks and perhaps someday soon, I would be able to share these new haikus with him.

"But I don't know how to write hike-ooos," Ivy said.

"I shall teach you then. Perhaps tonight," I suggested.

"I don't have to write my hiking-ooos about a snake, do I?" Iris asked as she edged around the snake and continued along the north shore path toward Castle Rock.

"You may write about anything you wish," I assured Iris.

"But first we should play Shut the Box with Friend Anne," Ivy suggested.

"Oh, yes. Friend Anne loves Shut the Box," Iris said.

"Indeed! That sounds like a splendid plan," I said.

After we returned to Castle Rock, we sorted out the mail, and I surprised the girls with their letters: one for each of them from their mother. Not being able to read quite yet, the twins were happy to let me read their letters to them. Then they traded letters and tried to read them to each other.

"Mummy doesn't say when she will be coming back," Iris noted.

"No she didn't. But all is well, and we're having a great time here, are we not?" I asked, hugging both the girls.

The telegram that arrived the day after the ball had not been from Charles; it was from Edwin saying that his mother had fallen and broken her ankle. As Mrs. Dillworth didn't have any daughters, but only a daughter-in-law, she had asked if Lily could assist when she arrived home from the hospital. Lily had left early the next morning. Her letter to me thanked me for watching after the twins as they surely would have been underfoot at the Dillworth home and besides they would be happier there on Grenell with me than at home with their governess.

Anne held up a letter and waved it at me. "I have a note from Friend Elizabet. It seems that she's to be married."

"Yes. I'm sorry. I quite forgot to tell you that I ran into Elizabet at the ball the other night."

"Oh, so that's how she knew your nieces were visiting. I was wondering how she'd come across that piece of information. She's invited us to a children's lawn party at the Frontenac later this week," Anne said.

"Can't we make excuses?"

Anne said nothing but looked at me with her calm, practiced, emotionless face, and I knew that we could not.

"The girls will love it." Anne paused, then asked if there was a letter from Charles.

I shook my head. It had been four days since the ball, and I had yet to hear a word from him.

"Rose?" Anne asked.

I shook my head again. I hadn't heard from Rose since she'd left. Daily I wrote two short, cheery notes—one to her and one to Mother— in hopes that one day I would hear from both of them. "Only a letter from Sophie," I said, holding it up. "She's with child again. This will be her third. She's hoping for a boy this time." This, of course, made me think of Lily. The birth of the twins had been difficult, and she's been told she would never bear children again. Edwin, of course, wanted a boy and an heir.

Anne had said after talking to the doctor about the twins' delivery, it was a miracle that Lily survived—and a miracle that the twins had survived.

Lily embraced this news, deciding to be grateful for her little miracles rather than to be disheartened by not being able to bear children again.

As the girls continued to look at the letters that Lily had sent them, I went to the camp below to retrieve the sewing project I had worked on after they had fallen asleep last night. We had read a tale in *The Blue Fairy Book* called "The Forty Thieves." In it, Ali Babba, the hero of the story, had climbed a tree to hide from a troop of thieves. This had prompted a discussion on tree climbing. It seems that a neighbor boy is forever scampering up trees. He even fashioned a tree house from stray scraps of wood. Both girls longed to climb trees like their friend and explore his tree house, but it was impossible in their frilly white dresses. As soon as they drifted off to sleep in each other's arms, I had set on my surprise project, thankful that I had enlisted Anne's help. She had been diligently working on it all day.

"I have a surprise for you," I said, holding the two bundles behind my back.

"What is it?" the girls asked, running to me and jumping up and down in anticipation. From behind my back, I withdrew a bundle for each girl.

"What is it?" Ivy asked, tentatively holding up something that looked like very baggy Turkish-style pants with ankle cuffs.

"They are bloomers. New Women wear them to ride safety bicycles. And while not fit for wearing to a tea party or out in public—besides riding a safety bicycle, of course—I think bloomers might be the perfect thing to wear while climbing trees."

The girls cheered. "May we put them on now?"

"Yes, of course. Use my room, and carefully place your dresses on my bed so they don't wrinkle."

They returned wearing their new bloomers and white shirtwaists.

"Shall we try them out?" I asked.

The girls nodded.

"Now off to the tree!" I said as I opened the door. "No, this way," I said pointing to the path the led up behind our cottage. Off the path toward the center of the island was a huge spreading oak with low limbs. I gave the girls a boost and they scampered up the tree.

I spread a quilt on the ground below and watched them. Ivy climbed high into the canopy while making monkey sounds. "Do you think this is how Jambo would climb a tree?" she asked.

Iris straddled the large low branch that was as thick as a keg. "I couldn't do this in a dress," she said, leaning back against the trunk.

As I watched the girls, I was a little jealous, wishing I had had a pair of bloomers at their age. I picked wild daisies that grew near the rock I was sitting on and wove the daisies into wreaths for my nieces to wear. Eventually, Ivy climbed down and joined Iris on the fat lower branch. "Do you think this is a fairy tree full of fairies in the gloaming?" Ivy asked her sister.

"I think this branch is like the bowsprit of a great sailing ship," Iris said.

This made me smile as it indeed was the size and shape of a bowsprit.

And so the two pretended they were sailing across the sea rising and falling on the waves.

"Here you go, you two," I said handing the daisy wreaths to the girls.

"I now crown you Princess of Grenell, Princess Ivy," Iris said in a regal voice as she placed the daisy crown on her sister's head. Ivy reciprocated by crowning her sister Princess Iris with the same royal flair. The two giggled and hugged each other, and when they looked up and out across the water, they were distracted.

"Look! Look! There is a skiff coming to shore," they shouted out.

"The man rowing is very tiny with a long, white beard and an odd hat," Iris said.

"Perhaps he's an elf," Ivy suggested.

I didn't turn, thinking it was part of their imagined journey.

"Truly, Auntie, an elf in a skiff is coming to shore. I think he is coming to our dock."

I looked out, and indeed there was a skiff that seemed to be rowing to our dock.

"May we meet the elf?" the girls asked.

"Quickly, girls, let's hurry back to Castle Rock so you can change back into your dresses."

I lifted the girls down from the tree and followed the path back to Castle Rock. Once out of their bloomers and in proper dresses again, the twins skipped down the spiral path ahead of me. Anne had gone ahead of us to see who was in the skiff that had come ashore, not to our dock but to the shelving rock two lots upriver from us.

"Here they come now," Anne said. "I'd like to introduce Dr. Gifford from Oswego, New York. Dr. Gifford, this is Marguerite Hartranft and these are her nieces Ivy and Iris Dillworth."

The man was quite a bit taller than the girls had imagined but still shorter than most. He had a long white beard that trailed down to his belt. His hat, indeed, was very odd. It had the widest brim I'd ever seen and a high crown shaped like a chocolate drop. There was intricate embroidery scrolling along the upturned edges of the brim and around the crown of the chocolate drop. Braided-leather cords wrapped around the crown and went through holes in the brim to become chin straps. He took off his wide-brimmmed hat, exposing thinning white hair with a very pink scalp showing through. He bowed deeply. "Good day, ladies," he said. "A pleasure to make your acquaintance."

"I like your hat," Iris said.

"Why thank you," Dr. Gifford said placing the hat on his head again.

"What kind of hat is that?" Ivy asked.

"This, my dear, is a genuine leather charro sombrero. Purchased it a few years back when I visited the New Mexico territory. Thought it would be perfect for rowing on the river. Sombra means 'shade' in Spanish. So it was like buying my own shade for the trip. These stampede strings keep the hat tight to my head so that I don't have to swim for it. Otherwise, a gust of wind sends if flying. Would you like to try it on?"

The girls nodded excitedly.

"See here! What's this? I've never seen anything like this in all my years of doctoring. It looks as if daisies are growing out of her head," Dr. Gifford exclaimed.

The girls dissolved into giggles at this silly notion.

"Daisies aren't growing out of our heads," Ivy said.

"They are daisy crowns. We are the princesses of Grenell," Iris added.

"Oh, I see," Dr. Gifford said, bowing regally to the little princesses. "With your permission, your majesties, may I remove your daisy crowns, so you can try on my hat?"

"But of course!" the girls said in unison.

As Dr. Gifford let the girls try on his hat, Anne explained to us that Dr. Gifford had left Oswego, New York, which is on the south shore of Lake Ontario, and rowed in his skiff all the way to Grenell Island.

"My goodness! How long of a trip was that?" I asked.

"Hmmm. By my calculations, I'd say it's upwards of sixty miles," he said.

"Sixty miles?" Ivy asked. "How long did it take you to row sixty miles?"

"Oh, I wasn't in a hurry. I rowed slowly, taking in the scenery. When a man gets to be my age, it's the journey, not the speed, that's important. You young'uns today are always thinking you have to get places quickly. Did you ladies hear about the New York Central passenger train locomotive number 999 that just a few months ago pulled a passenger train between the New York towns of Batavia and Buffalo at a rate of 112 miles an hour? Outrageous! Don't think man was meant to go a hundred miles an hour. Not for me! But, then again, I'm an old man and I have the time for rambling."

"Did a train really go one hundred miles an hour?" Ivy asked, looking at Dr. Gifford warily, thinking perhaps that he was telling us a tall tale.

"Yes, Ivy. Dr. Gifford is correct. I read about it in the paper," I said.

Dr. Gifford nodded gravely. "Now I know most of these fishing guides around here can row thirty miles in a day easily. But I'm an old man and spend most of my time in a doctor's office—thus the need for bringing along my own shade. So I took my sweet time, rowing a little and drifting a little."

Dr. Gifford sat down, leaned back against the skiff, and gestured for us to do the same. "At night, I would pull the skiff ashore, make a fire, stretch my canvas top over the side of the skiff to the ground and sleep beneath that. It was a lovely trip. I rented this lot from the Grenells and plan to spend a week or two. Nice to know I have nice neighbors and a lady doctor. Nice to know I have someone to turn to if I get sick or injured."

"Let us know if you need anything," I said rising to my feet and taking the girls by the hand. "Will you be renting a tent?"

"No need. I'll just tip the skiff on its side and throw a tarp over it to make a lean-to as I did on my trip here."

The girls broke away from me, ran ahead, and took Anne by the hand.

"Aunt Marguerite promised to teach us how to write hike-ooos tonight," Ivy said.

"But first, we want to play Shut the Box with you!" Iris exclaimed.

CHAPTER
thirty-five

"It was so nice of you to include us. The girls are so excited," I said as I stepped aboard the *Mamie C.*

"Miss Hartranft! Delighted to see you again," Mrs. Clark said, grasping both my hands and kissing me on the cheek.

Yesterday afternoon, we'd received a telegram from the Clarks inviting us on a short excursion on the *Mamie C.* with the Kerr family. The twins jumped up and down when I told them we were spending the day on a private steam yacht. I wanted to jump up and down as well. It had been days since the ball, and I had not heard a word from Charles and I was anxious to see him again.

I'd introduced the twins to the rest of the Kerr family while we were waiting on the dock. I introduced them to the Clark family as we boarded.

"If the girls would like to see the bow of the ship, I'd be happy to take them," Lois offered. I nodded my approval, and she took the girls by the hands, and walked to the bow with the rest of the Kerr family just as the *Mamie C.* edged away from the Grenell Island Store dock.

Mrs. Clark nodded toward the salon. I opened the door and we settled into the plush club chairs. I looked around expectantly, thinking I would find Charles there as I had not seen him on the bow when the yacht arrived.

"We wanted to do something nice for the Kerrs after all they did to help Charles this summer. My goodness, after the Princeton outing, he was here at their place as much as he was at our cottage. And I've missed seeing you now that Charles has gone back to Chicago."

It was as if all the air had been sucked out of the salon. I blinked hard, for this was the first that I had heard that Charles had returned home.

I looked at my hands, gathered my wits, and looked at Mrs. Clark expectantly hoping she would say more as I didn't trust my voice to say anything right now as my throat was thick with emotion. Meanwhile, my mind was repeating the phrase "Charles is gone" over and over in my head. He'd left without saying goodbye. Was I never to see him again?

"I'm so sorry that Dr. Ashbridge couldn't join us. I was looking forward to meeting her," Mrs. Clark said.

I swallowed hard and tried to speak clearly, hiding the hurt and confusion over the revelation of Charles's departure. "She's disappointed as well, but we received an urgent message that Mrs. Schiller was ill and asked the doctor to attend to her."

"Is Mrs. Schiller a cottager or someone staying at the Pullman House?"

"A cottager. The Schillers own the first cottage on the Grenell Island Park side of the bridge. They call it Ojibway Inn," I said, bending low to look out the porthole windows on either side of the salon.

"Indian names are so popular along the river. Do you know the meaning?"

"Flossie—Miss Bixby—says it's the name of a tribe of Algonquin people," I said.

"Yes, yes. Miss Bixby, your roommate at Penn. Charles said she is studying anthropology?"

I nodded.

"How I wish she could have come along, but she is away now, is she not?"

"Yes, she is at the American Canoe Association rendezvous. Perhaps we will see the canoes and sailing canoes out in Eel Bay."

"I'm not familiar with this end of the river. Where is Eel Bay?"

"It's on the other side of the Narrows, the body of water we will cross en route to Grand View Park. We are going through the Narrows now," I said, indicating the palisades on the starboard side of the yacht.

"Have we passed your cottage? What do you call it?"

"Castle Rock. It's a bit of a joke. If you look back, you can see the large castle being built at the crest of Grenell for the Sharples family. He's calling it Bungalow. I'd quipped that if that was a Bungalow than our tiny cottage was a castle."

"Is it tiny?"

"Indeed! Our cottage is about the size of your parlor."

"Oh, how lovely and just right for you and Dr. Ashbridge."

"Yes, we are quite comfortable."

"Some days, I wished we had something a little simpler. A little less grand. So much fuss with china, silver, and staff," Mrs. Clark said she entered the salon.

"What a lovely salon," Mrs. Kerr said as she came through in the salon door. "How long have you had the *Mamie C.*?"

As the two discussed decorating of the *Mamie C.*'s salon, my thoughts drifted away. I only heard "Charles is gone" echoing in my head. But I roused myself from my stupor to hear Mrs. Clark say to me, "We thought we would treat you and the Kerrs to a nice luncheon at Grand View Park. I hope you don't mind going again."

"Not at all. I rowed over to the bakery not long ago. Their rye is my favorite. I'll probably purchase a loaf to take home with us."

"I didn't know they had a bakery. I heard they have a wonderful toboggan slide and an excellent bathing beach. I trust you brought bathing costumes for you and the girls," Mrs. Kerr said.

I nodded.

We soon landed and had a lovely lunch before we all changed into our bathing costumes.

I waded into the river from the beach. Once waist high, I lunged forward into the waiting arms of the river. Ah! The cool, clear freshness of the water revived my jangled nerves. I forgot all else. I swam out away from the beach using the breaststroke so I could keep my hair dry.

"Girls! Come swim with me," I called to them, motioning them toward me.

The girls weren't interested in swimming. They only wanted to slide down the toboggan slide. They scampered up the stairs.

I swam back so I could watch them slide down.

"Are you sure it's not too high for them?" asked Mary Mason who was standing at the bottom of the slide watching the girls as they reached the top. I wanted to tell Mary Mason that Ivy had climbed even higher in the oak tree the other day.

The girls put the sliding mat down and climbed aboard. I wasn't sure which twin was first and which twin sat behind her sister with her arms wrapped around her midsection. "Watch us, Aunt Marguerite! Watch!" one called out. Then they yelled, "One! Two! Three!" They pushed themselves off the flat platform at the top. Squeals of delight pierced the air as they dashed down the slide and splashed into the water below.

The two girls stood, laughing, panting, and dripping with water.

"Move out of the way so others can slide down," I instructed.

Laughing so hard they could barely stand, the twins grabbed the mat and sloshed toward me.

"Did we get you wet, Aunt Marguerite?" one asked.

"Just a little! And I thought I was standing far enough away."

"Oh, do come with us this time. Please," they implored, pulling me toward the shore.

It seems the more I declined, the more they insisted. Eventually, I gave in to their pleas and climbed the stairs. This slide was nearly twice as tall as the Pullman House slide. It was a little unnerving to look down at the water below. So instead, I looked out at the two islands referred to as the Robinson Group. From this height, I could see all the way to Canoe Point on Grindstone Island. That made me think of Flossie. And I could hear how she might chide me to go ahead and push off. So I did. I felt the air rush at my face, and my stomach felt like it was flipping upside down. I plunged into the water with such impact that water went up my nose and my mobcap flew off. High above me, I could hear the twins clap and cheer. It took me a moment to gather my wits, grab my mat, and move out of the way so they could slide down after me.

"Again. Again!" The twins insisted.

"Once was enough for me," I said. They shrugged away their disappointment and ran back to climb the slide one more time.

"So much for not getting my hair wet," I said as Mary Mason and Lois approached.

"Such adventurous little girls," Mary Mason noted.

"They're turning into real river girls like you and Lois," I said. "They have learned to swim, fish, row, and perhaps when Flossie returns –if they're still here—she'll teach them to paddle a canoe."

"What about sailing?" Lois asked. "We'd be happy to take you and the girls out on *Tiger* and teach you to sail."

Mrs. Clark was wading nearby, and as she approached, she let out a little squeak and fell to her knees. Mary Mason, Lois, and I hurried over to help her to her feet.

"Luckily it's shallow here, and I didn't get my coiffure wet," she said as we raised her to her feet.

"I hadn't anticipated getting my hair so wet. I'm afraid I'm in need of serious repair," I said.

"Come, let's see if I can help you pin your hair up, Miss Hartranft," Mrs. Clark said motioning toward the shore.

"Please, do call me Marguerite," I told her.

"Then I insist you call me Sarah," Mrs. Clark said as she took a step toward the shore and winced.

"Did you twist your ankle?" I asked.

"No. Only stepped in a hole. But I will take your arm to steady myself so I don't fall again." She looped her arm through mine.

"Certainly," I said, smiling at Mrs. Clark.

"So what do you hear from Charles these days? Has he finished his book?" Mrs. Clark asked as we waded to shore.

"He hasn't said," I said, feeling my chest tighten at the mention of his name.

"He never quite explained what emergency sent him dashing into the night. It must have been something quite urgent. By the time we arrived back to Comfort Island that night—it was quite late as you might imagine—Charles was gone. Of course, we didn't realize until the morning that he had left before we returned. He had packed all his things, left a note saying that he decided to stay in Alexandria Bay that night as he had an early morning train and didn't want to inconvenience us with an early morning trip to the steamship dock. But he must have known that the staff would have been happy to row him over. We're still unsure how he made it from Round Island back to Comfort."

By now we had reached a bench and sat. "Thank you, my dear,

for your assistance," she said patting my arm. She paused then, looking first at me, then out at the water. "Did he ever disclose the nature of his emergency?"

"No. He didn't."

Mrs. Clark reached down and rung out the bottom hem of her swim costume and turned to look up at me. "I don't mean to pry, but it's all so puzzling. Did he receive a telegram? How was he alerted to this emergency? At the Frontenac, of all places?"

"I'm afraid I do not know the answer to that question," I said, following her example and ringing out the bottom hem of my bathing costume.

"Here, dear, let me help you re-pin your hair," she said, turning my face toward hers as she took out loose pins and put them in my hand.

Once my hair was secured in a bun again, she stopped and gazed directly into my eyes. "So he didn't say anything to you? He just said he had an emergency?"

I looked down and bit my lip slightly as I tried to think of an appropriate response. "No, he said he needed refreshment. He did not go toward the refreshment table. He simply left the ballroom."

This bit of information seemed to startle Mrs. Clark. She was quiet for a moment, as she pondered my revelation. "Marguerite, you have heard from Charles, haven't you?"

I gulped hard, batted my eyes lids to blink away tears, and shook my head.

Mrs. Clark gasped, bringing one hand to her throat and placing the other on my hand. "My stars. He just left? Without a word?"

I pressed my lips together and nodded.

"For no reason? Did you argue?"

"No, but . . ."

"I can't imagine. He is quite fond of you. He'd even asked me . . . he'd hinted at . . ."

"There was an awkward moment just before he left," I said, turning from her gaze to look out over the river. I looked down at my hands before I continued. "We were speaking with my friend Nora—Mrs. Withers." The word *friend* left a tinny taste in my mouth. "Nora is a bit of a fabulist."

"A fabulist?"

"A person who composes or relates fables."

I had chosen that word carefully. It was from the Latin word *fabula* meaning "story" but over the years, fabulist has developed a second meaning beyond 'storyteller.' A fabulist is a liar, especially a person who invents elaborate, dishonest stories.

"Go on."

"Even as a schoolgirl, Nora was known for embellishing. As outrageous as her stories about me were that night, there somehow was a kernel of truth in everything she said making it hard for me to deny them outright. The things Nora said about me were clearly upsetting to Charles," I said looking down at my hands again. I noticed that my fingers were still slightly pruned from my time in the water.

"This is unacceptable," Mrs. Clark said, her words more forceful and agitated than I'd ever heard her utter before. I feared she was going to ask me where she might find Nora so she could confront her.

I could tell that her mind was working hard trying to figure out this dilemma.

"But later? Were you able to explain yourself to him?"

I shook my head. "I never had the chance. He left. Went straight out the door and I've . . ." the words caught in my throat. "I've never seen or heard from him since."

"To leave without explanation, to not respond to your queries. Unacceptable. Utterly unacceptable," Mrs. Clark said.

I realized then that her irritation was not with Nora, but with Charles.

"Mr. Clark is leaving for Chicago tomorrow on business. I will see to it that he gets to the bottom of this."

I felt color rise in my cheeks. The thought that Charles would think that I had sent the Clarks to intercede on my behalf filled me with shame. "Mrs. Clark, I don't think . . ."

A piercing scream shattered the afternoon calm, bringing us both instantly to our feet. Lois, Mary Mason, Mr. Clark, and the Clark boys rushed to the base of the toboggan slide.

I rushed to find the twins, splashing into the water. Mancel had one of the twins in his arms, blood gushing from the top of her forehead. Lois picked up the other twin and cradled her against her shoulder.

"What happened?" I asked going to first one twin and then the other. Both appeared injured.

"We'll explain later. I think we need to get this girl to a doctor as soon as possible," Mr. Clark said.

"Anne should be home by now. It's just the other side of the Narrows."

"Sir! You there!" Mr. Clark called out. "We're in need of one of your skiffs. We will return it immediately and compensate you then."

The man waved his compliance, and the Clark boys rushed off to tie the skiff to the stern of the *Mamie C.*

"We will be back to pick you up later," Mr. Clark said waving to Mr. and Mrs. Kerr and their sons. Mancel had one twin and Lois the other. Mary Mason and Mrs. Clark escorted me aboard the *Mamie C.* and lent comfort where they could. The Kerr boys helped untie the lines and push us off as we settled in the salon. Mancel transferred the more severely injured twin to my arms. Mary Mason found a towel and brought it to me to hold against the gash at the top of her forehead. Blood covered her face, and she sputtered slightly as blood dripped into her mouth.

The *Mamie C.* flew across Eel Bay. I heard the Clarks shout as *Mamie C.*'s whistle shrieked, warning other boats to get out of the way. "We're almost through the Narrows," said Mary Mason, patting my back. "We're almost there." We slowed as we approached Grenell. Mr. Clark called out for Dr. Anne, shouting that we had an injured child aboard. His calls alerted the Pabsts and the Pratts, who rushed toward the two-plank dock to help.

It was too shallow for the *Mamie C.* to dock at Castle Rock. We would have to transfer the girls to the skiff and row to shore. The wounded twin was only whimpering now but cried out when Mancel took her from my arms.

"Hush. Hush," I said, trying to soothe her. "We're almost there. Mancel will hand you to me once I'm in the skiff."

I climbed into the skiff and Mancel lowered the twin into my waiting arms, then helped the other twin into the skiff. He climbed aboard and rowed in long, sure pulls to the Castle Rock dock. Prof. Pabst and his brother Carl were there to take the twin from my arms. Prof. Pabst carried one twin, and Carl carried the other up the spiral path to the cottage.

Grenell 1893

I thanked the Clarks and the Kerrs, then followed them up the spiral path.

Anne was already tending to the twin with the gash on her forehead.

"I'm sorry Aunt Marguerite," the other twin said climbing onto my lap and hugging me. "Will Iris be alright?"

It was only then that I knew which twin was which.

CHAPTER
thirty-six

"You're not going to wear one of your day dresses?" Anne asked when I ushered the girls up the spiral path and into the cottage for breakfast.

The twins were wearing their Sunday best for Sunday school this morning: white frilly dresses with wide, pink satin sashes. I had combed out Ivy's honey-brown hair, pulled the top layer back, secured it with a barrette, and added a large pink satin ribbon. I suggested to Iris that we leave her hair down and pin the bow on the side of her head, saying, "That way your hair covers the bandage on the left side of your forehead." But Iris had protested, insisting that her hair be styled the same as her twin's.

"Do you like our hair bows, Friend Anne?" Iris asked.

"Ivy's loops were bigger than mine," Iris reported, "but Aunt Marguerite fixed them so that they are a perfect match—just like us!"

I smiled and did not point out that Iris's bandage made it very easy for me to tell for the first time in their short lives which twin was which.

"How are you feeling this morning?" Friend Anne asked Iris. "You are looking well."

"Fine. It's tender when I touch it, so I don't," Iris said with a shrug.

"How are your teeth, Ivy? Still wiggly?" Friend Anne asked.

Ivy nodded. "Do you think they might fall out?"

"Well, they are baby teeth. If they do fall out, they will be replaced by permanent teeth eventually."

I bent down and checked Ivy's teeth. Her gums had been red and tender yesterday but looked much better this morning. Iris's bandage didn't allow me a peek at her injury. I rubbed my own forehead instead. I felt a sudden heaviness in my chest, wondering if there would be much of a scar.

As if sensing what I was thinking, Friend Anne whispered in my ear. "I took care to take tiny stitches. There won't be much of a scar. Besides, it's right below the hairline and very easy to hide with her hair once the bandage is removed."

I nodded, hoping she was right.

"No fancy day dress for you, Marguerite? No Sunday best? No matching hat? No crocheted gloves?" Anne asked of me again as she brought a skillet of scrambled eggs to the table.

"I couldn't sleep last night after the girls went to bed, so I decided that I should pack away the dresses. I'll ask Nat to send them all back to Helen. I don't need them anymore."

Anne nodded slightly to acknowledge that she had heard. I saw a momentary flash of surprise cross her face but it quickly disappeared as she continued serving scrambled eggs to the girls.

After breakfast, we washed the girls' bright and shiny faces, took them by the hands, and walked along the North Shore Boulevard to the Gardner Cottage. From here I could see that the large boathouse on Murray Isle was nearing completion. The worksite was thankfully quiet today as it was Sunday—a day of rest.

The twins were excited about Sunday school. They had never attended a Sunday school before and were full of questions. Anne was raised a Quaker. I was raised Catholic. Therefore neither of us had ever attended a Sunday school class.

"You are the first! You will have to share with us all that you learned," I said as we turned inland.

I heard the music before I saw the long line of people on the south side of Gardner Point.

"Where's that music coming from?" Ivy asked, looking skyward as if expecting an angel playing a harp to drop from the sky.

"That is our neighbor, Prof. Pabst. He's playing the pump organ from inside the Gardner cottage." The rich notes emanating from the cottage aroused in me childhood memories of going to church with my parents. I could feel the music resonating deep within my chest. The music was moving, both spiritually and physically.

"Is that the school?" Iris asked.

"That is the Gardner cottage. Mrs. Gardner and her husband own three guest cottages on the island, though she stays in that tent over there so she can make sure her guests enjoy the summer on the island. The service is outside. Perhaps the Sunday school will be held inside."

Mrs. Gardner had been on the island as long as I have. She and her husband, William, stopped to visit the Pratts the year I was sixteen, my first year on the island. The next year they bought Gardner Point, a narrow finger of land that poked out into the ribbon of water between Grenell and Wilsons Island. The guest cottage sat in the middle of the point, and, from the long line that had formed, it seemed they were holding the service on the upriver side of the cottage.

"Why are we waiting in line?" Ivy asked.

I rose up on my toes and peeked around a few hats. I saw Mrs. Gardner—Eunice—greeting everyone and introducing them to to a small man in a black suit with a clerical collar.

"Mrs. Gardner is welcoming everyone to Gardner Point," I said.

Iris leaned out and peered around the group to see for herself. "Is that man her husband?"

"No, dear. I think that is the minister who will be conducting today's service. Mr. Gardner is in Syracuse managing their boarding house."

Another family had arrived. Mrs. Hudson ushered her four children in line behind us. She seemed to have two separate families: a boy and girl in their teens and then two younger girls, who looked to be younger than the twins. Perhaps they were four and six?

"Good morning," I said to Mrs. Hudson.

"How fares thee?" Anne asked, slipping back into a traditional Quaker greeting.

Mrs. Hudson gave us a nervous smile as she fussed over the girls' sashes, making sure their bows were perfectly tied.

Just when I wondered if Mrs. Hudson had come alone with the children, I saw Mr. Hudson in the distance. He'd stop to chat with Mr.

Reeves. After patting his back and shaking his hand, Mr. Hudson strutted our way. Mr. Hudson was a small, slight man, but always walked with his nose in the air and his chest puffed out as if trying to seem bigger than he really was.

When he noticed us, Mr. Hudson raised his chin higher and looked down his long, thin nose at us, before he nodded a greeting. "Good day, ladies. Surprised to see you here," he said.

My face flushed at his comment as he was probably right. If the girls weren't here and excited about attending Sunday school, I probably would have rowed to Clayton and attended morning Mass at St. Mary's.

"What a beautiful morning for a service," I said, smiling broadly to hide my embarrassment.

Prof. Pabst finished a hymn with a long, resonant chord. Gardner Point was suddenly silent, so I heard Mrs. Hudson tap her husband's arm sharply before she whispered, "Marshall! That was rude."

"I only meant that Catholics and Quakers usually don't attend Baptist services," Mr. Hudson whispered back.

Iris tugged at my elbow, and I leaned over so she could whisper in my ear, "What's a Baptist?"

Thankfully, we had reached the front of the line, so instead of answering, I patted Iris's hand and pulled her forward to introduce her and her twin to our hostess.

Mrs. Gardner is a spry, industrious woman with intelligent eyes. According to the Kerrs, who had stayed at the Gardner cottage, Mrs. Gardner was a most genial proprietress, who instinctually anticipated the needs of her guests. Because of her attention to detail, her three guest cottages were in high demand and usually rented to well-to-do families from New York City, Philadelphia, or New Jersey.

Mrs. Gardner introduced us to the Rev. Stoddard, a slight man with a high forehead, well-maintained mustache, and large ears. He had an easy smile and expressive eyes that brightened as he greeted us. He bent down and spoke to the twins and shook their hands.

Harry, the Gardner's fourteen-year-old son, ran over to his mother to ask where he might get more chairs. She quickly gave him instructions and he darted off to comply. "Please . . . make yourself comfortable the service will begin shortly," she said turning back to us. We thanked her for her hospitality moved forward.

The point was well-shaded by a large, sprawling maple with tiny oak saplings beneath. Several dozen chairs were lined up beneath the shade of the tree and facing the cottage. Quilts were spread on the ground in front of and on either side of the row of chairs. The Kerr sisters greeted us. Lois indicated the young family standing next to her. "We'd like to introduce you to Mr. and Mrs. Bakewell and their two children, Euphemia and Allen. They have rented the Gardner cottage for the season," she said.

"How fair thee today?" Anne asked as she nodded toward the young couple. Mrs. Bakewell was holding a young child who looked to be around two years old and Mr. Bakewell held the hand of a young girl who appeared to be about the same age as the twins.

"Thomas—Mr. Bakewell, that is—is father's first cousin. When Father graduated from Western University of Pennsylvania, he worked for a law firm founded by his uncle William Bakewell, Thomas's father," Lois informed us.

"Thomas attended the same university as Father, though many years later. He is a patent lawyer like his father, who pioneered patent law," Mary Mason added.

"We live in such a wondrous age of discovery and invention," Mr. Bakewell said.

Quite a few people were arriving and Mrs. Gardner urged us to find a seat. "Please sit anywhere you wish. The girls may sit up front on the quilts."

"Perhaps Euphemia—Effy—would like to sit with the twins," Mary Mason suggested. As the chairs looked like they might all be filled, Anne and I along with the three young girls, decided to sit on the quilts near where the Kerrs and the Bakewells were sitting.

It was a beautiful morning for an outdoor service. The sky was clear, and the bright sun glinted off the water. Behind the chairs was the beautiful view of Wilsons Island and the tiny islands of Huckleberry and Little Huckleberry. We enjoyed the view while we waited for the service to begin as more islanders continued to stream in. Soon all the chairs were filled.

"There they are," Mrs. Bakewell announced and nodded to Mr. and Mrs. Curtis and family who were speaking with Rev. Stoddard and Mrs. Gardner. Mrs. Bakewell raised a gloved hand and waved when they turned to look for a place to sit.

Leonard Curtis is T. B. Kerr's law partner. His family was much younger than the Kerr offspring. They had four children—two girls and two boys ranging in age from nine to three. "We have room here for the children," Mrs. Bakewell called out. "Dr. Ashbridge, Miss Hartranft, have you met the Curtises?"

"No, but I have heard much about them from Mary Mason and Lois," I said.

Mrs. Bakewell introduced us to Mr. and Mrs. Curtis. Mrs. Curtis insisted we call her Lottie. Then, Lottie introduced their four children: Bessie, Helen, Leonard, Jr. and Alfred. We barely got the introductions out of the way before Rev. Stoddard disappeared around the corner of the house. The congregation faced the two open windows of the Gardner cottage. Inside the cottage, Prof. Pabst started another organ hymn with a dramatic chord. Rev. Stoddard appeared at the end of the porch to face the crowd assembled on Gardner Point. Below the railing, Mrs. Gardner had placed vases of flowers—sunflowers and fire lilies.

After the hymn, Rev. Stoddard welcomed us to the first religious service on Grenell Island, thanking our hostess, Mrs. Gardner, for making it possible. I was impressed that such a big booming voice emanated from such a small man.

Before the sermon, Mary Mason and Lois gathered the children and shepherded them off to Sunday school inside the cottage. During the sermon my attention was sometimes lured away by the twitter of small birds hopping about the leaves above gathering tiny moths. Despite Rev. Stoddard's spirited words and powerful voice, I was distracted by the lap of the water upon the shore and the soft breeze whiffling through the great maple boughs above.

After the service, we exited the way we had entered. The line moved slowly as each person stopped to thank Rev. Stoddard for the service and Mrs. Gardner for providing such a beautiful setting. We were told the girls would be finished with Sunday school soon, so we went to the path and waited for them.

There we met Mrs. Stoddard, who was holding her one-year-old daughter, Lillian. We chatted with her as we waited. Soon, three girls holding hands came skipping from the cottage. Effy is slightly taller than the twins, with hair a shade darker, but from a distance, they looked like triplets. She was in the middle, each twin holding one of her hands as if they were sharing a special prize between them. They were eager to tell us about Sunday school.

"We heard a story from Miss Lois about Noah's ark," Ivy said.

". . . and then, Miss Mary Mason had us sing a song," Iris continued.

"All the other children knew it . . .

". . . but it was new to us . . ."

"Even Effy knew it," Ivy said indicating their new friend.

"I've been singing that song since I was as a little girl," Effy said.

"What song was it?" I asked.

"It was very pretty. It was called 'Jesus Loves Me.'"

"Ah, yes," Anne said, "We know who wrote that song, don't we, Marguerite?"

"You do?" the twins asked in unison.

"Does she live on Grenell?" Effy asked.

"No, but she visited Grenell years ago." I described Anna Warner to the girls. "She lives on an island as we do. It's called Constitution Island and it's in the Hudson River right across from West Point, where there is a school for army officers."

"Do you see her often?" Effy asked.

"No, but we write often."

"Next time you write to her please tell her how much we love her song," Effy insisted.

The Bakewells came then and took Effy by the hand. The girls said goodbye to their new friend. Then with Ivy on the left and Iris on the right, they took each other's hand and started off on the Park Avenue path back towards Castle Rock. "I can't wait to tell Mother about Sunday school," Iris said to Ivy.

"We can sing the song for her," Ivy said and started singing the refrain to "Jesus Loves Me" as they walked along the path.

I cringed. "I'm afraid this will become a problem."

"The song?"

"Yes."

"Lily won't mind, but Mother will not be happy. It happened before I was born—before you were born—but it lives large in Mother's memory."

"You must be referring to Philadelphia's Summer of Blood," Anne said as we followed the twins as they turned onto the North Boulevard path.

"Indeed. What year was that?"

"I'm not sure—1844 or thereabouts. Two Catholic churches were burned, and twenty or thirty people died in the riots."

"Riots! How awful! And my mother told me it started over whether Catholic children should be forced to sing Protestant hymns at school."

Anne nodded. "I remember my father speaking of it. Irish and Catholic neighborhoods were targeted. The anti-immigration nativists drew cartoons of ethnic stereotypes of Irish and German immigrants depicting them as drunken rabble-rousers, papists, and threats to the peaceful order of the United States."

"Hence the reason our parish founded a Catholic school and why we were cautioned not to be friends with Protestants," I said, following the girls up the spiral path to Castle Rock.

"From what you tell me about what happened on Carleton Island earlier this season, anti-Catholic sentiments still linger today."

CHAPTER
thirty-seven

"Auntie! How exciting is this? Another steam yacht ride!" Iris shouted. The strong southwest wind swept her honey-brown hair from her face, exposing the bandage on her forehead.

Both girls gripped the bow railing of the *Alert* as we steamed away from Grenell, passed Wilsons Island, and headed toward Maple Island. "Look! There! What a big bird! What kind of bird is that?" Iris asked, pointing to a large blue-gray bird wading along the shore at the head of Maple Island.

"It is a great blue heron," I said.

Startled by our approach, the heron stretched out its long S-shaped neck, pushed off with its long legs, and took flight. Even above the chug of the *Alert*'s steam engine, we could hear the flap of the large wings. The bird had a six-foot wingspan at least. The heron flapped slowly and deliberately, then let out a loud, indignant squawk as he crossed our bow.

The girls laughed. "He's grumpy!" they said in unison.

"I suppose he didn't like us disturbing him while he was fishing," I said.

The heron folded its neck back, resting its head on its shoulders, and rowed the air with strong, rhythmic flaps of its wings. Its long spindly legs dangled behind, and it flew in front of the *Alert* as we plied the waters between Maple and Bluff. It was as if it knew where we were going and was leading us from Maple to the head of Robbins Island. But at the foot of Bluff Island, the heron gave up its escort, peeled off, and glided toward the American channel and Round Island. I turned away from the heron and faced the tall rock rising out of the water. I told the girls about the first time I had climbed the great towering rock at the foot of Bluff to sing the patriotic songs on the Glorious Fourth.

"I want to do that," Iris said.

"May we climb to the top and sing sometime?" Iris asked.

I reached for their hands and squeezed them. "Perhaps someday, if you are ever here on the Glorious Fourth," I said.

"We're so close to the shore!" Ivy noted, a tad concerned.

"The water is very deep here," I reassured her. "Captain Bertrand and Mr. Haggard have steamed these waters many times before and know exactly where to go." The girls turned to look at the man at the throttle in the wheelhouse behind us and waved, then turned their faces back into the wind, their long hair trailing behind them like streamers. As we passed the head of Bluff and turned starboard toward Grindstone, the wind caught the tops of the waves and sprinkled us with chilly spray. The girls giggled, and the sun glinted from the wet droplets on their faces.

"Perhaps we should go into the cabin," I said as I ushered them toward the salon door. The *Alert* was a tad larger than the *Mamie C.* and a little more utilitarian: a wooden bench ran around the inside of the salon, which was devloid of decorative molding, oriental carpet, and elaborate lamps to light the interior. The steamer spent her days ferrying parties between islands and as of late, had been chartered by Charles Emery for the season to push barges of quarried stone between Robbins and Calumet.

"Did you get wet?" Anne asked as she reached in her reticule for a handkerchief.

"Just a little," Ivy said as Anne dabbed away the droplets from Ivy's face. I did the same with Iris.

"It felt as if the river kissed me!" Iris said, and I felt a shiver run through me. I had had the same sensation my first year on the river.

By the time we had steamed past the cut between Bluff and Robbins, the bow was out of the wind, so the girls and I returned to the bow. The twins asked the names of the little islands on the starboard side and the one lone island on the port side and were surprised when I did not know their names. I smiled at this, touched that the twins thought their aunt knew everything about the islands. How could I impart to them that no one knows all the facts or secrets sprinkled in this great blue waterway? This "unknown" sprinkled amongst the islands, bays, and coves was what made the islands so mysterious, so captivating, so endearing.

"Is that where we are going?" Iris asked, pointing to a large cottage on the north side of a wide bay at the head of the island.

"I think perhaps it is," I said. "I've never stepped foot on Robbins."

The girls said nothing but turned to me with wide eyes.

"The island is privately owned by a Mr. Emery. He is building a large cottage across from Clayton and purchased the Frontenac Hotel on Round Island a few years ago. He started a farm here on Robbins with orchards and hothouses to grow food for the hotel."

I looked, but from here I couldn't imagine that this was a garden isle; it looked full of rock, pine, and oak just like Grenell.

"Is that Mr. Emery?" Iris asked, nodding to the man on the dock.

"I'm not sure," I replied. "But I think it may be Mr. Shoemaker, who is in charge of the farm. He's asked Friend Anne to advise him on the placement of beehives on the island. He's the one who sent the *Alert* to pick us up at the Grenell Island Store dock."

The man on the dock was tall and sported a well-groomed mustache. And while spotlessly attired, his clothing and slouch hat indicated to me that the man who waited for us could not be the millionaire Mr. Emery, the tabacco tycoon.

Once securely at the dock, the man stepped forward, welcomed us to Robbins Island, and introduced himself as Mr. Shoemaker, the farm manager.

"How fair thee today, Mr. Shoemaker?" Friend Anne asked in her typical Quaker greeting as she ushered the girls in front of her on the gangway. "I am Anne Ashbridge."

"Ah, the famous Dr. Ashbridge. I hear you are quite the expert on bees."

"My profession, of course, is as a medical doctor, but I have always had a fascination with apiary management."

"Well, well, who do we have here?" Mr. Shoemaker asked, taking note of the twins.

"May I introduce Miss Hartranft of the University of Pennsylvania and her nieces, Ivy and Iris."

"Ah? Another apiary expert?" Mr. Shoemaker asked, taking my hand and shaking it lightly.

"I'm sorry to disappoint. My expertise is in Greek and Latin. Friend Anne and I share a cottage on Grenell and my nieces and I have tagged along. I'm curious about your island farm and thought the twins could learn something of its management."

"I see. I see," Mr. Shoemaker said nodding genially. "I would love to show you around. Feel free to ask questions."

"My first question is about this lovely house before us. I was wondering if this was the keeper's house that was formerly on Calumet?"

"Indeed it is! Mr. Emery had it moved here on the ice last winter and it has become my headquarters. Come come. I have a shay waiting."

"What are you calling the island these days? Sam Grenell had intimated that perhaps it will now be called Emery's Island," I said.

"Indeed, I've heard it called such," Mr. Shoemaker said as he indicated the direction of the awaiting shay. "Mr. Emery has owned the island for a few years now, but most of the locals still refer to it as Robbins Island, though the official name has always been Picton after some British military man who fought with Wellington at Waterloo. I dare say the Robbins family has been so thoroughly associated with the island for decades now that it will always be called Robbins."

"We have two Robbins families on Grenell—Hyland Robbins and Elridge Robbins," I said, taking the twins by the hand and walking beside Mr. Shoemaker.

"I think they are all related somehow. The Robbins family has always homesteaded here on this island. Mr. Emery bought the island lock stock and barrel, though he did allow the Robbins family to remove some of the buildings."

"Yes, a wonderful farmhouse was moved to Grenell just this past winter," I said.

"The thick ice was very conducive to moving buildings," Mr. Shoemaker said, then continued. "There is a fine flock of sheep on the island. Just this spring, a flock of twelve ewes had twenty-five lambs. Three of them were black with white heads and tails." In the distance, we saw sheep grazing in a clearing.

The bay horse snorted and stamped as we approached. "I hope we're not too crowded in the shay," Mr. Shoemaker said indicating the two-wheeled horse-drawn vehicle. "It's meant to seat two."

"I think Marguerite and I can all squeeze in and be quite comfortable with the twins on our laps," Anne said as Mr. Shoemaker handed her up into the shay. Once we were settled with the girls on our laps, Mr. Shoemaker climbed aboard, took the reins and gave them a shake.

"Look at the baby lambs!" Iris called out as we passed a field dotted with sheep.

"So sweet! May we pet them later?" Ivy asked.

"I don't think we should bother the mothers and their little lambs," Mr. Shoemaker said.

We next passed three hothouses, which he promised to show us later. Soon the orchards came into view. When Nat had mentioned two-thousand fruit trees, I thought he was exaggerating or perhaps he had misheard, but I knew when I saw the vast orchard in front of me that Nat had spoken the truth. The metal blades of a windmill creaked and scraped as it turned in the wind. The windmill pumped water to irrigate the orchards. Beyond the orchard, rows and rows of waist-high bushes stretched over a small mound and out of sight.

"This is our black raspberry field. The invention of the berry harvester makes it possible to conduct berry farming in such a remote location like this. As you can see, Dr. Ashbridge, honeybees would be a welcomed addition to our farm project to help pollenate the orchards and the black raspberry patch. I'm in need of your apiary skills."

Anne explained that it would be hard to overwinter the bees on the island due to the harsh North Country weather but that it was possible. She suggested the hives face southwest and have a windbreak from strong winds. She also suggested he dig a cellar, a place to put the hives in fall to help protect the bees from the severe winters. "The Coggshall brothers are the foremost experts in beekeeping in the country—some say the world—and not that far away in West Groton, New York. They can ship bees to you in a day via rail. You can have your bees installed and ready in the spring."

We stopped then and descended from the one-horse shay. While Anne and Mr. Shoemaker explored locations for the hives and the cellars, the twins and I walked back toward the hothouses.

"Look! The black raspberries are nearly ready to pick. May we pick a few?" Iris asked.

"Oh, girls. You know how raspberries stain. We'll have to save picking raspberries for a day when you are dressed for that adventure."

The air inside of the hothouse was heavy and smelled of fresh dirt and leafy things. A worker there invited the girls to look at the tomatoes that were developing. They were small and green and plentiful. "They are of the Autocrat variety," the young man told us. "Last year we had three record breakers, with two weighing four-and-a-half pounds and one weighing two-and-one-third pounds."

I blinked, unable to fathom what a four-and-one-half pound tomato would look like or how this spindly plant could support such a weighty tomato. Perhaps he was mistaken.

Anne and Mr. Shoemaker soon joined us and verified the weights of the tomatoes. After a quick tour of the hothouses, we climbed back into the shay and returned to the dock. Captain Bertrand welcomed us back aboard the *Alert*, and we waved goodbye to Mr. Shoemaker as we steamed away from Robbins across the channel to Round Island.

We arrived at the Frontenac dock just as the steamer *St. Lawrence* was pulling away. "Elizabet said she would meet us on the dock, but we're a little early," Anne said as we disembarked. The dock was busy with new arrivals to the hotel milling about. I searched the crowd, looking for a large ostentatious hat certain that when I found it, I would find Elizabet beneath it. I found such a hat, but the woman's hair was too fair to be Elizabet's.

"There you are! Oh my! You are early, and I'm so glad for it! Now we will have more time to catch up." I looked up to see Elizabet racing toward us with a smile on her face, her cheeks bright pink. I was nonplussed. My memories of Elizabet were of a serious woman who always wore a dour, disapproving look. Even more surprising was her attire. Instead of a tall hat with bird parts, she wore a sensible boater with a dark brown ribbon on the band and a narrower ribbon around the brim. She looked very sporty in a curry and tangerine striped shirtwaist with a jacket and a rainy daisy skirt, so-called because the shorter hemline made it easier to keep dry in wet weather.

"Please excuse my golf skirt. Vincent and I just finished a round of golf, and I didn't have time to change. I barely had time to get to the dock. I hope you haven't been waiting long."

Anne assured her that we had just stepped off the *Alert*.

"Oh my, Marguerite. You are as lovely as ever. Friend Anne tells me you are a teaching fellow at Penn?"

"Yes. I teach at the Graduate Department for Women."

"Oh, I imagine that you are an enthralling instructor. You have such a deep knowledge and passion for Greek and all things classic. Your students are indeed lucky. And these delightful young ladies must be your nieces," Elizabet said leaning down toward Ivy and Iris.

"Ivy and Iris, I'd like to introduce you to Dr. DuPont," I said.

"Pleasure to meet you, Dr. DuPont," the girls said in unison.

"Oh, please! While you are here, you simply must call me Auntie Elizabet. Promise tell me that you will."

The girls nodded compliance, and she took them each by the hand and headed up toward the hotel. "Today promises to be a fun day of games on the lawn. But first, a little luncheon. Are you hungry?"

The hotel had a tent on the lawn from where we watched as "Auntie" Elizabet helped the girls get sandwiches, cake, fruit, and a huge glass of lemonade. A member of the hotel staff put our plates and drinks on a large tray and carried it to our picnic spot. Turkish rugs were laid on the lawn. We settled in a shady spot and enjoyed our luncheon. On the veranda, an orchestra played as we ate.

Once finished with their lunch, the girls joined the other children playing in the center part of the lawn.

"I'm so happy you could join me today," Elizabet said. "The girls are a delight."

"You mentioned in your note something about getting married?" Anne asked.

Elizabet blushed and said, "My fiancé promised to stop by after his tennis match. I do want you to meet him, Anne. He is a wonderful man. I met him working at a clinic in New York. And well . . . I've never thought of myself as the marrying sort. Never wanted to subjugate myself to a man. But we are true partners. We've started a medical practice in the Murray

Hill district. He treats men, and I treat the ladies and we confer on both."

As Elizabet continued to describe her medical practice with her fiancé, Vincent, I looked out at the children playing on the Frontenac lawn. The girls were playing the game of graces, tossing a wooden, ribbon-covered hoop to each other using two dowel-like sticks. The boys were playing battledore, batting about a shuttlecock with a wooden-framed battledore covered with parchment. The goal was to keep the shuttlecock, a cork trimmed with feathers on top, in the air without allowing it to fall to the ground. I was struck by how similar the scene was to one I'd seen on one of the many ancient Greek vases where the Greek athletes were using paddles to hit something that looked very much like a shuttlecock. The memory of sitting next to Charles while we looked at sketches of pottery flooded me with tender memories. My cheeks reddened at the thought.

"But listen to me go on. How about you, Marguerite? Are things serious between you and the young man I met with you at the midsummer ball?" Elizabet asked.

"No. Nothing serious. We've only met a few weeks ago."

The children were now playing bean bags and taking turns walking on stilts. Once all the children were finished with their lunch, it was time for the main event: the potato race. A number of lanes were marked out on the flattest portion of the lawn. Potatoes were placed at intervals along each lane, and a basket was placed several feet behind each lane. The boys went first. Their task was to retrieve potatoes one by one, returning each potato to the basket before returning for the next. The first to collect all the potatoes in his lane was the winner.

When it was the girls' turn, Ivy barely beat Iris, who immediately turned to apologize to her sister and promised to share the prize. The boy's winner and the girl's winner were each called to the judges' table, where they were awarded their prizes. Ivy was awarded a beautiful souvenir silver spoon while the boy received a gold scarf pin.

Each child at the party was presented with a small kite. As the children returned to their parents with the plea to help them fly their kite, a correspondent for *Daily on the St. Lawrence* beckoned the potato race winners over so he could record their names for the newspaper. The winner of the boys' potato race was named Will. When the correspondent asked for the correct spelling of his last name, Will went to retrieve his mother. The correspondent turned to Ivy. The young man was quite taken with Ivy's insistence that both twins won and would share the spoon. I helped with the spelling of their last name just as Will's mother arrived, and I suddenly found myself face-to-face with Nora Withers.

"Well, well, I didn't expect to see you at a children's lawn party, of all places. Is there some symposium going on at the hotel that I'm not aware of?"

My mouth opened, but no response came forth. It was as if someone had punched me in the stomach. I found myself gasping for air.

Nora seemed not to notice my inability to speak. She ruffled young Will's hair. "I see you've met my eldest. Who might these lovely girls be? Perhaps Lily's daughters?"

By now, Anne and Elizabet were approaching the podium. Seeing their faces helped me find my voice. "Nora, what are you doing here? I - I thought you were only staying for a week," I managed to squeak out.

"Oh, the boys were having such great fun with the Myers' children, that they asked us to stay on at their cottage."

Nora turned and saw Anne and Elizabet.

"Congratulations," Anne said to Ivy.

Nora turned back to me. "So this is a lady's outing only? Where is that young man who was escorting you the other night? Mr. Bartman from Chicago—if I remember correctly."

"I'm here as the guest of Dr. DuPont. You remember Dr. Ashbridge, I assume," I said.

"Of course! How are you, Dr. Ashbridge?" Nora asked. "And now that I think of it, I seem to recall you mentioning a Dr. Elizabet DuPont back from your now infamous symposium days." Nora shot me a look that terrified me. What had I said about Elizabet in the past that she might use against me now? That was twelve years ago. But it seemed that Nora only remembered the unsavory parts of my letters.

"It seems that Miss Hartranft has forgotten her manners," Nora said, nodding to Elizabet. "So I suppose I must introduce myself. I am Nora Huffington Withers."

"It's a pleasure to meet," Elizabet said.

"Oh, no! The pleasure is all mine. At last, the infamous Dr. DuPont. After all the stories that Marguerite told me about you." She tsked-tsked and raised her eyebrows for emphasis. "I'm delighted to meet you in the flesh."

"Really," Elizabet said, tilting her head and eyeing me warily.

I was frozen to the spot. Was Nora going to embarrass me again? My stomach churned in anticipation.

"Strange," Elizabet started casting an inquisitive eye towards Nora. "In all the years that I've known Marguerite, she's not once mentioned your name to me. How do you two know one another?"

"Oh, we go way back. We were classmates at Misericordia Academy," Nora replied.

Elizabet's eyes widened, and she placed her hand on her chest as if to hold back her shock at this revelation. "Schoolmates, you mean. Certainly not classmates!" Elizabet exhorted.

Now Nora looked perplexed. "Yes, classmates," she insisted.

"Now that is a shock," Elizabet said, opening her parasol and holding it over her head.

"Why is that?" Nora wondered.

"Oh, you look so much older than she. I wouldn't have been surprised if you had told me you were her teacher. You look ten years her senior."

Nora's chin fell a full inch, revealing the bottom row of her sharp, kittenlike teeth. Gone were her smug smile and haughty glances.

"Mama, can we go now?" Will asked, tugging on Nora's skirt. "Henry is here with the dog-cart. Oscar is ready to take us back to the cottage."

"Well, it is indeed a pleasure meeting you, Mrs. Withers. Don't let us keep you. I'm sure Marguerite can fill me in on your . . . friendship." Elizabet drew out the last word like she was pulling taffy.

With that, Elizabet turned and took Ivy by the hand, squeezed it, and said, "Who would like ice cream?" Anne took Iris's hand, and the four of them moved toward the ice cream pavilion.

Nora stood rooted to the spot.

"Mama? Can we go now?" Will asked again.

I turned to face Nora. "Seems it's time to go. In light of what has happened the other night and this afternoon, don't expect to hear from me any time soon," I said and turned to follow Anne, Elizabet, and the twins. With any luck at all, I would never see Nora Huffington Withers again.

As the girls ate their ice cream, Anne, Elizabet, and I spoke of our day-to-day lives away from the islands. As Elizabet described her work as a doctor in New York City, among the well-to-do set, I studied her face. She seemed confident and sincerely concerned about her patients. She asked me about my students. I studied her face. She seemed completely changed from the Elizabet I had met in 1881 when I thought her to be haughty, dismissive, and condescending.

"I think I see the *Alert* approaching," Anne said.

"I'll walk you to the dock," Elizabet said.

Anne took the girls and walked ahead.

"I feel I owe you some explanation," I said to Elizabet as we headed down the broad walkway toward the dock.

"Oh, no explanation needed," Elizabet assured me. "I can spot women like Nora from a mile away."

"Women like Nora?"

"Jealous women."

"Jealous women?" I asked, failing to see how Nora would be jealous of me.

"Jealous women or women who continually compare themselves to others and come up feeling as if they don't measure up. Their jealousy usually takes either one of two tracks. First is the false pleaser. Women who over compliment and overpraise, in the hopes the other woman will do the same. I'll be frank. I loathe fawning, obsequious women. How degrading to stoop to bootlicking in the hopes of getting a compliment in return. Actually, I respect the Nora-sort a bit more."

"And the 'Nora-sort'?"

"Ahh! It takes more cunning, more conniving to be the second sort—the Nora-sort. They make themselves feel better by undermining others with gossip—better yet with innuendo. By smiling to your face and professing friendship to draw you out in order to collect more fodder to cast aspersions on you later. Sound familiar?"

"How do you know this?"

Elizabet laughed then. "Don't you know? I was Nora! I'm afraid I'm the one who owes you an apology. I was so jealous of you during our symposium. It was obvious to me that you were very young and here you were so knowledgeable and confident—a little bit of a know-it-all, I'm afraid. I don't mind telling you, but up until I met you, I was used to being the most beautiful and most intelligent woman in the room. I was trying to get my dear Friend Anne to come to New York, but she seemed more interested in mentoring you and living on that primitive island. I'm afraid I was very, very jealous. You've grown into a lovely young, woman. I hope you can forgive me for my bad behavior."

"I was surprised by such a warm welcome the night of the midsummer ball," I admitted.

"All I can say is that I'm in love and that has changed my outlook on the whole world," Elizabet said. "I hope that your relationship with Mr. Bartman proves as fruitful."

CHAPTER
thirty-eight

"We can't believe it! Another steamboat adventure!" Ivy said.

"I need you to be on your best behavior today," I told the twins as I followed the girls down a stairstep of tree roots and we navigated the rough terrain of the North Boulevard path.

Their "yes, Auntie" response was almost drowned out by the rustle of leaves. The boughs of a great oak above us bobbed in the strong north wind.

I'd awakened this morning before dawn as the north wind had been fluttering the sides of the tent. It was as if I were inside a living, wheezing beast. Outside, waves crashed against the rocky shoreline in a steady rhythm.

The wind had grown progressively stronger after sunrise. The strong wind made the hammer falls from the Murray Isle boathouse sound as if they were right here on Grenell Island. Meanwhile, the sounds of the worksite on the crest of Grenell were whisked away by the wind.

We turned onto Park Avenue, and as we moved inland, the world became quieter as we were no longer buffeted by the relentless north wind. We walked the base of Point Breeze to the Otsego peninsula. Point Breeze had been breezy the day I saw the areo-machine. But today it was still. We were in the lee of the wind.

As we neared the Susquehanna Club, we were greeted by Mr.

Burditt's nineteen-year-old granddaughter, Maud, who was visiting her grandfather for the month of August. Maud was dressed in a white skirt with a blue-and-white striped blouse and a navy blue jacket with leg-o-mutton sleeves. She was instantly taken with the twins, crouching down on one knee to greet them face-to-face. And the girls were equally enamored with the dark-haired, bright-eyed beauty from New York City.

"I was going to wear my boater," she said holding up a white boater with a navy blue band. "But Grandfather says there's quite a north wind blowing today, so I'll leave it at home." Maud trotted up the porch steps and tossed the boater on a table. "Come, girls," she said, taking the twins by the hands after she descended again. "Brainard is ready to row us out to the *Otsego*."

Maud climbed in the skiff first, then helped the girls climb aboard.

"Here you go, miss," a raw-boned youth said and offered me his hand, helping me into the skiff.

"Have you met Brainard Robbins?" Maud asked.

The gaunt lad looked to be around fifteen years of age. I nodded at him. "Not officially, but I've seen him around the island," I said.

"Brainard's father, Capt. E. G. Robbins built the Band House—which Grandfather now calls Grove Cottage—and the Susquehanna Club. He's captained the steamer *Otsego* for nearly twenty years now," Maud said as we pushed away from the dock.

"I heard Capt. Robbins moved a house from Robbins to Grenell this past winter," I said.

She turned to the young man in the skiff and said, "Brainard, I'd like to introduce Miss Marguerite Hartranft, who has a cottage on the north shore."

"Pleasure, ma'am," Brainard said. He nodded to me, looked over his shoulder, and started rowing to the steamer *Otsego* anchored in the bay between Otsego Point and Pullman. "You share the cottage with the lady doctor, right?"

"I do. She teaches at the Woman's Medical College in West Philadelphia."

"Where is Dr. Anne? I'd hoped she would join us today," Maud asked.

"She decided to stay ashore. She was out on a call last night at the

Schiller cottage. Mrs. Schiller is very ill. Dr. Anne thought she might be needed there again this afternoon."

"What happened here?" Maud asked, pointing to the bandage still visible on Iris' forehead.

Brainard maneuvered around the Kerrs' sailboat, *Tiger*, which was anchored in this deep-watered bay.

"A toboggan accident at Grand View Park," Iris said.

Maud placed a splayed hand across her chest. Her eyes widened with surprise. "You went down the slide at Grand View Park? It's so very very tall! You are so brave!"

"We went down many times," Iris told Maud.

"But the last time down, I ended up with Ivy's tooth in my forehead. I'd like to go again, but Dr. Anne says that I mustn't go underwater until my wound has healed," Iris said.

"I won't go unless Iris can go. I don't want her to feel left out," Ivy said.

"A very brave girl and a very compassionate girl," Maud said, patting both their knees.

"Maybe the next time we go, I can get a scar on my head, though I'd like to have mine on the right side, not the left." The girls looked at each other as if they were looking in a mirror pointing back and forth from a bandaged forehead to the non-bandaged forehead. "Sometimes when I look at Iris, my forehead hurts here! Like I was cut, too—only it doesn't show," Ivy said softly.

This was a daunting thought. I hoped Ivy didn't seriously consider injuring herself so that she would match her sister.

"Ahoy, Andrew!" Brainard shouted. "I see the white flag flying from the skiff. You fella's catch a muskellunge?"

The white flag, in truth, was an upturned fishing net planted in the front of the skiff indicating that they had caught a muskellunge.

"A musket fish?" Ivy asked

"No, muskellunge," I corrected Ivy. "Miss Flossie tells me that it is an Ojibwa word meaning 'great fish.'"

"It's about as long as we are tall," Iris said, gazing at the fish Mr. Gerard held up.

"Mr. Gerard is a well-known fisherman who is a regular at the Pullman

House. Andrew Merckle is his favorite oarsman," Maud informed us. "When Capt. Gerard isn't pulling fish from the St. Lawrence, he manages the ferry from Brooklyn to Manhattan." Maud leaned close. "I heard that his daughter is celebrating her birthday later this week and the Pullman House is throwing a party for her. She's turning thirteen. Perhaps you girls would like to come?"

The twins turned excitedly to me, waiting for an answer. "How kind of you to ask. We'll have to see. I'm not sure when my sister, their mother, is returning to collect them."

By now, Brainard had reached the side of the steam yacht *Otsego*.

"What a funny name," Iris said, looking up at the name painted on the side of the steamer.

"My grandfather is from Otsego County," Maud explained. "When the club members bought the south peninsula of Grenell back in the late 1870s, they named it Otsego Point, mostly for the county they lived in, but also because Otsego means 'place of the rock,' although some of the Indians where my grandfather lives say it means 'clean water'. Either way, it's the perfect name for this point of land, don't you think?"

I nodded in agreement.

"Let me get aboard first, and I will help the girls," Maud said as she quickly ascended the rope ladder, turned, and reached for Ivy's hand.

Once the girls were aboard, I climbed the rope ladder and joined the girls and Maud on deck.

Mr. Burditt was seated in a wicker chair and struggled to his feet as we approached. "Good day, Miss Hartranft! So happy you could join us! Eager to see Miss Bixby compete today in her Mohawk canoe. I hope the wind doesn't mar today's events."

"Grandfather, I'd like to introduce you to Ivy and Iris, Miss Hartfant's nieces.

"Welcome! Welcome! Have you met Captain Robbins?" Mr. Burditt said, waving us over.

"I've seen him from afar. He's always a blur. Always in motion. It's a pleasure to finally meet you face-to-face," I said.

"Pleasure, ma'am," Capt. Robbins said, tugging on the brim of his captain's hat. He excused himself to prepare the steamer for departure.

Brainard tied the skiff to the mooring buoy and untied the steamer line. "We're away, captain," he reported to this father as he climbed aboard.

Capt. Robbins tooted the *Otsego*'s steam whistle as we chugged past the Pullman House dock. Prince barked and ran the length of the dock with Jambo on his back. The people on the dock waved.

"I remember when this boat was called *Rockland*," I said to Mr. Burditt.

"My, Miss Hartranft! You have a good memory. I always hated that name. Back in 1887, Mr. Sayles and I purchased this boat. The arguments we had over the name! I finally gave in, but when he built the hotel, I bought out his share and changed the name to *Otsego*, a far more elegant name."

Despite the sunny skies, it was a blustery day with a fierce north wind. Once past Pullman House, we caught the wind, and the *Otsego* rolled to starboard and then back to port as we headed into the teeth of the wind. Waters are almost always calm in the Narrows, but today it was like a wind tunnel. The oncoming waves beat against the bow like watery fists. Fluffy white clouds were raked across the sky, and Eel Bay was pricked with white caps. The gale pushed the water into wild, rolling billows which broke into seething foam as they hit our bow.

"Not an ideal day for a canoe race," Maud said as we passed Canoe Point at the foot of Grindstone. The shoreline was lined with hundreds of canoes that had been pulled ashore. Inland, dozens of canvas tents dotted the campground. Flags and colorful pennants fluttered above every tent.

"Do you know what country those flags represent?" I asked the girls.

They pointed out flags from Canada, England, and the United States. The pennants represented canoe clubs from all over.

Capt. Robbins calmly steered the *Otsego* to the lee of two islands known as the Robinson Group. We droppped anchor just in time to see the start of the first race of sailing canoes. What pluck and skill it took to handle the sailing canoes in such rough water and strong wind. The winner capsized twice before completing the course.

The novice race was next and Mr. Burditt handed me a pair of field glasses so I could look for Flossie. "There she is," I called out, pointing to Chief Two Buttons's black-and-white birchbark canoe. Seventeen canoes started the race, but within the first few minutes, all but six had capsized. The six remaining canoes paddled on with the roaring gale tugging persistently at pennants flapping from the bows of the canoes.

I was so proud that Flossie was one of the six canoes still upright in the water. Flossie negotiated the first two turns around the buoys that marked the racecourse, but at the third, a wave caught her broadside and capsized her. A safety boat rowed over and helped her set the canoe upright. They offered to tow her in, but she asked them to assist her back into the canoe. Instead of paddling toward shore, Flossie paddled straight into the wind and for us. Once on the lee side of *Otsego*, Brainard helped the dripping Miss Bixby onto the steam yacht.

"I'm afraid I've dripped water all over your deck," Flossie said as Mr. Burditt approached.

"Pshaw! Welcome aboard. Brainard, gather some towels. Maud, could you prepare a warm cup of tea for our intrepid Miss Bixby?"

I toweled off Flossie's wet hair and wrung out her wet skirts before she sat in a deck chair. Maud tucked a warm blanket around her. After she had been served a piping hot cup of tea, Mr. Burditt asked about life at the American Canoe Association camp. Flossie reported that there were eighty-eight tents in the main camp and about twenty tents at Squaw Point, the ladies' annex. All in all, there were about 140 canoes and 250 canoeists.

"The biggest tent—right in the middle of the main camp—belongs to J. H. Rushton. Can't miss it. It has a huge green pennant with 'Rushton' in big, white letters on a towering pole in front of the tent. Mr. Rushton brought a full assortment of canoes and replacement parts in case of mishaps. And he donated a bunch of paddles to be awarded as prizes."

"Rushton is a canoe manufacturer?" Mr. Burditt asked.

"Yes, from Canton, New York," Flossie said,, warming her hands on the china teacup. "Rushton shot to prominence back in 1886 when a sailing canoe he designed won the A.C.A.'s International Challenge Cup."

"Yes, yes," Mr. Burdick said, raising his chin and cradling it in his hand as he searched his memory. "I believe I remember hearing about that. A chap named Gibson. Also from New York?"

"Yes, Albany. A member of the Mohican Canoe Club. The entire club has been fascinated with my genuine Mohican canoe. They came en masse to see it the other day, and I gave the club instructions on the Indian paddle stroke."

"So what is camp life like?" Maud asked.

Flossie took another sip of her tea, settled the cup back into the saucer, and smiled. "Great fun! We're a lively lot. High jinks, boisterous capers, jolly events day and night. Impromptu parades in outlandish costumes spring up at all hours. There are big bonfires at night at which various clubs stage minstrel shows or a burlesque circus. Last evening, the Peterboro tent hosted a sideshow. We were all asked not to throw cabbages at the actors as they were not insured." Flossie threw her head back and laughed at the memory before she continued. "There was a bearded lady, a fat lady who sang a ditty in a tremulous tenor. Like the bearded lady, the fat lady was a man—but you've probably guessed that. A rollicking time!"

Maud refilled Flossie's cup and she took a sip before she placed it back on the table. "Some nights, the women stay in Squaw Camp and have our own fire just for us. One night we had a dance performance. The prettiest was the rhythmical dancing of the butterfly queen performed by a Miss Muckleston of Kingston. There was also a nobby Highland fling, and Winnie, a girl from Brooklyn, did a Carmencita act with great agility and modesty. One night we sang songs by the campfire: "Alouette," "The Cat Came Back," "The Boating Song," "Home by the Sea," "The Paddle Song," and other songs like that—accompanied by a string quintet."

"We saw lots of Canadian flags," I prompted.

"Yes there are quite a few Canadians here. There is a large delegation from Toronto. I met Fred Falls. He writes for *The Daily Mail*. Who knows! I might be written-up in the paper! But the Cataraqui Club of Kingston has the largest Canadian delegation—ninety members. Their tents are the center of attention most of the time. From what I can surmise, they think they're royalty. One guy—Alderman John S. Skinner—is quite the dandy. The rest of us think nothing of bathing in the river, but he hesitates to do so. I've heard he has a full-length tub in his tent so he can stretch out and soak after a long day in the canoe. Can you imagine?"

Flossie raised her cup to take another sip of tea, but, remembering another tidbit, she set it down abruptly. "Oh! And listen to this! The Cataraqui Club brought a piano. They didn't arrive with a piano but went and got one after the Vesper Club hosted a sing-along. The Vespers are great singers, not bad musicians, either. They had guitars, violins, mandolins, and a cello. We sang and sang and voted 'Susan Brown' as the official A. C. A. camp song of 1893. At noon the next day, a piano arrived on the barge. Not to be outdone, the Cataraqui Club sent an envoy to collect another piano."

Everyone listened intently as Flossie continued to talk about racing canoes and their owners. Another race started, and everyone stood and went to the rail to watch. Flossie stood, her gold-and-silver curls springing to life as they dried.

"Here, let me put a drier blanket around you," I said removing the damp blanket and putting a dry blanket around her shoulders.

Flossie pulled me closer. "We had quite an interesting visitor to the Squaw Camp the other evening," she said." Her name is Miss Anthony. She's a Quaker and so like our Dr. Anne, she prefers to be called by her first name, Susan. She is staying with the Sargent family on Sargent Island, not the one here in Eel Bay, but the one down in the Summerland group below Alexandria Bay. She is quite prominent in the suffragist movement. She's giving a talk later this week at the Tabernacle at Thousand Island Park. I would really like you to meet her."

"Sorry, Flossie, but I have my nieces here," I said, nodding my head toward the twins who were standing at the rail with Maud.

"Bring them along!"

"They are only seven years old," I said, thinking of how Rose and Mother would react if they found out that I went to a suffragist meeting and took Ivy and Iris with me.

"Seven is great. Seven is perfect. They will learn so much about life and the world."

"The answer is no," I said quietly.

"You are afraid of what Rose and your mother will say."

"That notion does play into my decision."

"So many of the things Mrs. Anthony said to me made sense. I hope you will reconsider."

"I'm sorry, but even if Ivy and Iris weren't here, I probably wouldn't attend."

"Why not?" Flossie asked as she rubbed her hair with the towel.

"I work so hard trying to make the men I work with think of me not as a *lady* professor, but as a professor that is the same as they are. The best compliment I received last year was when they were talking freely in my presence and then apologized because they forgot that I was a woman; they thought of me as their equal until that point."

Flossie sighed as she folded up the towel. "Marguerite, you are a walking contradiction."

"Thank you. I'll take that as a compliment. Like Walt Whitman, I resist being fit into a pigeonhole. As Mr. Whitman says: 'Do I contradict myself? Very well, then I contradict myself, I am large, I contain multitudes.'"

"Ah, you and your Whitman quotes. You are like Ruth with her Franklin quotes. I love you anyway," Flossie said, giving me a hug and soaking my shirt front in the process.

"I really must be getting back," she called to our host and hostess. "Thank you for your hospitality."

"Thank you for an inside peek at A.C.A. camp life," Maud said.

Mr. Burditt escorted Flossie to the rope ladder and helped her descend. Once she was settled inside her canoe he had secured to the side of the steamship, he handed her the paddle.

"I'll be back to Castle Rock soon," Flossie said, waving and then paddling off toward Grindstone. "Oh, and don't forget the A.C.A. Carnival is tomorrow night, weather permitting."

"Enjoy the rest of your time on Canoe Point," I called after her, but I doubt if she heard me over the wind.

We watched the remainder of the races, which were made that much more exciting by the turbulent waters. We had spent most of the day on the deck of the *Otsego* which despite the mooring on the lee side of the Robinson Group still rocked and swayed and bucked. We retreated inside the salon occasionally for respite from the wind and for lunch. But the constant rocking of the boat—the struggle to stand upright when the wind seemed intent on flattening us to the deck of the boat—was very draining. By the time the last canoe race was held, the twins were exhausted and fell asleep in my arms as we steamed back to Grenell. Once safely moored back at Grenell Island, Brainard kindly rowed us back to Castle Rock where I was surprised to find Lily waiting for us on the dock with Anne. Lily lifted Iris, from my arms, and Anne carried Ivy. We laid them in the tent in the lower camp.

The wind had died down a lot since midafternoon, so I lit a small fire on the shoreline to warm up, and Anne brought us tea. "I'll leave you two to speak of family matters," she said retreating to the cottage above.

"How is your mother-in-law?" I asked.

Lily smiled. "Not much can get her down. She's a force of nature."

"Like the wind today?"

"Very much so."

"How is she getting on with her broken ankle?"

"Luckily, it wasn't broken. Only badly sprained. Before I left, she was up and about with a cane. And it's no ordinary cane: it's ebony with a large engraved handle. You know my mother-in-law—only the best! I fear for the servants, though. Every time they try to help her from a chair or up the steps, she slaps their hands or shoves them away and screams at them that she is not an invalid. I'm afraid she will turn her ebony cane on them and hit their shins or the side of their heads. I'm afraid for her as well. The servants think twice before helping her when she truly does need help."

"I noticed a bandage on Iris' forehead. Did something happen?"

"I'm so sorry," I said and recounted the incident at Grand View Park.

"My goodness! So sorry, the girls put you through such worry. Luckily Dr. Anne was here to stitch her up. I'm sure with your care and Anne's healing hands, Iris will be none the worse for the wear."

We stared at the fire for a few moments. The sky was darker now, and the fire glowed brightly. The logs crackled. Lily hugged her arms to her chest and asked somewhat tentatively, "Any word from Charles?"

I shook my head.

"Give him time. He appreciates you for your mind. I'm not sure many other men would."

"Father did."

"Yes . . . Father did," Lily said softly.

"That reminds me of something Rose said when she left. She hinted that I somehow caused Father's death?"

Lily sighed heavily but continued staring at the fire.

"So you know about this?"

She nodded, poking at the embers with a long stick.

"For how long?"

"Does it matter what they think? It's not true."

"They?"

Lily looked at me then, her eyes full of sadness. "Of course, *they*. Mother and Rose, that is. I have no idea which one came up with the idea, but the two of them keep the idea alive."

"Mother? Mother thinks that I'm the cause of father's death?"

"Who knows exactly what they think? Mother is so so entrenched in her role as a widow. She can't get over the feeling that Father was taken from her too early and she can't blame herself or the doctor so. . ."

"She blames me."

The fire popped, spitting out a hot ember in my direction. I quickly leaned forward and brushed it from my skirt.

"You'll see. It will pass like this wind today. Eventually, the idea will blow itself out, and things will be fine. Like this night. There will always be 'wind' with those two. But you can learn to navigate windy waters. Sort of like spending a week with my mother-in-law."

I hugged Lily, grateful to have a little sister so wise. What would I do without Lily?

A log fell then, it was like our own little fireworks!

The next night the water was calm, so I rowed Lily and the twins to Eel Bay where we watched the American Canoe Association Carnival. Each canoe had been fitted with poles fore and aft and strung with small colorful Japanese lanterns. Over a hundred canoes paraded single file around a raft, that sent skyrockets streaking into the night sky. The calm waters of Eel Bay twinkled with the reflected light. A truly magical evening. The perfect last night for Lily and the girls.

Lily and the twins left mid-day the next day. Nat helped me take down the tents. We packed them up, and he rowed them back to the Hunkerson barn on Grindstone to be stored.

That evening after we had finished washing the supper dishes and I had hung the dishtowel on the rack to dry, we went out onto the porch to enjoy the sunset. Flossie had returned to Castle Rock, her two-week adventure with the American Canoe Association finished.

I settled in the wicker rocking chair, and Anne sat in the wooden rocker. Flossie was setting up her cot in the front room.

"I miss them," I said rocking back.

"Ivy and Iris?" Anne asked as she set her rocker in motion.

"Yes." My wicker rocker squeaked while her wooden rocker creaked, setting up a steady rhythm between us.

"Did you ever want to have children?" I asked as I watched the setting sun paint the sky over Murray Isle in dazzling color.

Anne's rocker creaked a few times back and forth before she replied. "I suppose the thought had crossed my mind now and then. But medicine is the all-consuming purpose in my life. I see my students as daughters I never had."

I nodded.

"And you? It's not too late for you."

"I'm twenty-eight. I'm afraid time is running out for me."

Anne slowed her rocker, and reached out and put her hand on my arm. "I'm a doctor. You still have a decade of childbearing years ahead of you," she insisted. She held me still, and the silence of the night held us fast for a moment before she resumed rocking.

I let the squeak and creak of our rockers carry the conversation for a while as I pondered that fact. I shifted my attention to the lawn below where two brown square scars, matted and brown, marked where the tents had stood. My thoughts drifted to Mother and Rose.

"The lawn will recover. Give it time. Trust me. A month from now the grass will be green again."

"It will take some time; the grass is so compacted and brown," I said. The patches might be green again but not with grass; they would be filled with weeds. I wasn't sure the lawn would ever be the same again.

I looked up at the lightning tree. I had had similar thoughts when the great white pine on the shoreline was struck by lightning. It had survived. Yet it was a third of its original size. As I gazed up, a flock of grackles whooshed in, alighting on the tree amidst a variety of whistles croaks, and squeaks that drowned out the noise from our rockers. The grackles sounded like a bunch of rusty gates swinging in the wind. They hopped about the pine needles sending white moths fluttering into the sunset sky. The grackles hungrily devoured them.

We heard the screen door shut as Flossie joined us on the porch.

"I'm leaving midmorning tomorrow to listen to Susan B. Anthony's talk at the Thousand Island Park Tabernacle. I'm hoping both of you have reconsidered and will join me."

"I have to agree with Marguerite. I'm not one to join organizations in protest of the status quo—to carry placards or wear ribbons."

"But you are an instructor at the only medical school for women in the world. You would really help our cause," Flossie insisted.

"I prefer to lead by example, not by protest. Marguerite wants to be known as a classics professor, not a woman classics professor. Likewise, I don't want to be known as a woman doctor. I want to be known as a doctor."

For once, Flossie said nothing. She sighed and went back into the cottage.

The flock of grackles reached a high pitch with their calls and clear whistles. Then in a *whoosh*, they took flight en masse, swirling from the tree in a shape-shifting cloud. One grackle remained in the white pine, then took flight and flapped frantically to catch up with the flock. The birds moved as if they were one giant, raucous, living being, swooping and soaring in intricately coordinated patterns across the water on their way to Murray Isle. Their squawky calls diminished. The creaks from our rocking chairs seemed exceedingly loud in the sudden quiet. As the evening hush settled upon us, the chorus of bugs grew louder, and we sat mute, taking in the remnants of the day.

CHAPTER
thirty-nine

The night was heavy. The darkness wrapped around me like a damp, heavy blanket. After three days of north wind, the air was still. So still. So quiet. So dark. Sleep would not come. No wind. No breeze. I heard Anne's bedsprings creak as she rolled over. I doubted she was able to sleep either. Lightning flashed far and distant, lighting up the silent night. The storm was too far out to hear the thunder. I waited, hoping sleep would come. At times like this, thoughts of the night of the midsummer ball at the Frontenac plagued me. Keywords repeated over and over in my mind as well as the last final words, "I need to get some refreshment." Charles went the opposite way—out of the ballroom, into the night, and gone. Cinder*fella* running away from the ball. Was I supposed to chase after him? Like Cinderella, did he leave a clue behind that I did not find?

Lightning flashed again. There was now a hint of a breeze, but not enough to stir the pines or ruffle the cedars.

What had been so urgent? Perhaps Lily was right. Perhaps he had fallen ill and too embarrassed to admit it. But to pack up and leave that night? It was a mystery to me.

I shut my eyes. Imagining a scene in my mind's eye, I saw a fairy with a wand tap Charles on the head, and he was gone. I opened my eyes, and there was another lightning flash. Seconds later, the low grumble of thunder followed. The frequency of lightning increased. The thunder boomed louder.

The wind and rain arrived at the same time. The cottage creaked and moaned as the west wind slammed into it. Anne and I were both up in an instant, running to shut the windows against the rain. Once closed, we stood at the main room windows for a while staring into the darkness. When the lightning flashed, the world momentarily seemed like it was in the middle of a day—although a day without color, a black-and-white world soon plunged back into darkness.

"The storm should clear the humidity. We should both try to get some sleep," Anne said before she returned to her bedroom. There were no raindrops on my bedroom window. So I opened it again. The row of cedars outside my window blocked the rain but allowed the sweetest smelling breeze in. Rain pounded on the roof, drowning out the words from the night at the Frontenac. Surrounded by a cedar-laden scent, I drifted off to sleep. I couldn't have slept more than a few minutes when I heard another pounding. It sounded as if someone were knocking on our door.

"Dr. Anne?" I heard a deep voice call out.

I reached for my bed jacket.

Anne, accustomed to being awakened in the night for emergencies, was at the door before I was.

"Mr. Gardiner! You look like a drowned rat. Marguerite, bring some towels."

"No need, ma'am, I'll be going back into this soup as soon as the good doctor is ready. Hate to take you out into the rain, but it's Mr. Carlisle, Doc. He's taken a turn for the worse. And please, ladies—call me John."

"I'll dress and get my bag," Anne said disappearing into her dark room.

John Gardiner was the oarsman and all-around jack-of-all-trades for the Carlisle family.

"May I put the kettle on for some tea?" I asked.

"Been drinking coffee all night, miss. Tryin' to stay awake in case Mrs. Carlisle needed me for anything. Another cup and I'd float away."

Accustomed to getting dressed in the middle of the night for emergencies, Anne was back, dressed and ready to return with Mr.

Gardiner in record time. She quickly wound her long braid into a bun and pinned it into place. She flung her waxed canvas cape around her shoulders, buttoned it closed, and grabbed her Gladstone doctor's bag.

"My umbrellie is outside, ma'am," John said, holding the door open for Anne. "We'll need it to screen us from the wind. That wind makes the rain feel like prickly needles."

"As soon as the store is open, see if you can send some breadstuffs for breakfast," Anne said to me as she ducked beneath John's open umbrella.

I nodded.

I dozed here and there but was afraid I would oversleep. The sun didn't rise that day, but instead, the dark night was traded for a gray, dreary morning. The rain had not stopped, but it had slowed to a drizzle. I quickly dressed, pulled my hair back and wound it into a bun. I started off on the long way—clockwise around the island—to the store, figuring the north shore would be too wet and slippery. I would have to negotiate the farm, which would be muddy, but at least it was flat there.

It was still drizzling when I opened the store door, and I was surprised to find a crowd of people standing inside. It was so early, long before the mailboat was due to arrive. Obviously, like me, people had come to the store hoping for news about Mr. Carlisle. The air was heavy with the smell of wet wool. The dour expressions on the careworn faces and hushed tones indicated that the state of affairs was dire. Even Aunt Lucy was at the store, and I wondered if I'd ever seen her there before, so far away from her kitchen and chickens. She was serving fat wedges of soda bread to the assembled crowd.

When the word came that Mr. Carlisle had passed on, most lingered, sharing memories of the man.

"Only sixty-four years old," someone tsked.

"I remember when he came to the island. Think it was 1885. Fell in love with the place. Bought the lot and built Jersey Heights the very next season," Mr. Reeves said. "He introduced so many people to the river."

"He was always talking up the Thousand Islands—Grenell Island in particular."

"Quite the fisherman."

"Loved fishing."

On and on the comments went.

Many reported seeing him on the porch on Sunday, only two days ago.

"His color had improved, and I thought he was on the mend," Mr. Harnois reported.

"Wishful thinking," Lois Kerr whispered to me. "Mother said that Mr. Carlisle came here to die. We've had him in our prayers every night and day since his return to the island."

Aunt Lucy quickly disappeared. "Gotta get to my kitchen," she said and I knew she would spend the rest of the day cooking for the Carlisle family. Others followed suit, and by noon baskets of food were being carried toward Jersey Heights.

When I inquired about breadstuffs, Herb told me that plenty had already been sent.

I went back to Castle Rock to wait for Anne to return. I took out the great yellow book, *Leaves of Grass*. Like that time after Dempsey died back in 1881, I read "When Lilacs Last in the Dooryard Bloom'd." Mr. Whitman wrote that poem after Lincoln's death. I read it over silently, then closed my eyes, put my hand on the page, and recited the words by heart.

When I heard footfalls upon the spiral path, I closed the great book, rushed to the door, swung it open, and stepped out onto the rock. I was surprised to see a halo of gold-and-silver hair. "Oh, it's you," I said.

"Sorry to disappoint," Flossie said, crestfallen at my rash greeting.

"I'm sorry That was not a proper welcome." I explained that Anne had left in the middle of the night to attend to Mr. Carlisle, and word about the island was that he had died. I was waiting for confirmation from Anne.

No sooner were the words out of my mouth than Anne appeared at the door. Her walking skirt was still soaked through. She took off her waxed cape and gave it a good shake, droplets of water spraying everywhere. I opened the door and took the cape from her. "I'll hang this up for you," I said.

"I must change," she said crossing the front room and heading toward her room. She stopped at the door with her hand on the doorknob and paused there for a long moment, as if collecting her thoughts. Then, without turning, but still facing the door with her head down she said,

"Mr. Taylor—Mr. Carlisle's cousin from Round Island—is coming to accompany the body back to Newark at four this afternoon. Thankfully, he has stepped in to make all the arrangements. I need to sign the death certificate. I was hoping you would come back to the Carlisles' with me as you have met Mr. Taylor, and I have not."

"Most certainly," I said.

Anne pushed through her bedroom door, then closed the door behind without responding.

Flossie looked at me wide-eyed. I nodded toward the screen door. We stepped outside. I quietly shut the screen door behind me.

"I've never seen Anne so affected. She's always so stoic in her professional dealings. In her everyday life as well," Flossie whispered to me.

"Anne has attended many deaths since I've known her. Sometimes it affects her strongly," I said.

"But Mr. Carlisle has been ill a long time. His death was not unexpected."

"It's more about the person. She has known and attended to Mr. Carlisle and his family since they came to the island. I never realized until now, but Mr. Carlisle did resemble her father a bit. About the same age, too. My guess is she is remembering her father's death."

"I was hoping to talk you into coming to the Susan B. Anthony talks today, but I see that is impossible now."

"Yes," I said, relieved. I was dead set against attending and grateful that Flossie wasn't going to try to convince me. Flossie can be relentless.

The tea kettle whistled, and I went in to make a pot of tea. Anne emerged from her room looking drained. I insisted she sit at the table, then brought the tea.

"Have you eaten at all?"

"No," she replied. "I'm not hungry."

Ignoring this last bit of information, I prepared a tray with sliced cheese, fruit, and bread. Despite her protestations that she wasn't hungry, Anne ate. Flossie excused herself and went to Thousand Island Park for the lecture, telling me, "Since it's a two-day event, I'm staying with a woman I met at the A.C.A. I'll keep Anne and the Carlisle family in my thoughts and prayers."

It was gray all day until around three. By the time we left to go back to Jersey Heights, there was a break in the clouds to the west. The heavy gray-blue clouds above were perfectly mirrored in the water below. Then a yellow-orange crack appeared on the horizon. Here and there in the dark clouds above, pockets of light appeared. Shafts of sunlight poured from the cracks and splashed onto the water below. As the Carlisle staff gathered the family's baggage for departure, the heavy clouds slowly drifted eastward, and the late afternoon air grew warmer and brighter.

People from all over the island came to pay their respects to Mr. Carlisle. They lined the shore of Otsego Point and watched as Nat and other boys carried down the trunks and bags for the family's journey back to Newark. Looking east, I saw that the docks of Pullman House were crowded with onlookers. Skiffs dotted the water as some people had rowed over to watch the great man leave Grenell. Soon the steamer *Nightingale* appeared, approaching Grenell from downriver. The steamer captains of other vessels, aware of *Nightingale*'s mission, steered clear of Grenell Island Park. It was as if everything and everyone on the river had paused to mourn the passing of Mr. Carlisle.

Anne and I entered the Carlisle cottage, Jersey Heights, nodding wordlessly to the bereaved family. Mrs. Carlisle and her grown daughter, Nettie, were accompanied by Mrs. Carlisle's sister and her children.

Anne introduced herself to Mr. and Mrs. Taylor, who had just arrived from Round Island to accompany the family back to Newark. I nodded to Mr. Taylor and conveyed my condolences. He nodded back and continued up the stairs to greet Mrs. Carlisle on this somber day.

John Gardiner had enlisted the help of Capt. E. G. Robbins, Hyland Robbins, and George Grenell to help carry the body to the steamer. Each took a corner of the litter and carefully carried the sheet-covered body down the long steep stairway leading to the dock and up the gangway to the *Nightingale*.

Flags at Pullman House, Susquehanna Club, Edgewater, La Roche, and Point Ida all hung limply at half-mast. The *Nightingale* blew her whistle long and low as it slowly pulled away from the dock. The crowd on the shore stood motionless watching the *Nightingale* as she swung into the channel and headed upriver to Clayton. All steamer traffic in the channel paused in deference.

Grenell 1893

Just as people began to stir and move toward their own cottages, a steamer from downriver sped into the quiet yacht basin. Its wake rocked the steamer *Otsego*. The sailing yacht, *Tiger*, bobbed at its mooring. Everyone paused and turned to watch the steamer land at La Roche's dock. Before it was properly tied up, uniformed men with guns drawn poured from the vessel and raced up the stairs toward the Griswold cottage. La Roche is mere yards from where Anne and I stood on the porch of Jersey Heights. We could hear shouting, a scuffle, and then silence.

"Whatever is going on?" Anne asked.

"Were those Pinkerton detectives?" I wondered aloud.

Anne shrugged. We gripped the rail in front of us and waited. No one had left the Pullman dock. Everyone's eyes were fastened on La Roche cottage. Moments later, the Pinkerton detectives appeared on the porch. Two left the porch marching shoulder to shoulder down the front steps. Behind them, two more detectives followed with a man between them. They each held an arm of the man as they escorted him down the steps. Two more detectives followed. Emily came out on the porch then, dabbing at her eyes. Her sister, Delia, wrapped a comforting arm around her. They stood on the porch, and, like the residents of Grenell Island Park and the guests of the Pullman House, watched Prof. Gabriel—Emily's angel—being led away from La Roche in handcuffs.

When we returned to Castle Rock, Anne immediately went to bed.

I was tired but too restless to sleep. Besides, there were still hours of sunlight left in the day. As sad as Mr. Carlisle's death was, the arrival of the Pinkertons and the arrest of Prof. Gabriel had unnerved me. Try as I might to adhere to the three gates—to eschew gossip—I couldn't help wondering how I could find out what was going on at La Roche. In case Anne woke, I wrote a note that I was going to the store on the pretense of getting mail.

As I suspected, the Grenell Island Store was a hub of activity. Half the island stood outside on the lawn just outside the store. Wild stories about Prof. Gabriel's arrest filled the air: he was a spy sent from France; he was a kidnapper; he tried to rob the bank in Clayton; he was the mastermind of a whiskey-smuggling ring. While I didn't engage in any of these discussions, I lingered and listened. I almost wished Flossie were here. She would readily question everyone without compunction.

Eventually, the heavy sense of guilt I harbored at indulging in gossip got the better of me and prodded my return to Castle Rock. The wild accusations and speculations had only made me feel more restless, more curious. I decided to take the long way back on the boardwalk side of the island. I walked slowly listening intently to the conversations pouring from the porches. Everyone was talking about the Gabriel arrest. As I reached the Grenell farm, I was happy to see Nat. Leave it to Nat to ferret out the truth or at least the closest version of it. "Do you know what's going on?" I asked.

Nat filled me in on what he knew as we walked through the Grenell farm. Nat had heard that Miss Delia noticed she was missing checks from her checkbook and had traveled early last week to the bank in Clayton to inquire if there had been any checks written on her account. Indeed, there were! Several checks had been forged with her signature and a sizeable amount of money withdrawn from her savings. Delia immediately suspected her new brother-in-law. "Miss Delia said she had never trusted that man. Not from day one. She didn't hesitate to hire the Pinkertons to sort out the matter. That they did, and right quick!" Nat told me.

I went back to the cottage and peeked in on Anne. She was still fast asleep. She might very well sleep until morning. I was secretly glad that Anne was asleep as she would never approve of my probing into this incident.

I sat and thought about poor, poor Emily. "He married her only for the money," many at the store had insisted.

"Why else would such a dashing young man marry an old spinster?"

I thought of her love of the French language and teaching. "Couldn't he have married her for her mind? For their mutual love of language and learning?" I asked myself aloud. Though dead tired, I couldn't sleep. I tossed and turned all night dreaming of Prof. Gabriel and Charles. Sometimes they were the same person.

I woke and, through my window I could see tiny patches of St. Lawrence blue through a curtain of cedar boughs. It was as if a dozen pair of blue eyes were winking at me through the branches. I thought of the first time I saw the St. Lawrence. It was the most remarkable blue: regal blue, a true blue, a loyal blue. It was like the blue eyes of my one true love.

The blue eyes of my one true love. That is what I thought the very first time I saw the St. Lawrence. That thought floated to my consciousness often when I looked at the river. Did that fleeting notion mean that my true love would have blue eyes? Charles had brown eyes. Perhaps that meant Charles was not my true love. I wasn't sure I believed in the notion that there was just one person for me out there.

It was the Greeks who had come up with the notion of soul mates. Plato wrote about it in his *Symposium* in the speech by Aristophanes. According to Greek mythology, humans had been created with four arms, four legs, and one head with two faces. Thinking these creatures too powerful, Zeus split them apart. Now, all our lives we search for our other half to make us complete again. When we meet that person, the realization that we have met our matching half should hit us like lightning. I thought of the day on the *Nightingale* when I first saw Charles on the bow and then later on the shore. There was no lightning. No instant recognition. No revelation.

Perhaps Nora did me a favor.

CHAPTER *forty*

"Good morning, Miss Marguerite."

I had been bailing out the skiff from yesterday's rain when I heard Nat and looked up to see him walk around Sentry Rock. My heart leaped when I noticed that he had a telegram in his hand. So many possibilities. Mother? Rose? Charles? But then again, it could be Lily. Telegrams were often bad news. I hoped with all my heart that it was good news.

"Thank you, Nat," I said, taking the envelope from him.

"Do you want me to wait for a response?"

"No. Thank you."

I sat on the dock, put my feet in the skiff, and stared at the envelope in my hand. I wasn't sure whom I wanted to hear from more. As soon as Nat had disappeared into the dark lot, I carefully pried open the back flap of the envelope.

> Meet at your dock today at two? STOP.
> Much to talk about. STOP. Charles.

Charles. If he were meeting me at two, that meant he was in the islands now. How long had he been here? What did he wish to talk about? Had he spoken to Mr. Clark in Chicago? Was he on Comfort Island now? Did he mean for me to take him for a row in my skiff? I finished bailing the skiff just in case, then went back to the cottage.

I checked my bodice watch. It was ten. What would I do for the next four hours?

"Have you heard yet from the university about your class schedule?" Anne asked. She was sitting at our table sorting through a folder of paper.

"No," I said. "Not yet. I expect to hear from them shortly. Classes begin in a month."

"I have quite the class schedule this year. And I've also received several inquiries for the room vacated by Keiko. I was hoping you could read through their letters and give me your opinion."

"Of course," I said, happy to have a diversion.

After I had reviewed and discussed the inquiries from those wishing to be our new housemates, I pulled the telegram envelope from my pocket and put it on the table. "I heard from Charles this morning."

Even Anne couldn't hide the look of surprise that crossed her normally placid countenance. "What did he say?"

"He wants to meet me on our dock and . . . talk."

"I see."

Anne suggested we have our midday meal then, but I wasn't hungry. I settled for bread and butter and a cup of tea. After our meal, Anne suggested we straighten pantry shelves. By the time we finished, it was a quarter till two.

I considered pinning the cameo to my high, stand-up collar but wrapped it in a handkerchief and slipped it into my pocket instead. I was prepared to give it back to him. I put on my boater. It wasn't windy today, so I wouldn't need a hatpin. At the last minute, I decided that it would be better to be safe than sorry and secured the boater in place with two large hatpins. Feeling prepared for anything, I walked down to the dock to wait for Charles.

I figured he would be walking from Pullman House and wondered if in the daylight he would be able to find his way. I sat on the dock, with my feet on the skiff seat, and looked toward the bridge to Pratt Point just in case. I could almost see the end of the Pratts' bridge from where I was sitting. I heard oars dipping into the water and turned to see who was rowing around Pratt Point and was surprised that it was Charles.

I watched as he tried to figure out how to turn the skiff, causing a zigzag approach to our dock.

"Good afternoon," he called out when he was only yards away.

"Good afternoon," I said. I reached out, grabbed the gunwale, and pulled him toward the dock.

"Ready for a row?" he asked. "It's a nice day for it."

"Yes." I climbed into the skiff and sat on the seat behind him.

He turned and looked over his shoulder, perplexed. "I thought you would sit across from me," he said.

"I am. You row from the center seat when you are alone, but when others are in the skiff, you sit directly on the seat in front of you and face the opposite direction. That way the boat will be better balanced and we'll be looking at each other."

"Oh," he said. He stood abruptly. The skiff wobbled dramatically and tipped dangerously toward the water side of the skiff. I lunged low in the opposite direction, reaching for the dock. Charles somehow regained his balance and didn't plunge headfirst into the river.

"Keep your center of gravity low as you shift seats," I advised, holding onto the dock and steadying the skiff. "Have ever rowed a skiff before?" I asked. "I mean besides your row from Pullman House to here."

"Not as often as you have, but I'm learning," Charles said reaching forward to readjust the oars for his new position in the skiff.

I pushed off from the dock. Charles settled the oars onto the oar pins and grabbed the grips. Like Mr. Quigley on his first attempt, Charles dug too deeply into the water with the oars.

"Shallow. Slow. Steady," I said.

He complied, and we slid gracefully toward Murray Isle.

"Where are we going this afternoon?" I asked.

"I don't know. Do you have a favorite spot?"

"I do. I call it Cathedral Cove, though officially on the charts it's called Escanaba Bay. Row towards the Narrows.

"Where is that?"

I pointed and he turned to look. "The palisades there," I said.

He rowed and I waited.

Should I be the first to say something about the night of the midsummer ball? I pressed my lips together. He was the one who had sent the telegram. He had written that he had something to talk about. I waited.

I looked out across the water. The sunlight glinted, sparkled, and flashed across the surface. Looking west, I saw that Maple Island and Robbins Island appeared melded together into one landmass.

I scrutinized the shoreline ahead of me. In the past few years, cottages had sprung up on Murray Isle like mushrooms after a rain. I could hear the hammering coming from the huge boathouse downriver. Construction for a large hotel was to begin soon. I'd been told It would be twice the size of the Pullman House. There were great plans for the newly formed park. Lake Minnetonka was to be created in the center with interior lots around it, and even a small-gauge train was planned to run around the exterior of the island. I wondered briefly if I would see puffs of steam and hear a clanking bell or train whistle as the train chugged around the island. The coming hotel would bring another boom of cottage building.

As Charles rowed north, Maple Island and Robbins Island seemed to move apart, and I could see the space between them. Then the opening between them was starting to close again as we neared the foot of Murray. I fought the urge to look at my watch. How long had we been silent in the skiff? Did he intend to say something?

"About the night of the midsummer ball," I finally ventured.

"I was wrong to leave," he interjected. He kept his eyes on his feet as he rowed. "I don't know where to begin."

I was flooded with questions. What had been so terrible that he had felt the need to return to Chicago? How did he get back to Comfort Island? I remained silent. The only sounds between us were the dip of the oars into the water, the creak of the leather bindings around the oar pins, and the sound of the water against the hull as we glided through the water.

Charles looked from side to side as if concerned that he was not rowing correctly.

Tired of waiting, I finally spoke. "I should have told you that I am older than you are."

He looked up at me then and paused mid-stroke. The oars quivered in midair. Droplets dripped from the oars, making a chain-of-circles pattern on the water's surface as we slowly drifted toward Murray on the momentum of his last pull.

"You're older than I am?"

"Yes. Probably four or five years. I should have told you that I'm a teaching fellow and not a student at Penn."

"Oh, that. That doesn't bother me. Not a whit. It only improves my opinion of you."

"Was it the ghost, then?"

"Ghost?"

"That dilapidated building behind you high up on the rocks is Cliff House," I said, pointing to the looming structure. "It's rumored to be haunted. Remember the night of the searchlight excursion? The story about the ghost parade?"

Charles stopped rowing and looked over his shoulder.

"Nora claimed that I was the source of the rumor, that I concocted a hoax, pretending to be a ghost to scare the patrons at Hub House. I didn't. I assure you."

"Anyone who knows you, knows that that is preposterous," Charles said as he began rowing again.

"What was it, then?" My tone was sharper than I intended, my exasperation evident.

Charles paused for a moment, looked at me, then looked over his shoulder to check his progress. Once satisfied that he was going in the right direction, he turned forward and rowed with renewed urgency. A look of consternation crossed his face while he dug deep with the oars. I remained silent and waited as we rounded the foot of Murray. He mushed his lips together and pulled hard on the oars again. "It's that you're Catholic," he spat out.

"Catholic?" I asked. Had Nora said something about me being Catholic? I thought back to that horrid night, sifting through things Nora had said, cringing at the memories. She had said something about a convent. And then the words *wayward Catholic daughter* surfaced in my memory.

"Is being Catholic so repugnant to you?" I asked.

"Not at all. But I had planned . . . There were fireworks that night. Right?"

"I suppose, but we left early." *Though not as early as you*, I wanted to add.

"I . . . I had planned . . . during the fireworks that evening . . . to ask you for your hand in marriage." He paused then and asked which way to go. I pointed to my left, indicating the entrance to the bay I referred to as

Cathedral Cove. He pulled on the wrong oar and went the opposite way.

"Pull on the other oar," I instructed.

There was no need to go quickly now. Charles pulled on the oars lightly, and there were long pauses between pulls on the oars as he tried to come up with the words.

"Mother has been insisting that I find a wife. She keeps telling me I need to settle down. That's rather comical, actually," he said with a forced laugh. "No one could be more settled than I am. All my life, my classmates have ridiculed me for being so methodical. Plodding. Black Bart. Not at all like my older brother. He's a bit of a ladies' man, always a different woman on his arm. But I suppose by 'settled' Mother means moving out of my father's house and into a house of my own. Finding a wife. Starting a family."

The sound of the skiff skimming across the top of lily pads startled Charles, and he turned around to see what had caused the skiff to sound like it was gliding over fabric.

"What do I do?" he asked, seemingly afraid to dip the oars into the water lilies.

"We could just sit here and enjoy the silence," I said. "I love this spot." I looked up at the hemlocks that hung out over the water. Their presence was dark, thick, and stately on the rocky shore. A kingfisher swooped out of the hemlocks, diving low over the water before letting out a *rat-a-tat-tat* alarm call.

The water was like a millpond here, so sheltered from the wind. I marveled at the peace. The silence. I breathed in the calm. I wondered briefly if someday the shoreline of Cathedral Cove would be lined with cottages and a small-gauge train would chug around the edges of this sacred place. The world around me was changing so rapidly.

"Until I met you, I never thought that would be possible," Charles said.

Lost in my own thoughts, I looked at him, perplexed. "That what was possible?"

"Day after day as Mother prattled on about the importance of finding a wife, I would think, 'What would I do with a wife? What should we talk about over the morning table? Curtains and servants and all those mundane things that my mother talks of?' But then I met you. You would be more than a wife. More than a woman to share my household with. You share my passion for all things classical. With you, there would always be something to talk about."

I bit my lip. He was right. We could always talk about the ancient world, but could we talk about today? Our life in today's world?

A dragonfly buzzed by. I slowly raised my hand, and it alighted on my finger. Here, I was not worried about anything. This pocket of quiet seemed frozen in time.

"Why do you like this place?" Charles asked.

Perhaps there was hope. Perhaps we would be able to talk about more than life two-thousand years ago.

"It's the quiet that attracts me. It feels sacred . . . like a cathedral."

His head dropped a little at that word, and he looked at his hands.

"I had planned to ask for your hand in marriage that night. During the fireworks. But . . ."

"But I'm Catholic, and that's a problem."

"Not to me but my mother. Mother has never cared for . . ."

"Catholics."

Charles brightened and looked at me. "But Mr. Clark hit upon a compromise." He shifted in his seat and leaned forward. "You could remain Catholic. You wouldn't have to convert. You could go to Mass every day if you like . . . All Mother asks is that you promise to raise our children Episcopalian."

A frog hopped from the nearby shore and landed with a plop. Ripples spread out from where it landed.

"Is that amenable to you?" he asked.

"Actually, it is amenable . . . to me."

His face brightened and he dug into his inside jacket pocket for something.

"But, Charles, you see I have a mother, too, and her feelings about Episcopalians probably match your mother's feelings about Catholics."

"You don't have to decide now. I brought you an invitation. Well, technically it came to the Clarks but they graciously passed it along to me . . . us."

I took the envelope from his outstretched hand. I pulled from it a piece of birchbark. Scrawled in dramatic handwriting across the thick white surface was a clever invitation. In quaint language it invited the recipient to "an informal hornpipe in ye boathouse."

"I'm not sure where Murray Isle is, but Mrs. Clark assures me it isn't far from Grenell. Do you know where it is?"

"Well . . . yes. It's rather close. This island surrounding you at this moment is Murray Isle. The Murray Hill Park boathouse is across the water and a little upriver from me. I've been watching them build it all summer."

Charles didn't seem in the least chagrined at not knowing where he was. "So you'll go with me? We could waltz and I . . ."

"I'm sorry. I can't go. After you . . . left . . . I returned all the borrowed gowns to Mrs. Sharples. I sent them back to West Chester. I have nothing to wear."

Now it was Charles's turn to look perplexed. "What's wrong with what you have on?"

"I'm wearing a shirtwaist and a walking skirt. I can't wear this to a ball," I said.

"I don't mind. It doesn't matter to me."

I thought how true that probably was. "But our mothers care. Mrs. Clark cares. The social world around us cares. I'm sorry. My answer is no." I'd wasted so much of my summer worrying about what clothes to wear. My passion for fashion was about as dead and dry as the brown spot in the lawn the wardrobe tent had left.

"Mrs. Clark will be happy to lend you a gown," Charles suggested.

I knew this was also true. Seeing me in her gown on Charles's arm would make Mrs. Clark very happy. I shook the thought away. This was not about making Mrs. Clark happy. "I'm sorry. I have to say no to the ball."

He pressed his lips together and let out a sigh.

"Have you been writing haikus?" I asked.

The ends of his tight-lipped mouth turned up into a half-smile.

"Yes. Not every day, but a few on the train from Chicago."

"Did you bring them with you?"

"No. Have you've been writing haikus?"

"Every day."

"Did you bring them with you?"

"No."

"But will you send them to me?"

I nodded.

I put my head back and stared at the tops of the hemlocks that encircled us. I'd have to write a haiku about Cathedral Cove. Then I noted that the sky had grown darker. I looked west and saw the tops of the trees were stirring dramatically. When I heard distant thunder, I jerked to attention. "I think we need to head back. Quickly," I said.

While I didn't have the same sensibilities as Hunk to be able to predict the weather, I could smell rain in the air.

"What? Now?" Charles asked.

"Now!" I insisted.

Charles fumbled with the oars, afraid of sticking them in the water through the thick layer of water lilies.

"Here," I said, reaching out my hand to beckon him forward. "Stay low and move to the center seat." He complied. I moved to the center seat beside him.

I think for an instant that he thought I wanted to seal his proposal with a kiss because he looked surprised when I moved to his former seat, then nodded my head for him to sit where I had sat. "Stay low!" I reminded him.

The moment he was seated, I dipped the oars in the water. I pushed forward on the left and pulled backward on the right, causing the skiff to make a 180-degree turn. Charles grabbed the gunwales. I rowed hard and swiftly toward the entrance of the Narrows. Once past the foot of Murray, I could see that I was right: there was a storm approaching. I saw a flash of lightning. The wind had picked up, but only small furrows of water pushed this way from the west. There weren't whitecaps—yet. I picked up my pace. By the time I was in the middle of the waterway between Murray and Grenell, the first whitecaps appeared. I angled the skiff a little toward where Dr. Gifford had camped so that the whitecaps didn't hit us broadside. It was easier to row into the wind so I was heading upriver of Castle Rock. Once near the Grenell Island shoreline and a bit more sheltered from the wind, I turned parallel to the shore and rowed downriver toward Castle Rock.

We barely got the skiff secured at the dock before the rain grew more intense. At first, it fell in huge fat droplets and then in a solid curtain of rain. We were instantly drenched.

"So glad you made it back safely," Anne said holding the door open so we could rush in. "I have the kettle on for afternoon tea. I trust you will join us, Mr. Bartman?"

"Thank you, no. I've never cared too much for tea."

"A glass of water then?" Anne asked.

"No, I'm fine."

"Please, have a seat," Anne said indicating a chair at our table.

Charles removed his wet jacket and I hung it on the back of an empty chair.

"Your hair is soaking wet," I said retrieving a towel from my room that I handed to Charles so that he could dry his hair. Luckily, my boater had kept my hair relatively dry. I was lucky I had secured it with not one but two hatpins.

I placed a shawl over my wet shirtwaist and sat down. The tea smelled most inviting as Anne poured a cup for me. I reached for the jar of cloves and then the jar of cinnamon imperials.

"Whatever are you putting into your teacup?" Chalres asked.

I looked at Anne and smiled. "It is a ritual of ours. I first added cloves and cinnamon imperials to my tea here at Castle Rock. Of course, we called it Camp Anne back then."

"Interesting."

I dropped two imperials into the cup and watched the ruby-red coloring swirl into the tea as the imperials dissolved.

"Well," Anne said turning toward Charles, "what brings you to Grenell this afternoon?"

Charles seemed taken aback by her directness. He obviously wasn't used to conversing with Quakers.

"An apology and an invitation."

Anne stirred the tea without clinking the spoon on the cup then lifted the spoon and watched it drip before she silently placed it on the saucer behind the cup. "Yes. I suppose an apology was in order after deserting Marguerite at the midsummer ball." Her back was ramrod straight and her eyes piercing as if challenging Charles to disagree.

Charles stammered a yes

"And the invitation?"

"To the Murray Hill Park Boathouse Ball."

I handed the invitation to Anne, who read it with interest.

"Are you planning on attending?" she asked me. But before I could respond, she turned to Charles and said, "And if she does attend, what assurances does Marguerite have that you will not desert her again? Quite shocking after you made such a fuss about the importance of escorting her home the night of the searchlight excursion."

Charles looked positively undone.

"I'm afraid it's a moot point," I said. "I have nothing to wear now that I sent all my gowns back to West Chester."

We sipped our tea in silence.

"Look at that!" I said after my last sip. "No more rain. The day is sunny and bright again. I guess it was just a passing storm."

"Poor timing for a row is all," Anne said. "Perhaps there is a rainbow."

I stood and shook out Charles's jacket. The shoulder section was still quite damp. "Let's see if there is a rainbow." We stepped outside the door and saw an arch of a rainbow beyond Pratt Point.

"Would you like me to help bail out your skiff?" I asked Charles.

"Bail?"

"Remove the rainwater that accumulated so your feet won't get all wet when you row back to Pullman House," I explained. "Come I'll show you."

"Thank you for your hospitality, Dr. Ashbridge," Charles said to Anne, who only nodded an acknowledgment before she returned to the cottage.

I removed the tin can I kept under the forward seat of my skiff and went back to Charles's rented skiff. I pushed down on the bow so the water ran forward, then scooped the water out. I was amazed at the amount of water that had accumulated in the skiff in such a short time. As I bailed, Charles stood behind me shifting his weight from foot to foot.

"There. It will be lighter and easier to row," I said brushing droplets of water from the front of my walking skirt.

"So you will consider coming to the Murray Hill Park Boathouse Ball?" he asked sheepishly as I wiped off his seat with a towel.

I stood and looked over his shoulder and saw the brown patch left by the wardrobe tent.

"Perhaps you need time to think about it?" Charles asked when I didn't respond right away.

"I'm not sure balls and frivolous parties are important to me. I much prefer a quiet row on the river."

"Mrs. Clark said as much."

Ah! So it was Mrs. Clark who had concocted this afternoon's row, apology, and invitation.

"Thank Mrs. Clark for her kind invitation, but I'm afraid I have to decline. Let me help you into the skiff."

I almost forgot that I had the handkerchief-wrapped cameo in my pocket. "Wait," I said. "I need to give this back to you."

"This is a lady's handkerchief, not mine," he said as he started to hand it back to me. That's when he noticed that there was something inside. Recognition flashed across his face. He unwrapped the cameo and held it in his hand. "What? No!" he said and gazed down at me with a hurt look in his small, dark eyes.

He took my hands and pulled me closer. "Marguerite, this is for you, whether you go to the ball with me or not. Whether you marry me or not. I hope that you will consent to both. Regardless, this cameo is for you. My grandmother told me to give it to the woman I love." He dropped down on one knee then. He looked up into my eyes as he put the cameo back into my hand, closed my fingers around it, and wrapped his fingers around mine. "You are that woman. This cameo—and my love—will always belong to you."

Touched and a tad embarrassed, I wasn't sure what to say as Charles continued to hold my hands and stared up at me.

"Please say you'll go to the ball," he whispered to me. "Please say you'll marry me."

The word yes was somewhere inside of me. Part of me thought it might bubble up and I'd blurt it out. I kept my lips tightly clamped together. The sound of the river was softly whispering to me, *Wait! Think!*

I pulled Charles to his feet. "You've given me much to think about. I will consider your marriage proposal seriously, I promise. But I truly have nothing to wear to the ball."

CHAPTER
forty-one

"How long will you be gone?" Flossie asked.

Anne and I shared a look. Flossie had been acting very odd since she had returned from her two days at Thousand Island Park. She seemed very excited that we would be away from the cottage for a while.

"We're going to a lot-owners' meeting at Pullman House, after which Mrs. Harnois has invited us to Point Ida for luncheon," I said.

"So-o-o-o," Flossie said, rubbing at her chin as she looked up to the sky, calculating in her head. "So you'll be back around two o'clock?"

"Well, I hoped that we could stop by and see how Delia and Emily are doing since we'll be right there next to them at Point Ida."

"That's thoughtful," Flossie said as she followed us down the spiral path.

"And I heard that the Kerrs and Curtises are leaving soon, so I thought we might say goodbye to them while we are just a hop, skip, and a jump from Glimpses and Edgewater," I said.

"Splendid! So three o'clock or perhaps later?"

"Why is it so important to know precisely when we will be back?" I finally asked.

"Because I'm preparing a surprise supper for you tonight, and I really don't want you to know what I'm preparing," Flossie said.

"I see," I said. But I didn't. I'd never known Flossie to cook or bake anything.

"So you're leaving now and definitely won't be back before three. Oh! I need to borrow the skiff to go to Thousand Island Park for supplies. Supplies for our surprise supper, that is. With your permission, of course."

Anne and I nodded our approval, though, I wondered why she would need to row to Thousand Island Park when we had an adequately-stocked grocery store here on the island.

"See you after three o'clock," Flossie said, dashing toward the skiff.

"I only hope the cottage is still standing when we return," I said to Anne as we edged around Sentry Rock and headed toward Pullman House.

Prof. Pabst was just leaving his porch and joined us. We asked if he knew what this lot-owners' meeting was all about. He had heard that there was a movement afoot, especially at this end of the river, to organize summer residents. "A few weeks ago there was a meeting at the Frontenac and a new organization was formed called the Thousand Island Protective Association. The owner of the Grenell Island Park cottage Edgewater, Leonard E. Curtis, was elected president, and Charles Emery as vice-president," he told us.

"A protective association? To protect whom from what?" Anne asked.

"From what I understand, the purpose of the organization is to deal with grievances with transportation companies, mail, and telegraphic services, as well as other nuisances affecting the health or comfort of the summer residents. But I think they are also concerned about thefts from the cottages."

"Has there been a problem with theft?" Anne asked.

Prof. Pabst nodded gravely. "Especially in the grander cottages when they are unoccupied."

We didn't have much in our small cottage, but I would hate to see it broken into and ransacked.

"But I also heard that the meeting may be about building a church on Grenell. We can't go on imposing on Mrs. Gardner Sunday after Sunday. Her current renters, the Bakewells, were most amenable to having a religious service while they were there, but we can't assume all renters will be as receptive. So perhaps I'm all wrong and this meeting might have been called to mobilize residents to build a church—an endeavor I would whole-heartedly support," Prof. Pabst said as we turned onto St. James Place.

By the time we reached the Pullman House, the lobby and salon were crowded with people. It seemed nearly every lot-owner on the island was there. Mr. Hudson was the organizer of today's meeting. He stood front and center, with Sam Grenell on one side and Colonel Sayles on the other side. Perhaps I was still prickly from the "Quaker and Catholic" comment he made at Gardner's Point, but he seemed to cast a withering look when he saw Anne and me enter the parlor.

I saw someone wave to us and was pleased to see Alice sitting a few rows back dressed in her black widow's weeds. This was her first public appearance on the island since she had arrived in May. Anne and I threaded our way through the crowd toward Alice. We barely had time to say good morning and settle into our seats before Mr. Hudson called for quiet.

The meeting rambled on for hours. As Prof. Pabst had surmised, the gathering had dual purposes: the organization of an island association and the importance of building a church on the island. Colonel Sayles took the opportunity to announce that Pullman House was to be electrified this fall. Besides being fitted with electric lamps, by next spring, there would be a bell in each room that could be rung from the office. Likewise, each room would be connected to the office via an annunciator. This news was met with *oohs* and *ahhs* from the crowd.

Not to be outdone, Sam jumped up and declared that he would be paving St. James Place from the head of the island to the foot of the island. In addition, he would install a system of streetlamps to light the way at night. With this, the crowd broke into spontaneous applause. Sam hooked his thumbs behind his lapels and looked triumphant. I glanced at Aunt Lucy. She shook her head in dismay. She knew better than anyone Sam's propensity to promise more than he was able to deliver.

Eventually, it was decided that Grenell Island Park needed an association to represent the wants and needs of the Grenell Island Park lot-owners. The smug smile on Sam's face was replaced with a grimace when Colonel Sayles was elected president of the new Grenell Island Park Association. Mr. Hudson was elected secretary. A committee was needed to draft a suitable constitution and bylaws. Colonel Sayles and Mr. Hudson immediately volunteered closely followed by Sam Grenell. "If need be," Colonel Sayles said after Sam was added to the committee, "we will have the association duly incorporated."

"Incorporation?" Sam asked incredulously. "What we need is a banquet! We need an annual island banquet for all the island residents—one with a suitable program of music and toasts," Sam said raising an empty hand as if toasting the banquet idea. When the cheering subsided, dates were bantered about and soon the date for the first annual banquet was set for August 11, 1894. At that time the organization would hold an election of officers.

After the formation of the new association, talk turned to the need for a new church. Capt. Robbins spoke in favor of a church being built at once. Rev. Stoddard made an impassioned speech in which he called Grenell Island Park "the grandest place on the river so arrayed by nature that it is designed to be the most densely inhabited in the near future."

At that, Sam stood again and this time promised he would donate to the newly formed association the pick of any unsold lot on the island for the construction of a church. The crowd cheered. Sam basked in the accolades shouted forth. The lot-owners were atwitter with ideas and suggestions. Despite having several Baptist ministers on the island, the majority of the people in attendance were in favor of an Episcopal church.

I looked at Anne and sighed. It was the first reminder since Charles's proposal of the momentous decision I had ahead of me.

A church committee was appointed consisting of Prof. Pabst and Mr. Babcock. They were instructed to raise funds and submit a plan of action—if possible by next week. Prof. Pabst passed a sheet of paper requesting pledges for money. Four-hundred dollars was pledged on the spot.

There was much excitement after the meeting. The group lingered and talked about the glorious future of Grenell Island Park. Slowly people edged toward the door and out into the bright sunny day.

"Marguerite, might I have a word with you?" Alice asked as we stepped through the Pullman House doors.

"Certainly. I'm so happy to see you here today," I said, moving to the far end of the veranda and away from the exiting throng of lot-owners.

"It has been a very solitary summer, but I felt that, as a lot-owner, I really needed to attend the meeting."

"I'm so glad you did."

"I wanted to thank you for whatever you said to Olivia. I know you had words with her that weekend my sister was visiting with Jessie and Mabelle. She's been fishing nearly every day since. So nice to have fresh fish but it has brightened her mood as well. I'm afraid she's taken her father's death quite hard."

"I only reminded her that she shared a passion for fishing with her father and she would be fishing for two from now on. I thought it a great way for her to honor her father's memory. I'm glad to hear her spirits have improved."

Alice smiled and nodded. "What a lovely notion. And . . ."

"Yes?" I asked when she hesitated.

"I hope I'm not speaking out of turn, but . . ."

"Go on," I urged her.

"I was wondering about the young man I've seen you in the company of as of late."

"Mr. Bartman?"

"I was wondering if . . . Well, are things serious between the two of you?"

"We only just met in June. He has a passion for classics as do I and we have discussed a possible future together . . ." I was not ready to publicly state that Charles had asked for my hand in marriage.

"But?"

"Compromises must be made."

Alice smiled then. "With marriage, there are always compromises. I don't know this gentleman. I only heard you speaking the night you returned from the searchlight excursion . . ."

I reddened at the memory. "I apologize if we woke you."

Alice leaned forward and placed a comforting hand on my arm. "I assure you that you didn't. I was already awake. But I wanted to advise you . . . that . . ." She paused, searching for the right words. "My mother successfully married off all five daughters. It was important to her to know that all her daughters would be 'taken care of.' It's a very traditional thought. I dare say your mother probably thinks the same way."

I nodded.

"But in the end, we need to be willing—and able—to take care of ourselves as there is no assurance that our husbands will always be there to take care of us."

I put my hand on hers. I thought of my mother who refused to take care of herself. Days after Father's death, she moved in with her son-in-law and daughter. From her father's house to her husband's house to her son-in-law's house. To me, it seemed as if she was not running to the protection of a man but running away from herself.

"So you must know exactly what you are willing to compromise, because once you give up your hard-won independence, there is no going back," Alice advised.

"Thank you for your wise words," I said as we walked back toward the veranda steps. "I promise you I will do just that," I told Alice as we descended the steps. Anne was speaking to Lottie Curtis near the stairs.

"There she is," Lottie, said smiling at me broadly. "I was helping Dr. Anne pass the time as she waited for you." She turned back to Anne. "I'll stop preaching and let you get to your luncheon. Thank you for listening to me," she said.

We bade farewell to Alice and Lottie then headed toward Point Ida.

"What was that all about?" I asked as we turned from St. James Place onto Ontario Avenue.

"It seems Lottie is very impassioned about women's suffrage. She feels that the ideal that 'a woman's place is in the home' is passing. She feels that women can capably care for their homes and take part in civic affairs. Furthermore, with a background in civic affairs, a woman is better able to train her children to be good citizens."

I nodded. I wondered briefly if, because I work side by side with men, that I had gained a different view of the world.

We discussed this notion as we reached the spot where Ontario Avenue truncated at St. Marks Place. We looked up at the backside of the Harnois cottage. "It looks much different from down here than it does from the waterside," Anne noted.

"No porches here on the back," I said.

"But what a view they have from those porches." We walked around Mr. Fox's store and to the path that led to the Harnois cottage, which was perched on the ridge of rock that I refer to as the female camel hump.

Grenell 1893

Aime Harnois, a prominent Watertown contractor, bought the acre lot on the channel side of the island in 1890 and built a lovely two-story cottage with a double-decker porch that wrapped around the front three sides of the cottage to take advantage of the commanding view. Before they bought the island property, Aime and Fanny had a lovely fourteen-year-old daughter named Louise. Sadly, Louise died. Heartbroken, the couple decided to have another child and at age forty, Mrs. Harnois gave birth to little Ida. She became the apple of their eye. Ida was five when they bought the property and named it Point Ida in her honor. Reminded of this, I was encouraged that I was certainly not nearing the end of my childbearing years.

Once on the porch, I knocked quietly on the screen door. Ida, now eight, jumped out from behind the door, startling Anne and me. "They're here!" Ida shouted as she turned and ran to another room in the cottage. Several rounds of "They're here. They're here!" echoed off the walls as Ida ran through the first floor. Then there was silence. We stood on the porch, waiting to be admitted.

We heard Ida pound up the stairs as she called out, "They're here!"

"Yes, yes! Ida, I hear you. They're here. You can stop screaming now," Mrs. Harnois said from somewhere in the house. We heard footsteps on the stairs and then Mrs. Harnois stumbled into the front room. "But where are they?" she asked.

I cleared my throat and Mrs. Harnois saw us on the other side of the screen door.

"Oh, dear. Ida didn't bother to invite you in but just left you standing on the porch? Please forgive my daughter's discourteousness. We've tried to teach her proper manners, but Ida is so willful. She prefers to do as she pleases. Her insolence will be the death of us both. Not that I don't want to invite you in, but I have a table set up on the other side. I thought we would luncheon on the veranda. It's such a lovely day." Mrs. Harnois opened the door and stepped out on the porch, and we walked around to the west veranda, where a lovely table was set for luncheon.

Before I sat down I turned and looked out at the scene in front of me. What a view they had! The Griswold sisters and the Carlisles were a little higher on the rock, but Point Ida had a lovely view of the Susquehanna Club and Edgewood to the west. Looking straight out, I could see Twin

Island and steamboats traveling up and down the channel. Looking east, was a great view of Pullman House. Beyond that was Castle Francis and Rock Island Lighthouse.

Mrs. Harnois was a buxom woman with small eyes and a permanent scowl. She started wearing spectacles a few years ago, and my theory is a lifetime of squinting caused the scowl on her face for she did not have a sour disposition. Self-consciously, I rubbed at the spot between my eyes, wondering if the last few days of pondering and worrying had created a permanent furrow there.

Mrs. Harnois immediately asked us about today's meeting at Pullman House. "Mr. Harnois attended, of course, but had pressing matters in Syracuse and left forthwith. He should be back on the island the day after tomorrow. Oh my! Such an eventful week with Mr. Carlisle's passing, then that dreadful affair with Mr. Gabriel. Poor Emily! How does one recover from such a betrayal?"

Mrs. Harnois's cook served a tray of sandwiches and glasses of lemonade.

"I hear you're leaving soon," Mrs. Harnois said as she offered us a sandwich from the tray. "Of course, we must be leaving in a week or so when the school bell rings. But if the weather is like this we may stay. What could Ida possibly miss at school that would require us missing such splendid days on the river? But whether we go or not, we will certainly be back at the cottage on the weekends through October. So glad we had the fireplace put in."

Mrs. Harnois babbled on as we nibbled on watercress sandwiches. Ida appeared soon after the cook had placed a lovely tray of jumbles and tea cakes in the center of the table. Ida reached out and grabbed a currant jumble and took a bite. "Mamma, you promised you would play croquet with me this afternoon."

"Not now, Ida. We have guests."

Ida took another bite of her jumble and brushed the crumbs from her face. "Did you see the new seawall Papa had installed last fall?" she said through a mouthful of cookie. She pointed out to the lawn below. "It's two hundred feet long. Papa had a barge full of soil brought in for the lawn. There used to be rocks under all that grass. Then they rolled it flat so it's perfect for croquet. Of course, Mr. Curtis had to put in a wall and extend his lawn, too. But Papa thought of it first. Mamma says that Mr. Curtis is nothing but a big hairy monkey."

Mrs. Harnois choked slightly on her bite of tea cake. She swallowed quickly and washed down the bite with a little lemonade. "Now . . . now, Ida, I don't believe that I called Mr. Curtis a monkey."

"Yes, you did! You said, 'Monkey see, monkey do.' You said Mr. Curtis copies everything Papa does because he doesn't have an original idea of his own," Ida insisted.

Mrs. Harnois looked at us and rolled her eyes. "My how the child exaggerates."

"But Mr. Curtis's lawn is too slanted to make a good croquet court. I'd like to see him try. The balls would roll right off into the river. Come now, Mamma! You promised me a croquet match," Ida said, pulling on her mother's arm and sticking out her lip. "You promised!"

Unable to bear any more whining from Ida, Anne and I stood, thanked Mrs. Harnois for the wonderful luncheon, and excused ourselves.

It was a short walk from the Harnois cottage to the Griswold cottage. The Griswold sisters were reading in a large wicker couch on the porch. Emily greeted us with a huge smile. "So nice that you came to visit," she said, rising to her feet and motioning for us to join them on the porch. "After the scene the other day, everyone has stayed away. I suppose they are afraid of being raided by the Pinkertons." Emily was trying to make light of the situation, but I could see the strain behind the smile.

"Not at all," I said, giving her a kiss on each cheek.

"Do sit down. It's a pleasure seeing both of you," Emily said as we sat in the rockers on either side of the wicker couch.

"How are you getting on?" Anne asked.

"Same as before," Emily said. "What would I do without my devoted sister? Always so kind and understanding."

"Pshaw. It's been you taking care of me for years." The two reached across and held each other's hands. I was glad to see that there was no finger-pointing or blame—only the resolve to move forward with their heads held high.

Biddy came out and offered lemonade, but we both declined.

Anne and I spoke then of our upcoming class schedules and new housemate.

"We're making the rounds," I said, rising. "So happy we caught you at home so we could say good-bye until next season."

"Saying good-bye is always the least favorite part of the season," Delia said.

"How long will you stay on the island?" Anne asked

"We'll stay as long as the weather holds. As long as it's warm and sunny, we'll be here on the porch drinking in this wondrous view."

After more hugs, more kisses on the cheeks, and more promises to write, we left La Roche.

From there it was a short walk to Glimpses on Point Breeze. We walked around the back of Jersey Heights, which was already closed and shuttered for the season.

"Do you think Mrs. Carlisle will sell?" Anne asked.

I didn't know. Some widows did sell. Others, like Alice, continued on.

When we knocked on the door at Glimpses, Mrs. Beardsley, the proprietress, told us that the entire Kerr family had left on *Tiger* for the last sail of the season. "They are packed and ready to leave on the morning train," she told us.

"Please give them our regards," I said.

"Would you like to write a note?" Mrs. Beardsley asked.

"That would be lovely," I said and she disappeared inside the cottage for paper and pen.

While we waited, I described to Anne the airship that had brought me to Point Breeze my first morning on the island.

"How very curious," Anne said, staring off toward the mainland as if she could imagine the aero-machine I had described flying across the channel. "Was it ever revealed whom the men were or what their purpose was?"

Mrs. Beardsley returned and handed me two sheets of writing paper and a fountain pen. "My brother-in-law, Mr. Haskell, looked into it. He too is an inventor. When I wrote to my sister about the airship, Mr. Haskell immediately remembered an article about an airship in a past issue of *Scientific American* that was written by a Dr. Martin Braun, a surgeon from Cape Vincent. Though we're not a hundred percent certain, we think Dr. Braun was the inventor of the craft we saw."

"I wonder why he didn't come forward to take credit for the flight?" I asked.

"James—Mr. Haskell— says Dr. Braun already has two patents on airships and is probably trying to perfect his craft for a third. Inventors are secretive with their inventions. There are so many men who would steal the ideas of others rather than working on their own ideas. Hence the need for patent attorneys like our guests, Mr. Kerr and Mr. Curtis."

I nodded as I wrote a quick note of thanks for everything the Kerrs had done for me this season. I was so fortunate that the sighting of the aero-machine had brought us together. I looked forward to exchanging correspondence over the winter and reuniting with Mary Mason and Lois next season.

I checked my bodice watch as we left Point Breeze. It was only two-thirty, too early to return to Castle Rock, so I suggested we stop to see Aunt Lucy and her chickens and then perhaps little Alma and Mavis.

Alma was sleeping. Grace and Charlie were chasing the young pullets about the yard—my first clue that Aunt Lucy was not there. When I asked, Grace Grenell told us that Aunt Lucy had gone to visit the Pratts. George was still toiling away on the structure that would eventually be both his store and home. Charlie told us the large storefront windows at the front of the store would arrive next week.

So instead of visiting with Aunt Lucy, we decided to walk around the head of the island and then up the hill to assess the progress of Mr. Sharples's Bungalow. We hadn't yet reached Bay View when we heard two bicycle bells ring out.

"Miss Hartranft, is that you?" A young woman called out. "It is! We had hoped we would run into you," said a lovely, young woman in a gray-and-blue wheeling costume. Their brakes squeaked as they slowed to a stop in front of us. It was Yvette Sawyer and Thomas Quigley.

I placed a hand across my chest. "I don't believe I've ever seen a bicycle on Grenell Island Park before. What a surprise!"

Yvette tilted her head back and laughed. "This is the smallest of islands we're traversing today. We are on an adventure! Wheeling our way across the islands from Clayton to Westminster Park."

"However will you accomplish that?" Anne asked.

"You didn't fly across the water between islands, did you?" I teased, thinking of the wheelmen beneath the aero-machine I had seen earlier this season.

Mr. Quigley let out a boisterous laugh that ended in a girlish titter. It took him a moment to recover before he continued. "No, I hired a scow to take us to the head of Grindstone. We got off at Buck Bay and took Head Island Road to Middle Road to Swiftwater Point Road."

"Middle Road has been my favorite so far," Yvette said.

"What? I thought you liked Round Island and all the swanky people we saw there," Thomas said.

"No! I preferred the rolling farmland of Grindstone," Yvette told Thomas and then turned to Anne and me to describe the golden fields of hay. "The farmers were haying. They had teams of horses, first cutting and then raking cut hay into windrows. Oh, the sweet smell of fresh-cut hay! It was positively intoxicating. Further on we saw fields where the hay had been raked into cute little stacks all lined up like a row of pointed hats."

Thomas pointed downriver as if we could imagine the road on Grindstone. "The scow met us at the end of Swiftwater Point Road then ferried us to Round Island. Our ride down the middle of Round Island went very quickly! We almost beat the scow to the Frontenac steamboat dock."

Yvette laughed and placed a hand on Thomas's arm. "If it weren't for all the people on the promenade between the Frontenac Hotel and the dock, we would have! We were certain we would be able to beat him from the Grenell Island Store dock to the Pullman House dock but I'm rather glad we met you instead. I was afraid you might have left for Philadelphia."

"We're leaving on the third," I said.

"I do, too! Back to Princeton," Thomas said.

"And I've been thinking about attending Syracuse University in the fall—if it's not too late to enroll," Yvette said.

I smiled, happy that Yvette was considering furthering her education.

"So, from here, you're headed to Wellesley Island?" Anne asked.

Thomas and Yvette nodded.

"I heard there is a new road from Thousand Island Park to Westminster Park," Anne said.

Yvette nodded enthusiastically. "Yes, we've already cycled it several times."

"Six miles of flat road that hugs the southern shore of the island,"

Thomas said.

"It's a wonderful ride. Great views of the river and the parks on the mainland—St. Lawrence Park and Point Vivian," Yvette reported.

"Are you dining in Westminster?" I asked.

"Oh no! We'll turn around and ride back to Coast Avenue," Thomas said as if six miles were a mere six blocks.

"Besides, the sun is setting earlier and earlier these days. We don't want to be caught out in the dark," Yvette said.

Thomas looked at me and winked. I have a feeling he wouldn't mind being caught out after dark with the vivacious Yvette.

"Safe travels to you," Anne said as the pair prepared to resume their ride.

"Good luck on getting into Syracuse University. Let me know if you need any help with your application," I called after them.

We continued on down the South Boulevard boardwalk, where I was surprised to see that Bay View was already shuttered for the season. "They're gone? I didn't get a chance to visit with Grace, Addie or Jessie at all!" I said.

Anne said nothing but slid me a reproachful look.

"I know. It's my own fault. I spent a lot of time at Thousand Island Park and on excursions with the Clarks. Did you get to visit with them at all? Did Maud and her new husband visit Bay View?" Maud, the eldest of the four Hinds' girls, had married Fred Roseboom two years ago.

"Yes. Maud is doing quite well. In fact, rumor has it that she is expecting the birth of her first child in February," Anne said.

"How exciting! The Hinds' first grandchild."

"I bet that baby will be photographed often. You remember that Mr. Roseboom is a photographer, right? He specializes in photographing babies. I heard last fall he photographed seventy-two babies in one day."

"Remarkable!"

We had hoped to see the Reeves family, but they were nowhere in sight—probably out fishing. As we continued on our way from South Boulevard to Park Avenue and up the steep Highland Avenue to the Bungalow worksite, I wondered what else I had missed at Grenell Island Park. While I had loved spending time with the Clark family and Charles, I had missed seeing my island family. That's how I'd come to think of our island community—for the ninety days of the summer season, we were family.

We barely caught Arnie as the work day was winding down. Most of the workers had already left for the day. We took a quick walk around the site. The walls were taller. Arnie felt certain they would have a roof on before the snow flew and the winter would be spent working on the interior of the great structure. Uncertain if I would see him before we left, we said our goodbyes for the season, then took the path to the Bungalow dock on the north shore.

We heard hammering and we turned toward Castle Rock. I had assumed the hammer falls were from the Murray Hill Park boathouse. I thought it odd that they were still hammering as tonight was the night of the ball. But as we neared Castle Rock, the hammering grew louder, and I soon discovered that the hammering was coming from our cottage. What sort of meal was Flossie preparing that would require a hammer? Anne and I shared a look. I checked my bodice watch; it was a few minutes after three.

"Flossie, we're back!" I called out from the base of the spiral path.

We heard voices and shushing. Flossie stuck her head out the screen door. "Have you gotten the mail yet? The afternoon post should be here by now. Why don't you row! And it's a lovely afternoon. Once you pick up the mail, maybe you could row around Maple Island before you come back!"

Anne and I shared a look.

We rowed to the post office and picked up the mail. There was a letter from Charles. I opened it before I got back to the skiff, thinking perhaps he would insist that I attend the ball with him tonight and inform me that he was bringing a dress of Mrs. Clark's for me to wear. Inside was a note that simply read, "Thinking of you." Three haikus were written on separate slips of paper. I tucked them back into the envelope to read later. I told myself I was not disappointed. I was relieved. Would I really want Charles to force me to go to the ball when I had made it very clear that I did not wish to attend?

As recommended, I rowed us around Maple Island before we returned to our dock at Castle Rock. "They're here!" I heard for the second time today as Flossie left the cottage and trotted down toward the dock. She seemed to be calling out to alert someone of our arrival, so when we walked up the path to the cottage, I wasn't surprised to see a tall woman wearing a carpenter's apron over her shirtwaist and walking skirt standing on the other side of the screen door. The woman brushed her hands together before brushing sawdust from her wavy dark hair, which was pulled back from her face and secured in a small knot at the back of her head. She had large blue eyes and a broad, captivating smile.

"Anne, Marguerite—I'd like to introduce you to Mrs. Merrill. I met her at Susan B. Anthony's lecture at Thousand Island Park. I engaged her to create something for you. Come!"

Flossie pulled Anne and me into the kitchen, then turned us toward the front corner of the room.

Anne gasped and placed both hands across her chest. "Heavens above! What have we here?" It's not often that something takes Anne by surprise, but the newly constructed, built-in corner cabinet did just that.

The cabinet had four sets of double doors, one on top of the other, from floor to the ceiling. Anne couldn't resist opening door after door. Though it only took up one small corner of the room, the cabinet provided much-needed storage for our tiny cottage. Until now we had only two shelves for both dishes and pantry items.

"I don't know what to say! Thank you so much, Flossie. This was very thoughtful of you," I said, grasping Flossie's hand.

"Anne and Marguerite, I'm so grateful you let me stay at Castle Rock for days! Weeks! It's the least I could do. Luckily, I met Mrs. Merrill, who—while not a carpenter by trade—is quite handy with a hammer. She suggested the design."

"And you managed to do all this in one day? Astonding!" That was quite a statement for Anne, who was not given to hyperbole. "The cabinet is ingenious in design and Quaker-like in its simple style and efficiency of purpose. It's perfect!" Anne told Mrs. Merrill.

"Mrs. Merrill is a most remarkable woman, but we can speak more about that over dinner. I've made stew."

We turned then to see a pot of stew bubbling on the cookstove. "If everyone will wash up, I'll serve," Flossie shooed us toward the washbasin.

"Have you ever cooked anything before?" I asked, raising the first spoonful of stew to my lips. I paused and sniffed at it. It smelled delicious.

"I'll have you know that I used to make lots of soups and stews when I lived with my father. But I haven't cooked much since going off to college."

I blew on the steaming spoonful, then took a tentative taste, which was rich and beefy, but the flavor of the potatoes and carrots came through.

We enjoyed several bites of the warming stew before Flossie said, "Remember that I said that Mrs. Merrill was a remarkable woman? She's actually a woman of prominence."

"Well, I don't know about prominence—perhaps back in Kansas." Mrs. Merrill smiled at Flossie.

"Alright then, we'll let Anne and Marguerite decide," Flossie said, letting let her spoon clink on her bowl. She stood and, with a grand hand gesture indicated Mrs. Merrill who looked a tad embarrassed by this introduction. "Anne, Marguerite, may I introduce Mayor Merrill. She is the first woman mayor in the United States."

Anne's eyebrows went up at that. My mouth fell open a bit. "Is that true? Are you the mayor of your town?"

"I'd read that women gained the right to vote in local elections in Kansas a few years back," Anne said.

"Yes, back in 1887," Mrs. Merrill said, motioning for Flossie to sit down again.

"What prompted you to run for mayor?" I asked.

"That's just it," Mrs. Merrill chuckled. "I didn't."

"This is a great story! Wait until you hear this!" Flossie said shifting excitedly in her chair and leaning forward.

"We have two parties in our town of Argonia, Kansas—the Farmers' Alliance and the Free Soil Party. As a prank, the Free Soil Party—who was against women in politics—put my name on the ballot for mayor. I suspect their line of thinking was that if a woman were soundly defeated, that the women of the town would be humiliated. Such a humiliation would discourage women from running for office for a long, long time. Why they picked me, I haven't a clue. Didn't even know about it until after the polls opened as the ballot wasn't public until the day of the election. Well, it didn't take long for word to spread. Shortly after the polls were opened, representatives of the Farmers' Alliance sent a delegation to my home with two questions. First, they asked: If elected, would I serve? Next, they asked: If elected would I support the Farmers' Alliance platform? My answer was yes to both questions. The Farmers' Alliance spread the word for their party to vote Merrill. By now the Women's Christian Temperance Union had caught wind of my candidacy, and they voted en masse for me. By the end of the day, I had secured more than two-thirds of the votes for mayor and won by a landslide."

I had not heard about the lady mayor from Argonia, Kansas.

"How does your husband feel about your mayorship?" Anne asked.

"Proud as any woman is about her husband who is a mayor, I suppose," she said, eyes bright as she blew on a spoonful of stew.

"And you're a carpenter too?"

Mrs. Merrill savored her spoonful of stew and answered after she swallowed. "Well, not by trade. My daddy was a carpenter, and since he had no sons, I helped out a bit," she said.

"Tell me," Anne began, rising and walking toward the front room windows. "After this morning's meeting, I've been thinking it would be nice to put shutters on the windows to help protect the cottage from the elements and as a deterrent to intruders. How difficult would it be to make shutters for the windows?"

Mrs. Merrill joined Anne at the window and ran her hand around the molding. "It would be a relatively simple job. You should be able to do it yourselves. I'd be happy to teach you. You know the saying 'Give a man a fish and you feed him for a day. Teach a man to fish and you feed him for a lifetime.'"

"But I'm supposed to leave tomorrow morning. I want to help," Flossie lamented. "I suppose I could catch a later steamer and train. Wait. I'll be right back!" Flossie pushed back from the table, rose, and was out the door, rushing off to the Pullman House to talk to the ticket agent.

"The ticket office closed an hour ago," I said checking my bodice watch.

"I have a feeling that won't impede a determined Flossie," Anne said, returning to the table and clearing away the dishes.

We had finished the dishes and were enjoying a cup of tea while listening to Mayor Merrill tell tales of life in Argonia, Kansas, when Flossie burst through the door, still panting from her dash back to the cottage. "Can we finish by three tomorrow?"

"If we get started early enough," Mayor Merrill said, her eyes bright and a captivating smile on her face.

After Flossie rowed Mrs. Merrill back to Thousand Island Park, the three of us settled on the porch. Lots of private steam yachts were heading toward the Murray Isle Boathouse for the ball. I kept my eyes peeled for the *Mamie C.* but did not see it. The *Nightingale* was busy bringing guests from Round, Grenell, and Thousand Island Park. There were lots of lights inside. Rose-tinged patches of light poured out of the boathouse windows and glistened on the water below as they floated over the wakes of the steamers. Merry laughter of the early arrivals greeted the next steamer. Soon harp and violin music poured out into the night. We could hear the rhythmic steps of the happy dancers echoing off the floor. I shut my eyes and imagined happy couples whirling about the room. The boathouse rafters echoed with mirth and gaiety. As the night wore on, couples wandered out of the boathouse and walked along the dock. A big moon shone from above and covered the rippling waters with a silvery sheen.

"Regretting your refusal to attend?" Anne asked.

"Not at all," I said. "Today would have been a different day if I'd had to spend it getting ready for a ball."

"What?" Flossie asked. "You were asked to the ball and you said no? Who asked you?" She looked at my face, then at Anne's. "Charles? He's back? He asked you to the ball and you said no?"

I nodded my head slightly.

"When did all this happen? When were you going to tell me?"

"There wasn't much to tell," I said. "He came to apologize."

"And?"

I shrugged.

"Fine! Don't tell me," Flossie said brusquely and stomped back into the cottage.

Anne reached over and patted my hand.

I shut my eyes and knew that it was best for me to keep my own counsel. I needed to look deep inside for the answers for the dilemma ahead of me.

I shut my eyes and enjoyed the music as the orchestra started another waltz.

CHAPTER
forty-two

Mayor Merrill was there shortly after breakfast with all the supplies and tools for the day's project. After we carried the beadboard for the shutters and the boards for the cross pieces from the dock up the spiral path, Mayor Merrill assigned tasks. Anne measured; Flossie sawed; and I drilled holes in the cross pieces with a brace and bit.

Mayor Merrill repeated the phrase 'measure twice cut once' dozens of times and was as good as her word. After she measured and re-measured each window with her wooden folding ruler, Mayor Merrill gave the dimensions to Anne, who used a metal L square to draw the dimensions onto the beadboard. The measurements were checked again by Anne and rechecked by Mayor Merrill.

Mayor Merrill taught us the finer points of each of our jobs. "Why am I drilling a hole in these cross pieces?" I asked after I readjusted the brace and bit to be perfectly perpendicular to the board before I started drilling.

"The crosspieces help give stability to the shutters. They will help keep the beadboard from warping over the years. The crosspieces will also provide a nice handle to hold onto as you put up and take down the shutters. The shutters will be secured to the windows with a wing fastener on each side of the window. We need a rounded half-circle with a diameter just a bit larger than the length of the wing fastener so we can turn it. Flossie will be sawing the crosspiece boards in half later."

I nodded, though it seemed she was speaking in a foreign tongue I didn't understand. I only hoped that by the end of the day, I would understand this new vocabulary.

Our initial tasks completed, we switched to new tasks. Anne hammered. I planed the bottom edge of the shutter with a hand planer. And Flossie screwed in the wing fasteners.

"Remember to keep it at a thirty-degree angle," Mayor Merrill reminded me. "See how the window sills are slanted down so rain flows away from the window? You're shaving the bottom so it will fit snug against this slanted surface. This will help make the inside of the cottage watertight against that north wind which will blow snow up against the windows."

After all the drilling, sawing, hammering, and planing, we cleaned up our worksite, sweeping away the sawdust. Meanwhile, Mayor Merrill was labeling each shutter on the backside in pencil so we would know which shutter went with which window. She added arrows so we knew where the planed edge was properly lined up with the slant in the sill. All that was left was painting the outside of the shutters white. This I could do in my sleep. No instruction needed.

With that, Mayor Merrill packed up her tools and headed down to her rented skiff.

"Thanks so much for all the help," I called after her as she rowed away.

"I didn't do a thing. You did it all yourselves. The next time you have a project, you'll be able to tackle it yourselves."

Just as Mayor Merrill rounded Pratt Point, Nat came into view. After Anne and I helped Flossie load her things in his skiff, we walked with her to the Grenell Store dock to say goodbye. We would be joining Flossie in West Philadelphia in a few days' time.

"We're going to need some tools," Anne noted as we walked back to Castle Rock.

That night after supper we made our lists for next year's improvements and the tools we would need. After dinner, we went out on the porch to watch the sunset.

Nothing matches an island sunset, yet each is different. Some are vibrant. Others are more subdued. Last night's sunset was a soft peach with a swatch of misty lavender in the middle. The peach faded, and the lavender darkened into a deep purple. I wondered if I could capture this particular sunset into a haiku, so I ducked inside the cottage to retrieve my notebook and pencil.

I'd received not one but two letters from Charles today. One in the morning and another in the afternoon mail. After I had changed into my nightdress and brushed my hair one hundred strokes before plaiting it into a long braid, I carefully slit open the envelopes with my letter opener. Each envelope contained three slips of paper, a haiku written on each. Nothing more.

Charles's process for writing haikus was the opposite of mine. He fully formed the haikus in his head before writing them down. I needed a pencil and notebook. I always started by writing down keywords, then rearranging the images on paper. I smiled when I read his haikus—two were about clouds, and the other was about a blade of grass bejeweled with morning dew.

I closed my eyes, searching my memory for inspiration. I wrote three haikus, using several pages of my notebook to do so. Once finished, I wrote the haikus out on slips of paper, one copy for Charles and a copy for me. I put the haikus for Charles in an envelope and the copies for me in the wooden box.

I turned the knob on my finger lamp until the wick dipped back inside the burner. The light in the room grew dimmer and dimmer until the flame was finally extinguished and the room was plunged into darkness.

The darkness seemed to magnify the insect noise outside. In the distance, I heard the loud piercing call of the saw-whet owl. The first time I heard it, I thought I might be hearing a ghost from Cliff House. It was Hunk who informed me that the noise had come from the tiny owl that migrates from upper Canada down to the lakes for the winter. The saw-whets fly through here about the same time every year. A few years ago, while out for a late-night swim, I saw a pair of huge, bright yellow eyes staring at me from the lightning tree. I thought it was a cat at first, which would be as odd as seeing an owl. Despite the large eyes, the owl was tiny. It could have fit in the palm of my hand.

Hearing the saw-whet owl tonight of all nights made me think of

Charles saying that I looked like Athena and that he wouldn't be surprised if I had an owl. Charles appreciated me for my mind, not the gowns I wore.

I shut my eyes and imagined how my first visit to Rose and Mother might go after I returned to West Philadelphia. I imagined telling them of my proposal. They would be so happy. But all that would be dashed when I told them of the compromise.

Then there was the ultimatum Rose had issued earlier this season: Come live with us now before it's too late! Rose's assurance that with her help she could have me married off by next spring and delivered safely into the hands of a husband who could properly look after me rang in my ears. She had said "or else," but she'd never actually spelled out exactly what "or else" might mean. Two months had passed without a word. Perhaps the "or else" meant: Or else we will have nothing to do with you.

It was so important to my mother and older sister that I marry and marry well. Marrying Charles would meet this requirement. Yes, I would have to give up my teaching fellowship, but I could help Charles in his endeavors. Would Mother and Rose approve of that? What if I didn't tell them about the compromise. I would be hundreds of miles away in Chicago. Would they know? Could I keep it a secret? Perhaps after I was married—when they saw me in all that opulence living alongside the Pullmans and the Heaths—raising our children Episcopalian wouldn't matter as much. But I knew that was a lie. No amount of wishing would change that. The high-pitched screech of the saw-whet cut through the night and brought me back from my imagined world to my tiny bedroom at Castle Rock. I heard my father's voice: *When you start lying to yourself, all is lost.*

Perhaps Charles and I would never have children, and all this worry would be for naught. But I wanted children. And if I had my way, I would raise them Quaker. In my mind's eye, I saw an outraged Mrs. Bartman, Mother, and Rose pulling at their hair and crying out. For some reason this thought made me chuckle to myself. I rolled over and felt myself relax. Tomorrow was our last full day on the island. I needed my sleep.

The saw-whet cried again, and another saw-whet—perhaps as far away as Murray—answered it. The two called back and forth in the night. Their calls lulled me to sleep at last.

CHAPTER
forty-three

Our last full day on the island was a day of changes. First, Capt. Taylor sent word that the water was too low for the *Minnehaha* to pick us up at our dock. We hadn't much in the way of cargo: two steamer trunks, several crates, four valises, and Anne's Gladstone doctor's bag. Still, this had to be transported to the Grenell Island Store dock.

Next, Nat arrived with a grim forecast. "Hunk says it's best to get your baggage to the store today. If you wait until tomorrow, it'll get mighty wet." Hunk's weather predictions were so accurate that I often wondered if he were predicting the weather or conjuring it.

That sent us into a flurry of packing. I made sure my books were safely packed in the center of my steamer trunk.

Hunk showed up late that afternoon to help Nat transfer our baggage to the store dock. "Don't you worry," Hunk told me. "I know your precious books are in that trunk. I'll make sure everything is well-covered with a tarpaulin on the lee side of the building. Nothing will get wet."

"Keep those letters comin'," Hunk said as he rowed away from the dock. "Our winters are mighty long and your words are like a ray of sunshine."

"Have a good winter!" I called after him, wishing I had spent more time with Hunk this season.

After Hunk and Nat left with our baggage, we walked around the island and said our good-byes: Uncle Sam, Aunt Lucy, and the chickens, of course; Alice and the girls; Mavis and Alma Mae; and the Reeves. There would be letters through the fall, winter, and early spring, but it would be a long while before I would see my island family again. Alma Mae would be the most changed. I remembered saying good-bye to Otis Pratt last year, not knowing it would be the last time. Life was precarious. Precious.

By sunset, we were packed and ready. We retired early but I barely slept. I spent most of the night in that vexing in-between state. In-between sleep and wakefulness. In-between summer and fall. In-between wanting to marry and wanting to stay independent. In-between wanting to please my mother and older sister and wanting to please myself. I listened for *the Voice*, if only to prove to myself that it wasn't Edwin. If it were Edwin, I'd hear it in West Philadelphia, wouldn't I? I chased that thought away. That was silly Nora nonsense, and I wouldn't waste any time trying to explain it away. Still, I wondered and wished I could summon *the Voice* at will. Why did it always sound so comforting and reassuring? Was it *the Voice* of my one true love? These questions plagued me as the hum of locusts slowly faded away and the long night wore on. I turned over again, pulling a quilt up over my shoulder against the cool air drifting in through the north window as the first few raindrops danced atop the rooftop. The rain that Hunk predicted had started.

I shut my eyes, and the next time I opened them it was lighter outside. The day dawned gray and lavender. I sat up in bed, stretched, and breathed in. The air was moist and fresh, such a comingling of scents: pine, cedar, and the smell of the river. No place smells quite like this. It's the most glorious cologne in the world: a scent that invigorates and soothes at the same time.

I rolled over then and looked out the window. A breeze puffed out my gauzy curtains and sucked them back to the screen again.

A month from now, I would be so busy with classes, lectures, and grading papers that my life here will have seemed like a dream—a dream that would sustain me through the long, non-island time of my life. This island season went by far too quickly. I'd wasted so much time dithering over clothes and hair and not enough time fishing and staring at the sunset.

I turned over and placed my hand on *Leaves of Grass*, that great yellow book that brought me to this island in the first place. I always carried *Leaves of Grass* with me in my valise. While I would trust Hunk with my life, my 1881 copy of *Leaves of Grass* signed by the Good Gray Poet himself was too valuable for me to leave in the hands any porter.

I reached for the great yellow book and hugged it to me. My bookmark, which Floisse had made for me of leather and Indian beads, stuck out the top. I knew what page it marked. Last night I had asked for a bit of wisdom from the Good Gray Poet. I balanced the book on its spine, shut my eyes, let the book fall open, and then let my finger fall and point to a line. On page 175 is a continuation of the poem "A Song for Occupations" and my finger pointed to this line:

> *Happiness, knowledge, not in another place, but this place, not for another hour but this hour.*

The Good Gray Poet never disappointed.

I got up and dressed and was surprised when I left the room to find Anne in the front room dressed and ready for the day. "How did you sleep?" I asked.

"Not well. I never sleep well the last night on the island." She stared out the front room window as if she were searching for something. "It's as if each time I leave this place, I leave another piece of myself, and I have to wait eight months to be whole again."

I joined her at the front room window. Even on this gray day, the vista was breathtaking. To the right, we could see the granite palisades of Wellesley Island. The top of Murray was studded with rows of white pine and darker hemlocks, their bristly spires poking into the thick gray clouds above. Fingers of fog meandered between the pine boughs.

"We shouldn't start a fire, so we'll have a meager breakfast. Water. Cheese. Bread and butter. It will get us to our first train stop, where we can have a more substantial meal," Anne said removing butter and cheese from the icebox.

We hadn't added any ice to the box in the last three days and the twenty-five-pound block had melted away to a tiny chunk about the size of a snowball. I put it outside on the rock when I emptied the drip pan. As I wiped out the inside of the icebox, Anne set the breakfast table.

We ate in silence. A poet's meal for such a poetic morning. We washed up the dishes and put them in our new corner cabinet.

"I think the rain has stopped—at least for the moment," I said. "We'd better get the shutters up while we can." We scurried outside and were barely able to install all the shutters and secure them with the wing fasteners before the rain started again. The interior of the cottage was now dark and cold. We had moved our rocking chairs off the porch last night, but drug them back out on the porch and watched the rain as we waited for Nat. Luckily the wind was from the west, and we were protected from the blowing rain by the screen of cedars to our left. The rain pounded on the roof and rocks so hard that it was impossible to talk. The rain pummeled the ice chunk on the rock. I watched the ice twist, melt, and dissolve in the relentless torrent of rain. We watched and waited. The Good Gray Poet's words echoed in my head: "Happiness, knowledge, not in another place, but this place, not for another hour but this hour."

As the rain slowed, we saw Nat appear from behind Sentry Rock. His slouch hat was pulled low on his head. The rain fell, running off the brim and over his raised jacket collar. Nat trotted up the spiral path. "There's a break in the weather but another wave of storms on the way. I suggest we go now."

We quickly put our rockers in the cottage, locked the door, and hurried down the path. We put on our waxed-canvas capes and pulled the wide hoods over our heads. I climbed into the skiff, put my valise on my lap, and tucked it under my cape to protect it if it started to rain harder before we reached the store dock. Rainwater sloshed in the bottom of the skiff around my feet. No time to bail. We untied the lines and pushed off the dock. Nat began rowing at a lively pace toward the head of the island.

"Wait, wait! I have something for you," we heard someone call out. We turned to see a figure rounding Pratt Point and rowing our way.

"Who is that?" Anne asked.

I squinted at the back of the figure rowing toward us. It was a short man with a tight-fitting hat. "Is that Mr. Tetsuka?"

"Indeed! That's who it is," Anne agreed.

"So sorry to be late," Mr. Tetsuka said as he pulled up next to our skiff. He tucked the oar inside his skiff, reached out, grabbed our gunwale, and pulled his skiff next to ours. "I finished late last night and then the rain came." He placed a brown paper-wrapped package in my lap.

"This is a gift form Keikosan for you, Miss Marguerite. The letter explains all," Mr. Tetsuka said handing me an envelope.

"We've got to go or we'll get drenched," Nat warned.

"Goodbye. Safe travels," Mr. Tetsuka said as he pushed away.

Nat pulled hard on the oars. I turned and waved to Mr. Tetsuka. "Thank you! Goodbye!" I called back, unsure what I was thanking him for. We could see rain beyond Maple. Once we cut through between Wilsons Island and Grenell I could see the line of rain had reached Maple. We were able to make it to the store porch before the major rain. There we saw our baggage safely tucked under an overhang and covered with a tarpaulin.

Mrs. Kilborn brought us cups of coffee. It was strong! I sipped it slowly, enjoying the warmth of the cup in my hand. When we finished our coffee, Anne asked about the package. It was wrapped in brown paper and tied with twine. I carefully opened it so I would be able to wrap it up again to protect it on our upcoming journey. "It's a shadow box," I said, looking at the box with a glass cover. "But it's so dark that I can't see what's inside. I think it's . . ." the words caught in my throat, and tears instantly sprang to my eyes.

"What is it?" Anne asked.

"It's Rose's tortoiseshell comb." The broken comb had been painstakingly reassembled. The pieces that were missing were replaced with what looked like gold or silver. The missing rhinestone pieces of the vine motif at the top had also been replaced with dots of silver.

I opened the letter and in her careful, neat printing she wrote:

> Mr. Tetsuka has repaired the tortoiseshell comb through the Japanese art of kintsugi. The pieces that could not be found were replaced with silver or gold. Kintsugi is an art form, but also a philosophy, built on the belief that our flaws, our mistakes, our misunderstandings are as beautiful and important in our lives as our accomplishments. Sometimes when we repair what is broken in our lives, our lives become more beautiful and more precious. Embrace this misunderstanding with your sister, and create between you a more unique, more beautiful, and more resilient relationship.

A tear dropped from my eye and I quickly pulled Keiko's letter aside so it wouldn't drip on it, smearing the ink. Instead, the tear fell on the glass of the shadow box and slowly slid down. I handed the letter to Anne to read, turned, and peered into the dark box. The haircomb was now a work of art, too precious to wear.

"Very profound," Anne said.

The steamer came right on time in the middle of a big blow. Only a few passengers were onboard, most bound for a train in Clayton. The porters wheeled our tarpaulin-covered baggage aboard. Once we knew our baggage was aboard, we raised our hoods and made a dash for the steamer. The driving rain pelted us at every step.

The inside of the steamer was thick with the smell of wet wool. The windows were fogged up, and I wiped the condensation away with the sleeve of my dress, hoping to catch the last glimpse of Grenell as we steamed away. I could barely hear the steam whistle shriek as the thrumming of the rain on the steamer drowned out all other sounds.

The wind drove the rain almost sideways. The water churned until it was frothy and gray. The wind blew the top of the waves across the water so it looked as if it were wearing a tulle veil.

A woman who was already aboard was quite discomfited and called for the purser. "How can the captain see where he is going? Perhaps we should turn back."

"I assure you, ma'am, that the captain knows the river."

"But there are so many rocks. How does he know where they all are?" she asked.

"The captain doesn't need to know where all the rocks are in the river; he only needs to know where the rocks aren't."

The simplicity of that statement struck me. I didn't need to know every rock in the situation ahead of me. I only needed to know where the rocks weren't. I pondered that notion as we steamed upriver through the storm.

Once safely dockside at the Clayton town wharf, I tucked my valise under my waxed-canvas cape, pulled the hood over my head, and hurried to the covered platform for the train. Anne stood next to me as we watched our baggage loaded onto a cart and wheeled to the baggage car.

"Are you coming?" she asked as she headed toward the sleeper car.

Grenell 1893

"In a minute," I said. Anne nodded as if she understood that I needed a few moments to be alone.

As soon as she climbed into the sleeping car, the wind picked up, the skies opened again, and windblown sheets of rain swept downriver. Watching the wind-pushed waves was mesmerizing on this gray and dreary day. Rain or shine, I could find happiness in this place, in this hour.

Rain dripped from the eaves and splashed on the pavement in front of me, threatening to drench the hem of my walking skirt. It was time for me to board the train. My choice ahead of me was not an easy one. The river needed to be a part of this decision. This was a point on which I would not compromise.

Whatever I decided, I knew the river would always be here, waiting for me.

Acknowledgements

A book is never written in a vacuum. Many thanks to Grenell Island and Murray Isle residents who provide tidbits and encouragement for my Thousand Islands Series, especially the Sweetapple family of Grenell and Billie Jo Radecke of Murray Isle.

All writers need extra eyes and insights to take a manuscript from rough draft to final draft. Special thanks to my first readers Linda Cregan and Janet Smith-Staples for their suggestions. Huge thanks to my copyeditor Tracy Schoenle. Her attention to detail is staggering.

Above all, a heartfelt thanks to my talented family. First, thanks to my daughter, Michelle Argento, who puts in countless hours as my book designer. Next, thanks to my son, Rob McElfresh, the story wizard, who easily zeroes in on a story's deficiencies and offers poignant suggestions. And finally, what would I do without my husband, Gary? He keeps the household running, leaving me free to write. How lucky am I to find someone who is such a great cook and a proofreader? He's the whole package.

Author's Note

Grenell 1893 is a work of fiction. My goal in writing this series is to give readers a sense of what life was like in the Thousand Islands in past years. I have strived to be accurate in language, dress, sensibilities, and day-to-day life of the times.

My narrator, Marguerite Hartranft, is 100% fictitious—although her last name is borrowed from my husband's ancestors. John Hartranft was a Civil War general and 17th Governor of Pennsylvania and a distant relative of both my husband, Gary McElfresh, and of Marguerite.

Fictitious Marguerite interacts with historical figures from the islands. Those familiar with the islands will recognize names of the more famous Thousand Islands summer residents: George Boldt, Charles Emery, George Pullman, etc. Grenell residents will recognize family names long associated with our island: Grenell, Reeves, Gardner, Sharples, Stoddard, etc. I have thoroughly researched historical figures who are mentioned in the novel. Unfortunately, I often have no idea of their appearance, personalities, or mannerisms. Their interactions with Marguerite are purely imagined.

I scoured the newspaper archives looking for events of the 1890s. Some of the events happened a few years before 1893, others a few years after 1893. Here are a few of the events I have moved around in time:
- On Grenell, the grand "castle" at the crest of the island was actually not built until 1895.
- Keiko Okami actually graduated from the Woman's Medical College of Pennsylvania in 1889, not in 1893. As far as I know, Keiko Okami never visited the Thousand Islands.
- While Swami Vivekananda did visit the Parliament of Religions in Chicago in 1893, he did not visit Thousand Island Park until 1895.
- The American Canoe Association held their annual rendezvous at Canoe Point on Grindstone Island from 1884-1888 and again in 1896. In 1893 the A.C.A. held their rendezvous at Brophy's Point on Wolfe Island.
- The Thousand Island Park bridge across South Bay was torn down in June of 1893.
- The wedding between Albert Gabriel and Emily Griswold was performed on the rock in front of the Griswold cottage in 1884, nearly a decade earlier. Albert was arrested for forgery two months after the wedding. However, he was not arrested on the island. He was arrested at their home in Adams, NY. As far as I know, he was arrested by the local authorities and not by Pinkerton National Detective Agencies.

- Generally, I usually only move things in time. In this novel, however, I actually moved a cottage. My apologies to the owners of Mosquito Lodge as I have moved it from its location on Rainbow Avenue to Park Avenue in Thousand Island Park.

Some readers may find some words used in the book "politically incorrect." In the 1890s, Native Americans were referred to as Indians and nonblack performers portrayed black roles in blackface. The description of Frank Taylor's campfire, was taken from a newspaper account. My intent in using the 19th-century descriptions was not to offend but to be historically accurate. These were different times. The fact that some readers might be shocked only proves that our society has become more inclusive, respectful, and evolved.

I'd also like to acknowledge *Grenell 1893*'s "guest time travelers." Relatives of Grenell Island resident Linda Hendley have stepped into the past and made an appearance in Grenell 1893. Mrs. Merrill, Autumn Morley, Paige Stieding, and the Tingley sisters (Lisa, Tressa, and Dresden) traveled back in time to 1893. Linda Hendley's mother, Mrs. Merrill, was the first woman mayor of Richland, WA in the 1960s. I imposed on Mrs. Merrill the true story of Susanna Salter of Argonia, KA, who was our nation's first woman mayor.